I0727897

Once Upon a Time:

Three tales from the Romance a Medieval Fairy Tale series

DEMELZA CARLTON

This is a work of fiction. Names, characters, businesses, places, events and incidents are either the products of the author's imagination or used in a fictitious manner. Any resemblance to actual persons, living or dead, or actual events is purely coincidental.

Enchant: Beauty and the Beast Retold

DEMELZA CARLTON

Book 1 in the Romance a Medieval Fairy Tale series

One

Three girls perched on the battlements, breaking their fast in the watery spring sun as they discussed the lone rider they'd spotted from their tower room.

"I think he's a knight come to sue for my hand in marriage," declared Anita, the oldest.

Arya sniffed. "Your hand isn't the bit he's most interested in, I'm sure. Anyway, knights wear armour, and he has none. I think he's one of Father's sea-captains, come to tell good news about his voyage."

Anita nudged Zuleika, the youngest, with her slipper-clad foot. "What say you, baby sister? Is he a knight or a sailor?"

Zuleika closed her eyes and cast her mind toward the man. She alone of the three had inherited her mother's skill for magic, and she practiced whenever she was able. "He comes with grim purpose. A duty he fears but will perform. I can't help but feel he carries my fate."

"Father wouldn't promise you in marriage to anyone until he's found husbands for the two of us. You're safe," Arya said. "Anita had better take a closer look, to make sure he's handsome enough for her."

Anita hushed them both as the man reined in his horse before the closed gate.

"Open up in the name of the king!" the man in the king's colours demanded, rapping smartly on the gate with his gloved fist. "I ride at the king's command and woe betide those who stand in my way!"

Safe behind the crenellations, Zuleika called, "What is the king's command?" She stuck her head out so she could see the man's face, though her sisters tried to pull her back.

"I bring a summons for the Lady Zoraida. The king has need of her." The man brandished a scroll case.

Zuleika's heart sank. This was a matter of

magic, she was certain of it. The king would not be happy when he found out her mother had died two winters past of an ailment that stole her breath until she breathed her last. Even her mother's healing powers had been no match for it. "Then you'd better come in. I'll order the guards to open the gates."

Her sisters hissed at her to stop, for Father had ordered the gates kept closed for their protection until his return.

"He's one man," Zuleika said. "But if we don't let him in, he will return with an army to bring down the walls. I will do as he asks, and send him on his way. Father need never know."

This last was a lie, she knew, but it worked to calm her sisters. Zuleika's heart pounded in her chest, for today she would step into her mother's shoes and become the enchantress.

Two

Zuleika ordered the steward to serve the man refreshments in the dining hall while her maids dressed her hair. Like her sisters, she often wore hers uncovered, but if this strange messenger wanted to consult with the lady of the house, then she would dress like one.

She had learned at a young age how to step silently through the rushes that covered the stone floors. So when she appeared at the man's side, almost from nowhere, she had the satisfaction of seeing him start.

He recovered quickly, and bowed. "Lady Zoraida. I am Sir Ryder, a messenger sent from the king. I am to give you this and await your reply." He held out the scroll case gingerly, as though he thought it might bite him.

Zuleika resisted the urge to transform the case into something with teeth, and took it from him instead.

She unrolled the scroll, and read the message twice before she dropped it on the table next to Sir Ryder's empty ale cup.

"Do you know what this says?" she demanded.

He dropped his gaze to the rushes, crackling under his shuffling feet. "Mostly, my lady. If you don't accompany me back to the capital, I'm to take your children instead."

Only a coward threatened children. "Then King Thorn shall have his curse," Zuleika vowed. "But it comes at a price. He must leave my family alone."

"You have my word, Lady Zoraida."

Zuleika waved to summon a servant. "Prepare a room for Sir Ryder. I'm sure he wants rest after his long journey. I shall be in my bower." Her mother's bower, but the knight didn't need to know that.

"Yes, my lady." Mildred looked worried enough not to expose Zuleika's subterfuge. "If you will follow me, sir?"

Zuleika held her head high as she marched out of the hall and toward the stairs that led to the tower that had been her mother's. It was no different to the maidens' tower she shared with her sisters, and yet…it was a completely different world. Mother's bower held her books and scrolls; all her favourite curios from her travels all over the world, and seemed filled with the heady power of potential, of what might be.

When Zuleika crossed the threshold today, destiny wrapped around her. The room might be filled with her mother's things, but it was her domain now.

Three

Zuleika rode alongside Sir Ryder, her head filled with as much doubt as her belly felt full of butterflies. Not about the curse she had created at the king's command. She knew her spell was perfect. Perhaps she had been a little heavy-handed on the curse aspect, but it was her first and she intended it to be a powerful one. No, her fears were far simpler. She had never travelled outside her father's lands before and to go to the capital for an audience with the king terrified her more than she was willing to admit. This was destiny at work, she knew, but that didn't mean she had to like it.

The journey seemed almost too short, for in no

time at all she found herself riding through the gates at Sir Ryder's side. Their arrival at the palace provoked a flurry of activity. A small army of maids flanked her and hustled her into a sumptuous apartment, where they washed the dust from her skin, dressed her hair in a fashionable style, and laced her into a gown fit for court.

The lavender gown suited her, for it was only a shade lighter than her violet eyes. The maids had pinned her long hair to the back of her head and so weighty was it that she found it a challenge to bow her head even the slightest bit. Instead, she was forced to lift her nose into the air like the most prideful princess imaginable. How her sisters would laugh if they could see her now.

When Sir Ryder returned to escort her to the throne room, Zuleika expected to see the whole court present. However, she found the room empty except for herself, Sir Ryder and the stern-looking man seated on the throne – the king, she presumed. She dropped a brief curtsey, as her mother had taught her, before raising her gaze to meet the king's.

His eyes hardened. "You are not Lady Zoraida," the king said. He turned to Sir Ryder. "I ordered you to bring me a witch, not some little girl."

Sir Ryder started to stammer out an excuse, but Zuleika was having none of this.

"You sent a letter demanding a curse, or her children," Zuleika said. "So that my mother may lie peacefully in her grave, I came in her stead, carrying the curse you desire so ardently. And I am no child, but a woman grown." This last was stretching the truth a little, but Zuleika knew girls were often wed at younger than her sixteen years. Besides, she knew no child could create the powerful curse she carried for the king.

The king waved imperiously. "So, cast your curse then, girl, for your insolence tries my patience."

Zuleika's eyes flashed. "I already have."

"Your Majesty," Sir Ryder corrected. "His Majesty King Thorn prefers to be addressed as 'your Majesty'."

Zuleika saw more arrogance than majesty in King Thorn's demeanour, but she chose not to argue. "Your Majesty," she said. "I have created the curse you require, and cast it on this looking glass. It is no ordinary looking glass, but one which allows the beholder to see any person or place they desire, no matter how distant." She unwrapped the bundle in her hands and held up her mother's looking glass. "The moment your enemy looks into the mirror, he is cursed."

The King gestured for a servant to bring the mirror to him. His large hands dwarfed the delicate item. "Anyone who looks in this mirror is cursed or just my enemy?"

"The owner of the looking glass is cursed by gazing into it," Zuleika said. "Your Majesty," she added as an afterthought.

King Thorn's brow creased. "So if I send my enemy this farseeing mirror as a gift, the first time he uses it, he will be cursed, correct?"

Zuleika nodded.

"But if I were to look into it now," the king said, "will the curse harm me?"

Once again, Zuleika nodded.

King Thorn passed the mirror to a servant, who wrapped it carefully back in its cloth. "When my enemy gazes into his gift, what will happen?"

Zuleika swallowed. "His reflection will reveal the darkest, most beastly aspects of his nature, which will become visible to all those who look at him. His lands will no longer offer welcome; they will appear forbidding to anyone who approaches them. His castle walls will appear impossibly high. The entrance to his lands will disappear, along with all those who are loyal to him. He will be hideous, friendless and doomed to live in the dreariest place in the world, because he carries his curse with him wherever he goes." Zuleika couldn't help but express her pride in what she felt was a curse worse than death.

The king laughed. "So he will have no army, no supporters, and no woman would look at him for long enough to bear his sons." He clapped his hands. "You have done well, little witch. I think I shall keep you." He dismissed her with a wave of his hand.

"But my family, your Majesty," protested Zuleika. "Your letter said if I cast this curse, then my family would be safe."

King Thorn rose to his feet, no longer smiling. "You dare question the king's honour, girl? I gave my word that your family will be safe, and so they shall be. You, however, seem to lack the most basic womanly virtues of silence and obedience. In my service, you will learn both." He beckoned to Sir Ryder. "Take her to her room, and see that she stays there."

Four

Zuleika ate little at dinner, retiring early. She worried what her father would think when he returned home to find her missing. Did the king intend to keep her prisoner forever? Not that her sumptuous chamber was anything like a prison cell. She knew there were dungeons beneath the palace where the king kept and tortured his prisoners. Enchantress or not, she was not powerful enough yet to avoid the cells if she displeased the king.

Despite the crackling fire, she shivered in her thin shift and crept into bed. Beneath the blankets, she could believe she was safe at home in the tower room she shared with her sisters.

At least, she could until the door creaked open

and the king walked in. He wore none of the finery he'd sported in the throne room earlier that day. In fact, if it weren't for his short tunic, the man would be completely naked.

Zuleika sat bolt upright in bed, pulling the sheets up to her chin. "Your Majesty," she began uncertainly, "I believe you may have wandered into the wrong chamber." She swallowed. "You see, this one is mine."

"Everything in this kingdom is mine," the king said. "This palace. This chamber. Everyone and everything in it." He seized her blankets and ripped them from the bed. Cold seeped through the thin sheet that was now Zuleika's only covering, before he tore that away, too.

She scrambled out of bed. "Then I shall find somewhere else to sleep, sire," she said, trying to hide the tremor in her voice.

He strode forward so they stood face-to-face, though he towered over her. "Did you not hear me, girl?" He pointed at the bed. "Take off your shift, lie down and serve your king." As if to demonstrate, he pulled off his own tunic, so he stood in all his naked glory.

Zuleika did not find him glorious at all. Shaking with fury, she said, "You said my family would not be harmed. You lied. A king with no honour is no king at all."

King Thorn slapped her face so hard she landed on the bed, stunned. "Before you open your mouth again, you will remind yourself that silence and obedience are a woman's greatest virtues." With one mighty hand, he tore away her shift. "It is an honour to lie with the king and bear his children, even if they are bastards." He climbed onto the bed, pinning her beneath his weight.

Zuleika tasted blood from where she'd bitten the inside of her cheek at his slap. She summoned all the power within her as she said, "Shed a single drop of my blood, and you will never sire a living child."

The king seized her throat so tightly, she could scarcely breathe. "To curse the king's treason, girl. But you are no witch. You are powerless. And I shall prove it by putting a bastard in your belly tonight. You will practice silence and obedience or I shall choke the life from you." His grip tightened, cutting off her air. "Do you understand, girl?"

Zuleika nodded.

A moment later, when the king took her maidenhead, she was grateful for his chokehold, for she didn't have the breath to scream.

Five

The king snored, yet another thing Zuleika did not like about the man. She dressed as silently as she could, determined to leave before he woke. She had little else but her lavender court dress to cover her blood-slicked thighs, but blood was power to an enchantress. She would wash when she was safe. She tiptoed to the courtyard. No one stirred as she dipped her fingertips in her own blood to cast her mother's best and least known spell: a portal to take her away from here.

She traced a doorway in the air. Now, instead of castle walls, she saw snowy peaks. The mountains near her home.

Zuleika glanced back, considering whether to claim her mother's mirror back, complete with the curse, but she did not. The mirror was tainted by the king's touch, much as she had been, and she had honour, even if he had none. He and his enemy could have their curse, in exchange for her family's safety. She would flee and never return.

She paused only to pack a few things from her mother's bower before Zuleika opened another portal, to a beach, this time. In the warm, salty water, she washed all traces of King Thorn from her body, before she healed her hurts. There would be no child. The king might not believe it yet, but he had activated the spell she cast on him when he shed her blood. His fate was sealed.

Zuleika pulled her enchantress' mantle closer about her. She accepted her fate, but hers would be far brighter. This she swore on her mother's grave before she left it behind, too.

Six

"Master, Sir Ryder has arrived." Greta dropped a clumsy curtsey.

Prince Vardan looked up from his dinner. "Whatever is my brother's favourite lackey doing here?"

"Bringing you birthday gifts from the king," the knight replied, ambling into the great hall as though he and not Vardan owned it. He selected a saffron bun and bit into it. "He sends his best wishes upon your coming of age."

Vardan watched Sir Ryder devour the cake like he'd never eaten one before, choosing not to comment on the man's lack of manners in taking food before it was offered. That one pastry invoked the laws of hospitality, where neither would betray the other while they remained under the same roof. He didn't relax until the knight had washed it down with a mug of ale.

Then Vardan said, "But my birthday is still a fortnight away."

Sir Ryder shrugged. "His Majesty wanted to be certain his gifts arrived in time. Would you like to see them?"

Vardan's brother did nothing out of affection, he knew. There was no love lost between the brothers, especially not since Thorn had claimed the throne. Vardan had asked for, and been granted, what his brother had called the dubious honour of becoming the new Trade Master of Beacon Isle when he came of age. Vardan had thanked his brother and hightailed it out of the capital on the first available ship. If he hadn't, he was certain that he would either find poison in his food or be accused of some plot to assassinate the king. Besides, Vardan was not cut out for court life. The politics of the palace were too petty for him. He wanted to be doing things, and managing the country's largest and busiest harbour would be a welcome relief. He'd take a sea captain over a courtier any day.

"Did he send me a wife?" Vardan asked, only partly in jest. One of the other reasons he'd left court was because his brother had planned to marry him to some barren widow twice his age so that he could get his hands on the islands that were her dowry. When Vardan took a wife, he intended to marry for love, or at least for affection. He wanted a woman who enchanted him, not one who reminded him of his mother.

Sir Ryder laughed. "No. I think he's still looking for one of those himself. But if you fancy a ride…" He gestured toward the open doors.

Vardan gazed into the bailey, and was surprised to meet the eyes of a horse. Nothing like the sturdy ponies that roamed wild on Beacon Isle, this creature had all the hauteur of an emperor. Black as the ocean at night, he seemed to have the same seething turbulence, as if the moment a man had the temerity to mount him, the horse would show him no mere man could command the sea.

"He's magnificent. A mount suitable for a prince, or even a king. I'm surprised my brother was willing to part with him." Vardan approached the animal, whose bridle was held by Marshall, the head groom.

"Only the best for the prince, he said," Sir Ryder told him. "He wanted me to make certain the stallion is to your liking. I am not to leave until I have seen you ride him."

Vardan eyed the horse critically. "Tell me, has my brother employed a witch? One who has cursed the horse so that when I attempt to ride him, I shall be thrown off and killed?"

Sir Ryder's eyes grew wide with what Vardan thought was genuine astonishment. "Your Highness, no! The king would never wish to curse the horse ridden by his beloved brother."

Vardan believed the knight, but he still didn't trust his brother. "Very well. Saddle him, Marshall, and let Sir Ryder have the first ride."

Despite the knight's protestations, in the end, Sir Ryder mounted the horse and took a turn around the bailey. The stallion's steady gait was as smooth as the rolling waves. A thing of beauty.

Reassured, Vardan accepted the reins from Sir Ryder and sprang into the saddle. A short walk took them to the gate, where Vardan urged the horse into a gallop. The fields beside the road flew past as Vardan laughed for sheer joy. His brother had given him a magnificent birthday gift. Perhaps Thorn finally felt secure enough in his kingship that he no longer imagined his younger brother as a threat to the throne. Vardan hoped so, for he had no intention of usurping his brother's place. He intended to live out his life as the Trade Master of Beacon Isle, the place he loved most. Every time he walked into his grandmother's rose garden, it was as if the old queen were alive once more, and he was a boy filled with hope for a future that seemed so bright. And now when he rode out on his water horse, which he would call…Arion, he decided, he could almost fly to the harbour to greet the ships coming in to trade goods from all corners of the world.

When he returned to the bailey, breathless with laughter and the thrill of the ride, he thanked the knight profusely for bringing his brother's gift, and told him to convey his gratitude to the king.

"There is another gift, more valuable still," the knight replied. He held out a beribboned box, big enough to hold a book, maybe two.

Yet when Vardan took the box, it felt too light to be books of any kind. "What is it?" he asked, shaking it.

Sir Ryder seized the box, stopping him. "It is very fragile, Your Highness. You must be careful."

Feeling like a chastened child, Vardan opened the package with exaggerated caution. Inside the box was a cloth-wrapped bundle, and inside the cloth was…"A lady's looking glass?" Vardan exclaimed, lifting the offending item up to the light. Oh, it was pretty enough, with jewels cunningly set into the shape of a flower on the back, and a quick rub of the surface revealed his reflection, staring back at him, trying not to laugh at such a strange gift.

"An enchanted looking glass," Sir Ryder corrected. "Now you are so far from the capital, the king wished you to be able to still see the goings-on at court. You merely have to breathe on the mirror, speak the name of a person or place, and when the mist clears, you will see what you seek, as clearly as if you were there. You could see the king at court, or his bride on their wedding day, without ever leaving your island. You could even peek at the future queen when she's bathing, to see if she is comely enough for the king." He winked.

Vardan tried to hide his disgust as he wrapped the mirror and stowed it back in its box. As if he would use such a powerful object to peep at women to stimulate his own lustful desires. Perhaps chivalry really was dead in the rest of the country. Not here on Beacon Isle, though. "Perhaps later," Vardan said. "Please convey my thanks to the king for his gifts. How long will you be staying? I shall have the servants prepare a room for you."

Conscious of being a good host, he made sure his guest was settled and that his staff knew to pay the knight every courtesy before Vardan carried the box to his solar.

Much later that night, weary of listening to Sir Ryder's tales of the latest intrigues at court, Vardan retired to his bedchamber.

Try as he might, he could not sleep. Could a magical object truly let him see things far away? And if it could, why would his brother part with something so valuable?

Finally, he rose from his bed and padded to his solar, where the mirror lay in a patch of moonlight. The flower on the back seemed to glow purple, but he was sure it was either his imagination or a trick of the light.

What would he want to see? Vardan truly had no desire to spy on women in the privacy of their chambers. Nor did he want to see his brother lording it over everyone in court. The *Whale*, one of the ships due this week, had been delayed, though, and there were tales of pirates to the north. If there were pirates in his shipping lanes, Vardan wanted to know as much about them as possible, so he or his small navy could hunt them down. The Trade Master of Beacon Isle had no mercy for pirates.

He breathed on the glass. "Show me the *Whale*." The looking glass glowed purple, and

Vardan gasped in shock.

Seven

Zuleika travelled the world. Like her mother before her, she journeyed from place to place, seeking out those children who showed a spark of magic. Nothing like as powerful as hers, of course, but enough to make them dangerous without the knowledge they needed to control their powers. On their name day, she would appear to give the child a blessing, which in truth was the gift of knowledge they would need in later life. Once they discovered their powers, the girls – for they were always girls – would have the necessary knowledge to make use of them. Some girls were destined to be healers, while others possessed the power to communicate with animals. One girl appeared to have the extraordinary ability to manipulate destiny – not just her own but that of other people, too. Some had the gift of illusion, or power over plants and other simple creatures, and one particularly gifted child had the power to manipulate air currents. She looked forward to finding out how these girls chose to use their powers. For good, she hoped, so that they would follow her example.

Zuleika prided herself on being a good witch, by which she meant she did no harm to those who did not already deserve it. After all, she did not wish to end up like the djinn. Djinn were powerful magic users like herself who had used their powers for their own personal gain, to the detriment of others. When they caused so much trouble that they came to the attention of the rulers of the day, they had been sentenced to enslavement. Not to a person, but to an item, and anyone who possessed that item also possessed mastery over the djinn.

Of course, djinn were clever, and quite capable of influencing their masters. Recently, the ruler of a desert city had requested her assistance to rid himself of a particularly pesky djinn who insisted on tampering with the city's only water source. She'd dealt with the djinn, all right, cramming his loincloth-clad behind back into his lamp before hiding the lamp in a cave so protected with enchantments no one would release him. But when she returned to the city to collect her payment for a job well done, she found that the problems with the water supply had worsened in her absence. The man who'd hired her blamed her for the faults in his ancient plumbing and threw her out of the city. Or he tried to, anyway. An enchantress as adept at portal-casting as Zuleika was couldn't be kept out of anywhere for long. She'd taken great satisfaction in turning the ungrateful bastard into a frog, before tossing him into his own water supply so he could investigate the pipework himself. She'd left him a loophole, so he could break the curse, if he didn't want to live out the rest of his life as a frog, but she hadn't made it easy for him. Such was the life of a good witch.

She had returned home on occasion, ostensibly to check her mother's books and notes when she was asked to enchant items with unusual properties. That pair of dancing shoes, for instance, which the girl had managed to lose at a party, so that the prince pursued her all over the country to return her precious shoes.

First Arya, then Anita had found suitable men they wanted to marry, so both now lived with their respective husbands and, the last she'd heard, children, too. That left her father alone in the keep, so she made it a point to visit him as often as she was able. She only stayed for a day or two before leaving again – she didn't want the king to get word of her presence. There was no telling what that dishonourable man might do, to her or her father.

This time, when she arrived in her mother's bower, she found her father waiting for her. He started from the couch, as though from a deep sleep. Evidently, he had been waiting for some time.

"Hello, Father," she said. "What is wrong?"

"Zuzu, you're here," her father said, rubbing at his eyes. "My ships. I have lost all my ships. Wrecked, sunk, boarded by pirates… Who knows? But they are lost. And without them, we have nothing but this keep. I need your help, Zuleika. If anyone can find my lost ships, even one of them, for that would save our fortunes, it is you. Will you help me?"

"Of course, Father," she said warmly. "Which ship did you hear from last?"

"The *Rosa*. Her cargo was to be your dowry, dear girl. Purple silk, vair and amethysts exactly the colour of your eyes, to make you gowns fit for a queen. The king has not taken a wife yet, and I had hoped to send you to court so that you might enchant him. But the *Rosa* has disappeared, along with all your finery. She left port on schedule, but she should have arrived in the harbour by now. I fear all is lost."

Biting back a protest that she'd rather die than dress up for the king, Zuleika merely nodded. "I will not fail you, Father. I will find your ships and their cargo. If pirates have taken them, they will rue the day they were ever born." And searching for them would take her far from King Thorn, she thought but did not say.

Father fell to his knees. "Thank you."

A father should not kneel before his children, least of all to her, Zuleika thought, as she helped her father to his feet. "Think nothing of it. I am a dutiful daughter, nothing more." And one who had no desire to be queen.

Though she had been home scarcely more than a few minutes, Zuleika prepared to cast another portal, not to a place, but to a ship's deck. She bit her lip, tasted her own blood, touched her finger to her tongue, and drew the doorway. When her blood touched the earth, the doorway glowed and opened. Zuleika stepped through.

Eight

Zuleika took in a deep breath, as she always did when arriving at a new place. Except that this time, there was no air to breathe, only water. Deep beneath the surface, Zuleika's lungs filled with seawater, and she began to drown. Her flailing legs kicked something hard – the ship, or the seabed? She wasn't certain. Desperately, she drew a doorway, then another, and a third. No light meant no portal, and no portal meant she would die. Zuleika bit her finger, watching the blood stream in the current, as she drew a fourth doorway. She thought she glimpsed light, before her eyes were forced to close. It might have been a portal, or it might have been heaven beckoning her home. She wasn't sure which she welcomed most, but darkness dragged her down, and she knew no more.

Nine

When Zuleika regained consciousness, she couldn't feel her body. The one exception was her throat, which burned like she'd swallowed liquid fire. She coughed weakly, relieved to find her ears still worked.

"What is it?"

"Is it a bird?"

"No, I saw a flash, like lightning. That be no bird."

"It's a girl!"

"A corpse, more like. She's not moving."

"Her dress is soaked through. She'll freeze, laying out here in the snow like that. Feel her skin. Cold as ice, she is."

"See? A corpse, like I told you."

"She's no corpse, you old fool! She still draws breath. We better get her inside and warm before she perishes of cold."

"But the master…"

Zuleika heard what sounded like a slap.

"Shhh. You'll scare the maid to death."

Zuleika wanted to tell her rescuers that she feared little any more, but her voice died in her damaged throat. For when she opened her eyes, she saw no one at all. Nothing but a walled garden, shrouded in snow. Her eyes drifted shut, and the darkness embraced her once more.

Ten

"With respect, master, it won't be enough. One, perhaps two more ships, and the cellars will be full. Your storehouses were full months ago. If we don't find a way to shift this cargo off the island soon – "

A bolt of what appeared to be purple lightning arrowed down from the cloudless sky, followed by a sharp crack that echoed off the courtyard walls.

Vardan waved Rolf into silence. "What in heaven's name was that?" the prince asked.

"Hopefully not something in the cellar," Rolf said drily.

Vardan laughed. "I hope you're right, my friend." He clapped his steward on the back and hurried to the nearest window overlooking the rose garden. At least, the expanse of snow smothering his grandmother's garden.

"It's a girl!" Inga exclaimed.

Vardan stared. Sure enough, the housekeeper was right. Lying on the snow was a woman whose scarlet dress made it look like she lay in a pool of blood. Perhaps she did.

"Is she hurt?" Vardan demanded.

Sven, the gardener, muttered something unintelligible.

"I don't think so, master," Inga called up. "Cold, yes, frozen nigh to death in her wet things outside in this weather, but her eyes opened for a moment there, and she still draws breath. We must get her inside before she takes a chill, if she hasn't already."

Most men would have called for more servants, Vardan knew, but he wasn't most men, and he was curious. Just as lightning did not strike out of a clear sky, women dressed in scarlet did not suddenly appear in rose gardens. Vardan smelled magic at work, but he wasn't yet certain whether it was good or ill. After what had befallen him, he no longer had any love for magic or those who practiced it.

He took the steps two at a time until he reached the garden, then trudged through the snow to where he could look upon the strange woman's face.

What he'd taken for a dark veil was instead the girl's unbound hair, as rich and dark as the sable furs in his nearly full cellar. He wondered idly whether her hair was also as silky to the touch. His hand reached out almost of its own accord.

"She's quite the beauty, isn't she, master? Though she's mighty pale. Perhaps it's the cold. With a little colour in her cheeks, there wouldn't be a man in the kingdom who could ignore her when she walks by," Inga said, as if reading his thoughts.

"She would not walk," Vardan found himself saying. "She would ride. A horse fit for a queen."

Inga cleared her throat. "Before you go riding with her, master, we must get her warm. Inside. For that we need a strong man more than a horse who can carry the maid – "

"I'll do it," he said. The girl was surprisingly heavy in his arms, but he realised that most of the weight was her waterlogged, half frozen clothes. "Have a room prepared for her. In the meantime, I will take her to my bed – "

Inga made a disapproving sound. "The queen's bedchamber would be better, master."

Though his grandmother no longer lived, they

would always think of her favourite rooms as the queen's chambers. "Yes. Of course, you are right. I shall take her there."

He carried the mysterious girl up the steps to the corridor his grandmother had claimed as her own. The windowless bedchamber was exactly as she had left it, right down to her shell combs on the table.

"Put her on the bed, master," Inga ordered, and the prince obeyed.

He regretted it instantly, as his arms felt strangely empty once he released the girl. "Surely you should turn down the bed first, so I can place her under the covers? I wouldn't want her to be cold." He reached for her again.

"Not in her wet things. I'll help her into some dry clothes before I put her to bed, master," Inga said. She waited a moment, before she added, "I will have to undress her. It would be unseemly for you to stay."

It took a moment for Inga's words to register. Unseemly. Undress. No, he did not watch women undress without their knowledge. Whoever this girl was, she deserved to be shown every courtesy. Vardan wasn't sure what had come over him, that he could forget such a thing. Thank heaven Inga had taken the liberty of reminding him.

"Thank you," he said fervently. "Treat her as an honoured guest. Send word when she wakes."

He hurried back to his solar, where he was glad to find Rolf no longer waiting to discuss cellars, storehouses and other such mundane matters.

There was a woman in the house who occupied all of his thoughts. Pale features, dark hair, who rode into his rose garden astride a bolt of purple lightning. If his grandmother could see the girl in her chambers now, and the distraction she drove her grandson to, the old queen would call him a fool.

A fool who could think only about how the girl was being undressed in those chambers right now…

For the first time in his life, Vardan's fingers itched for the magic mirror that would allow him to see all that happened in the queen's bedchamber, but he resisted the urge. He would see plenty of the girl, for unless she could summon another bolt of lightning to ride away from the island, she would be trapped here for some time. Just like everyone else.

Eleven

Zuleika drifted in and out of consciousness, aware of women's voices rising and falling around her, but too drowsy to understand their words. She had a body, and a bed, or so it seemed, but her time in the ocean and in the snow afterwards had sapped so much of her strength that there was little else she could do aside from lie in bed and sleep.

Not since the night the king violated her had she felt so weak. No man had taken advantage of her this time, though, she was certain. Years ago, in a longhouse where victorious warriors believed they had the right to lie with any woman of their choosing on the night of a glorious victory, she had performed a tricky little spell on herself, intending it to be more of a precaution than necessary protection.

Instead, Zuleika had woken to find a man writhing in agony on the pallet beside her, while lightning coursed over her skin. No man had tried to touch her since, so she wasn't sure if the spell would be quite so strong a second time, but the lightning flared into life when anyone approached her with harmful intent, warning them away. She hadn't felt the tingle of her lightning shield here.

"She has such soft hands. Highborn, no doubt," one woman said.

"You should have seen the dress she arrived in. Silk, it was, I'm sure, though the water ruined it. Some princess, perhaps," a second female voice remarked.

"How'd she get here, then? Princess or no, she managed to make her way from the sea, through at least three locked gates, and into the master's rose garden. It must be magic, I tell you. Perhaps she is cursed, too."

"Well, aren't you a bushel of sunshine, then? Maybe destiny sent her here to break curses, but she won't do none of that if you scare her." A snort. "I ask you, does she look cursed to you? Not a mark on her, and I undressed her and put her to bed myself. Blessed, more like. Maybe she's exactly what the master needs."

The master could not have her, Zuleika thought, digging her teeth into her lip. A single drop of blood was all it took to recast that lightning spell. Her body might be weak, but the magic in her blood was as strong as ever.

"Aren't you taking her tray?" the second woman asked.

"No, I'll leave it a little longer. She might wake, and want a bite to eat. If I ever slept as long as she has, I'm sure I'd be famished."

"Has she said anything yet?"

"No, not a word. Not even in her sleep. She is a mysterious maiden, this one."

The voices faded as the women left, Zuleika presumed. Still, she waited until she could no longer hear them before she dared to open her eyes.

The room looked as richly decorated as any of the rooms at the palace, though the bed hangings and the tapestries had faded over time. Whoever lived here was not as rich as they once were, or perhaps they'd simply placed her in one of their less sumptuous guest apartments. The walls were not plain stone, but plastered, so she definitely knew she wasn't in the king's palace.

She sat up cautiously, relieved to find no lightheadedness. She didn't have time to be ill; she needed to find her father's ships. But for that, she would need her strength.

Zuleika examined the tray on the table beside her bed. A small loaf of bread, some fish and a jug of what she discovered with a cautious sniff was wine, not ale. Either she had travelled further south than she'd realised, or she was a guest in a prosperous house indeed. So whose was it?

Adding it to the long list of questions already burning in her mind, Zuleika broke her fast. She drank sparingly of the wine, knowing she would need her wits about her in this strange house.

When she was sated, she ventured out of bed. Her first few steps were tentative, but when she realised that she had regained enough of her strength to walk, Zuleika's steps quickened as she explored her chamber. The fine shift she wore, while not hers, was serviceable enough to protect her modesty, but it was hardly appropriate to wear once she left the room.

A chest at the end of the bed held gowns, but when Zuleika lifted one up, she found they were made in a fashion she had never seen anyone wear before, except in some of the old books her mother had inherited from her mother. Old gowns, in a chamber with faded hangings. The former owner of both no longer lived, Zuleika surmised, so she would not object to her borrowing her clothes.

She dressed in the most practical gown she could find, one of dark green wool. When she tried to place the matching veil on her head, the weight alone made her head ache, so Zuleika resolved to go with her head uncovered. She combed and braided her hair, wishing she owned combs as fine as these, carved of some sort of shell that caught the light and warmed it with rainbows.

If she met the master of the house, she would ask him what they were made of and where they were from, so she could travel there and obtain her own, Zuleika promised herself. In the meantime, she intended to explore the house and find out a little more about how she'd come to end up here.

Her door opened smoothly. Evidently, she was a guest and not a prisoner. The corridor outside her room was open to the frosty air, so she was glad she'd chosen wool and not linen. Nevertheless, she returned to her room to pull a cloak out of the chest to wrap around herself against the cold. Properly attired, she ventured out once more.

She peered over the sill of the glassless window and found the view as cold as the air. A courtyard smothered in deep snow, walled in so she couldn't see anything but the sea of white. Perhaps they did intend to keep her prisoner, and they felt the walls would keep her in so that no locks were necessary. The were certainly high enough.

Zuleika strode briskly along the colonnade, headed for the shelter of a darkened corridor at the end that she hoped led deeper into the house. Torches burned in the wall sconces, leaving streaks of soot along the white-plastered walls.

She bit her lip, tasting blood once more, and whispered a seeking spell for her father's ship. The spell sparked and died. Her father's ship was too far away for her spell to reach it. Frustrated, Zuleika tried again, thinking of the silk her father had promised her when the ship came in. Silk she had no need for, but no matter.

The spell ignited in the air before her, weaving like a firefly as it led her deeper into the house. Zuleika stumbled after it, paying no heed to her surroundings as she followed the light to her destination – the cavernous cellars of the building. These were nothing like the cellars in her father's house, or the dungeon cells she'd seen in other places. These stretched beneath the building, the vaulted ceilings turning the warehouse into a veritable cathedral of commerce, for it was piled with goods of all kinds. Chests and barrels, stacks of timber, stone jars and bundles of cloth, statues and…she lost track of all the things she saw in the warehouse.

Her spell hovered over a particular chest, balanced precariously on top of two barrels. It was closed, but not latched shut, so she lifted the lid. Zuleika gasped at the sight of silk, exactly as her father had described it. This was her father's cargo…but where was his ship?

Her hand darted out, almost of its own accord, to stroke the fabric, as soft as she'd imagined. This silk had never touched the sea – salt would have marred its sheen. The chest had been removed from the ship before it sank to the depths where she'd nearly drowned. How, then, had it arrived here?

One thing was certain: whoever owned this house had no right to the stolen goods in his cellar. His wealth was no more his than any of these things. The master they spoke of was a dastardly pirate, the scum of the earth and every merchant's enemy. Whatever curse lay on him, she was certain he deserved it, and more.

She found a pry bar and began to open the tuns

stacked around the chest, all marked with her father's brand. They were filled with vair, the grey-blue squirrel pelts royal courts found so fashionable of late. Carefully tucked between the pelts of a particularly full tun was a small chest, the size of her mother's jewel casket. Zuleika opened it with shaking hands. The chest was full of amethysts, all the same shade of violet she had seen so many times in her reflection. Just as her father had described them.

Zuleika sank to the floor, overcome by a mix of fury and frustration. More than half the room contained her father's cargo. A fortune in imports, which he believed lost. If this remained here, he was ruined. But if she could return it to him, even without his ships, he could buy new ones. And where were the crews? Had they perished when pirates attacked, or had they been enslaved? She was no innocent, she'd seen slavery the world over. No man or woman was spared hard labour when taken prisoner in war. But a pirate who sold slaves? The master here was despicable indeed. Perhaps Zuleika would turn him into a form fitting his nature. A pig, perhaps. A bristled boar. Or a form that would teach him the error of his ways? Then she should transform him into a minnow, or a small crab. Or perhaps a squirrel, covered in grey and white vair.

That would be fitting.

Zuleika rose. She added a squirrel pelt to the jewel casket and closed the lid. She tucked the chest of amethysts under her arm, striding out of the room to find somewhere she could cast a portal home to her father. She would show him the casket as proof that she had found his missing cargo, before she returned to this house to seek vengeance on the worthless pirate who had stolen it.

She marched through the corridors, searching for a way out that she simply could not seem to find. The snowy courtyard taunted her, but she could not cast a portal there. Smaller spells could be cast in air alone, but something as substantial as a portal needed to be anchored in earth – soil or natural stone, not the flagstones beneath her feet. The snow in the courtyard was too deep for her to reach the earth. She needed to leave the house and venture outside.

She whispered a spell to guide her to a way out, and found herself in what must be the great hall of the house. This was grander than her father's, its white walls stretching up to an arched ceiling much like the cellar downstairs. She had never seen a building like it. She crossed the room and reached for the bar fastening the great doors.

"Stop, thief!" Someone seized her around the middle.

Another set of hands snatched the chest from her grip as she fought her captors – more than one, she decided, as someone tipped her hood over her face, blinding her. She struck out behind her, hoping to land a blow on her cowardly assailant, or one of them, at least, but instead she tripped over the hem of her cloak. Her head hit the door she'd failed to open, and the blow stole her senses.

Darkness won once more.

Twelve

"I thought I told you to inform me when she awoke," Vardan said, staring down at the girl. Now she lay on the stone floor instead of the snow, but her closed eyes and the swelling bruise beneath her hair taunted him for being a bad host who did not properly protect his guests.

Inga must have run from the other end of the house, for she was still breathing hard. "Nobody told me, master. This is the first I knew of it, and it looks like she's no longer awake, anyway."

This wasn't Inga's fault, Vardan told himself, but it was hard to contain his anger. The girl was hurt, for heaven's sake.

"Who did this?" Vardan demanded. "She's just a slip of a girl. No need to clout her over the head.

Inga here could probably restrain her."

Rolf coughed out a laugh. "She's more than a mere girl. Threw me across the corridor, she did, before she tripped over her own cloak and hit her head. I'll wager this one's a witch. How else did she get here?"

Vardan wet his lips. "I don't know, but I mean to ask when she wakes. Again. What did you say to her to make her attack you, Rolf?"

"I called her a thief." Rolf twitched the corner of her cloak aside and revealed a small casket. "She was carrying this."

Vardan lifted up the box. "From the cargo of the *Rosa*," he noted, tracing the merchant's mark on the side. He lifted the lid. "She's quite a discerning thief, then. A fine squirrel pelt, and a veritable treasure trove of jewels. What are these purple stones called?"

"Amethysts, master," Inga said. "Just the right shade to match that fur, too. The girl has a fine eye for colour."

A magical thief with fine eyes, who could match Rolf in a fight. Against all his normal inclinations to imprison her for being a thief, instead he felt the unfamiliar desire to protect her.

Vardan badly needed to speak to this girl. She sounded like the most remarkable woman he'd ever met, and he didn't even know her name yet.

"I'll take her back to her room, and this time, I intend to be there when she wakes up," Vardan said, once more scooping the girl up in his arms. Ah, that felt better. She was much lighter than before, though more heavily dressed, so her clothes must have been soaked through when she arrived. How had she made it from the ocean to his rose garden?

He added that to the list of things he wanted to ask her. In the meantime, he carried the welcome weight in his arms to her bed. After all, it wasn't like she could leave the island. She was trapped there as much as he was, whether she slept in a dungeon or the queen's bedchamber.

He settled her in her bed and sat down to wait. Answers would come soon enough

Thirteen

Some sound must have startled her into alertness, for Zuleika didn't wake willingly. Her head ached more than ever, but she strained to hear the noise again.

There it was – a breath, blown out forcefully as if in impatience.

Keeping her eyes closed, she cast her mind toward the heavy breather. A man, as she suspected. He radiated a strange combination of boredom and curiosity. Curiosity for the future, while he endured the tedium now. A guard, she guessed.

She opened her eyes slowly, expecting to see a dungeon, or at the very least, to find herself thrown outside into the snow. Instead, she saw she'd been placed in a bed. Possibly the very same bed she had recently vacated. She couldn't be certain, for in the dark room it was hard to discern whether there were hangings at all, let alone whether they were faded or not. What worried her most was that her lightning shield had not triggered when someone had attacked her. Either the spell was ineffective, which she doubted, or her assailant had not intended to harm her. Yet both explanations were impossible. Zuleika snorted. Enchantresses achieved the impossible on a daily basis.

"You may feign sleep for as long as you like, my lady, but you and I both know you are awake," a male voice said. It came from a shadow in the corner – a hulking shadow, but a man-sized one.

Years had passed, but Zuleika still heard that voice in her darkest dreams. He was no guard.

Try as she might, she would never forget King Thorn, and her very bones quaked in the terror invoked by hearing that voice. But she was not defenceless today. "Threaten me with whatever you wish. I will never remove the curse." She took a deep breath before continuing coldly, "It is no less than you deserve."

She prayed that he would not hear the frightened fluttering of her heart. Damn the king for what he had done, and for the memory possessing the power to scare her still. Zuleika vowed that she would leave this encounter the victor today. If he took so much as a step toward her, she would turn him into a toad. He deserved all that, and more.

As if he could read her thoughts, the man she thought was the king laughed. "You do not even know my name, let alone what a man like me deserves, though I daresay you are right. You must have been listening to servants' gossip, for only they believe that the curse can be removed. Who can blame them? They suffer, too, but they live in hope that the curse one day will be lifted. Why else would my storehouses be so full?"

Zuleika saw red. "Your storehouses are full of stolen goods which do not belong to you. The true owners slide into poverty, while you grow ever richer. That makes you a thief, sir, and a pirate. Synonymous with pond scum." She wished she had had the temerity to tell the king that when they first met. How dare a man who owned so much power already steal from upstanding merchants like her father? A toad was too good for him. A maggot might be more fitting.

Yet again, the man laughed. Zuleika began to wonder if she was in the presence of the king at all, or simply some madman who sounded like him. "You call me scum and sir in the same breath. As for my being a thief… That is what my servants say about you. They say you were caught carrying out a casket of jewels. What say you to that, Lady Thief?"

She bridled. "My father's ship was carrying those jewels home to me. I merely took what is mine. I am no thief."

"And neither am I, despite the contents of my storehouses. They, too, are the result of my curse, but if you have listened to the servants gossiping, then I am sure you know more than I do about our affliction. Tell me, lady: how would you break the curse?"

Dread settled in her stomach of a different sort. It dawned on her that this man wasn't the king, and she had no idea what he was cursed with. Even for an enchantress of her skill and power, tampering with an unknown spell was dangerous. And yet…breaking curses was what she was best at, though it wasn't as satisfying as animal transformations.

"I know nothing of your particular curse," she said cautiously, "but perhaps if I knew more, I might know someone who can help." Only a dark witch cursed those who did not deserve it. If he was cursed unjustly, she was honour-bound to help him. She drew herself up, trying to sound as authoritative as a queen, though she sat in her shift in the bed and not on a throne dressed in royal robes. "But only if you are not a pirate, and you swear that you intend to do no harm. Who are you, sir?"

The hunched shadow in the corner became a tall pillar of darkness as the man rose to his feet. "Lady, I am Prince Vardan, Trade Master of Beacon Isle, and no pirate. While you are my guest here, no one shall harm you."

He was right about that last part, Zuleika thought, but did not say. She wished she could see his expression, so she could judge if he was lying. It was on the tip of her tongue to tell him to step into the light, but if he sounded like the cursed king, and bore a curse of his own, he probably had been blessed with good looks to match those of the king. She had no desire to see Thorn's face or any like it ever again.

"And you are?"

Zuleika's mind raced. Beacon Isle was part of King Thorn's territory, which meant Prince Vardan must be his brother. That explained the similarity. If he knew her true identity, he might return her to the king. Not while she drew breath, she vowed. She would rather die than become King Thorn's whore. She chose to feign ignorance. "I am sorry, your Highness?"

For the third time he laughed. "You honestly can't expect me to believe that your parents named you 'Sorry'. Beauty or Belle I would believe. Especially Belle, for your voice does have bell-like qualities, and your beauty is already the talk of the house. In fact, if you do not give me your name, I shall give you one. Lady Belle, the mysterious maiden who appeared in the snow."

"Your Highness is too kind," she murmured. "I am certain there are many ladies here far more beautiful than I."

Vardan barked out a laugh. "None that I have seen this week. But, as you say, you know nothing of curses. Least of all the kind of curse that turns a man into this." He unshuttered his lantern and held it high, so that she might see his face.

Zuleika recoiled in horror. What she had taken for a man, was in fact something so hideous she could scarcely bear to look at him. She wasn't even sure what creature he'd been transformed into. Some sort of monstrous…feline? Canine? Bear? And were those…tusks, or horns?

He lowered the lantern before she could decide, hiding himself in the shadows once more. There was no laughter this time. "So you see, Lady Belle, that there will be no breaking of my curse. Do you still wish to know more?"

What had he done to deserve such a fate? The curse she had visited upon his brother for her brutal rape was mild in comparison to this. Perhaps Vardan was a pirate after all, and a worse man than the king. If he deserved this curse, he would not dupe her into removing it. In the unlikely event that he had been cursed unjustly…then she would help him. But she would take her time to determine the truth of the matter before she made her decision.

"I do, your Highness," she said with her eyes closed.

"Then on the morrow, you shall have a tour of Beacon Isle." And with that, he swept out of the room.

Fourteen

He should never have unshuttered the lantern, Vardan scolded himself. He could not explain the strange urge that had taken hold of him, to show himself to her as though he expected her reaction to be different to anyone else's. The horror in her eyes when she'd seen his face…

Horror, but not fear, he reflected. At least that was something. And she had agreed to tour the island with him, which he had to admit had surprised him. He'd never taken anyone on a tour of Beacon Isle before. What would a lady wish to see?

He would ask…who? No one knew her. He didn't even know her name, for she'd meekly accepted the teasing moniker he'd thrown at her without a murmur. Yet a moment earlier, she'd been as fierce as a she-bear, calling him a pirate. Synonymous with scum…a lady of some education, then, who spoke her mind even as she read his own. For she'd known about his distaste for pirates, he was certain of it.

And for all his thirst for answers, she hadn't told him anything. He hadn't counted on her being so clever. For a woman so beautiful…it seemed almost too much that she had a mind to match.

He needed to spend more time with her. His idea to take her on a tour of the island had been a good one, he was certain, but he wanted more time before that, too. Time to set her at her ease, to persuade her that however hideous he looked, he was still a man of honour, and she would be safe beneath his roof. Safe enough to spill some of her secrets into his ear.

"I'll invite her to dinner!" he exclaimed.

"Very good, master," Inga said behind him.

He whirled. "How long have you been following me?"

"I have not left, master. After I undressed her, I waited outside in case I was needed. I hope you will change her mind about breaking the curse."

So Inga had heard everything, it seemed. Vardan wasn't surprised. "Any advice you'd care to offer me on that count? For I have yet to find a woman who can stare at someone as beastly as I am and not shudder in disgust."

"Love is not all about how one looks, master," Inga said reproachfully.

"Beasts don't love. Only men do that."

Inga grasped his arm. "And women. Don't forget that, master. Of all her children and grandchildren, the good Queen Margareta loved you best of all. She would want happiness for you. If you can win this lady's heart and break the curse, then – "

"Then men will fly, we will enjoy fresh strawberries every day, and King Thorn will declare that Beacon Isle is its own kingdom, to be ruled by what the ancients called a democracy, or a republic, or some other mythical name. Do not let your hopes rise too far, or their wings will melt and your spirits will fall so low you will have no hope left." Vardan closed his eyes. "I am sorry. This bitterness shall pass. I will set my hopes low: that she will one day look at me without disgust, and that she will share a meal with me."

"Invite her to supper, then, master, for if it is dark in the great hall, you can better hide in the shadows."

Vardan nodded sharply. "I shall. Who knows?

Perhaps one day I will not need to hide."

Inga sounded sad. "I hope that day comes."

Fifteen

Zuleika waited until she was certain he was gone before she climbed out of bed and dressed. It wasn't until she realised she didn't know who had removed her clothes, she wondered whether he had done it. The laces she was trying to tie dropped from her numb fingers. No – surely not. The green woollen gown had been neatly folded in the chest, much like it was when she found it. A prince would not know how to fold gowns. Like his brother, he probably only knew how to tear them off helpless women.

No, her clothes had been cared for by one of the mysterious maids she had yet to meet. As if to prove a point, someone knocked tentatively at the door.

"My lady?" It was a woman's voice this time. "The master has supper served in the great hall. If you are feeling well enough, you are invited to join him." A pause. "But if you are still unwell, I shall bring a tray."

Zuleika was not so lazy as to wish to make extra work for the maids. "I will join him."

"Very good, my lady. Will you need my help to dress?"

Zuleika considered the laces she'd given up on. "No, I think I can manage." After all, she'd travelled to many places in the world without a maid, and managed to dress herself. But supper alone with the prince in the great hall… Now, that called for something a little more fancy than the green wool travelling dress she had chosen earlier. Instead, she chose a red velvet one, the colour of wine, much finer than the red dress she'd arrived in.

She took her time with the shell combs, knowing that the more beautiful she looked, the more information she could extract from the prince. For all his talk of a curse, no magic had touched the cargo. And where were the crew? If he had captured them and sold them as slaves…

Zuleika shook her head. If the man was a slaver, then he deserved his fate.

Instead of her boots, Zuleika chose a pair of soft slippers she found in the chest. They fitted her so well, it was almost as if they had been made for her. She felt a peculiar urge to dance. Later, she told herself. Once her investigations were finished, her father's cargo had been returned to him, and the man responsible for sinking his ships had tasted justice.

She needed no spell to guide her to the great hall this time, for she knew her way. A good thing, too, for it appeared that her lengthy preparations had made her late for dinner. The prince sat at one end of the long table, while a place was set for her at the opposite end. Platters of more food than two people could eat covered the wooden surface between them. When Zuleika sat down, she found the lighting so dim that she could scarcely see her food, let alone the man at the other end of the table.

"Do you normally eat in the dark, or do you simply dislike the sight of me?" Zuleika asked the prince.

He pretended not to hear her, though she was certain that he had.

Zuleika folded her arms across her breast. "I will not eat what I cannot see. I need more light."

Silence swelled for a moment between them,

before the prince clapped his hands and called, "The Lady Belle demands more light. She wishes to see."

Zuleika heard the sharp intake of breath behind her, followed by scurrying feet. Perhaps the prince did like to eat in darkness. Minutes passed, before Zuleika heard the tramp of feet. Not one pair, like before, but a veritable army of servants, bearing light. When they came into view, it was her turn to gasp. For there were no servants in sight. All she could see was a row of lit candles, marching in midair. Yet she had heard the sound of feet on stone.

Djinn, was her first thought, or another enchantress like herself. "What is this magic?" she demanded.

The prince gestured at his hideous visage, now clearly visible in the bright illumination. "It is merely a part of my curse, Lady Belle," he said. "Not even the strongest man on the island wishes to share a meal with me, for one look at my face turns his stomach. I did not wish to ruin your appetite for supper. My cook may be invisible, but her sturgeon pie is the best in the region, if not the world."

Invisible servants. No wonder Zuleika hadn't seen her assailant. There had been nothing to see.

Reluctantly, Zuleika returned to her seat. She met the prince's eyes squarely across the length of the table. Though he looked hideous, more beast than human, his eyes were the exception. His eyes missed nothing, and right now they were evaluating her reaction to his enchanted servants. She refused to be found wanting. She tore her gaze from his mesmerising eyes, and surveyed the now well-lit table. "You recommend the sturgeon pie, you say? Then I must taste some."

Before she could work out which pie was the one in question, a pie-laden plate rose off the table and flew toward her. It stopped at her elbow. A respectful female voice asked, "How much would you like, my lady?"

Invisible servants, Zuleika reminded herself. Beside her stood an ordinary maid who simply had the misfortune to be invisible. Zuleika indicated a generous slice, which appeared to part itself from the rest of the pie before floating to her plate. Even for an enchantress, accustomed to using magic every day, it was disconcerting to see floating food. She forced herself to smile directly at the prince as she picked up a knife and cut herself a small portion of pie. She popped it into her mouth without dropping her gaze.

Her eyes widened in surprise as she realised the

prince was right about his cook's skill. The sturgeon pie, with its mix of salt and spice, and perhaps even a little cheese, was indeed the best she had ever tasted. Zuleika hastened to scoop up another bite.

"What do you think, Lady Belle?" the prince asked.

Zuleika swallowed. "I think," she said carefully, "that your strongest men are weak indeed. I would gladly share a meal with a far more frightening man than you, if it meant more of that delicious pie. I have half a mind to try to steal your cook."

"My staff are loyal to me, even despite the curse. You would have better luck trying to steal a casket of jewels from my storeroom, and you have seen how badly that turns out." His voice held a warning edge.

Stealing from one's host was a gross violation of the laws of hospitality, as Zuleika well knew. She lowered her gaze. "I meant no disrespect to your household, your Highness."

"Vardan," he corrected. "I am a merchant prince, more than a royal one. Yes, I rule this isle, but not because of my birth. To everyone else here, I am the Trade Master of Beacon Isle. From what little I know of you so far, Lady Belle, I suspect you call no man your master." He smiled in what appeared to be amusement, but his eyes held a challenge.

"In that, you are correct, Vardan," she said sweetly. "Will you tell me more about how you came to be cursed?"

Vardan's gaze wandered around the room. "You may go," he said, waving his hands.

If Zuleika closed her eyes, she could almost imagine the servants clearing the room, leaving her alone with the prince as the candles formed an honour guard down the length of the table between them. "How do you know they are all gone?" she asked. "Someone could be standing silently in the corner, and you would never know."

His enormous shoulders rose and fell in a noncommittal shrug. "So it is true what they say, that there is no loyalty amongst thieves. Lady Belle, you betray yourself every time you open your mouth. Servants will listen to the master's private conversations, and mine will learn all my secrets whether I will it, or no. Loyalty is how I know they will keep their mouths shut about it outside my household. But what I will tell you this evening is no secret. In fact, they know the story so well that they will add their own details to it and I will not be able to get a word in. You will forgive me if I'm selfish enough to wish to keep your attention to myself. We get so few visitors here."

Zuleika felt his eyes on her again. "Then tell your tale, oh, selfish prince. Why are you cursed?"

He lifted his goblet and drank deeply from his wine. "Those are two different questions, but the answer to both is the same. In truth, I am not certain, but I shall tell you what I know." He took a deep breath, then continued, "As my brother's herald is my witness, I retired one night, an ordinary man in a household of ordinary servants. On the morrow, I awoke to a household in uproar. Every man, woman and child in my employ had been cursed with invisibility, and when I emerged from my chamber, I was as you see now. Why I became impossible to look at, instead of invisible like the rest, heaven only knows. The only person in the house to escape the curse was my brother's herald, Sir Ryder. He had recently brought me a name day gift from my brother, the king. He took ship the following morning, bearing a message to my brother, asking him to investigate this curse which had befallen us.

"Some time later, my brother's answer arrived. His inquiries revealed that I had offended a powerful witch, who would never lift the curse as long as she lived. His advice was to hunt the woman down and slay her."

"And did you?" Zuleika blurted out.

"What do you take me for?" the prince demanded. "I am no coward, slaughtering defenceless women, witch or no. And even if I were to dishonour myself so, I am still not stupid. The curse a witch casts with her dying breath is far more powerful than any she casts in life. Damn near unbreakable, or so I have heard. And it is not just me she would curse. The whole population of Beacon Isle depends on me to break the curse we are already under. So I sent another missive to my brother, asking him to bargain with her. What must I do in order for her to lift the curse? I offered wealth, lands, pledging myself to her service, but her answer was none of these. The witch said I had rejected her charms when she offered herself to me, and if she could not have me, then she would make me so hideous, so repulsive, that no one else could bear to look at me. She would lift the curse if I pledged my love for her, or if a woman, more beautiful than she, fell in love with me in my current form. As my honour will never abide the first, and no woman will look at me, the curse is no closer to being broken than on the day the witch cast it."

"So you plan to seduce me?" Zuleika asked.

The prince laughed so hard he nearly fell off his

chair. "Good heavens, no! Perhaps some of the servants, especially the more romantically inclined maids, hope I will do so, but you are safe from me, Lady Belle. I am not my brother. I do not seduce maidens for my own pleasure."

"Then you're a better man than your brother," she said vehemently. "He deserves this curse, not you."

Vardan laughed softly this time. "Ah, he would never refuse a woman's affections. But if the witch were to appear before me now as a beautiful maiden like yourself, I would still choose the curse over dishonour for I would not dishonour her. So you see, I am not blameless in this matter."

"I still wish to help you, if I can," Zuleika ventured. "It sits ill with me to let a wicked witch have her way."

The prince inclined his head. "Tomorrow, I shall show you the rest of Beacon Isle, and you shall see the extent of her curse. Then perhaps you will see how pointless it is to oppose a witch so powerful."

"No witch is invincible," Zuleika said. She thought of her own brush with death, mere days ago, when she had nearly drowned. The prince's servants might well have saved her life bringing her in from the snow.

"Perhaps not," he agreed. He stretched his arms up behind his monstrous head, fixing his gaze on her. "Now, Lady Belle, I have satisfied your curiosity, while mine hungers for answers. It is time for you to tell me how you came to be lying in my rose garden."

Zuleika swallowed. "It is?"

Sixteen

Haltingly, she told a tale about being aboard her father's ship, before finding herself in the water. She fought not to weep as she described how close she had come to drowning, but still she continued, "And then I found myself in the snow, where your servants found me." She cast her eyes down and sipped from her goblet.

Rolf had made his suspicions clear. In his opinion, the girl had heard the rumours that Beacon Isle was haunted by the ghosts of those who had once lived here which kept everyone else away, but she'd dismissed them as mere stories. Vardan couldn't blame her for that – he did not believe in ghosts, either. So she'd come here to search for the treasures the pirates had left in their cavernous lairs around the island, Rolf had insisted. The very fact that when she woke, she'd headed straight for the cellars to steal something precious confirmed it in Rolf's eyes.

But not Vardan's. Oh, he admitted it was possible. But he'd searched the casket of jewels twice, and found nothing but the pretty purple stones. Of all the jewels in his cellar, they were perhaps the least valuable of the lot. Why choose that when she could have had gold or rubies or diamonds?

Unless she'd just taken something at random to prove to someone else that she'd found the lost ships' cargo. That certainly fitted with her arriving her by magical means. She must have had help from someone.

Yet he'd lifted her from the snow himself – he'd felt the weight of water in her clothes, and smelled the salt from the sea. He didn't doubt her sincerity now when she spoke of near drowning.

How, then, was she here? And why?

Vardan wanted to pound his fist on the table and demand answers, but the girl had evidently been through quite an ordeal. That she could tell him anything at all was a miracle in itself. So instead, he forced himself to soften his tone. "And you know nothing of who pulled you from the water, and brought you to my home?"

She paused to swallow more wine. "No, your Highness. I saw no one."

Not even when she'd arrived here, as his invisible servants had frightened her so much she'd fainted. For all her strength of character, he must remember that she'd not long since awoken from a swoon. She was as delicate as the first spring flowers that ventured through the melting snow. Precious. In need of protection.

His heart stuttered in his chest as her gaze met his. Unflinching. Without horror or fear. Merely…curiosity, he decided. Perhaps it took more to satisfy her than he'd realised.

"Ask it," he suggested.

Her eyes widened. "Ask what?"

"The question dancing on the tip of your tongue. The one burning in your mind. Ask it," he said.

"It has occurred to me that while I have eaten this pie, you have not touched it. Is that a part of your curse? That you cannot eat, or enjoy food?"

Vardan shook his head. "No."

"Then is it poisoned?"

Lady or no, Belle had far more knowledge of the criminal classes and political intrigue than any respectable woman should have. What kind of woman suspected her food might be poisoned?

"No." He rose from his chair, marched down the length of the table and broke off a piece of the pie. He ate the whole slice while he stood before her, then washed it down with a goblet of wine poured from the same flagon Greta had used to fill her cup. Not once did his eyes leave hers. Finally, he swallowed and said, "You are safe here, Lady Belle. My servants are loyal and would not poison my food, or yours, and I will not hurt you. You have my word of honour."

For a long moment, her eyes stared into his, reading his soul, or so it felt. "Are you truly as honourable as you say, Vardan?"

He felt the peculiar urge to take the girl in his arms and kiss her. But that would hardly be honourable. Perhaps another time, when she knew him better and had learned to trust him. And they had found a way to break the curse. Then he might be permitted to kiss her without her recoiling in horror. "I hope so," he said fervently, both in answer to her and his own unspoken desires.

Seventeen

Later that night, Zuleika tossed and turned in her bed, knowing the prince hadn't believed her vague description of how she'd found herself in the water and then in the snow. She'd mentioned her father's ship, though, which had seemed to satisfy him, at least a little. When she told him the jewel casket she'd taken from his storeroom contained amethysts her father had bought for her, he'd grown suspicious. Now, she found it hard not to laugh. He'd believed the part about her being aboard a ship, which was a lie, but when faced with the truth that the jewels were hers, he didn't believe her. Men made so little sense.

She'd begun to discern expressions in that ghastly face of his, too, almost as if he was human.

Well, he probably was still human, despite whatever the jealous witch had changed him into. Why change him into some sort of hybrid between beast and man, anyway? A toad or a squirrel would have been fine, and much easier. And why curse his household along with him? That part made no sense at all. Surely she had not tried to seduce them in addition to their master.

Zuleika shook her head. She had stumbled upon the strangest, magical mystery she had ever encountered. Her good sense told her to find some bare earth or rock tomorrow and cast a portal home to her father, to tell him she'd found his cargo.

Except…she still didn't know how it had ended up here, nor how she'd transport it home. Vardan hadn't told her everything, either, she realised. He kept his secrets, just as she kept hers.

Perhaps if she toured the island with him, as he'd planned, she could persuade him to drop his guard and tell her the full story. Maybe even enough to allow her to lift his curse…

Not by falling in love with him, of course. She had more powerful means at her disposal that he knew nothing about, and she wanted to keep it that way. For all his trepidation against antagonising the other witch, Zuleika had little to fear from her. She was a fully-fledged enchantress who conquered djinn, for goodness' sake. A witch who wasted her power on complicated curses when simple ones would do would be no match for Zuleika.

If she defeated the witch and restored the prince and his household to their former state, he might be so grateful that he'd help her bring her father's merchandise home. Now that would be worth the delay.

With that settled, Zuleika drifted off to sleep.

Eighteen

A persistent tapping on the door woke Zuleika. With no windows in the room, it was difficult to tell the time. If it was Vardan trying to enter, he could tap until his fingers fell off. He spoke of honour and of being nothing like his brother, but words were cheap. When a man sole into a girl's chamber by night to have his way with her, then he showed his true mettle. Zuleika had locked and warded the door, so the only way in was if she allowed him entrance.

"Who is it?" she asked.

"It's Inga and Greta, m'lady. We brought your breakfast and fresh clothes for your journey."

Zuleika thought she recognised the voice. "Did you find me in the snow?"

"That was me, m'lady. I needed help to carry you in, before I shooed the menfolk out so I could take off your wet things. Your beautiful dress was ruined by the water, so we brought you something new."

Zuleika climbed out of bed and unbarred the door. She blinked for a moment as the corridor outside appeared empty, before she remembered the curse. "I can't see you, but you're still here, right?"

"Yes, my lady," the voice said, somewhere to Zuleika's left. Right above the floating breakfast tray. "You need not fear us. We're just ordinary women, the same as those in your household. You can't see us, what with the curse and all, but we'll make extra noise so you can hear us, and if you see things floating, that's because we're carrying them."

Zuleika stepped aside to let the tray, and presumably the woman carrying it, into the room. A second set of steps shuffled in behind the first woman.

"I have your clothes, my lady," a nervous voice said.

Unlike the breakfast tray, Zuleika couldn't see any clothes. "Where?" she asked.

"I'm carrying them in my arms, my lady. I will

lay them out, so you can see them." True to her word, the girl shuffled over to the bed, where a blue gown materialised from thin air as it spread across the chest. "It's the master's favourite colour, my lady. He won't be able to take his eyes off you when you wear this."

Zuleika suppressed an unladylike snort. "You expect me to seduce your prince to break the curse? I'm not sure it works like that."

"But if he falls in love with you, and he won't be able to help himself, he will be the most charming prince imaginable. One you won't be able to help but fall in love with," the girl said dreamily.

"Greta's head is turned at the thought of all this romance, but she is right about the master. He is charming when he wants to be, and a good man, besides. We know why the witch cursed us as well as him. She knew we'd do everything humanly possible to help him break the curse. There are far worse men in this world than Prince Vardan, my lady. He is a rose among thorns, and no mistake." The older woman set the breakfast tray on the table beside the bed, as if to emphasise her point.

"You both believe I can break this curse," Zuleika marvelled. "What if the king is wrong, and the witch left no such loophole to break the spell?

What then?"

The bed creaked as a depression appeared in the mattress, as though a heavy weight had settled on the edge. "Then my heart will break long before the master's. I have buried two children since the affliction turned us invisible. Two children whose faces I never saw, between birth and death. What fate is that for a child, to never see his mother's face, to never see a single smile?" Inga's voice shook with unseen tears. "My lady, I love the master as if he were my own son, and if bringing him happiness would let me see the face of my children once more, I would do anything. I beg you, if there is even the smallest kernel of compassion in you, help the master to break the curse."

A tear slipped down Zuleika's cheek. She could not refuse a mother's heartfelt plea. "I shall do whatever I can to help," she promised the woman.

Plump hands seized Zuleika's. "Thank you, my lady. And in return, I will help you. When the master sees you today, you will look like a queen."

"A princess, at best," Zuleika corrected. "You are not trying to tempt the king."

"A queen," Inga repeated firmly. "We want you to look too good for the master, so that he tries his hardest to win your heart. If you had only seen him before the curse, you would understand why a witch would want him for herself. He was the handsomest prince ever born. Why, even the king himself was jealous of him."

Zuleika reached for her loaf of bread and nibbled on the end. "Very well. Where do we start?"

"With the queen's jewels."

Zuleika choked. "The king's mother is here?"

Inga laughed, and even Greta tittered.

"No, my lady. Not Queen Katerina. The master's grandmother, Dowager Queen Margareta. This was her chamber, and the gown you wore to dinner last night was first worn by Her Majesty at her son's coronation. I can show you the coronation tapestry, if you like. She sewed it herself, so it shows the detail of the dress quite clearly."

Last night she had dressed like a queen. No wonder Vardan had stared at her so. Wearing his grandmother's dress, no less.

"You sound like my father." Zuleika sighed. "His ship carried silk and jewels and fur to make me a court dress so that I might tempt the king into marriage."

"They belong to your father?"

Present tense, not past, Zuleika noted. She

nodded.

"I will speak to the seamstress. If the cloth is yours, perhaps she can make something of it. If you help his brother to break the curse, perhaps the king will be so grateful that —"

"NO!" Zuleika interrupted, louder than she'd intended. She hurried to explain, "If I break the curse, as you say, I will be in love with the prince. The king can look elsewhere for a bride." Or a whore, she thought but didn't say.

"Yes, my lady."

Though she couldn't see Inga's face, Zuleika was certain the woman was smiling.

Nineteen

After enduring an interminably long toilette, Zuleika was finally allowed to make her way to the great hall, where she was told the prince waited for her. He had evidently grown impatient, for he was nowhere to be seen when she arrived. The heavy doors had been thrown open, so she ventured outside in search of him. The yard she entered sounded like it was full of people, but she could only see one – the prince. He stood in deep conversation with someone unseen, beside a magnificent dark horse. Yes, only a prince would own such an animal.

Zuleika gave the stallion a wide berth, as she made her way across the icy cobbles. The mare she presumed would be her mount seemed supremely unconcerned by the invisible people saddling her for the coming ride. Zuleika pulled off her glove and allowed the mare's misty breath to warm her hand, giving the horse her scent. "What is her name?" she asked the groom she knew to be in earshot.

"You are asking me, my lady?" At Zuleika's nod the man continued, "The master called her Embarr, on account of her swimming ashore from a shipwreck all by herself."

Zuleika nodded. The horse was yet another piece of the puzzle, for if she had come from a ship, she did not truly belong to the prince. "I think she shall suit me well indeed, provided she does not try to walk on water again."

The old man chuckled, which ended in a hacking cough. "Beg pardon, my lady. But Embarr here will not go near the water, not even to walk along the beach."

"Then she is a wise animal." Zuleika mounted the mare, aware of every eye upon her, including the prince's. She smoothed her skirts as he approached.

"Good morning, Lady Belle," he said. "Your beauty outshines the sun today."

Soft, feminine laughter floated out of the open door. Greta, Inga and several more, by the sound of it.

The girl she once was would have blushed. Zuleika the enchantress merely smiled.

The prince moved in close, and stroked the mare's neck. He dropped his voice so low it was barely audible as he said, "They will stop at nothing, won't they? I'd wager there isn't a member of my household not watching us now."

Zuleika ducked her head. In a low voice, she replied, "I believe you're right, your Highness. After all, they stand to gain much if the curse is broken."

His voice rumbled in his throat. "And yet they have made you irresistible. If the witch who cursed me had looked like you do now, I could not have refused her anything. Do you think they would cheer if I were to throw you to the ground right now, and ravish you here before them?"

It sounded like a jest, but the look in his eyes was too intense for levity.

Zuleika stiffened. "I think you would disappoint them. They believe they serve a good, honourable man. Not a beast who ruts with unwilling women."

A wolf. That was what he reminded her of right now. Something about him unsettled the mare, too. Zuleika nudged the horse forward through the gate.

"Make haste, your Highness," she called over her shoulder. "It is discourteous to keep a lady waiting."

She allowed Embarr to continue walking, until the clatter of hooves brought the prince to her side. She opened her mouth to say something else, but she closed it with a snap as they stepped out of the shelter of the high wall. The prince's house perched on a hill, overlooking the town and what must have been the harbour. The water was empty of ships today, though. If the prince owned all this, he was a wealthy man, with no need to resort to piracy.

She glanced at the prince, and found his eyes still fixed on her.

Before she could look away, he said, "I must apologise. I meant no disrespect. What I said, I said in jest. No more. My brother always said I had a fey sense of humour. I only wished to set you at ease in front of our audience, and instead I... I am sorry."

"If a man can jest about ravishing women, then what is to stop him following words with action? I assure you, rape is no joke, your Highness."

He seized Embarr's bridle, forcing her to stop. "I made a mistake, and offered you my apology.

You are correct that rape is no joke. But you are wrong if you believe that words said in jest are no different to a man's actions. I have never forced a woman, and I will not. I am not a beast. Whether you believe it or not, you need not fear me. I will not hurt you, Lady Belle."

She wanted to drop her gaze, but found she could not. No beast had ever looked so earnest. She wished she could believe him, if only for the sake of his household. She sighed. "Then perhaps we should start again. I shall bid you good morning, and ask whether you slept well?"

He released the mare's bridle as he relaxed. "It is a fine winter morning for a ride. I wish I had slept better, but a mysterious maiden danced through my dreams, disturbing my slumber with her secrets."

More flattery. "Ah, dancing maidens can be quite troublesome. I find it best to let them dance until they are exhausted, so that they fall asleep on their own, and leave you to rest."

The prince snorted softly. "So the maiden sleeps, but not I? That will not do. In order to sleep, I must dance, too."

A faint smile touched Zuleika's lips. "Then you must try it tonight, or the next time the maiden invades your dreams, your Highness, and let me know whether it works for you."

"Vardan," he corrected. "I am no one's Highness here. And as I have no doubt she will return tonight, if she permits me to dance with her, I shall give you a full report in the morning."

She laughed aloud. "As long as all you do is dance, your report will be fit for a lady's ears."

He grinned, showing more pointed teeth than any man should. "That I cannot promise. I am a man, after all."

Yes. She could not afford to forget that.

"A man who rides a rather splendid horse. I have no doubt he has an equally splendid name. Bucephalus, perhaps?" she asked.

"No, I am no general, and I have no desire to conquer the world. His name is Arion."

She nodded. "The speedy steed of the sea king. More noble still."

"A gift from my brother. He came on the last ship to enter the harbour before we were cursed." Vardan reined in his horse and pointed. "You see those rocks there? The ones that look like fangs? That's where the entrance to the harbour used to be. Now, we can't even get a fishing boat out at high tide."

That explained the absence of ships in port. "How did you get the ship out, then?" Zuleika asked, puzzled. "You say it entered the harbour, but there are no ships here now. How did it get out?"

He stared at her for a long moment before he answered, "By road. We built an enormous cart, harnessed every pony on the island to it, and rolled it from the harbour to the sea. It was all for naught, though, for it hadn't even sailed out of sight before she ran into another patch of rocks the lookout never saw until it was too late. Tore out the bottom of her hull and she sank like a stone. Most of the crew drowned, and those that did not...returned to port in their boats to spread stories of what they called Haunted Isle, not Beacon Isle, on account of the ghosts."

Zuleika blinked. "You have ghosts, too?"

He hesitated. "No, but...you shall soon see." He spurred Arion on, toward the town.

Curious, Zuleika followed.

Twenty

Either she was as practiced at pretence as the craftiest courtier, or Belle truly did not know about the island's haunted reputation. But how could she have heard about the island's treasures without hearing the ghost stories?

She had refused to wear any of his grandmother's jewels, too – which made her a strange thief. The casket of gems she'd tried to steal were worth far less than one of Queen Margareta's diamond or pearl necklaces. Yet Inga said Belle had done little more than touch the treasures before declaring them impractical for riding, and asked Inga to return them to the locked chest where they normally resided.

Only a peculiar woman indeed could resist

Queen Margareta's jewels.

Yet she had not refused the horse. Embarr was not as spirited a creature as Arion, but she was a horse bred for royalty. She seemed to accept Belle quite happily, and the lady's seat showed her a practiced horsewoman. Either her thievery ran to horses, or the lady kept a fine stable.

But if she was a member of the high nobility as she appeared, her manners were not those of a noble maiden, or at least not the women he'd met at court. She was courteous enough, but she did not bow her head in humility like most girls did. No, she held his gaze with considerable pride. She would never be any man's obedient wife, he thought, fighting down laughter at the thought. Should her father marry her to a weak man, she would undoubtedly turn into a shrew. But if she chose her own husband – and she certainly appeared old enough to be in her majority, and able to choose – she deserved someone who would continue to light that fire in her eyes that made them sparkle so. A woman such as her should never be broken by a bad husband.

If only he were in a position to ask for her hand...but what woman would accept him, looking the way he did? Even Belle with her piercing gaze would never see past the beast he'd become.

Twenty-One

Vardan slowed Arion down to a walk when they reached the first building. Zuleika followed suit. "Welcome to Harbourtown," Vardan said, spreading his arms wide. "A ghost town, now."

And so it looked, for not a soul was in sight. A pony plodded down the middle of the cobblestone street, pulling a laden cart. A cat dashed between the wheels and emerged unscathed. Spray of snow fountained up from the drift by the side of the road, as though a child had kicked it. As though…

Zuleika dismounted, wrapping the reins around her hand so she didn't lose Embarr in the crowd. A crowd she could not see, but she could hear.

The witch hadn't just cursed the prince's household. She'd cursed an entire town, bustling with people and businesses and all the things a place of this size should have. Even Zuleika couldn't cast a curse this far-reaching. No single spell-caster had done this. She would have had to cast dozens of curses to enchant this many people. It was…inconceivable that one witch would expend so much power to punish one man.

Zuleika moved in a daze, not looking where she was going, and she stumbled. She would have fallen, if not for her hold on the horse's reins. As it was, she landed painfully on her knees, tearing one of the lovely silk stockings Inga had insisted she wear. Now, the blue silk was stained purple with her blood.

Before she could think the action through, Zuleika touched her bloodied knee to the cobbles. "Show me what the curse hides," she whispered. She watched the spell eddy down the street as if blown by the wind, and as it went, people faded into sight. Men, women, children, going about their business as though there was no curse. But that wasn't right, either. The women's veils were crooked, for they could not see to set them straight. The children's hair was mussed, because no one ever saw it to admonish them to brush it. Two men stood outside the baker's in stained tunics, blissfully unaware of their need to wash.

The people of Harbourtown weren't only invisible to the world. They were invisible to themselves, too.

Before her eyes, children lived without ever seeing their mother's loving smile. Just as Inga had said.

Tears sprang to Zuleika's eyes. She must fix this. There had to be a way.

Strong hands seized her, lifting her to her feet.

"Are you all right?" Vardan asked, not taking his arms from around her.

The townsfolk stopped to stare. At their prince, with a strange woman in his arms. Realisation dawned on their faces, as men began to bow and women dropped curtseys.

"I am fine," Zuleika tried to say, turning her head so that she might see his face, but the words died in her throat. The beastly face – Vardan's face – that she expected to see was not there. Instead, she saw the face of King Thorn, an unspeakable monster she would never allow to touch her again.

She closed her eyes and released her hold on the spell, which dispersed its magic in a cloud of tiny stars only she could see. Zuleika dared to open her eyes, and breathed a sigh of relief as she saw Vardan's hideous visage once more. Unable to help herself, she lifted a hand to his cheek. It felt…smooth, like the skin of a man, and not a beast. The curse on him was merely illusion, she realised. Underneath it, he looked like…a beast.

Zuleika wrenched herself out of his grasp and straightened her cloak. "I am fine," she said finally, unwilling to look at him now. "I did not look where I was going."

"Perhaps you should stay on your horse. Her hooves are more sure than your feet."

Flushing with embarrassment, Zuleika climbed back on the mare. She knew he'd seen it, that moment of panic as she was helpless in a man's arms again. A man who looked like him, if only for a moment. "He is not his brother," she told herself. One glance at the prince confirmed it. How strange. The monstrous face she'd shied away from before was now a relief to look upon.

She met his eyes. Not his brother at all. "I think you are right." She swallowed, then continued, "Please, show me the town. I would like to see everything I can. I didn't realise the curse stretched so far. Whoever this witch is, she must be stopped."

Murmurs of agreement came from the townspeople lining the road.

"My brother told me her name. Something foreign, it sounded like. Zulu or Zollie or…"

"Zuleika?" she said, feeling sick.

Vardan nodded. "Something like that. He said if I didn't have the stomach to slay her, I should send her to him instead, and he would do the deed."

She should have killed the king instead of simply cursing him. Blaming her for a curse this huge? Zuleika had never met this man before, let alone tried to seduce him, and she'd certainly never cursed an entire town in a fit of pique.

"What did you tell him?" Zuleika didn't like the way her voice shook.

"That if he wants a woman, he can hunt her down himself. Beacon Isle is my responsibility, now more than ever. Do you not agree?"

Numbly, Zuleika nodded.

But inside, she felt far too much. The king was hunting her, he'd said. How far would he go to find her? A man with no honour might do anything, including breaking promises he never intended to keep. He might even hurt her family…

"You do not look well, Lady Belle. Perhaps you should rest a moment in the inn, and take some refreshment. Harbourtown's hospitality has earned it quite a reputation. The ships might not dock here anymore, but the innkeeper has not changed."

She allowed Vardan to help her off her horse and into the dim interior of the inn. People fussed around her, but all she could see was Vardan's eyes, filled with concern for her.

No, she was not the one in danger. Her father was, and somehow, she had to warn him.

Twenty-Two

The innkeeper settled Zuleika in a chair beside the fire while Vardan called for the speciality of the house.

"This is the best inn in Harbourtown, you'll see," Vardan told her. "Farlof's brother, Karl, has the largest farm on the southern part of the isle. If we're lucky, he might still have some of that dewberry wine." He cupped his hands to his mouth. "Ho! Elena! The lady wants wine!"

Zuleika frowned at him. "I said no such thing."

"Ah, you will once you taste it, my lady," a female voice said, before a tray floated into the room. "His Highness knows what he's about. When he was a boy visiting his grandmother on the island, you could tell the time by him. He'd be on my doorstep the moment the baking was out of the oven. And he still has a taste for them. That's the secret to why he chose to live at Beacon Isle and not the capital with the king. Saffron buns washed down with the island's own dewberry wine will be enough to make you want to stay forever."

Saffron buns? Zuleika had not tasted the spice more than once or twice in her life, but the curlicued cakes on the tray did look quite yellow, even in the dim light. And she could smell them – they must be still warm from the oven. Her mouth watered, but she didn't dare take one before the prince. She might be dressed like a queen, but she knew all too well he was far higher than she would ever be in the social pecking order. Royalty ate first. Always.

"Take one, my lady," Elena urged.

"After five years living under this curse, they see one pretty girl and forget I'm a prince," Vardan grumbled. "On Beacon Isle today, the woman who could break the curse ranks higher than royalty. How the mighty have fallen." He shook his head, but his eyes held amusement.

Still Zuleika hesitated.

"Oh, by all that's holy." Vardan seized a pastry and held it to her lips. "Bite, Lady Belle, and I promise you, you'll fall in love."

She blinked, but there was nothing magical about the cakes. No hidden love spell. Nothing but the buttery, spicy aroma that tempted her to…

Zuleika bit into the pastry, as cheering erupted from the prince. She took it from his fingers as she chewed the morsel. The saffron bun was every bit as good as it smelled. Light and crisp and just the slightest bit sweet. Before she'd realised it, she'd finished the whole thing.

Not even Vardan had made such a pig of himself — he was only halfway through his bun. "What is your verdict, Lady Belle?"

"The cakes are lovely," she said. "But I thought you said you were an honourable man. You are trying to seduce me with food."

"And wine!" he added, filling a cup and holding it out to her. "Don't forget the wine."

She took the cup, but she didn't drink. "You didn't answer me, your Highness."

"Vardan, and I believe I did. Food and wine, the best we have to offer, for my guest. There is nothing dishonourable in offering hospitality to a beautiful lady."

Zuleika heard shuffling footsteps, like someone trying to leave the room as quietly as possible. She stared into the depths of her wine cup in order to avoid his soul-piercing eyes. "But you are trying to seduce me."

"If there is a way to help my people and retain my honour, I will do what I must. If all I succeed in doing is to make you fall in love with Beacon Isle, as I have, then so be it. You are welcome to stay."

On a cursed island where the invisible people would be a daily reminder that there was a more powerful witch than her who worked for the king and was willing to blame her for inflicting this horror on the island. While her father worried.

Zuleika shook her head. "My father will be waiting for news of his lost ship. I must return home. Once you have shown and told me all you can about this curse, perhaps I can look in my mother's library at home for ways to break it." She drank the wine. Elena was right about her wanting more.

"First, you should check our library here. I'm sure it's far superior to anything your mother may have collected. My house used to be a monastery. The monks refused to stay in a building suffering under a curse, so they left, but they could not take everything. I'll show you on our return."

A monastery library wouldn't contain much about magic, but Zuleika held her tongue. She was fond of reading, and she would relish the chance to see his collection. He already knew two of her weaknesses – good food and wine. She didn't dare let him add a third: reading.

After all, she still didn't know how he'd come to be in possession of her father's goods. Or why the witch had chosen to target him for her curse. For all his talk of honour, there had to be something wrong with the man to justify such a punishment.

Either that, or she was missing something that might help her make sense of all this. She knew she wouldn't find the answer in any library, though – Vardan held the key to the curse, she was certain of it. How to extract it…she did not know. But she would enjoy finding out.

Twenty-Three

When Vardan was certain Belle had rested sufficiently – and they'd eaten all of Elena's saffron cakes, which was only to be expected – he suggested they continue on the tour.

He read her hesitation in her eyes – such a marvellous thing, to see another person's expression again! Her face was both delightful and expressive, a treat to observe – and offered, "Or we could remain here at the inn and resume the tour on the morrow, when you are better rested. We could return to my house, if you no longer wish to..." No longer wish to see any more of me or my island, he tried to say, but the words stuck in his throat.

She'd looked at him with such horror and fear

on the road outside that he'd nearly dropped to his knees under the weight of his despair. Could he have imagined the other times she'd looked at him and seen more than just a beast? Because the sheer intensity of the terror in her eyes for that moment had been enough to unman him. She hadn't been the only one in need of some wine when they entered the inn.

Yet she'd reached up to touch his face, and her terror had vanished. No one had touched him like that in a very long time. Like she actually wanted to.

A whisper of hope sent a shiver through his soul. Perhaps the curse could be broken by Lady Belle.

She rose and smoothed her skirt before reaching for her cloak. "I fear if I rest any longer, I shall fall asleep. I ate far too many of those delicious cakes. A ride in the crisp winter air should wake me up nicely." She paused. "Unless you are too tired of my company to continue, of course. I cannot have a tour of this island without a suitable guide."

Yes, she had recovered, Vardan decided, hurrying to fasten his cloak so he could follow her outside.

"I'll bring the next batch out in a basket, Prince

Vardan," Elena said. "And some wine. Your lady will want more, and so will you. Winning a lady's heart is hard work."

"You think I can win it, too?" Vardan asked bitterly. "Is there anyone on this cursed island who I will not disappoint when I fail?"

"I know some cheeky lads who like being invisible, so they can cause more mischief, but a good clout around the ears will sort them out. It certainly worked on you when you were a boy." Though he couldn't see it, Vardan knew she was smiling. Elena continued, "She has a playful heart, that one. I warrant she would dearly love to dance with the right man."

A man, and not a beast. Vardan sighed.

"The cakes you wanted, ma'am," said a younger voice.

Elena made an irritated sound in her throat. "Give them to the prince, then!"

The girl thrust the basket hard against Vardan's midsection. "There you go."

"Your Highness," Elena reminded her.

"There you go, your Highness," the girl said sulkily. Stomping footsteps signified that she'd left.

"The sooner you break this curse, the better," Elena said with feeling.

Vardan bowed his head. "I will do all that

honour permits."

"Don't forget the wine. It's in the basket, with the cakes."

Vardan nodded his thanks and carried his burden out to Arion.

He felt Belle's eyes on him as he secured the basket to his saddle. He mounted before he said, "Are you ready to see more of my domain, Lady Belle?"

She took a deep breath, closing her eyes in appreciation. "If that's another basket of those cakes you're carrying, I might just follow you anywhere."

Vardan offered up an earnest prayer that her words were more than jest. "They are," he said shortly. "So let's go." He set off at a walk, hearing the clop of Embarr's hooves following behind.

Twenty-Four

The buildings lining the harbour were a mixture of storehouses and taverns. Though she had never entered one, Zuleika recognised some of the waterside buildings as brothels. Many of the taverns were not yet open, for which she blamed the early hour, but the brothels never closed. Idly, she wondered if they did better business with invisible clientele. She considered asking Vardan, but a prince had no need to frequent a common whorehouse when he could follow his brother's example and turn his subjects into whores for his own private use. She sighed, only half listening as the prince told her how all the storehouses in Harbourtown were full, which was why he'd started to store goods in his cellars.

"Can't you just sell things?" Zuleika blurted out. "Full storehouses breed vermin, and goods can be damaged when they are stored too long. Especially foodstuffs. If they are full of the same things as your cellars, they are trade goods. Their value is not in being stockpiled, but in being sold to the right market, or so my father says."

Vardan nodded. "Your father is correct. But who would we sell them to, Lady Belle?" He waved his hand at the empty harbour. "There are no ships. No traders from east or west, though we used to welcome them daily. And if my people approach shore in their fishing boats, no one sees them. Others try to steal their goods, thinking the boats are empty, and no one wishes to trade with a ghost. Or me."

She hadn't thought of that, but Zuleika supposed it made sense. Still… "How do the trade goods arrive here if not by ship?"

"This is not our only harbour," Vardan replied. "Beacon Isle is bigger than you might think."

It still didn't add up in Zuleika's head. "But if there are other harbours, why are the goods not stored there, near the ships? And if you can transport goods from the other harbour to this one, why can't you send some of this cargo out on the ships when they leave?"

"There are no ships," he repeated.

"Why not?" she persisted.

"Pirates, and the curse, though we've found the curse quite convenient when it comes to combating pirates," Vardan said with a smile.

Zuleika was intrigued. "No one wins against pirates, or so my father says. They sail away to their secret bases, sell slaves and all their stolen merchandise, and live high until they find another ship to prey upon. They cannot be stopped, for as long as the secret bases remain and one man knows how to reach them, there will always be men willing to become pirates."

Vardan laughed. "Now that's where you're wrong. Let me show you."

Zuleika didn't understand her hesitation. Wasn't he offering her the knowledge she wanted? She mentally shook herself before she said, "All right. Show me."

Twenty-Five

Vardan guided Arion up to the cliff path, glancing back over his shoulder every now and again to make sure Lady Belle still followed him. He was worried about her swooning again, he told himself. Not admiring the purple fire in her eyes that kindled into life the moment they reached the clifftops.

For a woman who had almost drowned, she showed surprisingly little fear of the ocean. In fact, she seemed almost exhilarated by the stiff breeze whipping the sea into waves that boomed like battering rams when they struck the base of the cliffs. Or maybe it was the way the breeze plucked her hair from its braids and turned the silky strands into curls.

No wonder women kept their hair covered under veils. Unfettered, hers was…mesmerising. Once again, he wanted to reach out and stroke it. But he wouldn't, because to see her cringe away again would be another dagger to his heart. Once the curse was lifted, then she might look upon him with something that wasn't horror. Had all the islanders looked at him in the same way since the curse took effect? If so, perhaps their invisibility was a blessing and not a curse for him.

If the witch who cursed him planned things that way, she could hardly be the cold-hearted bitch his brother had said she was. For the first time since she cursed him, Vardan wanted to meet the woman. Or meet her again, as he'd evidently already met her but couldn't recall her. Why couldn't the witch have looked like Lady Belle, for he'd never forget a face or figure like hers. But even if she had, honour would have demanded he resist her advances.

Unless she'd looked like Lady Belle and he wanted to make her his wife.

He snorted. He'd known the girl for barely a day. He shouldn't be considering the possibility of marriage to her, or all that it entailed. Vardan owned that he had little control over his dreams, and the fact that she had been the maiden dancing naked through them did not mean he should be imagining undressing her now.

The lady's voice cut through his daydream. "You have the most peculiar smile on your face. Is there something special about this place, that it should inflame you with such love?"

You, Vardan thought but didn't say as he felt blood heat his cheeks. He doubted she would see it, though, for beasts did not blush.

"Yes," he said finally. "This is where I show you how one man with the knowledge of secret pirate bases can win against them all." He swung down from his horse, indicating that she should do the same. "We'll go on foot from here."

Lady Belle slid down gracefully, her boots barely making a sound as they landed on the windswept rock. The salt wind kept the cliffs free of snow through all but the coldest winters. "To where, precisely?" She tucked a wayward curl behind her ear.

What was it about her hair that distracted him so? Vardan shook his head. "Why, to the pirates' lair, of course." He laughed at her puzzled expression, and drew her to the very edge of the cliffs so he could point. "The cliffs along the northern side of the island are riddled with caves just like that one. And for a long time, pirates used these to store their stolen cargo. Some are even big enough to sail a ship inside."

"Truly?" Her eyes danced.

"Truly," he replied. "I will show you." He took her hand and pulled her to the very brink on the cliff.

Lady Belle balked, much like Embarr did when faced with the ocean waves. The horse nibbled at some of the hardy plants that had sprouted between the rocks, unconcerned, as her mistress dug her heels in with astonishing strength. "Unless you can fly, your Highness, there is no way you're taking me over that cliff. I like living, thank you."

He sighed. Reluctantly, he released her hand. "There are steps. See?" Vardan stepped over the edge and down the first three stone steps, worn smooth by wind, wave and the passage of many feet.

She blinked in surprise. "Down the entire cliffside?" Lady Belle swallowed, her eyes wide. "I may need your arm after all." Her hand was warm as she grasped his.

Vardan brought her fingers to his lips and kissed them lightly without thinking. Thank heaven she didn't pull away before he realised his mistake. "My apologies, Lady Belle."

"No need to apologise. I may not be

accustomed to descending from clifftops, but I rarely require a man's arm to walk." She proceeded to demonstrate that she was as surefooted as her horse as she followed Vardan down the winding steps to the cave.

The steps ended at a narrow stone ledge which at high tide was washed by the waves. Now, it was simply damp with spray and strewn with seaweed thrown up in the last storm. And slippery. "Be careful here, Lady Belle," he said, glancing behind to make sure she did not lose her footing. She'd hoisted her skirts a little to better see her feet, but Vardan glimpsed a shapely ankle and found himself longing to see more. Perhaps even the naked maiden of his dreams.

He trod hard on a piece of seaweed, and his foot shot forward, throwing him backward into her arms. His face ended up pressed against her breast for one delightful moment before he came to his senses and righted himself, repeating his profuse apologies.

Lady Belle did not seem inclined to forgive him. "As you say, Vardan. Do be careful." She did not take his hand again.

Sighing, he led the way.

Twenty-Six

It was panic that made her heart beat wildly when Vardan fell against her, Zuleika told herself. With his face pressed against her breast, he probably heard it through all the layers of fabric between them. The flush of heat she'd felt was mortification at being so close to a man, a man who looked like he did under the curse, as she well knew.

And there was a tingle of something more when he touched her, too. Something magical, that had nothing to do with being touched by a man. The magic that hummed so powerfully through him felt familiar, as though it liked her. She'd never felt anything like it. Magic didn't have feelings, or preferences for people. Yet each spell contained a little of the essence of its caster, because it was the caster's blood that fuelled the spell. Each essence was as individual as the caster, and this…this was not new to her. She must know the witch who had cursed Vardan.

Except that she didn't know many witches, particularly one whose magic was so dark it had no colour at all except black, for this curse appeared like a shadow across the island. The few witches she had met in her travels were mostly enslaved djinn, whose magic she'd needed to undo. Their magic naturally recognised her as an adversary, and buzzed with alarm at her approach. Vardan's curse seemed to hum with welcome.

No witch had ever welcomed her. Except her mother, of course, but her mother had lain in her grave these six years at least. Longer than Vardan had been cursed, so she couldn't have cast this enchantment.

Zuleika's hands itched to touch the prince again, to investigate the curse upon him more thoroughly. She forced her arms to stay by her sides. He was no different to his brother, and being overly familiar with him would not turn out well. She did not want to touch a man, nor have him touch her. Ever.

She ducked under a low overhang and stepped

into darkness.

Steel scraped across flint, and a moment later a torch flared into life. Instead of orange, this flame was the colour of bluebells.

"More magic?" Zuleika asked.

Vardan's eyes seemed to glow in the firelight. "We have no witches on the island, and none who are generous enough to use their magic to light the caves. Had we even a single witch, I would have asked her to help break the curse. No, these are driftwood torches, soaked in salt water. 'Tis the salt that burns blue." Vardan eyed her suspiciously. "Why such fear for magic, Lady Belle? Do you suffer from a curse, too?"

Zuleika choked back a laugh. Cursebreaking was her specialty. Not even the most powerful djinn could keep a curse focussed on her for long. "I do not fear magic," she managed to say. "But this island is already enchanted in ways I have never seen before. To a witch who could make a whole town invisible, I'm sure a little light is nothing."

Vardan nodded, as though he accepted her explanation. He held the torch aloft as he stepped out of the narrow passage. "This is the main cavern."

Zuleika gasped as the cave opened out into a

space that could have held the cathedral in the capital, so large was it. The floor stretched away into the darkness, outside of their circle of light, and behind her she could hear the splash of waves as the ocean made its presence known, though she could not see the water.

"This cavern is big enough to sail into when the tide is not too high, which is why it was a favourite among the local pirate fleet. They waited here until a rider from town told them a particularly rich cargo was leaving the harbour, and they'd venture out under cover of darkness to attack the unsuspecting vessel. Often, they unloaded their ill-gotten gains here so they could return for them and trade them in town, sometimes to the same merchants they'd stolen them from. I've known the same pelts to appear in the market no less than six times, sold to a new merchant only for it to be stolen again. Quite ingenious, really." Vardan smiled grimly. "Or it was, until I became Trade Master of Beacon Isle."

"So you discovered their ploy?" Zuleika guessed.

Vardan shrugged. "No, I can't take full credit for that. My steward, Rolf, suspected something like it, but it wasn't until the curse took effect that we knew for certain. You see, we changed overnight, and when the next day dawned, we were all as you see now. The pirates, however, were unchanged. Usually, they brought their stolen cargo from the caves by cart, working in the middle of the night to make sure no one saw them arrive or leave as they stocked their storehouses by the harbour. The morning they returned to trade…they entered a market empty of people. Or so they thought." He chuckled. "The panic had died down, so the villagers watched in invisible rage as some of their own, traitors that they had trusted, walked into town untouched by the curse. When they saw the town empty, they raced back to the cave…but not alone. Many followed them back to the pirate lair. Now, these pirates did not just steal cargo. Oh, no. They also sold the crews as slaves. Many townspeople had family members who had served as sailors, and no small number of these were enslaved by pirates. So what ensued in this cave…I can only describe as a bloodbath. The pirates were no match for their invisible, furious foes. There were no survivors."

Part of Zuleika recoiled in horror at the thought of the violence Vardan described, but a larger part of her revelled in triumph at the victory. For surely some of the enslaved crews had been her father's men. And the pirates' booty…

"What of the stolen cargoes?" she asked.

"What, no tears for the dead men, slaughtered right here where they stood?" Vardan asked, spreading his arms wide.

"Pirates are scum. Exterminating such vermin is a public service, I am sure. But what of the treasures stored here?"

If her all of her father's missing merchandise was still on the island somewhere, then all was not lost.

"Locked in my storehouses, secure and waiting for their rightful owners' return, Lady Thief," Vardan replied. "Look all you like. You will find no pirate treasures here."

Why did he not understand? "I am no thief," she said steadily, looking him in the eye. "And I begin to believe that neither are you. But it beggars belief that all the goods in your cellars and storehouses were once stored in this cave. Either it is bigger than it looks, or it was stacked to the very roof."

"This cave stretches for miles beneath the island, so it most certainly is bigger than it first appears. But you are correct. Not all the goods in my house or the whole of Harbourtown came from the pirate stash here."

Zuleika found herself nodding. "Like the cargo

from the *Rosa*. She was only lost a few weeks ago, a month at most. Long after you cleaned out this pirate lair. How, then, came all the goods to you?"

Vardan's smile looked more feral than any man should. Zuleika thought she glimpsed something of a killer whale in his features. "We have several fishing villages, and each has its own watchtower, built of the limestone quarried at the northern end of the island. Most nights they only fish for the fruit of the sea. But sometimes, when the lookout spots a sail…my people turn to hunting instead. And their skill is unsurpassed in these waters, except by sharks."

Now Zuleika shivered at his chilling tone. "That still does not answer my question, your Highness," she said slowly. "How did you come to have the cargo of the *Rosa* in your cellar?"

He studied her for a long moment before he said, "That, I think you will need to see to believe, but such a battle is hardly a suitable place for a lady. Even such a fearless one as yourself. So I shall take you to the nearest village, and let my people tell you about the hunt. Perhaps you will believe them more than you believe me." Vardan turned on his heel and headed out of the cave the way they'd come, taking the torch and its light with him.

Zuleika considered using magic to light her way, but she dismissed the idea as quickly as it had come. Vardan distrusted witches, and if he found out who she was…he might be far less hospitable. So she hurried after him, back to daylight where the death-drenched darkness would be merely a memory.

Twenty-Seven

Lady Belle barely spoke a word during the ride to the village of Storhem. Even when he grew so sick of the silence that he began telling her the names of the farmers and their likely crop next season as they passed each field, she merely nodded, looking like her thoughts were far from him and the cursed isle.

Perhaps she had only feigned indifference to the slaughter Vardan had witnessed firsthand. Had she known one of the pirates, then? A brother, perhaps, or the father she kept mentioning?

No, Vardan decided. Her father could not have been a pirate. She'd been raised a lady, and no pirate he'd met was capable of so much as looking at a woman without planning to dishonour her before selling her into slavery. Lady Belle could not have been any man's slave.

Or had the pirate been her sweetheart, a man she waited for? Her father could not have known about him, or he would certainly have stopped the match, as any good father should. Allowing such scum to so much as look at Lady Belle, let alone touch her…

Something clawed at his insides, twisting and ripping in ways that made Vardan clench his hands into fists around Arion's reins. Jealousy, he realised. Because pirates were scum, but they were still men. Barely more than beasts, but still men. Unlike him.

What would it take to break the curse, so that a woman might look kindly upon him once more?

No. Down that road lay madness. Hope was a curse all its own, for it tasted as sweet as mead even as it dulled his senses.

Banishing hope was a simple matter.

"Have you a sweetheart?" Vardan asked. Ah, that had got her attention.

Lady Belle stared at him. "What did you say?"

"Do you have a sweetheart?" he repeated patiently. "A man you are betrothed to, or wish to be. Or someone your father has promised you to."

The lady bristled. "I am not cargo or a slave, to

be bought and sold on a man's whim. I am of age, and both my hands and my heart are my own." As if to demonstrate, she tucked her cloak more closely around her so that it hid her hands. Her heart burned with pent-up fury — she could not hide the fire as it blazed out of her violet eyes.

For a wild moment, his own heart soared as he dared to hope again. But reality brought him back to earth abruptly. Vardan said, "Then I pity the man who has the courage to ask you for your hand, for your denial will undoubtedly drive him to despair. You are a rare woman, Lady Belle. Most women desire security, position, wealth or protection. Yet it seems to me you wish for none of these things. What desire drives you?"

She blinked, seemingly lost for words, but only for a moment. An impish grin lit her face. "Curiosity. First the fate of my father's ships and cargo, and now the nature of a powerful curse. I can't imagine being cursed and not doing everything in my power to break it. How have you not sought out a solution to your…affliction?"

Had she not listened to a word he'd said? "Of course I have. My brother — "

"Has it occurred to you that your brother might be lying, and that he knows less about curses than you do?" she interrupted, eyes flashing.

"Watch your words, Lady Belle. To speak ill of your king is treason."

Instead of calming her, this seemed to only incense her further. "Thorn is not my king. He is a deceitful, dishonourable louse who had the astonishing good fortune to be the oldest son of a royal family to survive into adulthood. If he knows anything about curses, it is because he has somehow enslaved a witch. Even then, she would be a poor witch indeed if she told him everything." She paused for breath, looked into his eyes, and continued, "I am sorry if my words grieve you, for I know the king is your brother. Perhaps he was a good man once, or has become one since I was last at court."

She knew him. She'd met Thorn, and she knew him. Her impassioned words proved it. Perhaps a little too much passion, though, as if she was trying to convince him of her hatred for Thorn. Women didn't hate Thorn. They flocked to his bed. Did that mean she was some sort of spy for his brother?

"I love my brother," Vardan said. "And I am loyal to the king." There. Let her tell him that when she carried her report home to the capital.

"But what if he is wrong, and love is not the way to break the spell? Loyalty is not the same as blind obedience. Another witch as powerful as the one who cursed you might be able to lift the enchantment. I have…heard such things can happen." She bit her lip, as if she wanted to say more but didn't dare let the words out.

Vardan snorted. "In folktales and legends, perhaps. If my brother had wished to lie, or give me bad counsel, he would not have given me such an impossible task to break the spell. Either seduce a woman when none will even look at me, let alone love me, or kill a woman who does not deserve it. You are a woman, Lady Belle, so you tell me: could you love me?"

Those violet eyes turned on him, and he dropped his gaze so he wouldn't see the pity in them.

"I am not the sort of sheltered maiden who falls in love with the first man she meets. I scarcely know you, Vardan. I do not understand how you could lay under such a fearsome curse for five years and not seek help to lift it."

Now he lifted his head to meet her gaze. No woman had looked at him the way she did, as though he was not a beast. "For five years, I have been busy. Discharging my responsibilities as the Trade Master of this island. Fighting pirates, as you shall see. And in all those years…you are the first woman who can stand to look at me. For five years, I have had no hope of breaking the curse. Yet today…I begin to believe it might be possible. I ask you again: could you love me?"

Long did he look into her eyes, for he was loath to look away, even as a tear slipped down her cheek. Only then did Vardan feel the shame he should have felt earlier, in driving a woman to pain and tears. He was not usually so unchivalrous.

"I am sorry. I should not have asked such a personal question. Can you forgive me, Lady Belle?" he asked.

She nodded, and her silence returned. Somehow, this time it was worse.

Twenty-Eight

Zuleika cursed herself for opening her mouth. Vardan was loyal to his lying brother, and as long as he believed the king over her, he would never understand that it took much more than love to break a spell as powerful as the one on Beacon Isle. If he would only listen…

She'd been so caught up in the curse itself that she hadn't seen his question coming. One she did not know the answer to. Could she love him?

She was capable of love, for she loved her family. She had no husband or betrothed, so if she chose, she could give her hand and her heart to any man she wished. If by some miracle Vardan turned out to be the complete opposite of his brother, despite looking like him under the illusion, then perhaps, it was faintly possible that, if he were charming enough and she stayed for sufficient time, that she might…maybe…be capable of such a thing. Possibly.

But she had no right to raise his hopes, because she knew it didn't matter. Even if she loved him madly and married him, the curse would remain. And until she relieved him of his affliction, she had no right to his heart or his gratitude, and no business falling in love with anyone.

She bit her lip as Embarr carried her into the fishing village, whispering a spell under her breath that would allow her to see what the curse hid once more. She knew better than to look at Vardan, but she found she needed little reminding this time. As evening fell, the villagers had stopped work for the day, and they seemed to be preparing for some kind of festival.

"What is the date? Is a saint's day, or some other holy occasion that I have forgotten?" she asked.

The villagers, who looked very much like those at home, stopped to stare, but none seemed ready to volunteer an answer.

"Please, will someone tell me what you are celebrating?" she persisted, her gaze sweeping across the dozen or so people before her. People who were not used to being seen.

Finally, a man stepped forward. He ducked his head a few times before he ventured, "If it please you, m'lady, the prince gave the order that a feast should be prepared to celebrate his…your visit to Storhem. We have the best of today's catch, and he sent word from Harbourtown that the baker was to prepare special cakes to your ladyship's liking. Two tuns of wine were sent from the prince's cellars…"

Hastily, Zuleika cut him off by expressing her thanks. This seemed to satisfy the man, who hustled the others off to the village square.

Vardan reached her side.

Zuleika allowed herself a glance at him before turning her head away. "Still trying to seduce me with food and wine, I see."

She heard him sigh. "I am merely trying to entice you to stay," he said. "As you say, you've known me for less than a day. Perhaps if you remain on the island longer, you will get to know me better, and perhaps even consider…" She heard him swallow before he finished, "Helping all of these good citizens by lifting our curse."

Stung, she turned to meet his gaze squarely. "I will help. But…" Conscious of the villagers who might hear her, and not wanting to smash their hopes as she had his, she subsided. Unable to stare at his face any longer, she dismissed her spell. Better not to frighten the villagers by seeing them when no one else could.

"Thank you," was all he said. No more talk of love, to Zuleika's considerable relief.

Twenty-Nine

Vardan tried to keep still in his seat between Lady Belle and the village headman at the high table in the village hall, but his eyes kept darting to look at her. It didn't help that they sat so close he couldn't help jostling her. It would be so easy to reach around her, pull her to him and kiss her.

And make her hate him for the rest of his miserable life, he didn't doubt.

She behaved like a proper lady, of course. Her eyes surveyed the noisy hall, though there was little to see except food disappearing from trenchers. She didn't look the least bit alarmed by the invisible crowd, and she even conversed with the headman's wife, who sat beside her. What was the woman's name? He couldn't believe he'd forgotten. He knew everyone on Beacon Isle.

Lady Belle's musical laugher stole his attention entirely. "Prince Vardan, is it true what Birgitte tells me? That when you were a boy, you once stole a fishing boat and led the other fishermen a merry chase around the whole island before they caught up to you?"

He'd forgotten that. "Yes," he said grudgingly, "but they did not catch up to me until I let them do so. I had a wager with my brother that I could singlehandedly sail around the island. There was a pretty maid we both liked and the winner of the wager would get a kiss, she said. So I rode up to Storhem, borrowed a fishing boat and set off. I sailed around the island, sure enough, and brought the little boat into Harbourtown, as proud as a prince could be. Then I gave the boat back to her owners. Not a scratch on her, I swear."

Lady Belle's voice dropped low so that only he could hear it over the hubbub in the hall. "What did your brother say when you won the wager? Was the maid's kiss worth all that effort?"

Vardan swallowed. This was the part he had never told a soul. "I do not know. When I arrived at the house, neither the maid nor my brother were anywhere to be found." Not by those who didn't know Thorn well, at least. For his brother…Vardan had found them doing much more than kissing. No, he did not want to remember that day, and he did not think it fit for a maiden's ears, either. Better for her to believe in chivalry and love and not all that animal grunting in the hayloft as two sweaty, naked bodies rutted like…well, beasts. Or that the girl had died trying to birth what Vardan assumed had been Thorn's bastard less than a year later. "How do you like the fish?" he asked.

"Delicious," she replied. "I have never eaten fish cooked with saffron before. It is far too rare a spice to use where I come from, and yet here, I see the whole village eating more saffron in this one meal than I have eaten in my lifetime before today."

Vardan frowned. "What do you expect? As you said earlier today, the purpose of trade goods is to be sold, not stockpiled, and when the goods are food…they must be eaten, or they spoil. Once the curse is lifted, we will be able to share the fruits of our saffron crops with the rest of the country, but while Beacon Isle is enchanted…we must use what we have. After all, without trade, we must grow all our own food. That includes spices."

Lady Belle stared at him. "Saffron is grown here?"

Hadn't he told her as much as they passed the crocus fields? "Of course. We rode past the fields on the way here."

It was her turn to frown. "I must have been so deep in thought about your curse that I did not notice. When we pass by there again, please remind me what I missed."

"Better to think about flowers than curses, Lady Belle. Thinking about this curse will not cure it, or someone would have lifted it already. Enough talk about curses for tonight. For cursed or no, this is a celebration feast and no feast is complete without dancing!" He roared the last word so that the whole hall would hear him.

Tables and benches scraped as many hands pulled them to the side of the hall.

"Dancing? Is that wise?" Lady Belle asked.

"Wise? Perhaps not. But enjoyable, certainly. I have never met a woman who did not dearly like to dance. Will you be the exception to that, too, Lady Belle?" Vardan prayed that he hadn't made a mistake. All the ladies at court loved dancing, and he remembered the rowdier village dances here when he was a boy.

"I own I enjoy dancing as much as my sisters, or any woman alive, but I meant is it wise to dance in a room full of people when most of them are invisible? I might not know the steps if the dances are different to those at home. What if I were to tread on someone's foot, or bump into them?"

Vardan laughed. "A lady as graceful as you would never do such a thing, I am certain."

"But, your Highness – "

The wooden door to the hall crashed open and a man stood silhouetted in the open doorway. Breathlessly, he announced, "Ship sighted to the south. Two pirate vessels, closing fast."

Of all the nights…Vardan cursed inwardly. There would be no dancing tonight. "Get her to safety," he called over his shoulder as he strode out of the hall. He should have checked the mirror this morning, as was his usual habit, to see if any merchant or pirate ships were nearby. He'd been so distracted by the woman that he'd forgotten, and the crew of this new ship might pay the price for his carelessness. The war against piracy was far more important than breaking some silly curse. Most days he remembered that, but today he'd been selfish. And now…

"Where are you going?" Lady Belle demanded from right behind him.

"Into battle, which is no place for a woman," he replied.

"You also said it was a battle I must see to

believe," she returned. Vardan wasn't sure how her eyes managed to flash in the darkness, yet they did.

"The aftermath, yes, but not from the middle of the fighting. We lose men and boats all the time when we hunt pirates. They know they have nothing to lose and for all our advantages, some of our men still die in the skirmish. If anything were to happen to you…if you were hurt, thrown into the water, drowned, killed…Lady Belle, you do not know what you are asking."

"I am not defenceless, you know," she said.

Vardan sighed. "But you are visible."

"So are you."

"Which is why I will not be part of a hunting party," Vardan explained patiently. "I climb the watchtower and command the fleet while the ghost boats surround the ships. They dispatch the pirates, bring the cargo to shore, and any crew who remain take the ship's boats to safety. We have tried offering them sanctuary at Beacon Isle, but word has spread that the island is haunted, and no superstitious sailor wants to land here any more."

"How can you possibly command ships so far out on the ocean?" Lady Belle demanded. "You cannot see them so far away. They cannot see you in the dark, and they could not hear you over the sounds of battle."

"We have a code of sorts," Vardan began, then stopped. Was that why she was here? To learn the codes so that she could share them with pirates? Surely not. Or was it the magic mirror she was after? That would be a prize indeed, if she knew about it. If she did not, he would not be the one to tell her. Let her believe the code was their only means of communication. "It is of my own invention," he added with considerable pride.

"And what do the village women do?"

"They keep house, clear away the remains of the feast, put the children to bed, and see that when the menfolk return from a hard night's work, there is breakfast waiting for them in the morning," Vardan said. As good wives should, he thought but didn't say.

"I will stand watch with you," she announced.

He cursed. "No, woman, you will not." Without another word, he kicked Arion into a gallop, sure she would not follow.

Thirty

Stubborn fool, Zuleika thought as she mounted Embarr. Did he honestly think she would allow farmers and fishermen to die in a battle she could end with a single spell? Or that she wouldn't do everything in her power to save the crew of the ship the pirates were attacking?

She cast a spell to guide her to him, and was surprised to find Arion only a few hundred yards from the village, tied up outside the clifftop watchtower. Zuleika left Embarr beside her stablemate and set off up the stairs to the top of the tower, where loud swearing had erupted from several throats, including Vardan's.

"Do we have enough people to take both ships? That pincer move is new. I want them all executed before they can pass word about that particular tactic on to their fellows."

"We're not sure, master," said a second voice. "We've never tried to take on two ships at the same time before."

Zuleika peered out of one of the tower windows as she climbed. The three ships were surprisingly easy to see, lit up by some peculiar kind of fire that floated on the water without extinguishing.

Magic. It had to be. First Thorn, now pirates. Would all the scum of the earth enslave witches? This would not be borne.

Already simmering with anger, Zuleika now blazed with fury. She bit down so hard on her lip that it hurt, but she barely noticed the sting. "Pirate scum, show your true form," she murmured. "Never to be men again until you repent your wicked life and vow never to return to piracy." The spell shot out in a bolt of violet fire, splitting into two as it homed in on the pirate ships.

She both felt and saw the spell take effect, bursting into clouds of purple sparks on the decks of all three ships. Only then did she see the fishing fleet close in around the vessels, looking eerily empty in the floating firelight.

Whispering a second spell, she sent it out across the waves to search for the witch, but the spell circled the ships without settling on anyone. If there was no spellcaster aboard the ships, how on earth could water burn so?

She hurried up to Vardan. Perhaps he could answer her question. "Send word to Sillhem to ready their boats," she heard him say. "Have the men of Raggarn ready to receive the cargo. And the women…ask them to pray and prepare for the wounded. This will not be an easy fight."

As she entered the room, two men swept past her, heading down the steps to carry out Vardan's orders. Vardan was too busy peering out the window to notice her, so she took a deep breath and cast her mind toward the ships. There was no fighting, merely the salvaging of cargo before the merchant ship sank. One of the pirate ships had rammed it, and water already gushed through the splintered bow.

So that was the *Rosa*'s fate. Impaled by a pirate ship. Had the *Rosa*'s demise been lit by the same strange candles dotting the sea surface now?

"How goes the battle?" she asked.

Vardan glanced back at her and swore under his breath. "I told you to stay in the village where it is safe, not follow me." In this light, he looked like an eagle now, with beakish nose and bright, searching eyes.

Zuleika took a step closer to him. "It seems safe enough here. No pirates, and the ships are so far away. I did not realise you could see so clearly from here, even at night."

He stared at her for a long moment before he said, "That's Greek fire. A strange substance that burns even in water. I've seen it cling to a man's clothes and burn him alive, no matter how many buckets of water we threw at him. Among men of honour, it is considered too terrible a weapon to use on an enemy, but pirates have no honour and will resort to such tactics to win. Battle is not pretty, Lady Belle, and one with pirates is uglier still."

So it wasn't magic at all. No wonder she had not found a witch. "I have seen it before. Naphtha, they called it. Water is the wrong element to combat it with. What you need is earth. You must smother it with dust."

"Better to smother the pirates who know how to make it, so that they cannot use it again," he said grimly. Now, he surely looked like a shark, the cold, predatory fish that killed without conscience. What kind of curse transformed his face from moment to moment? As if it did not simply turn him into a beast, but the beast that best reflected his thoughts at any given time. "The only good pirate is a dead one."

Zuleika agreed with the sentiment, but still she said, "There are not many men who know how to make Greek fire, as you call it. The secret was known to a djinn who was enslaved to a lamp in punishment for sharing the secret of its fabrication with his king's enemies." A particularly pesky djinn she knew to be safe in the same enchanted cave where she'd imprisoned him. "More likely, they stole a cargo that contained some of the stuff."

"Perhaps," Vardan said, his gaze returning to the ships. "We shall see what my people bring ashore." He pointed at the fleet of boats clustered around the three ships. As if on command, one peeled away from the cluster and headed for shore.

Finally, Zuleika understood. "You man the watchtowers, watching for pirates or ships in trouble. Then, you send out your ghost fleet to do battle with the pirates. Once they have defeated the pirates, they bring the cargo from the stricken ship ashore. Are all the ships sunk?"

"Not all. Sometimes, when we have enough warning, we can save the merchant ship and it continues on its way. But word has spread about the ghost fleet, so savvy pirates flee when they see us. Yet a pirate who flees is not defeated, so we remain vigilant, for we know they will return, as they did today. They may lack honour, but they are still men who learn from their mistakes."

Zuleika opened her mouth to tell him that the only men aboard the ships were his own people and the merchant ship's crew, but that would mean confessing to casting the spell that transformed the pirates. Sighing, she closed her mouth again.

Vardan continued, "There is little to see here now. If the boats are carrying cargo, the battle is won. They will work through the night to save what is aboard the ship before she sinks. You should get some sleep, Lady Belle. Ask the headwoman, Birgitte, to find you a bed here, or you can return to my house, if you do not mind the ride."

Yes, sleep sounded quite tempting around now. Spellcasting, especially multiple transformations, was tiring at the best of times, let alone at the end of a long day's ride and feasting.

"Then I shall bid you good night, your Highness, and thank you for a delightful day," she said. She made it partway down the stairs before she heard his response.

"The pleasure is all mine, Lady Belle," he said so softly she suspected he hadn't intended her to hear it at all.

The prince was a strange man to enjoy arguing with her all day. Grinning broadly, Zuleika descended.

Thirty-One

It was almost dawn by the time Zuleika reached the prince's home, but falling into bed was certainly worth the ride. She fell asleep almost instantly, safe in the knowledge that Inga and the other servants would guard her chamber until she awoke.

She slept late into the day, waking only when she heard Inga's voice calling her name. Well, not her name…the one the prince had given her.

"My lady, you must dress for the feast," Inga said.

No, the feast was last night. A noisy affair in the village hall where they served yellow fish, smothered in saffron. And then there'd been pirates…

"My lady, the prince insists that you must sit by his side at the feast. There is always a big celebration after a victory at sea and this one is a double victory, he says, with no men lost. The people are saying it is a miracle, which must be your doing. A lady who can perform miracles can surely lift the curse, is what they say in town. They all wish to see the prince's lady, and you must look the part."

Wonderful. Having hundreds of invisible people staring at her, filled with such hope, when she was still no closer to breaking the spell. She'd never found a curse she couldn't counter until now. How this one could elude her so...

"If you do not rise on your own, I shall tell the master. He will drag you from your bed," Inga announced.

Vardan in her bed? No. Oh, no. His brother had been bad enough.

"My head hurts," Zuleika said, sitting up. "I hope you have willow bark tea."

"'Tis cold, but it should still work," Inga replied, gesturing at the tray beside the bed.

Zuleika gulped down the tea, then tore into the saffron cake sitting beside it. It, too, was cold, but still as delicious as the ones she'd devoured yesterday.

Behind her, the door opened. "I have the dress, my lady," said Greta, breathless with what sounded like excitement.

"Show her," commanded Inga.

Fabric rustled as Greta laid the gown on the chest at the end of the bed, and Zuleika gasped. The dress was made of yellow silk, bright as the sun. She couldn't stop herself from reaching out to touch it, to see if it was truly real.

"It's beautiful," Zuleika breathed.

"It was aboard one of the pirate ships, my lady, in a chest with no merchant's markings. The master's steward said it looked like a queen's dowry, for the gowns are all new, but there was no woman aboard any of the ships."

Perhaps the pirates had killed her, or she had sent her dowry ahead of her marriage, Zuleika told herself, forcing her hand to leave the silk alone. "I am not a queen. It is too rich a gown for me."

"Half the villagers out there are ready to declare you the Blessed Virgin, Queen of Heaven, come to save them," Inga said grimly. "You have already worn the Dowager Queen's gowns, and this belongs to no one now. If not you, then who will wear it?"

"I suppose…" Zuleika began.

"In this gown, you shall light up the room. The

master will not be able to take his eyes off you, I promise." Inga swallowed. "If only for one night, my lady, in the hope that you can break this curse…please, would you wear it?"

Once again, Zuleika could not refuse the woman's earnest plea. And wearing the beautiful silk gown was hardly a hardship.

"I will," she declared. If only wearing the beautiful dress would be enough to break the spell, but Zuleika knew it would take far more than that.

Thirty-Two

This was a terrible idea, Vardan told himself as he took his place at the high table in his own hall. He'd spent all night overseeing the salvage operation, though it had not been necessary, because he knew without a doubt his dreams would be filled with her when he slept.

He had snatched a few hours' sleep in the afternoon, which had left him feeling more tired than ever as the maiden with the violet eyes had danced just out of his reach, laughing at him. He was afraid to look into Lady Belle's eyes today.

A woman who could discuss war, or at least the weapons used in one, and took pride in victory. A girl who understood shipping and commerce as well as most merchants. A lady who saw his brother for what he was. A remarkable beauty who arrived mysteriously by magical means who yet wished to help free him of his enchantment. Could a man find himself in love with a woman he had known for only a few days? Never had he experienced such desire for a woman. More than beauty, more than brilliance…some sort of magic drew him to her. Lady Belle, the lady who would never give him her hand or her heart, for she did not even trust him with her name.

He wanted to pound the table into splinters with his fist, destroying everything in the hall like the rabid beast he resembled until he quelled his frustration. He might tear the house down before that happened.

Benches scraped and pushed back from tables as the room fell silent.

Lady Belle, haloed by the afternoon sun streaking through the window, looking like an avenging angel in glowing gold. He had no doubt that she was the one who could break the spell. He wanted to fall to his knees in worship.

But that would not do.

Instead, Vardan leaped to his feet, realising that his people were more courteous than he, for they had already moved to stand for the lady.

Her knowing smile seemed to see straight into

his heart as she looked right at him for just a moment before her gaze swept the room.

Rolf cleared his throat. In his best sonorous voice, he announced, "The Lady Belle, our guest of honour."

Jealousy blazed through Vardan's body as she turned that smile on his steward before her eyes returned to Vardan.

"The honour is mine, receiving your hospitality as a guest in this hall," she responded in ringing tones. The tones of a lady used to speaking in court, so that she might be heard above the sly whisperings of the other courtiers. She followed this statement with a deep curtsey, spreading her silk skirt so it caught the light even more. Magnificent.

Vardan stumbled forward, feeling every eye upon him as he bowed and offered her his arm for the interminable walk back to the high table. Her hand rested on his arm so lightly it should have felt like no weight at all, but Vardan felt the urge to drop to his knees at every step. How could one woman hold so much power over him? It was almost as if she had cast a spell on him.

If only the curse could be broken by him falling in love instead of her. For his heart, his soul…he had lost all of them to Lady Belle.

159

Thirty-Three

Exhaustion seemed to slow the prince's steps as he escorted her to the high table. Zuleika said nothing as she matched his pace, keeping a happy smile on her face for all the onlookers she could hear but not see. The temptation to cast a quick spell so that she could see them all was almost irresistible, but removing the illusion that hid the prince's people would also reveal his true face, instead of the one he wore now.

Invisible servants helped her into her chair and pushed it closer to the table, as others did the same for Vardan. Tonight, they sat alone at the high table, but still close enough to touch. Close enough for conversation, Zuleika corrected herself, which would not be heard by the rest of the hall, who had begun talking amongst themselves again.

"Were there many injuries sustained in last night's battle?" she enquired as she selected some meat from the platter before her.

"None that I know of," Vardan replied. "My men are calling it a bloodless victory, for not even a drop of pirate blood was shed, or so they say. If they did not all tell the same tale, I would doubt it, but fifty huntsmen cannot be wrong. Pirates do not bleed green unless there is sorcery at work."

"If no blood was shed, how can anyone know it was green?" Zuleika asked.

Vardan shrugged. "One moment they saw pirates swarming the *Trinity*, and the next…they were gone, leaving nothing but some green scum on the deck where they had once stood. Only magic can do that, which means there must have been a witch on the *Trinity*. She was so close…and yet I let her get away. You are my only hope now, Lady Belle."

She longed to tell him the truth — that the only witch present last night was her, but he would never say her true name the way his voice caressed that silly nickname. He would spit curses, order his men to seize her and send her to his brother.

She would not let that happen.

Zuleika sipped from her goblet. The warm, spiced mead soothed her, reminding her of home, so she drank more.

"Will you give me hope, Lady Belle?"

Her breath caught in her throat at the prince's beseeching tone, barely a whisper away from outright begging. "There is hope, your Highness. All curses can be broken. The only question is…at what price?" she said.

He spread his hands wide. "What can I offer you that will make you love me? The deepest desire of your heart – if I can give it to you, it is yours."

"Love is not enough to break the spell," she said. "Even if I were to…" Those eyes! So much feeling, it was enough to rock her to her very soul. No woman could look into those eyes and be unmoved. Zuleika swallowed and managed to continue, "If I were to give you my heart, it would not be enough. It took magic to cast the spell, and only magic can break it."

"You have enchanted me, Lady Belle. I know no more powerful spell than the one you have cast over me since you arrived at Beacon Isle. You light up the whole island, though the evil enchantress cursed us with darkness." He seized her hand in his. "Please say you will stay."

He would not ask her that if he knew she was an enchantress, Zuleika was certain.

He released her. "I realise I have little to offer you until the curse is lifted, but if you could find it in your heart to help, and perhaps wait a little, I will send my men after the witch. Together, I am sure you can find a solution to this…affliction."

A floating serving platter, borne by an invisible manservant, cut their conversation short, to Zuleika's relief, as she concentrated on selecting something suitable from the selection before her. She had eaten almost nothing all day, and she was famished.

Fortunately, Vardan had a similar appetite, so they ate in silence for a little while, before someone brought more mead to fill her cup.

Instead of resuming their conversation, Vardan rose to give a toast. "To yet another pirate victory, and the health of our beautiful guest."

The hall erupted in cheering as everyone raised their cups and drank. The prince's pledge was the first of many, it seemed, as the other men in the hall took the opportunity to toast the health, good fortune and future of Zuleika and the prince, as well as that of their own people.

Just as Zuleika worried she'd run out of mead, someone blew a particularly loud blast on a horn.

A group of musicians she'd neither seen nor heard until now drew her attention to the alcove at the side of the hall. In truth, she still could not see them, but their instruments were visible, and the sounds they made as they tuned their instruments were certainly audible.

At least, it was until people started pushing the tables to the sides of the hall, making enough noise to drown out even the most determined horn blower.

"Would you like to dance, Lady Belle?" Vardan asked, rising from his seat only to bow before her.

Rowdy cheers urged him on.

She opened her mouth to repeat last night's protests.

"Since the curse, we only dance caroles in a chain. You needn't worry about the steps. Simply hold onto those before and behind you, and follow where they lead." He held out his hand. "I will not lead you astray, Lady Belle. You have my word."

This time, she believed him. He was no pirate, or her spell would have turned him into green scum the previous night. Vardan and his people did not deserve the terrible curse Thorn and his pet witch had visited on them.

She took a deep breath. "And I will do

everything within my power to free you from this curse. I give you my word, your Highness."

He grinned. "Then let's dance!" He seized her hand, pulling her from the dais and into the crowd below.

Thirty-Four

The warmth of her hand in his sent Vardan's heart racing like never before. No one touched him willingly, but this was so much more. She'd given him her hand. It might only be for a dance now, but he vowed it would be more if he could persuade her to accept him. Once the curse was lifted…

The music changed, signifying that it was time to break the chain they had woven around the room and form up into couples. Without thinking, he placed his hands at her waist and lifted her, spinning around like everyone else in time to the music.

Her laughter swirled around him, the most joyous sound he'd ever heard. Her hands landed on his shoulders, perhaps to steady herself, but he would never drop her. Instead, he set her gently on her feet, and led her through the steps of the couples' dance. Though her brow creased occasionally when she made a misstep, her delighted smile never left her face. Heaven, this was surely heaven.

Yet the song ended and Vardan bowed to his partner. She dipped a curtsey, keeping her laughing eyes level with his.

His voice was hoarse in his throat. "Another dance, Lady Belle?"

The room fell silent, so her breathless answer rang out through the hall, "Oh yes."

The musicians struck up a country dance tune, a lovers' dance that played almost nonstop on the May Day festival, when the winter ended. It should have sounded strange with the island still shrouded in snow, but tonight it was perfect.

Whispers spread like wind through the hall as people shuffled toward the walls, leaving space for the dancers. For the master and the lady he wished was his, Vardan realised.

In a room full of invisible people, he and Lady Belle danced alone. Her skirts flared out as she spun with the steps, before whirling back into his embrace. Every time he released her, his heart died a little, until she returned to him a moment later as the dance brought them back together.

He heard the village women sigh each time, echoing the burst of feeling in his own heart. Country dances were for peasants, not royalty or nobility, but right now he didn't care. The stateliest court dances were dull compared to the sparkle that lit her eyes as she danced in his arms. If the members of the court were ever to dance with such abandon, they would never agree to arranged marriages with people they'd never met.

Vardan would never agree to any woman but Belle after this night. Every moment she spent in his arms, he wanted to extend into forever. Could she...would she ever be his?

The song ended far too soon, and Lady Belle drew him toward where servants stood with trays of drinks.

"I have a thirst that must be quenched, your Highness. I have never danced quite so...energetically before. When my sisters spoke of court dances, they always sounded so...sedate. Not something I wished to take part in. Yet this...this...I feel like I could dance all night, though I shall quite wear out my slippers." A silk-clad foot peeped out from under her skirt, and she clutched at his shoulder to keep her balance.

She might have clutched at his heart, the touch jolted him so much. Vardan covered her hand with his. "With you, I, too, could dance all night, and all day, too. But the curse…"

Her eyes seemed to glow with violet fire once more. "I will find a way. There must be something in my mother's library. If – "

Her mother's library was nothing compared to the collection here, most of it illuminated in the monastery's own scriptorium. And this library held something far more valuable than books. "I have a better idea," Vardan interrupted. "Come with me."

This time when he took her hand, it felt like the most natural thing in the world.

"Won't the others notice?" she asked, glancing back. Another song played and from the sound of feet on stone, Vardan guessed that the dancers had returned to the floor.

"Perhaps, but this is not court. We don't stand on ceremony here. This is a feast to celebrate a victory – a victory they won, not I. We shall return before they have finished this dance."

"All right."

She allowed him to lead her out of the hall and into the part of the house that used to be a monastery. He bypassed the monks' cells without a second glance, but Lady Belle slowed.

"Are these…prison cells?" she asked.

Vardan laughed. "No, the monks slept here when it was a monastery. They are sleeping cells, much like in a convent, I imagine. None are held here against their will. Their faith compels them, or so the brothers say. I used to sleep in one when I was studying with them as a boy. For all that they have no fire, they are still warm, for they are above the scriptorium. A fire burns there year round to help preserve the books. I will show you."

"You are taking me to your library," Belle said slowly, her smile dawning once more. "I should like to see that."

"Then come." He tugged at her hand, and she came willingly, her steps quickening to match his. Ah, a lady who liked books. If Vardan wasn't in love with her already, he wold have fallen a second time. She was perfection itself.

He threw the doors open and led her inside. Candles lit the room, as always, but Belle's gratifying gasp as she surveyed a library that rivalled the great hall for size made him examine it anew. Even the king did not have so many books in his palace in the capital.

"It would take a lifetime to read them all," she breathed, reaching for the nearest shelf but stopping before she touched anything.

Vardan grinned. "A few years, yes, but not a lifetime. I know from experience." He coughed. "If you wish it, you may stay here as long as it takes you to read them all. A lifetime, if that is your wish." Oh, how he longed to kiss her. The way she looked at him now, as if he was a man and not a beast. First, they must break the curse. "But I have something I must show you."

He drew her to the window, where a chest held his most prized possession. He drew out the well-wrapped bundle, then paused with the heavy thing in his hands. "This is a magical object, but it will not hurt you," he promised. "You need only look at it, if you wish. I will not ask you to touch it if you don't wish to."

Vardan expected to see fear in her eyes, but Lady Belle merely nodded as she turned expectant eyes on the bundle.

He folded back the cloth, revealing a mirror as shiny as the day when Sir Ryder had first handed it to him. Before the curse. Now, it was his only view to a world he could never be a part of.

"Have you ever seen its like?" Vardan murmured.

To his surprise, Belle nodded. "My mother owned just such a looking glass. She kept it in her library, too."

"This is no ordinary looking glass, for it shows far more than the beauty of its owner. It was a gift from my brother on my name day. I check it every morning and every night for pirates and approaching ships, so that my people might be prepared for the hunt. It shows more than ships, though. This glass can show you whatever you desire, wherever it might be in the world." Vardan grinned at her surprise. "So you see, it is nothing like your mother's mirror. I only have to fog it with my breath, like so –" he breathed on the glass "– and focus on what I desire to see. Once the fog clears, the mirror reveals what I ask." Vardan moistened his lips. "What I long for most right now is to find a witch who can break the curse, as she slayed the pirates. If I am not wrong, it will show the crew of the *Trinity* in their boat, and among them…the witch." He held the mirror up so Zuleika could see. "What do you see, Lady Belle?"

Thirty-Five

Zuleika's own reflection looked back. Nothing more. She sighed. "I only see myself, your Highness. There is nothing magical about your looking glass."

Vardan frowned. "That isn't possible." He breathed on the glass again. "Show me the crew of the *Trinity*," he commanded. "There! See?"

Zuleika inspected the mirror again. This time, the prince was right. The mirror showed a tiny boat, dwarfed by dark, wintry waves as the men huddled together for warmth. And there it was. Men, without a witch or woman among them. "I see the boat, but no witch."

Without warning, the prince's head was beside hers, so close their cheeks touched. "I believe you are right. Then where is she?"

Zuleika swallowed. I am here, she wanted to say, but she didn't want to spoil such a perfect evening. If anything, she wanted to return with him to the great hall, so that he might hold her in his arms while they danced the night away. Was it so wrong to want one more night?

He cupped her cheek, shifting so he could look into her eyes. "Lady Belle…"

She squeezed her eyes shut. If she stared into his soul any longer, she would be lost. "That is not my name." She wanted to tell him, if only to hear him say her name with the same adoration as he used for her nickname, but that would never happen. Her name on his lips. His lips…

"Then tell me," he whispered.

Zuleika seized his head in her hands and kissed him. Clumsily at first, for she had never kissed a man before, but then Vardan recovered from his surprise and kissed her back. Just as in the dance in the great hall, she followed his lead, until she was so breathless she had to stop.

"Lady…"

Zuleika shook her head. "My mother once told me to beware the man who could steal my breath with a kiss, for he would steal my heart, too, and I would be lost."

"You are not lost here. I have you, and this will be your home, if you wish it." Vardan's arms tightened around her. "It doesn't matter what your name is. Not to me. If you do not wish to tell me, you will be Lady Belle for as long as I live."

Madness had seized her. She could become Lady Belle in truth, as the prince kissed her breathless. "Yes," she murmured, lifting her lips for another kiss.

Another, and another, as their tongues twined in a couples' dance that was far more intimate than their last. Breathless, yet gasping, lost and also unmistakably found in the prince's arms, feeling none of winter's chill as his love warmed her from the inside in places she had never felt heat before. She kissed him harder, growing bolder as her hands slid over his shoulders to feel hard muscle under his tunic. "Oh, Vardan," she sighed, cuddling against his chest.

"So you will stay, my fearless lady?" he asked.

Zuleika lifted her gaze to his face. Her answer died on her lips as her eyes widened in horror. A scream ripped out of her throat as she tore away from him and ran.

Thirty-Six

Her lips were sweeter than spiced mead as she kissed him, and Vardan knew this was no dream. For a moment, he dared to let his mind wander from kissing her to wedding her to bedding her…

Then she looked at him and it all went to hell.

Her scream still rang in his ears, freezing him in place as she bolted. Vardan let her go, for he knew what she'd seen. The beast, not the man. Yet she'd still kissed him, fangs and all, so that for one blessed moment, he'd believed…

In an unattainable dream. No one could love a beast.

On the other side of his house, the merriment continued, but in the privacy of the library, invisible at last, the master wept.

Thirty-Seven

Eyes open or closed, Zuleika couldn't help but see his face. Vardan's face, exactly like his brother's. She hadn't cast a spell, drawn blood, broken the curse…none of it, and yet the illusion had shown him as the most beastly creature of all: the king.

"My lady!"

Zuleika heard Greta's voice, but didn't see the maid, and still she ran.

What kind of curse turned a man into a beast one moment, and a human monster the next?

One she could not break. Because if she did…the man she loved would look like the man she hated most. No matter how hideous he looked while cursed, she could still bear to look upon his face. But to look at Vardan and see Thorn…

No. That was why she must go.

Zuleika bit her lip, whispering a spell of invisibility to cloak her own form. Now she was just another reveller as she returned to the great hall, unknown and unseen. The doors were open and the gates, too, for men who had drunk too much to remember or even see a chamber pot were relieving themselves in the snow.

Ah, men were the same everywhere. Pissing contests would always occur as long as men had their manhoods.

Would Vardan boast to his brother that he had kissed the girl, only for Thorn to laugh and say he'd bedded her before she'd even met Vardan? Well, she'd curse them both for it. Thorn with childlessness, and Vardan by not removing his existing curse. She could do it, she was certain, if she understood the nature of it. But she would not.

Instead, she would leave.

Zuleika marched out the gate, wishing she had thought to bring a cloak against the biting cold. No matter. She would not be outside for long. Snow had not fallen today, so the road was clear, though the drifts lay deep on either side. She touched a finger to her bitten lip, pausing only long enough to see it stained red with blood, before she traced a portal in the air. A portal home.

Her hand arched up, then descended, letting the single drop of blood touch the cleared ground. The portal glowed purple-white before the enchantress stepped through and both vanished from Beacon Isle.

Thirty-Eight

What kind of curse turned a man into a beast one moment, and a human monster the next? A week Zuleika had been home, since her father welcomed both her and the news that his merchandise was safe, if inaccessible under the watchful eyes of the master of Beacon Isle, yet it was Vardan who had occupied her thoughts every waking moment, and some of her dreams, too.

She resisted the thought for a week before she finally capitulated and ventured into her mother's bower. Hers now.

Instead of pulling out books at random, Zuleika sat in the middle of the room, as she had been taught to do, and breathed deeply for focus. When she felt she had achieved this, she cast a spell for wisdom and asked for the knowledge she needed to break the spell, something she should have done long ago.

An enchantress was gifted shortly after her birth by a more senior enchantress with all the collective knowledge she would need to master her craft. Millennia of experience, passed down through countless generations, the wisdom of the ages. She could ask for answers and receive them from the vast repository of knowledge, mixed with her own memories, but it required focus. And the right questions.

What kind of curse turned a man into a monster?

A curse that revealed the darkest, most beastly aspects of his nature, her memories whispered. So that they will become visible to all those who look at him.

What kind of curse transformed not just a man, but his lands as well?

A curse that forbids his lands from offering welcome to anyone who approaches them.

What manner of curse could turn the population of an entire island invisible?

A curse that makes all those loyal to a man disappear, when he is the island's beloved leader.

Who would sentence a man to suffer such a

curse?

No one. No one would willingly doom any man to such a fate.

Then how did Vardan come to be cursed?

The mirror. Her mother's mirror. Not one like it – the mirror itself. Far-seeing, irresistible…and cursed. Twice. By Zuleika's own hand.

How did he come to possess it?

He is the king's brother. The king made him a gift of the mirror.

Why?

Because the king sees him as an enemy. He sees everyone more powerful than he as an enemy. He is a treacherous snake who deserves his fate.

But Prince Vardan does not.

No. The prince deserves to be loved and to have the curse lifted. His people deserve to see their loyalty rewarded by the breaking of their curse.

Is it true, then, that love can break the spell?

Only if it was cast with love, or a loophole allowing love to break it. If there is no loophole, then only two people can break the spell. Either a caster more powerful than the one who cast the curse; or the caster herself. But the price will be high, especially when the spell is recast by a cursed item so many times. Better to build a loophole when a spell is first cast.

Zuleika's mouth grew dry, though she hadn't spoken a single word aloud.

And what if there is no single caster more powerful than the original one?

Then it will take a group of casters to use their collective power to remove the spell, but if that happens, they will see the damage this curse has wrought, and once the curse is undone, they will come after the caster. Enslave her like the djinn, for such wickedness will not be tolerated.

They would enslave her to the mirror, wouldn't they? So every day she could look upon the man she loved, knowing she had caused his suffering and that of all his people, when she could have prevented it, and see the hatred in his eyes.

Better to die than live as a slave.

Vardan and his people deserved to be free. No matter what the cost.

Thirty-Nine

Show me the girl. Show me Lady Belle. Show her to me.

The words echoed in Vardan's head all day and all night, tempting him to peer into the mirror to see her again, but he resisted. Why would he want to see the woman who was no different to anyone else? She couldn't stand the sight of him. So much so that she'd disappeared from the island not long after he'd made the mistake of kissing her.

Some of the villagers had admitted to seeing a flash of purple lightning that night, just as he had on the night of her arrival. Perhaps Thorn's witch had summoned Belle back against her will, but Vardan doubted it. The girl had run for a reason. And though he knew little of the lady, Vardan was certain Belle was no pawn in this game. Whoever she was.

Thorn's new queen, perhaps?

Jealousy burned him again at that thought, but there was little he could do to combat it. He wanted her in his arms, not his brother's, but if the lady did not want him…he would not waste his time pining after her, nor shed another tear. His moment of weakness had passed; he must be strong for his people, and continue to hunt pirates.

That's what he needed the mirror for. If he checked hourly instead of daily, what was the harm?

He breathed on the mirror, wishing to see the nearest pirate vessel, and the mirror flared with violet light as the image formed. Violet, just like Lady Belle's strange lightning. And her eyes. He'd never forget her eyes. Eyes that looked at him with what he'd thought was love, if only for a moment.

Vardan peered at the ship, trying to judge its location and how far it was from the island.

He did not feel the curse settling another layer of the spell over him and the rest of the island, as it had done every time he'd used the magic mirror. He had done this more than a thousand times — what was once more?

Forty

Zuleika opened a portal into the prince's library, hoping everyone would be asleep and not see her arrival. Sure enough, the room was empty, though the candles still burned. She knew what she had to do. Better to die than live as a slave, she reminded herself.

The chest was still there, and inside it was the bundle that contained the mirror. She unwrapped it carefully. Tears stung her eyes as she glimpsed the jewelled rose on the back, for it had been so long since she'd last seen it.

Zuleika lifted her mother's beautiful mirror, not daring to peer into it for fear she'd curse herself into revealing the frightened mouse she felt like right now. She wanted to know where Vardan was, so that she might see him one last time, but she also dreaded meeting him. If she did, she would have to confess everything, for he deserved to know the truth, and she couldn't bear to lie to him any longer, even if he would hate her, knowing what she'd done.

She balled her free hand into a fist, smashing it into the mirror. The glass shattered, sending shards into her hand and wrist. Blood trickled, beaded, then spurted as she pulled out the pieces. All the while, she held her bleeding hand over the broken mirror, telling it to break the curse, break the curse, break the curse, for every time it had been cast. Vardan might have looked into the mirror a hundred, a thousand, or ten thousand times in the years it had remained in his possession, and if it took a drop of blood to dispel each time it had cursed him, she might drain her body of blood and it would not be enough. But still she let it flow, pooling on the frame and the few fragments of silvered glass that remained. This was her fault, and only she could free the island of its enchantment. If it took her lifeblood, then so be it. She should have known better than to cast such a curse in the first place. If she lived, she would never curse another object again.

Zuleika fell to her knees, then slowly toppled

onto the floor, her attention only on the mirror and keeping her blood flowing over it. For Vardan. For his people. But mostly for him.

The room began to dim, and she knew she'd lost too much blood to stay conscious for long. If she knew the curse was broken, perhaps she could heal herself, but that would mean seeing Vardan, and if his eyes met hers, her heart would break at his hatred when her heart held only love for him.

"Lady Belle!" The one voice she both desired and dreaded spoke her name, or at least the name he'd given her. "You're hurt. Let me help you. How did this happen?" He raised his voice to bellow, "Someone help! Lady Belle is hurt! Fetch a physician. A surgeon. Someone who can help!"

"Do not...worry. I did this. It is my fault, and I must...repair the damage." Drawing breath was becoming difficult, but still Zuleika tried to speak. "My name is not Belle."

"You are my Lady Belle, and I love you," Vardan said, his eyes softening as he smiled. Like a man, and not a beast. A good man. Not a monster.

Running footsteps skidded to a halt. "Lady Belle has returned, and she's hurt. Send a rider to town for a physician!" Inga hurried to Zuleika's side, lifting the skirt of her pink gown a little so it wouldn't slow her down. A gown Zuleika could see.

The curse was broken. She had not failed him. Now it didn't matter that her vision had grown dim.

"Lady Belle, what happened?" Vardan asked urgently.

"My name is Zuleika, and I have broken your curse. I never met you before this winter, and if I had, I never would have cast it." She closed her eyes. Oblivion hovered close now. She could feel it.

"But…why?" he whispered.

"Because I love you," she said.

He gathered her up in his arms, pressing her close, but she did not feel a thing, for she had already succumbed to the darkness' embrace.

Forty-One

Vardan jolted awake, convinced someone had doused him in Greek fire and set him alight, but his chamber was dark. Merely a dream, he told himself, but his dreams were reserved for Lady Belle, the maiden who always danced just out of reach.

His heart constricted in his chest at the thought of her. Too long had he resisted the siren call of the magic mirror. If he saw her but once, and knew she was safe, he would be content never to think of her again. Or if he were to discover her scheming with his brother…what then?

Then he would know that she was truly lost to him, and he could mourn.

Resolved, he climbed from his bed and padded

to the library. In his childhood, the monks had worked there day and night, and true to tradition, the candles burned still. A warm wash of light to drive away the sudden chill in his heart.

Something was amiss. He could feel it.

Three steps into the room, he stopped dead.

She lay in a pool of blood, stretching out her hand for the magic mirror as if it could somehow help her.

He wanted to demand how she'd come here, where she'd gone, and who had hurt her, but most of all, he didn't want to lose her.

So much blood…

He bellowed for help as he dropped to his knees beside her, unsure what he could do. If he had a witch here now, he would trade his very soul for a spell that could save her life, but all he had were his two hands and a houseful of servants, none of whom knew magic or more than rudimentary healing.

He shouted for help again, and he saw her move, just the tiniest bit. Her face crumpled, as if in pain. She mumbled something that sounded like nonsense and he did his best to reassure her. Help would come. It had to.

A hand touched his shoulder. Fingers he could see.

Inga's voice roused the household, commanding them like an army in battle. Better she than him tonight. He couldn't turn his attention away from Belle. Couldn't lose her again.

She mumbled more nonsense before her eyes closed.

No. What cruel fate had returned her to him, only to kill her before his eyes?

"Why?" he begged of the heavens, but he got no answer except a sigh as Belle's breath left her.

Forty-Two

Zuleika opened her eyes, expecting an afterlife, but she only saw the dowager queen's bedchamber. She still lived. Her hand was terribly painful, and shrouded in linen bandages.

"The lady wakes." Vardan rose from his corner chair, much as he had the first time they met. Today, though, he was merely a man, and no longer a cursed creature. As Zuleika's gaze caressed his features for what she was certain would be the last time, she found it hard to believe she had ever mistaken him for his brother. Sure, both men had similar features, but the expression on Vardan's face and the soul shining through his eyes showed him to be a very different man. A man of honour, integrity, compassion and…for at least a little while, love.

"So many times I told you my tale, that I forgot to ask for yours. So, tell me, Lady Belle, or will you give me your true name now?"

She winced. "I already told you. The first name was a gift from you. It wasn't so different to my name. Not really. Zuleika means brilliant beauty. It is the name my parents gave me, and the rest of the world knows me by. Zuleika, enchantress, daughter of Baron Hans and his wife Lady Zoraida, also an enchantress, and the previous owner of the mirror enchanted with farseeing before I cursed it at the king's command." She swallowed painfully. "The very same mirror I smashed in your library."

Vardan drew the chair up beside the bed and seated himself. "It sounds like quite a tale, Lady Zuleika. Especially as I have heard that name before. I think I deserve to hear all of your tale now."

So Zuleika told him everything, starting with the king's courier, Sir Ryder, through to her escape from the palace. Tears rolled down her cheeks, but she didn't stop to wipe them away. She described trying to open a portal at the bottom of the sea, where her father's ship had sunk, and of finding herself in Vardan's courtyard. Finally, she told him about how she'd realised that the curse on Beacon Isle was indeed of her making, but magnified hundreds of times over, because of the mirror, and how she hadn't been sure she could break something so powerful, but she had owed it to him to try.

And when she was done, her vision so blurred by tears she could no longer see, Vardan walked out of the room without saying a word.

Her every instinct screamed to call him back, but she knew it would be no use. Vardan was free to live the life he deserved and love a woman as honourable as he was. Not a witch who was tainted with the darkness of her crimes.

Slowly, painfully, she pulled a gown over her shift, and made her way down to the courtyard. No one stopped her; no one even saw her. For a household that had once been full of invisible people, she was the only invisible one now without even a spell to make her so. No matter. She would not be here for long.

Zuleika bit her unbandaged finger and drew a doorway in the air. Her blood touched the earth and the circle was complete, opening a portal home. With one final glance back at the house on Beacon Isle, she stepped through the portal and left the island, and the prince, behind.

Forty-Three

By the time Lady Belle – no, Lady Zuleika – had finished her tale, Vardan wasn't sure whether he wanted to kill his brother outright or torture him for eternity. What Thorn had forced her to do, that she'd felt honour-bound to undo, even at the risk of her life…

He didn't want to believe it, but her eyes burned with sincerity through every word. How could he not believe her? The memory of her lying in all that blood was one he would never forget. Even now, she was deathly pale.

She had nearly given her life for him. If he'd taken the time to find out more about the curse earlier, he might have stopped using the mirror, might have saved her this pain. Damn him, if he'd taken his brother's advice and sought her out, even, none of this would have happened.

So when tears welled up in her eyes – tears because of the pain he'd caused her, through no fault of her own, he forced himself to leave the room. He had no right to embrace or comfort her, no matter how much he wanted to.

What comfort could he offer, anyway? She had run from him once. She didn't want him. But he was still deeply in her debt for breaking the curse.

She deserved vengeance for the wrongs Thorn had done her. Had done to them both.

Death wasn't good enough for him. And there was no honour in torture. Besides, Thorn expected some sort of attack from Vardan – he'd gone to great lengths to keep him here on the island, far from court. If Vardan did succeed in killing the king, he would be sentencing himself to a lifetime on the throne. A life he did not want, for his home was here. On a hill above what had once been the greatest trading port in the world. And would be again, he vowed.

If he couldn't take Thorn's life, he would take the one thing he loved most – his power. Thorn could keep his precious throne and his court. But Beacon Isle's storehouses contained the riches of most of the merchants in the civilised world.

Merchants who knew Vardan to be their ally. If he could control the trade routes with the promise of keeping them free of pirates, his humble seat would hold more power than all the thrones in the western world combined.

But to do that, he needed Rolf.

He shouted for his steward as he strode to his solar, already listing names in his head. He knew which merchants held the most power among their colleagues, and he must win those over first. Had much changed in five years? Vardan needed to find out.

Rolf had a scruffy grey beard that made him look old. Vardan found himself staring at the man he hadn't seen for five years and wondering how the intervening time had aged him.

"You bellowed, master?" Rolf asked. "If you wanted to tell me the curse has been lifted, I noticed it for myself. You summoned me before I could shave."

"No. I've thought of a way to empty the cellars and the storehouses, and build a merchant league like the world has never seen before."

Rolf lifted an eyebrow. "White Harbour has hardly been open for a day and already you plan to fill it with ships?" His lips twitched with amusement.

Vardan hastened to explain his plan, as enthusiasm kindled in Rolf's eyes. Yes, he believed the idea was possible, and it was a good one. But he had so many questions and suggestions that Vardan had to reach for some paper to start writing it all down.

Vardan wasn't sure what time it was when Inga burst into the room. "Where is she?" the housekeeper demanded.

She'd grown thinner under the curse, he thought, though he couldn't be certain. "Where is who?" Vardan replied, before realisation froze his heart. Who else would drive her into such a panic but the Lady Zuleika?

"Lady Belle. She's not in her room," Inga said. "You were the last person to see her, master, and her so weak and all. She's supposed to stay in bed and rest. Where is she?"

In her panic, the woman looked like she was ready to shake him to make him talk. No one had dared try that on him since he was a boy.

"She was resting in bed when I saw her last. Search the house and the grounds, if you must. Send someone down to Harbourtown to enquire if anyone has seen her," Vardan said. "She's too ill to have gotten far."

Even as he said the words, he knew they were a

lie. She could appear and vanish from his house at will, in a bolt of lightning. Weak as she was, had she run again? Not now. Surely not now.

"Find her," he said hoarsely. "Whatever it takes."

Inga marched out, so she didn't see Vardan grip the table to keep himself upright as his legs threatened to collapse beneath him.

"Are you well, master?" Rolf asked. He nodded at the prince's whitened knuckles.

Vardan passed a hand before his eyes. Without her, all his plotting would be a waste of time. She would be found, he told himself.

"I am well. Let us resume," Vardan said, and their discussion continued. Rolf recommended new names to add to the list of those to be approached first, then sent for inventories so they would know whose merchandise occupied the most space in the storehouses. Without the mirror and the invisible fleet, fighting pirates would be harder, but if they could persuade Zuleika to help with a spell or two…

Realisation hit Vardan like a blow. "The pirates. She turned them into scum."

"What did you say, master?"

"The pirates," Vardan repeated. "When the pirates attacked the *Trinity*, they disappeared, leaving nothing but green slime where they stood. She kept calling pirates scum, so that's what she turned them into. That's why I couldn't find a witch on the *Trinity*. She was here the whole time."

"So the Lady Belle truly was a witch?"

"Is a witch," Vardan corrected. "The Lady Zuleika, for that is her real name, said she is an enchantress. A powerful sort of witch, I understand. One who has no need of ships or horses, for she can ride lightning."

"She sounds like a powerful ally to have. Is she on these lists yet?" Rolf asked.

Vardan swallowed. "She has helped us so much already. We are deeply in her debt. All this is a small way I can begin to repay her for what she has done."

"Most ladies like flowers, gowns and trinkets. Love letters and poetry, even," Rolf offered. "Jewels – I know she likes those. A league of merchants is hardly the way to woo a maiden."

"When the snow melts, I shall give her every rose in my garden, but until then…I would rather lay the world at her feet. The Lady Zuleika is not most ladies, my friend."

"No, that she's not," Rolf said softly. He clapped the prince on the back. "Now, until we can persuade a witch to turn your sailors invisible,

I propose...."

They talked tactics for a long time, until the news arrived that she was nowhere to be found on the island. The lady had vanished as quickly as she'd arrived, just like before.

Feeling Rolf's eyes upon him, Vardan schooled the anguish away from his expression. "Then I shall stay here, while you act as my envoy to the merchants on my first list. Send word after every meeting, so that I might know the outcome. I want to know who is with us, and who is not, for the more who agree, the more the others will be swayed."

"And what of the lady?" Rolf asked.

Vardan's eyes flashed. "She is a merchant's daughter. Maybe even the daughter of one of the men on that list. She identified her father's mark on some of the goods in our cellar. If you see her on your travels...tell her....tell her..." He swallowed. "Tell her she is welcome at Beacon Isle at any time, for any reason, and that the contents of the library are hers, if she wants them."

Rolf whistled. "The monks won't like that."

"Bugger the monks. They left the books here with me when they deserted the island. They belong to the one person who saved it."

"Yes, master. When I find her, I'll tell her that."

Rolf's eyes glinted.

When. Vardan liked that. When he found her. Until that time came, he would live in hope. For now he was a man again, hope was his once more.

Forty-Four

Weeks passed. The snow melted and the roads turned into a quagmire of mud. Then that, too, dried, until there was little to deter anyone but the most timid horseman from reaching her father's keep.

Zuleika expected the king's men hourly, knowing it was only a matter of time before he discovered that she'd lifted the curse at Beacon Isle and was once again within his borders. Within easy grasp. He might not have a powerful witch at his disposal, but she was still weak from losing so much blood. Casting more than the most minor spell would tax her strength, leaving her as helpless as any normal woman in the hands of a much stronger man, and she swore she would die before she let the king touch her again.

No man would, for her heart belonged to his brother.

So she waited, and rested, and while she rested, she read. She read every book and scroll in her mother's bower, and when she was finished, she read them again. Never again would she curse an object as she had her mother's mirror, at least not without some safeguard in place to prevent the curse from enchanting the same person more than once. And never without some loophole that would allow someone else to break the spell without spilling her blood.

It hadn't escaped her that if she'd created the very loophole the king had invented, her love for Vardan would have broken the spell weeks ago, and he would never have needed to know about her powers, or that she'd cast the curse in the first place. There was no point in wishing Thorn's lies were true, though. Even if she were to cast a spell on him so that any lie he told transformed into truth, it would be too late to help her.

So, sighing, she returned to her books. She'd heard whispers about a witch who could weave the fates of men into real cloth on her loom, and she wanted to know whether it was possible before she sought out the witch to stop her. Cursing men was one thing, but taking their free will and rewriting their destiny? That went too far. She wanted to believe that the woman was merely a seer whose skills allowed her to illuminate a man's path to his desired goal, but if the stories were correct, she demanded a high price from her would-be clients, and those who chose not to engage her services found themselves threatened with ruin in the most horrible ways.

Shouts from the courtyard below dragged her thoughts from the dry manuscript before her. More voices than there should be in her father's house right now. Her time had run out – the king's men had come for her.

Zuleika sighed. She might not be completely recovered, but she was well enough to cast a portal. Were they just in the main courtyard, or had they overrun the keep already? Zuleika peered out the window. If she could make it to the kitchen garden…

She gripped the window sill, forgetting about spells or escape. The courtyard was filled with laden wagons, and more were plodding up the road to the keep. The shouts she'd heard were orders for every able man in the household to help unload the goods Zuleika recognised from the storehouses on Beacon Isle. Vardan had kept his word, and returned everything.

Zuleika flew down the steps to her father's study, where she found him in deep discussion with a man whose voice she recognised as belonging to Rolf, Vardan's steward.

"I already told you, he will accept no payment for the return of your goods," Rolf said irritably. "He's done this as an act of goodwill, because he needs merchants like you to join with him in league against pirates and kings who make doing business impossible, and he knows the losses you have already suffered. He asks but one thing from you." Rolf's eyes darted in Zuleika's direction, though he did not meet her gaze. "That you send him the Lady Zuleika."

Father's face turned red. "That's preposterous. Sell my virgin daughter to a rebel who opposes the king? Better I send her to court, where she will find a husband whose armies will fight this insanity. Why, the king himself has expressed his interest in my daughter for a bride. I'll not have her sold into slavery to a man who holds me to ransom!"

"Prince Vardan does not buy or sell slaves, Father," Zuleika said. "If he seeks to set up a league of merchants, doubtless he has heard of how fast I can travel, and he wishes to engage my services as an envoy to turn this league into a reality before someone breathes word of it to the king. If you join him in this, as your daughter, the other merchants will listen to me. Wouldn't it be a relief to only have to lose your ship to a storm, instead of so many other things? If only to save your fortunes alone, I would go, but to set up lasting trade agreements across the world? It would be an honour, Father." Now she found Rolf staring at her, and she met his gaze without flinching. "If the prince wants me, he shall have me."

If only he wanted her the way she wanted him.

Forty-Five

Vardan surveyed White Harbour with satisfaction. The ships had returned, as he'd predicted, and many brought letters from the merchants who owned them. Pledges of support, paeans of praise for his ideas, requests for reductions in port duties when they docked at Beacon Isle…they came thick and fast, but still didn't have the power to bring a smile to his face. Only one person could do that – the Lady Zuleika, if she returned to him.

Or Rolf, if he sent a letter saying the lady was on her way.

He ripped open the last letter and skimmed the first lines. This one was far from complimentary. The merchant who'd sent it couldn't decide whether Vardan was insane or merely a traitor, but he swore the king would hear of it, all the same. Vardan peered at the seal, trying to remember the man. Ah, now he knew him. He was the younger brother to the crone Thorn had tried to marry him to, years ago. That made him the king's man, or a man the king wanted to court.

Vardan was tempted to throw the letter into the fire and be done with it, but caution stayed his hand. Yes, Thorn would certainly hear of their merchant league, but there was little he could do about it when he did. That was the beauty of it – many ports were already in the hands of those who had been first to support Vardan. Even if Thorn sent troops or ships to attack Beacon Isle, they were one port among dozens around the world, in countries Thorn did not control. And the one port which had a fleet experienced in naval warfare and combating pirates.

Once Thorn realised his impotence, he would lash out at anyone who got in his way – especially those who brought bad tidings. Loyalty to King Thorn did not always mean a reward, for Vardan knew how treacherous his brother could be.

Vardan found paper and ink, and began to write a response to the merchant who called him mad. The man might be old and loyal, but he was not entirely stupid, and if he liked living, perhaps he would be willing to embrace what he'd once called madness. If he did not…be it on his own head. He could stand with the treacherous snake. Vardan had more men than he needed on his side already.

But all the men in the world could not equal one woman…

He sighed and sent up a silent prayer that someone would find her, and persuade Zuleika to return to him. If word of the league reached Thorn, it would surely reach her.

He hoped so. For all this was for naught unless one day he would be reunited with his Lady Belle.

Forty-Six

Some hours later, when the only thing in the wagons was a chest of Zuleika's belongings that looked pitiful compared to the full loads they'd carried up to the keep, Rolf offered her a seat beside her chest, but Zuleika declined. She was far more comfortable astride her own horse, even if little Lady was nowhere near as elegant as the prince's Embarr.

She rode tall and straight, like the queen her father had wanted her to be. He'd settle for her being a princess, though, she'd discovered, when she'd found him interrogating Rolf about the prince, particularly whether he had a wife. Her father had insisted she wear her violet riding habit, and do everything she could to make the prince think of her as a suitable bride, not an envoy.

Privately, she wasn't even sure he'd consider her an envoy, but the more she thought about the idea, the more she liked it. She would never be a bride, let alone Vardan's, but his merchant league had merit. Not to mention it would give him allies against the king, should Thorn choose a less devious attack than a curse. And she would get to see him again.

Rolf coughed, making her look up. He looked relieved to have finally secured her attention. "Beg pardon, my lady. But is it true what the master said about you being a witch?"

She considered not telling him, but where was the harm in telling the man what he already knew? Vardan kept no secrets from his servants, after all.

Zuleika sighed. "Yes. And when I was a child, I cursed a mirror on the king's command, which he gave to the prince. When I arrived at your island and discovered the result of the cursed gift, I did everything in my power to undo the harm that was done. I could not give back the lost time, or make up for all those years of invisibility, or – "

"Is it true that you nearly died to break the curse?" Rolf interrupted.

"Yes," she admitted, then hastened to add, "But I am much recovered from the ordeal. Why, I'm sure I could cast a spell before you could blink, if I needed to." Not that he looked about to attack her for being a witch, but it paid to be wary.

"Like the fast travel spell you talked about. Is that how you appeared on the island?"

Zuleika nodded. "I could, but I'm not sure I'd have the power to create a portal big enough to fit all of us, including the wagons. In fact, my portals are barely large enough for me. Certainly not big enough for a horse."

Rolf wet his lips. "So, if you wanted to, you could go back to Beacon Isle without having to take ship with us, and be there sooner. Like, today?"

And see Vardan sooner. "Yes."

"Then you should go, my lady. The master was very angry when you disappeared just as the curse broke. He said if we found you, to send you to him immediately."

Zuleika's traitorous heart beat faster at the faint hope that Vardan wanted to see her again. Perhaps he had questions about her past. Or he wanted to tell her to her face that she was no longer welcome on Beacon Isle, as if walking out of the room when she'd finished her tale wasn't clear enough.

"You would not mind?" she asked.

Rolf grinned. "I've been cursed for five years,

my lady, but I never saw magic cast before. Seems you're the good kind of witch, lifting the curse and all, so if I see any magic, I'd like it to be yours."

"A witch like me is called an enchantress. There are not many of us, and fewer still can cast portals," Zuleika said. "We try to do some good in the world."

"As you will, my lady." Rolf reined in his horse, and waited.

Zuleika slid from Lady's back, feeling very self-conscious with Rolf watching. Portal magic was difficult, but not particularly impressive. She bit her finger, and traced an arch in the air, squeezing out a drop of blood to hit the earth at the end. The portal to Beacon Isle glowed into life.

"Farewell, my lady. We will see you at Beacon Isle soon," she heard Rolf say as she stepped through.

Forty-Seven

As Vardan strode along the passage, he glimpsed a flash of purple in the rose garden. Could it be she? Instead of leaning out the window, he raced down the stairs into the courtyard. Row upon row of rosebushes stood sentinel…but no lady lay among them.

It was probably a good thing. While snow had lain deep in the courtyard when she first arrived, now she would find herself beset by thorns.

He approached the place where he'd first seen her. In place of the snowdrift, there stood a different white drift – this time made up of rose petals, not snow, as his grandmother's white roses were celebrating spring in true floral form. She'd called them her full moon roses, specially bred for their colour, which in the ancient language of flowers meant loyalty.

Here he saw the purple he'd glimpsed from the level above. In the midst of all the white roses, one rosebush had not yet burst into bloom as its companions had. No, this had extended a stem higher than any of the others, and it was crowned by a single bud that had just begun to open.

This rose was not white, like its fellows, but a particular shade of purple. Almost exactly like the pair of enchanting eyes that haunted his dreams.

For that was the meaning of purple roses, he remembered now: enchantment.

His grandmother would have liked the blue moon among all her full moons. She probably would have liked Zuleika, too – the lady who undoubtedly changed the colour of her roses through magical means.

Smiling, Vardan stretched out on one of the garden benches his grandmother had liked to sit on when he was a boy.

Throughout the rest of the house and Harbourtown below, people bustled about their business, but he enjoyed a moment of stillness. His grandmother's garden always brought him peace.

Forty-Eight

Spring had come to Vardan's rose garden far sooner than it had reached her father's house, Zuleika found. Some of the bushes had already burst into bloom, while the profusion of buds on others promised that spring had only just begun.

It was a far cry from the snow-filled courtyard she'd first arrived in. And so sweet-smelling, too. Zuleika took another deep breath, hoping that the memory of sweetness would be enough to help her keep her composure in her interview with Vardan. No, she would need more than just the memory. Reaching out, she plucked a purple rose from the nearest bush, and tucked the bloom into her braided hair.

"Now you've returned to steal my flowers, Lady

Belle?"

Zuleika whirled and found Vardan seated on a bench she hadn't seen, tucked under an archway twined with flowers. He rose.

"I...I didn't mean to..." she stammered. "And my name isn't – "

"Belle, I know," he interrupted. "But you have been Lady Belle to me so long, both before me and in my dreams, it is hard to remember you are also Lady Zuleika, powerful enchantress." He bowed.

Zuleika swallowed. "My power is less than it was," she admitted. "I lost a lot of blood. It will return, though, as I recover. Which reminds me that I have a proposal for you. When I heard of your plan for a merchants' league – "

"You came here with a proposal because of the merchants' league?" Disbelief registered on his face.

Zuleika shook her head. "No, I came because Rolf brought my father's goods, and told him that they came at a price. That I must come here immediately."

"I gave no such order," he snapped, then his voice softened as he continued, "Though I considered it. Many times. Rolf..."

Realisation hit Zuleika at the same time as she

saw it dawn in Vardan's eyes. "He lied," she breathed. "Loyalty. He lied to me out of loyalty to you, so that I would return to Beacon Isle. To you." His eyes. Once she'd seen them, she couldn't look away. Beast or man, those eyes spoke to her soul as he pierced her heart. She understood the loyalty that had driven Rolf. Now, she, too, would live or die for this man. Even if he never looked at her the same way as he had the night he'd kissed her.

She cleared her throat. "To be your envoy, I assume, as I suggested. I can travel quickly, and if I speak for both you and my father, I'm sure your league will exist before the year is out. If you give me a list of merchants, I shall go immediately – "

"You will not. Rolf and my men have the league well in hand." Vardan took a deep breath. "If you wish to help me, I have a different proposal in mind. One where you stay here on Beacon Isle, with me. If you wish."

"Of course, but I thought…after I was the cause of the curse afflicting your island, you wouldn't want me here. No one would."

Vardan grasped her hand. "You cursed a mirror, not me. My brother gave me a cursed mirror, not you. I looked into the mirror and cursed my island, not you. Yet you came to my aid, to our aid, and broke the curse, though it nearly killed you. None of this is your fault, Lady Zuleika."

She swallowed. "But it is. I still cast the curse so the king could give it to you. I had no idea it would be so powerful. Lifting it was the least I could do, when I knew no one else would be willing to die in order to correct my mistake. What else could I do?"

"I can think of a few things." He captured her other hand and brought them to his lips. A warm, tingling kiss drove all other thoughts out of her head for one blissful moment. "You are the only person alive who could break that curse?"

"Yes."

"And yet my brother told me to slay you."

Zuleika frowned. "That would not have broken the curse. The mirror was imbued with blood magic that only blood could dispel. Killing me would have ensured the curse was permanent."

Vardan inclined his head. "As you say. A curse my brother made you cast, which he gifted to me, and then lied about how to break it. He has woven a curious web to trap us both and keep us apart. Perhaps he fears what we can do together."

"With the league, yes — " she began, but he silenced her with a kiss. A kiss that stole her breath and her senses, because she wanted nothing more than him.

"With you by my side, he wouldn't dare try to curse me again," Vardan said. "Lady Zuleika, my brave Belle, would you do me the honour of becoming my wife?"

Zuleika felt lightheaded. For a moment, she thought she'd heard him say something else, something impossible, until she realised she must have heard wrong. Her soaring heart plummeted. "Your witch?" she asked. "I could cast protection spells on your person right away, but to protect the isle would take longer. I would be honoured to try, though."

He chuckled. "I have had enough of spells to last me a lifetime, and perhaps a second one after that. No, I want you to be my wife. The woman who will stand by my side when the league first meets."

Zuleika's heart soared once more. There could be no mistake this time. "I will," she said, lifting her chin.

"You will? You really will?" He beamed. "I will send someone to bring a priest directly. We will be married in the chapel today, and tonight..." He swallowed, his eyes shining. "Tonight I will truly make you my wife. Nothing would make me happier."

Could he truly mean that? With all her heart, Zuleika wanted to believe him.

Forty-Nine

She'd agreed to stay. With him. His Lady Belle would be his in truth – tonight!

Vardan could barely believe it. That very morning, he'd wondered if he'd ever see her again. Now…he could scarcely stand to let her out of his sight. Inga refused to allow him into the queen's chambers, though, saying that it was bad luck to see a bride before she was ready for the wedding.

Vardan had endured enough bad luck for a lifetime – as had she. Reluctantly, he retreated from his housekeeper's stern gaze. He'd do nothing else to jeopardise his future with Zuleika. She'd run from him twice now, and he didn't want to risk a third time. Not when she was so close to becoming his wife.

And tonight…

Vardan swallowed. He'd endured so long without a woman's touch, that the mere thought of bedding Lady Belle tonight…he prayed that he could be the charming prince she deserved, and not a beast in her bed tonight.

Fifty

In a daze, Zuleika found herself back in her old chamber, at the mercy of a delighted Inga and Greta. Some time later, she stood in the chapel wearing the same gold silk dress she'd worn when she danced with the prince. When she knelt, he dropped to his knees at her side, and they both said the vows which the priest told them made them husband and wife.

The moment they left the chapel, Vardan pulled her in close to give her another breath-stealing kiss. Zuleika thought he would carry her to bed then and there, for the desire in his eyes was unmistakeable, but he insisted on heading for the great hall instead for supper.

She ate, but she didn't taste a bite. As each

moment ticked past, it brought her closer to what she feared most about marriage. Even to Vardan. And yet…she did not want to delay the inevitable. When Vardan asked whether she wanted to dance a little after dinner, she summoned her courage and replied calmly, "No, I think I would like to go to bed."

Servants whispered as Vardan wrapped a proprietary arm around her waist and lifted her from her seat, but Zuleika did her best to ignore them. Her heart beat so fast she was scared he would hear it, but Vardan only took her hand and led her to a part of the house she hadn't seen before.

His bedchamber, she realised, entering the grand room that was much bigger than her windowless chamber. The bed, too, was enormous – big enough for a dozen people to sleep in. Fit for a king, or, tonight, a prince. And his bride.

Tears sprang to her eyes, though she tried to stop them. Vardan had his back to her now as he poured two cups of wine, but in a moment he would turn and see…

"You are the bravest woman I have ever met. One who, I believed until this day, was afraid of nothing. Yet now, you look terrified." He handed her a brimming cup. "Share the wine with me, and tell me your secret: what has the power to frighten an enchantress?"

She burst into tears. "The consummation."

"Ah." He sipped from his cup. "Me, too."

She stared at him. "Why?"

"The first time I kissed you, you ran away. If you found one kiss so terrible, what will you do if I don't please you in bed?"

Zuleika blushed. "It was not the kiss I objected to, but…has anyone ever told you how similar you look to your brother?" Her eyes begged him to understand.

Vardan clenched his fists. "One day, I will make sure my brother answers for the evil he has done. Whether to me, or to God, I haven't decided, but I swear on your life and mine, he will answer for it. I am not my brother, and I promise you that I will never hurt you. Never."

Zuleika wiped her tears away. "Not intentionally, no, but…" She felt like such a fool.

He seemed to understand. He sat on the edge of the bed, patting the spot beside him. When she sat, he said, "You drink your wine, for it's my turn to tell you a secret I never told anyone."

She sipped, and tasted dewberry wine. Relaxing a little, she said, "All right."

Vardan slipped an arm around her waist.

"When I was perhaps sixteen or seventeen, only a boy though I thought I was a man, I was sent here to the monastery to study. My brother had just claimed the throne and perhaps he thought it amusing to make a monk of me. My grandmother had other ideas. One memorable week, an envoy came into port, from some exotic southern city. My grandmother wanted to hold a feast, so I was invited to sup with them. The envoy was boring, droning about politics and trade agreements that held no interest for me, but he'd brought with him two girls I thought were his daughters. As a good host, I set about trying to entertain them with witty conversation."

Zuleika managed a small smile. "Were you as charming then as you are now? I'm sure they could not resist you."

Vardan coughed. "I was a bumbling fool, and they knew it. As the evening progressed, though, it turned out that the ladies were not his daughters, but courtesans who he'd brought to soften up the monarchs he met along the way. As I was a prince, they decided that included me, so they made a wager as to who could win my affections by the end of the evening. After a few cups of wine, they called off the wager, and retired to their chamber with me in tow.

"They made a man of me that night, but as I was young and eager and had little stamina, the ladies took to amusing themselves. I watched, wide-eyed, for some time, before I summoned the courage to ask them what they were doing. So…they showed me everything they knew about how to pleasure a woman, and in the morning, one of them bit her lip the same way you do and whispered to me that when I lay with the woman I loved, I would give her nothing but pleasure, every time. I don't know if she was a witch, but the way she spoke and the way she touched me, it seemed very much like a spell."

Zuleika wet her lips. "Only an enchantress could work that sort of spell, and I haven't seen any magic about you since the curse was lifted."

Vardan reddened. "Well, no, you wouldn't. She only touched me in one place, which you haven't yet seen."

Zuleika took a deep breath. "Show me." She gulped a mouthful of wine.

He laughed nervously. "As my lady commands." He shucked off his clothes until he stood naked before her. "There. My…manhood."

As it was level with her eyes, it was hard not to stare. She'd known Vardan wasn't a small man, and this part of him wasn't small, either. She concentrated hard, and found she could see the glow of what might be a spell, though certainly not one of hers. This glowed faintly blue, instead of her familiar shades of purple. She reached out and wrapped her fingers around him, feeling the pulse of his heartbeat but also the throb of what was definitely a spell.

He groaned. "If you're going to do that, I won't last long enough to consummate this marriage. Can you do something more useful with your hands, like help me unlace your gown?"

She drained her wine cup, set it on the table, and found herself in Vardan's embrace. His lips tasted of dewberry as he kissed her deeply. Between them, they managed to remove Zuleika's gown and the shift beneath it, until she stood in nothing but her silk stockings.

Vardan held her at arm's length for a moment, drinking her in. "You are the most beautiful woman I've ever seen. I hope I don't disappoint you."

He kissed her again, pulling her close. As their bare bodies touched, it felt like the lightning spell had ignited along her skin, but it hurt neither of them. They toppled sideways onto the bed, her hands caressing the hard muscles of a man for the first time in her life and she found she quite liked it. Harder still was his manhood pressed against her leg. She wrapped her hand around it again…

"Oh God, you don't know how much I want to be inside you. I love you, Lady Belle," he groaned.

…and guided him between her thighs. She gasped as he filled her, expecting to feel pain, but instead there was just the wondrous warmth of his body joined with hers, inside hers, as she urged him to show her what he meant by pleasure.

He found a perfect rhythm, surging in and out of her with as much gentleness as if it truly was her first time, as his kisses grew more heated and his hands…oh, his hands. Stroking every inch of her until she wanted to purr like a cat. But there was a different sound fighting to escape from her throat, as a sort of storm welled up inside her. Stronger than the tide, sweeping her away, she heard her own cry of joy mingling with his.

When she regained her breath, she asked, "What was that?"

Vardan chuckled. "That is what happens when a chivalrous man makes love to a woman. The lady must always come first." When he withdrew from her, she noticed that the glow around his manhood was gone, but she didn't mention it, for her glow of happiness was more than enough for both of them, she was certain.

Later that night, after they'd made love for the third blissful time, Zuleika privately decided that the courtesan's pleasure spell hadn't done much, because Vardan was such an incredible lover already. So she cuddled up to her princely husband, who was no longer a beast except in bed, which suited her just fine, and dreamily resolved that they would live happily ever after.

Dance: Cinderella Retold

DEMELZA CARLTON

Book 2 in the Romance a Medieval Fairy Tale series

One

"Now your father must teach you to dance." The words rang like a bell in Mai's head, for they were the last thing her mother said to her before she died.

But her father showed no signs of teaching her anything, if in fact he noticed her at all. So deeply was he mired in his grief that Mai wondered if he even remembered he had a daughter. He moved from snake to dragon to tiger, each pose as graceful as the last, until Father became a fighter and nothing more. She knew his prowess in battle honoured the ancestors and that Mother was one of them now, but with each blow he aimed at the air, he dishonoured her last wishes.

Mai was only a little girl, but she had made promises to her mother, too. She had vowed to love, care for and honour her father. So her sense of duty made her step into the courtyard and face the furious man who fought ghosts. His hand stopped a breath from her face.

"You should not be here, child," he said, his voice raw and breathless.

Her dark eyes brimmed with hope. "I wish to dance, too, Father," she said. "Show me."

He shook his head. "I only know the martial dance. It is the dance for highborn sons, not daughters."

"Mother said you must teach me."

Father dropped to his knees. "If it was her wish, then I must."

In the mud of the courtyard, Mai found her father again. His instructions seemed strange at first, but as her movements became more practiced and fluid, she understood that this was a dance, if different to the dances her mother had excelled in.

Every morning, she joined her father in the courtyard for their daily dance until the sun rose above the house walls and set his grey hair aglow. Many moons passed in this way, until one summer dawn. Father smiled, then he laughed and said, "You have your mother's grace, Mai. If she had ever picked up a sword, she would have been both deadly and beautiful."

Mai felt his eyes on her, reading her soul.

"I will not always be able to protect you, so perhaps it is fitting that you learn all that I can teach you, before I join the ancestors and your mother."

"You are not..." She swallowed. "You're not ill, are you, Father?"

"No, I'm not. But we never know how much time we will have, so we must make the most of it." He bowed his head. "Today, I will go on a journey. The new Emperor summons me to court, and I must obey."

Mai swallowed hard, blinking back tears. "Yes, Father. I will pray to Mother every day until you return."

Father smiled down sadly at his young daughter. "Living or dead, she will always bring me home."

Two

Months passed, for it was a long journey from their mountain village to the capital. Every morning, Mai made an offering at the ancestral shrine, before moving to the courtyard to practice dancing alone. If she closed her eyes, she could almost believe her father practised beside her, and she longed for the day when he would return.

One evening, as she placed her mother's favourite flowers in the shrine, she heard a commotion in the distance. She followed the shouts to the gate, where she could see what looked like a procession making its way through the village. Her heart stuttered in fear. Surely…not a funeral procession?

None of the people headed toward her house was

wearing white, she realised with relief, for even under the dust caking their clothes, the colours shone through.

Then something appeared around the corner of the last house in the village that made Mai stare even more intently. A box as big as a house, sitting on poles carried by several men, brought up the rear of the procession. This, too, was brightly coloured in red and gold, though dulled with the dust of travel. Curtains swayed in the doorway to the box, tempting Mai to climb inside.

The procession reached the gate and she raced across the courtyard to the veranda, where she would have a better view of everyone as they crowded into the yard. Especially the mysterious box.

The box bearers set their burden on the ground, right in front of the veranda steps. A man stepped forward and stuck his arm through the curtains, then pulled it out again, clasping a hand.

At the bottom of the curtains, a tiny, striped shoe poked out, not much larger than one of Mai's shoes. She clapped her hands in delight, hoping for a playmate. Yet the girl who emerged from the box was far older than Mai – she was a woman grown, despite her tiny feet. And the way her round belly bulged through her robes told Mai the girl would be a mother before long, just like the other women in the village.

The woman swept past into the house without noticing Mai.

Mai sighed and sat down. No other children to play with, no mother to tell her stories, and no father to dance with. The servants wouldn't play with her, either. A more morose girl would have sat there and sulked, but Mai was a cheerful child, so instead she rose and made her way to the family shrine. Her mother might not be able to tell her stories, but she could tell her mother one, about the arrival of the round-bellied girl with the tiny feet.

Mai gathered some flowers from the garden and climbed the steps to the shrine, only to discover she wasn't the only one paying her respects to the ancestors.

"Father!" she exclaimed, racing across the tiles to throw herself into Fu's open arms. "I came to tell mother about the new girl!"

"Her name is Jing, and she will be your new stepmother," Fu said gravely.

Mai squirmed out of his grasp so she could stare up at him. "That girl is not my mother. She'll be mother to the babies in her round belly, just like Mrs Wu in the village."

"No, she is not your mother, and yes, she will give you sisters to play with. But Jing is used to life in the Imperial City, not a country house like ours. Will you do your best to help her, like a good daughter?" Fu asked.

"For you, Father, anything. She is our guest, and we must be hospitable to guests," Mai declared.

Fu laughed softly. "No, child, she is not a guest. Jing is here to stay. This is her home now, but I think she would like it if you treated her like an honoured guest." He eyed her. "She does not rise early, for court women don't like to see the dawn. So we will resume our dancing lessons tomorrow at dawn. The army with the best trained troops is assured victory, remember. Have you practised while I've been gone?"

Mai nodded happily. "Every morning, Father. It is not as much fun by myself, but now you are back, it will be better."

"Do you use your wooden sword every morning?" Fu demanded, eyeing Mai's thin arms.

She shook her head. "No, for it is too heavy."

"It is at first, but as your strength increases, you will grow used to it. A dancer's skill is equal parts balance and strength. Your balance is good, but we must work on your strength."

Mai bowed her head. "Yes, Father. I will practise now, so that tomorrow morning I will be ready."

He clapped her on the shoulder. "Good girl." Fu glanced at her mother's funeral tablet. "Da Ying would be proud to see you dance."

Mai beamed. "Thank you!" She skipped out into the courtyard in search of her practice sword, forgetting about stepmothers or sisters or strange boxes, for they were nothing compared to the honour she intended to bring her ancestors.

Three

For the most part, Jing left Mai alone. Her increasingly rounded belly made her waddle around like the ducks in the pond at the bottom of the garden, to Mai's amusement, until one night Mai woke to shrill howls as first one, and then the other of her two half-sisters were born.

Lin and Lei's cries could be heard echoing through the house at all hours of the day and night, while Jing and the servants did everything in their power to quiet the babies.

Most days, Father could be found in the courtyard, training, as he had when Mai's mother had died, once again with a deep frown on his face. The frown turned into a smile whenever Mai joined him, though, and everything seemed right in the world once more.

For six years, they danced together every morning and night, as the two screaming babies turned into troublesome toddlers before growing into girls the same age as Mai had been when her stepmother first arrived. But when a child's piercing scream broke the dawn silence, Mai laid down her wooden practice sword and dashed into the house, certain Lin or Lei had been seriously hurt.

She found a manservant holding down Lei while Jing did something to the girl's feet that only made her howl louder. Jing shouted for bandages, which a maid handed to her. Jing wrapped the strips of silk around her daughter's feet before cramming them into a pair of shoes that even Mai knew were too small for her.

Lin watched with wide eyes until the manservant let go of her sister and seized her instead. Then Lin started to cry and struggle, begging her mother not to hurt her.

Jing grabbed the girl's shoulders. "Do you want to be a lady, and find a good husband, or be doomed to be an old maid like your sister Mai?"

"I don't need a husband," Mai protested. "I promised my mother I would take care of Father, always."

"There. Do you want to be a drudge all your life, or

a lady who is carried everywhere in a litter?" Jing pressed.

Lin stopped struggling. "I want to be a lady, and a bride to a handsome husband, just like in the stories," she whispered.

She climbed up beside the still-sobbing Lei and Mai watched in horror as Jing broke her daughter's toes, bent them beneath the soles of her feet and bound the whole mess up in silk bandages. Now Mai understood why the too-small shoes suddenly fit Lei again, for Lin's shoes slid on over the bandages as if she were years younger.

"There," Jing said, planting her hands on her hips. "Now, you must walk around the garden ten times before you may have breakfast. Go, go!" She shooed the girls off the bed.

Both of them cried out as they took their first steps, begging their mother to let them sit down again, for their feet hurt too much to walk.

"Ladies must have lotus feet like mine, or no husband will have you," Jing said. "You will walk, no matter how much it hurts, or you will not eat. Do you hear me?"

Both girls nodded. Holding hands, they hobbled outside.

Mai folded her arms across her chest. "How can you do such a thing to your own daughters? It is barbaric!"

When Jing turned to face her, Mai was surprised to see tears streaming down her stepmother's face. "I do what must be done, to give my girls a future. A little pain now is nothing compared to a lifetime of being unwanted. My mother spared me until my feet had almost grown too big, and I was lucky to get a husband at all. If not for the Emperor's command and your father's ignorance of court fashions, I would not have been married, for no other nobleman would have me. My daughters will have such tiny feet that even princes will marvel at them."

Mai drew herself up. "You will not do such a thing to me. If you try to touch my feet, I will make you rue the day you were born." She wasn't sure how, but she had heard a great hero in one of her father's stories say such a thing, so it must mean something very frightening.

Jing sagged, looking as haggard as though it was her own toes that had been broken today and not her daughters'. "No, I will not," she agreed. "You are too old, and your feet are too big. I should have bound your feet when I first came, but my pregnancy and the girls…I could not. You will never find a good husband now, Mai. Not with feet as big as yours. Just like your common-born mother."

"My mother was not common! She was a general's

daughter, like me, and her feet were perfectly sized to suit my father!" Mai snapped.

Jing marched to the cupboard and took down a pair of shoes Mai recognised as her mother's favourite. Beside them, Jing placed a pair of her own. "Times have changed since your mother was a girl. Perhaps she could make a good marriage with feet like this, but we have a new Emperor now, and in his court, they would call her an iron lotus, fit only to marry a fieldhand."

Mai stared at her mother's red silk shoes beside Jing's tiny striped slippers. "My mother's shoes were magical. She wore those the night my father fell in love with her, she said, and she kept them. She said the ancestors had blessed them with balance in all things, so that when she wore them, her balance was perfect, too."

Jing shook her head. "You don't understand, do you? It doesn't matter how well a girl dances any more. It is all about the size of her feet. You will never marry." She thrust the shoes at Mai. "Take these huge things away. Treasure them if you must, as a memory of times that will never come again. No amount of magic in your mother's shoes will make you marriageable. When you pray to the ancestors, pray that I bear your father a son, for with no husband, you will have no children to take care of you in your old age. No one to bring flowers to your shrine once you are gone."

Jing tossed her head and minced away before Mai could reply.

Weighted down with sorrow that her stepmother could hurt her sisters so, Mai made her way back to the courtyard. Her father was nowhere to be seen and her two sobbing sisters had collapsed on the steps, in too much pain to continue their tortuous circuit. She beckoned a maid over to tend to the girls, before resuming her search for her father. He would put a stop to this, she was certain.

Mai found her father in the shrine, lighting her mother's favourite incense. Normally, she waited until he was finished praying, but her sisters' pain would not wait. "Do you know what she has done?" Mai demanded. "She is torturing the girls. Breaking their bones! They will never learn to dance as you taught me. They can barely walk! And for what? To find husbands? What husband would ask for his wife to have her feet broken when she's just a baby, long before he even meets her, so she can wear smaller shoes?"

Father shook his head. "The new Emperor is nothing like the old. Many things have changed. Jing swears to me what she does is for our daughters' future. A future I fear I do not understand any more. I will not fight when I cannot win. The court of my youth is gone, along with the Emperor I served. It is a strange new world we live in, Mai. Your mother and I sought to protect you from it, but..." He squinted at her. "Are those her shoes?"

With trembling hands, Mai surrendered the shoes to her father. "Is it true that she wore them the night you fell in love?"

"She wore these every night, and every day, too," Father said. "I never saw her in any others until we were married. They were a gift from her fairy godmother, she said, enchanted with balance. Her godmother gave them to her after she got in trouble for losing her shoes. These shoes can never be lost. They will always find their way back to their rightful owner." He glanced down. "They should fit you now. Why don't you try them on?"

Wear her mother's magical shoes? Mai's breath caught in her throat, but she did as her father told her. Slipping one bare foot, then the other into the shoes, she found he was right. They fit her perfectly.

"You will be as beautiful as your mother one day, and even more graceful, I think. When it is time to find a husband for you, I will have plenty of men to choose from, who would beg for your hand," Father said.

"I don't want a husband, Father. I promised

Mother I would take care of you," Mai replied mutinously, pressing her lips together.

"That is Jing's job now," Father said with a sigh. "And her son, if she manages to bear one. You are young yet. A man might catch your eye the way I caught your mother's eye. Then, I will have no choice but to make the match you choose."

Mai looked her father in the eye. "I will never choose another man over you, Father. I promise."

Fu kissed the top of his daughter's head. "You are a good girl. Do not think too harshly of your stepmother. Your mother wanted you prepared for a different life, while your sisters will find husbands at court, like their mother did. Court life requires sacrifices that I hope you will never have to make."

He had that right, Mai thought but did not say. Not if all her ancestors and every dragon in the country teamed up to drag her to the Emperor's palace would she set foot inside the place. Especially if she had to bind bits of her body and pretend to be something she wasn't.

Four

Years passed as Jing taught her daughters court dances for their absurdly tiny feet, and Mai practised increasingly complex martial dances with her father. On her sixteenth birthday, he gave her a sword made especially for her. While Mai stood speechless with joy at such a thoughtful gift, her stepmother trotted into the courtyard with a scowl on her face.

"That is not a suitable gift for a girl!" Jing said. Ten years had not been kind to her. She had tried to give Fu more children, but none of them survived very long. "You should return it to the armoury, to await the birth of your son." She patted her belly with considerable satisfaction.

Mai suppressed a groan. When Jing was pregnant,

she made Mai do everything for her, including running errands she should send servants to do. Though she knew her father wanted a son, she hoped Jing would miscarry early this time, instead of giving birth to a stillborn child. Better than nine months of hope only to have them dashed at the end.

"If you bear me a son, my blacksmith will craft him his own sword," Fu said firmly. "This belongs to Mai. She needs it to practice, for a wooden sword is no longer enough."

"She needs a husband," Jing grumbled, shuffling back inside.

"For your next birthday, I will see about finding you a husband," Father said. "But in the meantime…will you dance with me, Mai?"

Mai smiled. "Gladly, Father."

Five

Jing's time came early and the house rang with her screams even as the midwife tried to quiet her. Mai's father prayed in the shrine, where he could not hear the screaming, so when a messenger arrived at the gate, it was up to Mai to meet the man.

He wore the Emperor's colours of red and gold, and the scroll case he carried on his belt blended in with his robes so completely Mai almost didn't see it until he reached for it.

She instinctively dropped into a defensive pose, thinking that he was reaching for a blade.

The man laughed. "Easy, boy. I bring a message from the Emperor. Though it is a declaration of war, it is not war on Yeong Fu, but a call for him to provide troops. Perhaps if you are lucky, he will send you."

Mai opened her mouth to tell the messenger that she was no boy, nor would her father waste her life in a war against the rebellious cities to the north, but a particularly loud scream issued from the house.

"Sounds like war is already here," the messenger commented. He thrust a scroll into her hands. "Your father might go to war just to get some peace and quiet." Laughing to himself, the man headed down the road toward the town.

Mai itched to unfasten the scroll and read the message it contained, but not even she dared to break the Emperor's seal. Instead, she carried it to her father where he knelt in the family shrine.

"What is it? Another dead daughter?" Fu asked without turning around.

Mai moistened her dry mouth. "No, Father. It is a summons from the Emperor. Calling you to war."

Fu made a disgusted sound. "No doubt throwing more lives away, trying to reclaim one of the lost cities in the north when it is too little, too late. Only a strategist like your mother could take those northern cities, but not even she could devise a way to hold them. The northerners breed so much faster than we do, and their would-be king sends them against us in greater and greater numbers. Better to broker a treaty than to besiege some northern city. The worst policy is to attack cities, as any decent general should know."

"But he is calling you to war, Father. You are the greatest general in the kingdom." Mai dropped to her knees beside her father. "If anyone can win, it is you." Mai's eyes shone with admiration as she gazed at him.

"The man who now calls himself Emperor made me retire when he foisted Jing on me. He ordered me to go home and sire sons to serve him as I served his father." Fu waved angrily in the direction of the house. "Even my stillborn sons are too smart to die in that man's service. They would rather founder in their mother's womb, and I cannot blame them. Let him take my sons, for the Emperor will not have me for this stupidity!"

A breathless maid entered the shrine, bowing deeply. "Master, young mistress. The mistress has given birth to a son!"

A live one, Mai presumed, by light of the Jia's joyful expression.

"Come, I must see this for myself," Fu said, rising. He led the way into the house, with Mai and the maid following close behind.

Jing lay in bed, a gloating smile on her face as she regarded the tiny, wrinkled baby in her arms, oblivious to the army of maids carrying out bloodied sheets and replacing the soiled linen around her.

"I have given you a son, husband," Jing said, pride

dripping from her every word. She held the squirming child out for his inspection. "I have named him Yeong Fu, after his father."

Fu laughed mirthlessly. "And when the Emperor sends more troops to take Yeong Fu to war, I will offer him my son. For this baby here will grow to manhood before General Li retakes the city he lost."

Jing's eyes grew wide as she swaddled the baby tightly. "What is this?"

"The Emperor has summoned me to recruit and lead an army of reinforcements north to assist General Li's siege of Dean," Fu said.

Jing clapped a hand to her mouth. "So you are going to war? How soon?"

Fu laughed. "I am not going anywhere, woman. Did I not say I would offer the Emperor my infant son in my stead? If he'd sent the Empress herself to command the siege, it might have a better chance than the one led by her brother."

Mai stared in wonder as Jing's eyes widened further. "But you cannot disobey the Emperor!" Jing cried.

"I can, and I have. He thinks he can send me to certain death under that fool's command. If the army doesn't die of disease or starvation, the garrison of Dean will cut them down just as they did last time. The Emperor sends me so that he may blame someone else for General Li's mistakes. It will not be me!" Fu's voice rose to a roar and baby Fu began to cry. Father strode out of the room, swearing under his breath about fools and those who didn't understand the first thing about war.

Mai turned to follow him out.

"You have to convince him to change his mind," Jing said. "Mai, you must. Or we all will die."

Mai stopped, and shot a scornful glance at her stepmother. "You don't understand the first thing about war. If Father says this is foolish, then it is."

"More foolish to disobey the Emperor than to go to war," Jing insisted. "In battle, men live or die, but when the Emperor sends his troops to crush a defenceless household like this one, not a fortified city, we will be slaughtered. You may play with swords in the yard, but one girl cannot hold off an army."

For once, Jing was right. Mai could best her father in training, but not an army of highly trained troops. And she didn't want to die. "I will ask him," she said.

Six

She didn't need to look far for her father, for Fu had chosen to take out his frustrations in a furious training session in the courtyard. Mai took up her sword and joined him, shifting from pose to pose as effortlessly as her father.

"You are a better fighter than me now," Fu said grudgingly.

Mai bowed her head at the compliment. "Thank you, Father, but I still have a lot to learn. I hope to live long enough to do so, though. Jing says that if you disobey the Emperor, he will send an army to kill us all. Even you and I together are no match for an army." She glanced around the yard. "And there is nowhere we can retreat to from their superior numbers here."

Fu lowered his blade. "Jing sees only a small part of the picture. Your mother would see it all, and know how to act, but without her, I have no grand strategy any more." He sighed. "If I disobey, one day the Emperor may send an army, if he is not too busy making war on cities where he has no business being. But if I obey him, my dishonour is certain. General Li is the Empress' brother and for all that he is a fool, he still commands the respect of his army. If I were to arrive at the siege of Dean, I would be under his command. When he offers battle, he will lose, just like he did the first time he besieged the city. And he will lay the blame on me. Perhaps my inexperienced troops, or my poor commands, or my insubordination, for I will not take orders from a fool. When word reaches the Emperor, he will move swiftly to seize my lands and all who live on them. He will kill my family, and he will kill me, because he only holds power as long as General Li is his ally. If I ride to war, we will all most certainly die. And if I do not…we at least stand a chance that the Emperor will forget about us. For the best chance of victory, a general must know when to attack, and when to defend, and when not to fight at all." He bowed his head. "Mai, this is not the time for fighting."

"A general who fears defeat cannot be victorious,"

Mai replied. "That is what you taught me, Father. The hope of victory will only result in defeat. It is strategy and planning that win, every time. And hoping to be forgotten…is no plan at all."

Fu smiled sadly and shook his head. "For a moment, I saw your mother looking out through your eyes. She always had a clear view to victory. Always. But without her…I am lost. If you were my son, I would send you in my place, so that you could learn the truth of war on a battlefield instead of just a training ground. True victory must be won, and contrary to what General Li believes, the best victories are bloodless ones."

Mai shook her head. "How can you win a victory without spilling any blood?"

"Through winning the hearts of your enemies," Fu replied. "I should send you to court as my messenger. Perhaps you could win the heart of the Emperor, or one of his sons. Maybe there is hope after all. I shall think on it, and tomorrow we will make plans to send you to court. For now, go see your stepmother, and tell her what I have told you." He shooed her away.

Mai's head spun. Sending her to court to seduce the Emperor? What hope did she have? Jing commented on her unmarriageable feet every time she saw her, until Mai knew no man would look on her as a possible wife, let alone a prince or the Emperor. She was better suited to war, like her mother.

If only she was a boy and not a girl…

"What did he say? Did you change his mind?" Jing demanded when Mai returned to her stepmother's room.

Mai shook her head. "He will not go to war. He wants to send me to court to be the Emperor's concubine instead, I think." She felt sick at the thought.

Jing snorted. "You? The Emperor would not even look at you. No man wants a wife or a concubine who plays with swords."

"There was one who did," Mai said slowly. "Long ago, when Sunxi first wrote his treatise on war, the Emperor asked him to prove it by training his concubines in the art of war. And he did."

Jing waved the words away like a bad smell. "That is nothing but a story. Soldiers carry swords, concubines need to be pretty. Your sisters will have all the accomplishments and beauty a girl needs to charm a prince, when they are old enough, but not you. You would do better to take up a sword and lead an army in your father's place. In court, you will only make enemies. More than we have already."

For a moment, Mai's heart soared at the thought of commanding an army, as her father had done. As her mother had, too, or so she'd said. When her father had fallen in battle with a near-mortal wound, she had rallied his troops to victory. Mai had studied ever tenet in Sunxi's treatise and trained every day for more than a decade. Why couldn't she command troops in her father's stead?

Because no army would follow a woman, not even the daughter of Yeong Fu and Da Ying. If she were truly a boy like the messenger had first assumed…

Mai raised her head and met her stepmother's gaze. "I will. I will dress in men's clothing and take up my sword and take Father's place. It is the only way."

As the words left her lips, Mai knew they were the right ones. She could bring no honour on her family here. But if she was victorious in battle…or even died bravely in battle, she would honour her ancestors and her mother by her deeds.

Jing's mouth fell open in shock. "You are too small to pass for a man. And your breasts…" Mai expected her stepmother to launch into a scathing lecture about the size of Mai's breasts, whose only virtue, according to Jing, was that they made Mai's feet seem small, but the lecture never came. "You must bind them, but an illusion would be better." Jing bit her lip. "Yes, I think I can do it."

"An illusion? What do you mean?"

Jing smiled, revealing blood on her teeth that had not been there before. "I shall cast an illusion, so that all who see you or your clothing while it is near you will believe you to be a man."

"But…surely only a witch could do something like that…" Mai faltered. She swallowed. "Are you a witch? Can you make me into a man?"

Jing made an impatient sound. "I cannot turn you into a man, girl. I am a witch, not a powerful enchantress, and a weak one at that. I can make things look like they do not, but I cannot change you. Do you want to look like a man, join the army and save your family?"

Mai lifted her chin. "I do. All warfare is based on deception."

Jing rolled her eyes. "You should have been born a boy. I can make you look like one, but you will have to make them believe you are a man, and not a girl. If the soldiers find out you are a girl, you will become nothing but a common whore. If they don't kill you." She wet her lips. "Either way, you will dishonour your family, so you will not be welcome back here."

Mai nodded. "I understand." And she did. She would not dishonour her mother or her ancestors. Da Ying's and Yeong Fu's daughter could only be victorious. It was in her blood.

Seven

Mai flexed her arms as she donned her mother's armour, amazed at the play of muscles she'd never seen on her arms before. No matter how much Jing said it was an illusion, they looked and even felt real. She itched to try lifting something heavy, like one of the big urns in the garden. It probably helped that she'd bound her breasts flat under her shirt, too. She felt...manly.

Even her mother's shoes had taken a more masculine appearance. They looked more like something her father would wear than the pretty silk slippers she knew and loved. Yet if she closed her eyes, she felt exactly the same. Her balance was the same as ever, and that was what mattered. She buckled on her sword belt and drew the blade from its sheath.

"Be swift as the wind. Plunder like fire, stand as firm as the mountains, and move like a thunderbolt," she whispered, as she did at the beginning of every dance.

She moved through the sequence of morning exercises she'd performed every day for as long as she could remember, noting the places where her armour restricted her movement, few though they were.

In the stable, she found her father's warhorse, saddled, packed and ready, as Jing had promised. Staring up at the huge animal, Mai almost doubled over as doubt punched her in the belly. She shouldn't be doing this. Girls didn't ride to war. If anyone in the army found out, she was as good as dead – to her family, even if she still breathed. It was one thing to spar with her father, who surely had gone easy on his daughter, but to fight armed soldiers in battle? She would die in a heartbeat. Now Mai felt queasy, too. If she rode to war, she would never return. Never see her family again. Her stepmother. Her sisters. Her father...

Mai wanted to run to the shrine, where she knew she would find her father, to bid goodbye to him one last time.

But she could not. If her father saw her like this, he would stop her. Even if it killed her, she had a duty to save her family from the Emperor's wrath.

She found the messenger camped just outside of town, on the outskirts of what looked like an army camp in a fallow field. Some of the men she recognised from the village, but most of them were unfamiliar. There were more men in this one field than in the entire village where she'd grown up. More than enough to slaughter her father's household, if commanded to do so.

All she had to do was walk in, and convince the men she was one of them.

Her heart sank, but Mai took a deep breath as she dredged up her courage. "All war is deception," she reminded herself under her breath. She rode up to the messenger's tent, reined in her horse and managed to dismount without falling. "My father sent me to captain his troops," she announced.

The messenger laughed. "And how many wars have you served in, boy?"

Mai felt her face redden. She hoped Jing's illusion hid that. "None," she admitted. "But my father has been training me for battle since I was six."

"Did you learn much?"

"Some," she said. "He said I could train for a lifetime, but learn more on one battlefield than in a decade of practice." She lifted her chin. "That is why he sent me."

This seemed to satisfy the messenger. "What's your name, boy?"

"Yeong Ma...oh!" Mai clapped a hand over her mouth in horror. She hadn't been here a minute and already she was about to reveal her identity.

"Yeong Mao?"

"Yyyes?"

"That is your name?" the messenger asked.

Mai nodded, not trusting her voice.

"I hope baldness doesn't run in your family, then. It would be a great pity to have a name meaning thick hair when you have none. Your men would have no respect for a general with a funny name." The messenger laughed, then gestured at the grass behind his tent. "You may set up camp beside me. In the morning, we march for Dean."

"Don't I get to decide when my men move?" Mai asked.

The messenger laughed so hard, he almost bent double. "These are not your men any more, boy. They belong to General Li, as do you. When we reach his camp, he'll make the decisions. My orders are to bring reinforcements, and I will. Untrained farm boys, most of them, but once the general's captains are done training them, even you might manage to kill a man in battle. Or die trying."

Mai smiled wanly and tried to hold back her tears as

she led her horse to what would be her campsite for the night. Men did not cry, she told herself. At least, not where anyone could see. Once she had her tent set up, then she could go to pieces at the thought of killing people. That she might die, she had come to accept, but that other men must die at her hands? The very thought made her shudder.

But if a stranger had to die to protect her family…so be it, Mai decided. There was nothing she would not do for those she loved. She might be a girl, but when the time came, she would have the heart of a warrior, until her heart beat its last.

Eight

"There is no greater pleasure than thrusting your sword hilt-deep in another man's heart," Prince Yi declared, demonstrating.

"My advisers told me you had never been with a woman before, but now I begin to believe it," Emperor Yun replied. "No wonder you don't have any sons yet. You're supposed to do the thrusting lower down, and into a woman."

"I don't slaughter women. I fight enemy soldiers in battle, and bring honour to our family name when I am victorious. That is my purpose, Father," Yi said, yanking his sword free of the practice dummy. A shower of straw came with it.

The Emperor sighed. "I know that is what you have

done, but I have more than enough generals. What I do not have is a suitably married heir to the throne, with children of his own to ensure the succession of our dynasty."

Yi's hands clenched around his sword. He whirled and lopped off the practice dummy's head. He wanted to hack the hapless straw man to pieces, but he feared even that would not soothe his frustration. "And what if I don't want to marry anyone, Father, let alone some suitable girl? Every maiden in court has feet so tiny she trots like a pig on its hind legs, and all they seem able to do is dance and giggle like animated dolls. All the same. Can you imagine one of them as Empress? Mother would have the poor girl for breakfast, while I go away to fight in the next war."

"We are at peace. Except for your uncle's foolish obsession with the city of Dean, there are no battles left to fight, boy," Yun snapped. "Sheath your sword. Preferably in your willing wife. One who can give you sons."

"So that in time, I will have this discussion with my sons, as you are with me?" Yi asked with a wry smile. Obedient to his father's wishes, he slid his sword into its leather sheath at his side. "I am not ready to settle down to a life in court, where I will grow fat as all I do is waddle between my wife's bed and your chambers, to advise you or carry out whatever minor errands you think suitable. Perhaps it is time to look at expanding our borders. That I would at least be good at."

"We are at peace!" Yun exploded. "We do not make war on our neighbours. Especially not while General Li keeps most of our army occupied in the siege of Dean. We are a nation of cultured, educated, enlightened…."

"How long do you think our neighbours will leave us alone if they know the noblemen of our court spend more time on poetry than swordplay? Some of them have never fought a single opponent, let alone a battle. The last battle I fought, they ran screaming from the field at the first sign of blood, for all the world like they were girls shrieking at a spider. Your cultured, enlightened courtiers are weak, Father."

Yun took a deep breath. "I know. In a time of peace and prosperity, we have the luxury of learning to write good poetry, instead of fighting for our lives. So that they may be weak…their rulers must be strong. The Empress and I protect our people with our strength, and that of the armies who serve us. One day, you will do the same, I hope, or your sons will."

"I serve you best in the army, Father. I have no patience for court. You know that."

"In time, perhaps you will learn patience, as I did. And learn to see the value of poetry. For no warrior is forgotten when his deeds are immortalised in a ballad the people love." Yun smiled. "Perhaps that is what you need. A woman who is your complement, your opposite, your partner. While you fight, she will compose poetry so that your descendants will recount your deeds forever."

"The only partner I want is one who can oppose me when I train. I have no use for a woman, unless she holds a sword. There are tales of warrior women of old, and even the old general, Sunxi, taught a king's concubines to fight. If I can train an army, I can certainly train one woman," Yi said.

"The only sword you want your wife to hold is yours. In bed. In the past, there were warrior women. Unnatural creatures that necessity forged into fighters. Those kind of women no longer exist, Yi." Yun sighed. "But I will make a deal with you. You are still young. Go to Dean, and end the siege. General Li listens to you. Enjoy the battle while it lasts. But when it is over…you will come home. I will hold a court ball and invite every noble maiden in the kingdom, and from their number, you shall choose a bride."

"I don't want a bride," Yi said through clenched teeth.

"Is it men you prefer, then?" Yun asked. "For ancestors' sake, boy, you don't have to love the girl. Just close your eyes and imagine she is someone else, poke her a bit, and beget some sons! You must marry.

I command it."

The Emperor did not issue commands to his son very often, and Yi was both a dutiful son and a loyal subject.

Yi sighed. "No, Father, I do not want a lover of any kind, male or female. I wish only to fight, for that is when I feel most alive. But if you command it, then I will obey. I will go to the siege at Dean, and when it is over, I shall return and marry whatever girl you wish."

"Whatever girl you wish, boy. You're the one who has to bed her, not me," Yun grumbled, but Yi could see his father was hiding a smile. The Emperor had gotten his way, as he always did.

At least Yi got one more campaign. And if General Li was in command, it would be a long campaign indeed. Yi wouldn't have to look at a woman again until the siege was over. Better yet, maybe his father would grow tired of waiting, and choose one of his brothers as his heir instead, leaving Yi free to command armies in the Emperor's name. Bliss, surely.

Nine

Mai rode at the head of an army, or at least she thought she did, until the city of Dean rose into view. What she saw made the troops at her back look like a troupe of travelling performers after a night of carousing. Tired, undisciplined and dirty. Mai barely noticed as the men were marched off to one of the fortified camps ringing the city around. She was too busy marvelling at the construction that had gone into besieging an entire city.

Dean itself was huge, its massive walls rising high above the surrounding plain, dwarfing the moat that seemed a mere puddle at its feet.

A second line of walls encircled the first, though they were thinner and made of timber. Tree trunks had been cut down and their tops sharpened into spikes to make these walls, which were broken by camps and watchtowers all the way along. Too many to count. How many men did General Li have? Not enough to man all of this, surely – hence why her father's people had been called up to enlist.

This didn't match her idea of battle. That involved two armies, clashing on the plain. The clash of swords and spears and the twang of bowstrings. How did one fight a war with all these buildings?

Mai pondered the question as she surveyed the encampment. Some of the watchtowers had wheels at the bottom, and were joined in pairs by a sort of skybridge between them. They were siege towers, then, capable of being wheeled to the wall and used to help the General's troops climb into the city. They looked complete, so why had the General not employed them for their purpose? Perhaps he did not have the men.

Still, it seemed foolish to keep the siege towers on display, where they were clearly visible from the city walls. The defenders would know what was coming, and have time to plan a defensive strategy against them. The besieging army would be at a disadvantage, heading into terrain they did not know. An enclosed city, no less, where the defenders lived and knew better than anyone else could.

Now, if they could tempt the city's forces out of the

gates, then the besiegers might have an advantage. But what could be tempting enough to entice them out? Perhaps…

"You're to report to General Li," the messenger said, interrupting Mai's battle plans. "I'll take you to the command tent, and then I can return to the capital. Where things are civilised."

Mai followed him into the biggest stockade, which sat on a natural rise on the otherwise flat plain. The General's tent was actually a wooden hut, built on a mound of earth in the middle of camp overlooking what appeared to be a training ground. The General himself was the only man in full armour, though he carried his helmet under his arm as he watched the troops training below.

No, not training. Sparring, Mai noticed with interest. She had not trained with an opponent since she left her father's household, and she was eager to learn to fight better against someone more skilled than she.

"This is the last one. Yeong Mao, Yeong Fu's son," the messenger announced, shoving Mai forward so that she almost overbalanced.

She righted herself before she fell at the General's feet. "My father sent me to learn the art of war, General," Mai said. "He has trained me well."

General Li snorted. "That's what they all say, right

up until they turn and run in battle. Cowards. Right. Whatever-your-name-is, go join the other young noblemen down there. First, we'll see how well you can fight, and then give you something to do."

He turned to speak to one of his aides, effectively dismissing her.

The messenger seemed mesmerised by the group of young men the General had pointed to. "Good luck, Yeong Mao," he said softly.

Mai swallowed. "Thank you," she said. "I wish you a safe journey back to the capital."

She joined the circle of boys, who formed a ring around two combatants. The smaller of the two, a boy perhaps a year or two older than Mai and not much bigger, struggled to hold his wooden sword aloft, even as he gripped the hilt with both shaking hands. The other boy – more a man, Mai decided, smacked his own wooden blade against the smaller boy's sword almost lazily, sending it flying across the circle to land at Mai's feet.

Mai reached down for the sword, which felt surprisingly light in her hand. Her father's wooden blades had a metal core, weighting them much like a proper sword, but this one was all wood. She looked up, intended to offer the practice blade back to the disarmed boy, but he now lay on his belly in the dirt, begging for mercy from the bigger boy whose blade merely touched the back of the downed boy's neck.

"Next," the victor drawled, letting his foe up.

The boy scrambled out of the circle as fast as his feet could carry him.

The next challenger was built like an ox. He would have no trouble lifting the light sword, Mai thought, as he tossed it from hand to hand like it weighed nothing. Then the challenger adopted a bold stance, knees bent, facing the victor of the previous bout.

"Try that on someone your own size!" the challenger called.

The victor strode forward, his muscles bunching as he delivered his first thrust.

The challenger managed a clumsy block, but his movements were too slow. He might have the strength to fight, but he had little practice with a sword, Mai decided. The victor delivered a series of slashing blows that his opponent barely managed to block in time, until one cut made it through, tearing through the fabric of the boy's tunic.

Mai glimpsed pale flesh for a moment before the boy dropped his blade, turned tail and ran out of the circle.

"The General will put him to good use, running messages in battle!" the victor said.

A few of the boys in the circle sniggered at this, but the laughter died quickly when they realised the man in the middle wasn't laughing. Instead, he pointed at those who had. "You, you and you. In that order. You're up next."

The boys ducked their heads in obedience, and the first one trudged across the dirt to meet his fate.

Without taking her eyes off the fight, Mai asked the boy beside her, "Who is he?"

"The Prince of Swords, Gong Ji," the boy whispered.

Gong Ji…the man's name was Rooster? Mai tried again. "Who?"

"Best swordsman in the kingdom, or so he says. No one's managed to beat him yet. The General said if we can stay on our feet for a turn of the hourglass in the ring with him, we will be assigned to his camp, and will lead troops in battle when we breach the city walls. The rest of us will go to different watchtowers to stand guard over the city."

Stand guard? There was no honour in guard duty. Leading troops into battle…if Mai wanted to earn honour for her family, then she must find a way to fight this Prince of Swords.

"How many have beaten the hourglass?" Mai asked.

The boy swallowed. "So far, none."

The Prince of Swords was a master swordsman indeed, then. An enemy she must know as well as she knew herself, for Mai to be victorious.

For the first time, she took a good look at the man, instead of his less skilled opponents. The prince lowered his head and barrelled into a boy, knocking him into the dirt. The prince was a big man, who used his size and strength to his advantage against smaller opponents like this one. He held his sword like a man who had trained for longer than Mai had, for he moved with a fluidity that spoke of experience with a good teacher. His sword truly was an extension of his arm – and a long arm, too. He used his bigger reach to attack his opponents before they had the chance to touch him, forcing them to defend against a fast flurry of blows that were designed to distract, not hit, until the prince saw an opening and took it. Not to hurt or to kill – no, he knocked his opponent down. In battle, his enemy would be trampled or run through, Mai knew. She suspected the prince did, too.

She watched him peel off his sweat-soaked tunic and use it to mop his face. Her belly sort of swirled a little, as if she was suddenly hungry for something. Strange. She'd eaten some of her travel rations only an hour ago. Why the sight of a man's muscled body made her feel hungry again, she had no idea. Yet as she stared, she realised he had an impressive collection of scars. Battle scars. The prince was a veteran of many battles, if his back was any indication. He would lead troops into battle. Perhaps he already had – many times. Now Mai's appetite took a different turn — she hungered for his knowledge and experience, so that she might lead troops to victory, too.

"Any of you other ladies want to come and dance with me?" the prince asked, turning slowly on the spot so he could meet the eyes of every boy who dared raise his gaze from the dirt. "Or will you all be standing guard on the watchtowers like the others?"

It was now or never.

Mai stepped forward. "I shall dance with you."

Ten

Even as Yi called out his final challenge to the circle of boys, he knew what their answer would be. He'd defeated too many of them for the rest to have the courage to face him. What was left were the cowards who were not fit for war. Bureaucrats who belonged in the capital, his father's new batch of aspiring poets, and...

"I will dance with you."

Yi looked up in surprise to meet the eyes of a boy he hadn't seen before. Small for his age or perhaps younger than the rest, he was hardly an impressive specimen, but he was no coward. His eyes brimmed with determination as he lifted the wooden practice sword in a fighting stance that even Yi had to admit looked convincing. The boy's small stature would be his downfall, though – he would be no match for Yi's strength, or that of an enemy soldier.

Yi considered rushing the boy, but decided to let him attack first. There was something different about this one. "I am ready," he announced, beckoning the boy to advance.

The boy stood firm and shook his head. "Where is the hourglass?" he demanded.

The forgotten timekeeper was produced and set back on its stool. Yi could feel the boy's eyes on him as he turned it and let the sand flow. "There," Yi said, moving to face the boy again.

The boy smiled, almost as though he was eager to begin. "I am ready," he said.

Yi had to admire his gall as the boy beckoned him to attack. Had he not been watching the other…well, one could hardly call them battles. Bouts, maybe. Very short ones.

"Then attack," Yi said.

The boy shook his head once more. He darted a glance at the hourglass.

Yi stifled a grin. So that was the boy's strategy. Stall until the sand ran out. If he would not attack, then Yi would.

Yi darted across the circle until he was two strides from the boy, then ducked his head and barrelled into him.

Or he would have, except where the boy had been a moment ago, Yi met only air. His foot connected with something, hooking under it, and he pitched forward. He tried to turn it into a combat roll, but his foot was caught and he sprawled on his belly in the dirt instead.

He'd tripped. Somehow, he'd tripped on uneven ground and fallen. It could have happened to anyone.

Yi rose to his feet, scanning the ground for the unseen obstacle. All he saw was a shoe, which matched the other one the boy still wore. He'd run so fast, he'd left his shoe behind for Yi to trip over. Fortuitous.

As if the boy could read his mind, he removed his other shoe and tossed it under the stool. Now he fought barefoot.

Yi tucked the lost shoe into his pocket. "We're not through yet," he said, raising his sword. Though the boy had no more shoes to ambush him with, Yi didn't charge again. Instead, he concentrated on speed, moving the wooden blade so fast none of the other boys had had a chance to block him.

Not so this one. He blocked every blow, stepping into Yi's reach instead of out of it, giving his shorter arms the advantage until he was so close every time he blocked, the hilt of his sword tapped Yi's chest.

Yi thought little of it – what were a few bruises from training? – until the boy slammed the hilt of his sword into Yi's solar plexus. Yi coughed, unable to breathe, but he knew it would be only temporary. He whirled away from the boy, putting space between them once more to give him time to recover.

Time he did not have. The boy harried him, trading blows every step of Yi's retreat until Yi managed to suck in another breath.

"Enough playing," Yi said sharply. He stepped forward, thinking to force the boy back with another flurry of blows, but he stood his ground. Still, he left an opening that Yi was waiting for. He bulled into the boy with his shoulder, determined to knock him into the dirt.

The boy twisted and Yi found he'd overreached. Already off balance, Yi stepped forward to right himself, but his foot caught on something again. This time, instead of falling on his face, he landed on his back, the breath knocked out of him once more. And there was no shoe in sight.

Honour forced Yi to his feet. He could not be seen lying in the dirt – not even if he was the victor of a hundred bouts today would they have any respect for him if this boy beat him. Grimly, he lifted his sword once more.

The boy held up his hand, palm out. "The hourglass is out of sand," he announced. "And I am still on my feet."

By the ancestors, so he was. Yi threw his sword in the dirt. "You boys, collect up the practice swords and put them away, then report to the General's aide for watchtower assignments." He pointed. "You, you and you will join the runners. And you." He glared at the boy who'd beaten him. "What is your name?"

The boy took his time handing his practice sword to one of the others, treating it with the respect of a real weapon and not the toy it was. Finally, he said, "My name is Yeong Mao."

"You were lucky, Yeong Mao," Yi growled. "Don't expect the enemy to trip over your lost shoe in battle. You must train, and train hard, if you want to remain in a fighting unit and not be sent to do guard duty like the others."

Mao's eyes darkened. "It was luck and skill that beat you. Or are you ashamed to admit defeat?"

He didn't seem to care that he was unarmed, or smaller than Yi. Mao took up a fighting stance once more, his hand taking the place of his blade.

This was madness. Yi didn't want some hot-headed youngster beside him in battle. He reached for one of the practice swords, determined to best this boy in the second bout. His honour was at stake.

"Do your worst," Yi spat.

This time, Mao attacked, blurring into motion so fast Yi barely saw him until Yi lay flat on his back again, and the boy bent over him.

"I'm going to kill you," Yi wheezed, fighting to drag air into his lungs as he clambered painfully to his feet.

"I'd wager this one will be first over the walls when we attack," General Li said, clapping his hands as he strode onto the practice ground. "Well done, boy. What's your name?"

"Yeong Mao," Mao repeated.

"Yeong Fu's son?" the General mused.

Mao nodded.

"You can share a tent with Yi here. Maybe even teach him a thing or two. Looks like he's getting rusty in his old age." General Li grinned.

Old age? Li was more than twice his age, Yi fumed. As for sharing a tent with the boy... He waited until the General moved out of earshot before he muttered, "One night. You can sleep in my tent for one night, but I want a rematch in the morning. No tricks this time."

Mao bowed his head, not bothering to hide his own grin. "Gladly, Gong Ji. Any time you wish to lie in the dirt again, I will help you."

"My name is Jun Yi," Yi bit out through clenched teeth. "Get it right, boy."

"My name is Mao, not boy," Mao corrected. His eyes flashed with an anger that equalled Yi's own. "And you are Gong Ji. A puffed-up rooster who is not as good in a fight as he thinks."

Yi lifted his fist to clout the boy, only to see his arm come up in an automatic block. Mao might be small, but he had some combat training, at least. "Tomorrow, we will test the truth of that," Yi promised. "And when I am done with you, you will be the chicken, not me, running away in fear."

Mao snorted. "We shall see."

Eleven

As Mai lay on her pallet, listening to Yi's breathing on the other side of the tent, her blood buzzed like it contained a swarm of bees. She couldn't recall ever being this angry at anyone before.

For what had felt like a perfect moment that stretched for eternity, she had stood in the ring opposite Yi in her first fight against a real opponent. And her performance had been flawless. Not even her father could have found fault with her today. The world had stood still while only she and Yi moved in it, and she had moved faster than he did every time. A deadly dance indeed.

How dare that puffed-up rooster claim her victory was because of some dishonourable trick?

For the first time in her life, she'd tasted triumph, and a moment later he'd trodden it into the dust by suggesting she'd won because of a lucky accident.

Unlucky, more like, that when she'd hooked her leg around his to trip him, his huge, lumbering foot had dislodged her shoe. Had she fought barefoot, the result would have been the same. Perhaps she should insist that they both fight barefoot on the morrow. Or if she went shoeless, he went shirtless, for the truth was that seeing his muscles so clearly had allowed her to almost read his mind, for the muscles of his chest gave away his next move before he made it. It had been easy to counter him, with so much warning.

She half expected Yi to attack her while she lay in bed, for a man so quick to assume dishonourable behaviour in others must be less than honourable himself. That was why she gripped the hilt of her dagger, ready to use it if the need arose, but his breathing grew even, as though he slept.

She listened a while longer, until she was satisfied that the man really was asleep, before she set her shoes alongside her bed, where they would trip him up if he approached her. Her dagger went under her pillow, within easy reach should she need it during the night. Then she rolled herself up in her blanket and sank into sleep.

Twelve

The eighth time Yi picked himself up off the ground where Mao had dumped him, he resolved it would be the last. "You win," he panted, bowing to the boy.

Mao gave a curt nod. "Just like yesterday." His eyes glittered with what Yi fancied was a warning.

"Just like yesterday," Yi agreed. He knew when he was beaten, though it had been a long time since anyone had been able to do so. He'd been smaller than Mao, and probably younger, too. He had long since surpassed his training masters. Perhaps Mao's master would be willing to train him, too. "Who taught you to fight like that?"

"My father, of course," Mao said, slipping his shoes back on his feet. The movement was oddly graceful, stirring something inside Yi that he didn't understand.

A memory, he told himself. For there was nothing about a boy putting on his shoes that could inspire any kind of feeling in him.

"And your father is Yeong Fu?" Yi asked, hoping he'd gotten the name right. It sounded vaguely familiar, but he couldn't place the man. That was strange in itself, for Yi prided himself on knowing every man at court who had some skill with a blade. A man who fought as well as Mao should be remembered. "Have I seen him at court?"

Mao shook his head. "My father is rarely at court. The last time the Emperor summoned him, I was but a small child. Too small and weak to even lift a wooden practice sword, though my father insisted otherwise."

A country noble, then, Yi guessed. Which made it all the stranger that he should know the man's name. "Did he train troops?"

Mao straightened with pride. "He trained me, just as he did all the other boys in his army, he said. He was a well-respected general who won many battles."

Not someone Yi had fought under, though. "Your father must be very old, then, if he has retired from commanding troops."

Mao opened his mouth to reply, then closed it again, as if to keep a secret from escaping. Interesting. Finally, he said, "That is why he sent me to war in his stead." He kept his eyes firmly on the ground.

A lie, Yi assumed, or only a partial truth. No matter. General Li had them sharing a tent. Mao could hardly avoid him. Whatever secrets he kept would leak out eventually, and Yi intended to be there when they did.

"How many battles have you fought in?" Yi asked.

Mao wet his lips. "None," he admitted. "How many have you?"

"Too many to count," Yi replied easily. It was true. He didn't remember any more. He had learned that the only battles that mattered were the ones you fought at the present moment, and the next one. "If I'd fought against someone like you, though, I wouldn't have survived."

Mao's mouth dropped open. "But…trained soldiers at war…fighting is what they are trained for. Not just a little practice in the yard every morning, like me."

"There is more to army life than fighting. They spend more time digging, doing camp chores and drilling than actually fighting," Yi said. "They train daily, but as a unit. A common soldier is not a warrior, or a fine swordsman. He is but one part of a company of men, who must all do the same thing at the same time when they are ordered to do so. They move as one, not as men."

Mao nodded thoughtfully. "A well-trained army is

as essential to victory as a good general, and capable officers. So my father says."

When the siege was over, Yi resolved to find Mao's father and make the man train him. If he could turn this small boy into a formidable fighter, surely he would welcome the Prince of Swords as his pupil. "But so is keeping the army well-fed. Come, I will show you the officers' mess, where you will find the worst meal you ever ate."

Mao's eyes widened. "Are we short on provisions? That does not bode well for victory."

Yi laughed. "Oh, we have provisions aplenty. You arrived at the head of a sizeable baggage train. The problem is the cooks are all army men. Just one of the palace cooks could turn every meal into a dream for your senses, but our cooks? The days when you can eat what they produce, it is a good day." It was on the tip of his tongue to say Heng, his manservant, was on good terms with the General's cook, so he rarely needed to visit the officers' mess, but Yi resisted. Let Mao learn what it really meant to serve in the army, instead of training at home with his father. The boy could surely fight, but something told Yi that he was too soft for army life. He still might turn and run in battle, like all the other noble boys he'd fought yesterday. Yi would take the city with seasoned fighting men, not boys. And young Mao was not a man yet. Though he might become one before Li ended the siege, at the snail's pace he worked at.

No matter. That would give him more time to win Mao over, so that his father would agree to train him.

Thirteen

Perhaps Yi was not so bad after all, Mai mused as she forced down another mouthful of bland food. She couldn't keep the smile off her face after what she felt was a fantastic training session that morning. Yi had fought hard, but she had fought harder, and victory was sweet once more. Especially when the man acknowledged it this time.

She had made some mistakes, she admitted, but Yi had not been quick enough to capitalise on them. On the morrow, she would improve.

In the meantime, she listened to Yi's tales of battles he had fought in. More than her father had, to hear the man talk. She had heard every story her father could tell more times than she could count, but Yi's were all new. Some were even fought here, on this very plain, on the rare occasions General Li had tempted the city's troops out to do battle. Those were fewer now the walls were up, but Yi admitted the city's army still ventured out to test Li's defences. It had been weeks since their last sortie – perhaps Mao would be lucky enough to join the next battle, Yi said.

It took Mai a moment to remember that the name was hers, but it was close enough to her own that she hoped she would soon grow used to it.

"We'll have plenty of poets to immortalise it, when you do get to fight," he said, laughing.

Poets? "What do you mean?"

He jerked his chin at the nearest watchtower. "Remember all those boys yesterday I sent to do guard duty?"

She nodded.

"Noble youths from court, most of them. Their fathers want them to serve in the army, but fighting is out of favour in my father's court. He favours poetry, and so do most of them. They might not know one end of a sword from another, but they are familiar with a calligraphy brush. I gave them the best vantage points to see whatever may come, and their best chance of surviving to tell the tale when they return to court."

Mai frowned. "So you deny them the honour of

dying in the Emperor's service, when that is why they are here?"

"There is honour in dying well in battle, but there is none when you die screaming, running from the battlefield like a pig fleeing slaughter. Honour is not earned through throwing away your life." He pointed at the common soldiers' camp below them. "If they fall in battle, it will be hard fought. They have entered the Emperor's service and trained every day for battle. But a boy who knows nothing of fighting, who has not trained a day in his life? They will be slaughtered, with no honour on either side."

Finally, Mai understood. Perhaps her desire to honour her ancestors by dying in battle would be a bad idea. She liked living, and if there was another way... "Why didn't you train them? The great Sunxi trained concubines to fight. Surely boys of the right age..."

Yi shook his head. "Not all men are born to fight, just as not all women are born to serve. Some choose a different path, or destiny chooses it for them." He laughed. "For those boys, I chose their path. One which has a future for them, and won't get me killed in battle as they run in fear at the first sight of blood. You'd better not turn out to be like them, Mao, or I'll find you a watchtower, too."

Mai laughed. "You tell tales of all the battles you have fought, but after fighting against you, I wonder that you survived at all. You're more likely to get yourself killed than anything I could do. Some fighter you are, Rooster."

It was Yi's turn to frown. "Will you stop calling me that?"

She leaned forward. "I shall stop calling you that when you are no longer a rooster. Beat me in a fight, and I will address you as your Highness, Prince of Swords, the best hero and fighter there ever was. Until then…I think I shall keep pulling your pretty tail feathers."

"Then another rematch on the morrow," Yi swore.

Mai inclined her head. "I look forward to it."

Fourteen

Weeks passed, every day the same as the last. Mai and Yi would begin the day with a new bout, and she would proceed to drop him on his back or his front or occasionally even his head until he cried enough for one day and sulkily slunk off to find breakfast. Sometimes, they would join the regular army in their training exercises, but at others, the General sent them on errands to the other camps.

The garrison inside Dean led sorties out to attack some of the camps at night, stealing their supplies and burning what they could, before sneaking back into the city. She'd seen the smoking aftermath of these raids, and occasionally witnessed a battalion marching out to help the camp while they were under attack, but no battle seemed to be in the General's plans. Yi believed the General's strategy was to wait here until the city starved, which would take a very long time with the city stealing their supplies to supplement their own. This kind of war seemed a very tedious business. So much for a campaign being as swift as the wind. Sure, the General might stand as firm as a mountain, but he moved more like a snail than a thunderbolt, and the only plundering going on was by the citizens of Dean, who understood the qualities of fire all too well, for they used it to great effect.

Many times, Mai found herself shaking her head. The commander of Dean evidently knew the art of war intimately, but the General did not. She began to wonder if her father was right, and whether Dean was the side that should win. After all, the better commander with the better army and the better terrain and all the supplies they needed would surely be victorious. She didn't dare mention that to Yi, though. Bad enough that her father might be a traitor, without letting the Emperor's son know she might be one, too.

She still slept with a knife under her pillow, but she now knew Yi well enough to be sure she'd never use it. For all his pride, he was an honourable man. And a protector of poets. If he wanted to kill her, he would do so in a fair fight, not in the darkness while she slept.

The food alternated between bland, awful and

burned, but it was mostly edible, so she bit back her complaints until she realised no one else was. Men whined more than Jing when they didn't like their food, she found.

She had to admit she didn't mind army life. Her mother had grown up with it, first with her father, and then with her husband, so it made sense that Mai would take to it as naturally as a duck to water.

Oh, duck. Mai's mouth watered at the thought of eating one that had been cooked properly, instead of the tough old bird the cooks had produced yesterday.

Gradually, she became known around the camp. Most of the men were too young to have served under her father, but they had grown up hearing the stories about him. One man even asked her if she'd do the honour of crossing swords with him in the training ring, if only so that he could tell his children he had fought with Yeong Fu's son.

Mai could not refuse him, so she told him to meet her after the next day's bout with Yi.

Somehow, word spread, so that when she and Yi arrived for yet another rematch, there must have been more than fifty men milling around, forming a crowd around the ring so that she could not even see the sand as she approached.

"What's this?" Yi asked irritably.

Several men turned, and all of them bowed at the

sight of the prince. Yi's name was on everyone's lips, along with Mai's father's.

The man she'd met only yesterday stepped forward. "Yeong Mao. Your Highness." He bowed. "When I told the others, they asked to come and watch. Some asked whether they, too, might have the honour of crossing swords with one or even both of you."

"Both?" The idea intrigued Mai. She had never fought at someone's side before.

Yi came to her rescue. "In my grandfather's day, he held tournaments where there was an event called a melee. There are two teams of men, and only one can emerge victorious. They fight together, like companies of opposing armies. Toward the end of the event, when many are injured, a winning team of two or three men have fought back to back until there is no one else left standing." He seemed to be struggling with something, but finally he added, "I cannot imagine a better fighter than yourself to have at my back in a melee. What do you say we postpone our rematch?"

Mai agreed. She listened while Yi laid down the rules, before she found her back pressed up against the warm wall of muscle that was Yi. She'd never been this close to a man before, and she rather liked it. Right up until she realised she had two soldiers rushing toward her, armed with wooden practice swords and more enthusiasm than anyone should have this early in the morning.

The fight. Of course. That's where her mind should be, she scolded herself. Not on the handsome man at her back whose behind kept rubbing against hers.

The sun was well up by the time Yi breathlessly called a halt to the mock battle. Bruised but exhilarated, Mai couldn't keep the smile off her face.

Yi used the hem of his robe to wipe the sweat from his forehead. "What did you think of that, boy? It's as close to battle as you'll get short of the real thing. Do you think you're man enough for more?"

Mai laughed in delight. "I want to do it again tomorrow, and the next day, too."

Yi stared at her. "You jest."

She shook her head. "Didn't you enjoy the challenge? So many different styles of fighting, so many different opponents, each thinking and acting differently so that you could lose yourself in a dance so complex you must rely on instinct and training and..." She sighed happily. "I was born for this."

"You're crazy," Yi said instead.

Mai laughed again. "Perhaps I am."

"A man as crazy as you needs breakfast. Shall we see what the cooks have burned for us today?"

For the first time, instead of stalking off in a huff, Yi joined her for breakfast. It would not be the last time, either.

Fifteen

Yi held still while Heng, his manservant, shaved him. Heng's hands were perfectly steady, but that didn't change the fact that he held a sharp blade very close to Yi's face. One slip could be disastrous.

"I don't know how you can let a man hold a blade to your throat without defending yourself," Mao commented as he bundled his clothing into a sheet from his bed. "If anyone got that close to me with a knife, I'd automatically block and disarm him."

Yi wanted to shake his head but he managed to resist. Heng wasn't done yet. "It's a matter of loyalty and trust. Heng and I have campaigned together for a long time. I've killed men who tried to attack him, so he's not going to kill me. I'm useful."

Heng snorted. "Enemy soldiers see him as a target. Stick near him. No one will bother to attack you, because they see him as a giant trophy they want to take home." He eyed Mao. "My family is noble like yours, but our lands are so small, there was nothing left for a younger son like me. As long as he's around, he makes life interesting. Sometimes campaigning, sometimes in court. It beats ploughing my father's fields with the villagers."

Mao nodded as if he understood.

"Are you a younger son, too?" Yi asked.

Mao laughed. "No, I am my father's firstborn. But I understand the desire to have more to my life than dreary days in a rural village. Ah, but a village does have one advantage." He bundled the sheet into a sack for his clothing and lifted it into the air. "I know who the washerwomen are, and where to find them. Here, I fear I might have to wash my own clothes in the river next time I bathe."

"Give them to Heng. He can take them and mine, too, before he fetches our breakfast," Yi said.

Heng faked a happy grin. "See, what did I tell you? Life is always interesting. Today, I become a washerwoman. Wait until some drunken soldier tries to find out what I keep under my skirts."

Yi laughed as Heng grabbed the bundle of clothing and sashayed out, hips swaying like a prostitute touting for business.

"He does a good job at shaving, you know," Yi said when Heng was gone. "Any time you want his help, just ask. For we are friends now, are we not?"

"Yes, we are friends," Mao admitted, "but I still feel strange ordering a man about. Maybe for a prince it is different, with so many servants in the palace, but at home, it was not like that. And I mean it about the blade. My father trained me too well. If I reacted as my training tells me to, I might hurt Heng without meaning to. I don't think we would remain friends after that."

Yi laughed, but he understood. He itched for battle, too. A siege like this was frustrating.

Sixteen

A commotion in the camp outside roused Mai from a deep sleep.

"Hurry, Mao, or we'll miss it," she heard Yi say. Something heavy landed on her midsection, and her breath whooshed out of her lungs at the impact. "Get your armour on!"

With Heng's help, Mai managed to don her armour, for Yi was already geared for war, capering around the tent like a court fool. She was still buckling on her sword belt when Yi dragged her from the tent.

"What's going on?" she mumbled, fumbling with the buckle.

"Another raid on the blockade. This time, we're sending reinforcements. We get to fight!"

Yi seemed ghoulishly excited about going out to kill other men. Mai wondered if he might be crazy after all. They joined the column of troops marching toward the city, which was lit by the orange light of flames licking toward the stars at a camp just north of their own.

When they reached the camp, Yi grabbed her arm and pulled her away from the other soldiers. "This way."

Screams erupted from the camp gates as the flames leaped higher.

Mai wasn't sure whether to run toward the sound or away from it. "What's happening?"

"They brought fire lances," Yi said. They rounded a section of wall and found the next section had been burned to ash, leaving them a clear view into the camp and the massacre at the gate. "Big bamboo tubes that explode and take down whole sections of wall, like this one, or many men all at once."

Mai's stomach churned. This was not the sort of fighting her father had taught her. She pointed at a box four men were wheeling toward the gate. "What is that?"

Yi stared intently in the direction she was pointing. "A cart, I think. I don't – "

A great gout of flame erupted from a pipe on top of the cart, dousing everything in its path in fire.

Mai looked on in horror as men caught in it screamed, then fell to the ground, writhing as they burned. Whatever the box was, it was monstrous.

"First fire lances, now fierce fire oil, and a box that sprays it," Yi said, awed. "So that's why the General has not attacked. If they're willing to risk one of these in a raid, they must have many more. All along the walls, ready to burn anyone and anything that comes close to the city."

"Not just ready to do it. It's doing it now!" Mai snapped, charging toward the box.

"What are you doing? They'll kill you!" Yi hissed.

"Not if I get to them first," Mai said grimly. She took the first man low in the gut, knocking him over so that his head hit the wheel of the cart, rendering him unconscious. Second, she tripped the man directing the nozzle spitting flames. The liquid spilled over his clothes instead, and Mai had to back away in a hurry as he became a flaming torch.

A third man stopped working the pump to stare at his fiery compatriot, so he didn't even see Mai's kick coming. He was unconscious before he hit the ground. Mai turned to deal with the fourth operator of the deadly box, only to find Yi extracting his sword from the man's belly.

"Your first battle, and you kill three men in the time it takes me to kill one. Did one of your ancestors sleep with a barbarian war god or something?" Yi asked.

"I didn't kill anyone," Mai defended herself. "Those two are just unconscious and that one set fire to himself."

"You'll be everyone's hero tonight," Yi muttered, before raising his voice. "This camp belongs to the Emperor, and anyone who is not loyal to him will burn like a torch!" he roared.

"It's the Prince of Swords! He holds the fire machine!" someone shouted.

Mai drew her sword as a group of men rushed toward them, only to recognise them as General Li's men.

"They're running back to hide in Dean now," another man said. "Look at them go!"

In the light of the still burning barricade, Mai could see men streaming back into a small city gate, before they barred it behind them.

Cheering erupted around Yi and Mai.

Mai couldn't understand it. She could still smell fuel and burning flesh, and there were corpses underfoot. What was there to cheer about? Men had died here.

Yi slung a comradely arm around Mai's shoulder. "I bet you feel like a big man now, your first battle and all." He looked just as deliriously happy as the others.

Mai couldn't seem to find the words to express the horror and guilt and sheer desolation she felt right now, so she just nodded and let Yi take her back to their camp while the others cleaned up what was left of this one.

Seventeen

By dusk of the next day, the wrecked camp looked almost as good as new, with the walls replaced already. A large barracks tent had become a hospital, filled with piteous groans from those who'd survived the burning touch of the flamethrowing machine or one of the fire lances. There were a lot of men not in the hospital, though, who seemed to be drinking everything in sight, but they raised their cups to toast Mai whenever they saw her. It seemed that Yi had spread the story that she'd disabled the flamethrower, and they looked at her like she was some kind of hero.

A hero who wouldn't be able to sleep tonight without having nightmares about the man she burned alive by accident. Already, she saw him whenever she closed her eyes, and his screams still rang in her ears, though they had only lasted a few seconds before the flames had silenced him forever.

For the first time, she noticed women roaming around the camp, instead of in their own little enclave on the far side of the cookfires. Mai knew they were camp followers, the women who served the army in various capacities in times of war. Not all of them were prostitutes. Some of them were soldiers' wives, like her mother had been, but the women she saw now made it clear they were not married...yet.

After seeing a steady succession of swaying hips, batted eyelashes and blown kisses as the women walked past her, she turned to find Yi grinning beside her. "So which one do you like?" he asked.

"I'm not in the market for a wife," Mai grumbled, picking at her tasteless dinner.

Yi laughed. "Not a wife. Just one night. After your first battle, it's tradition to take a woman. You being such a hero and all, they all want that honour. If you don't pick soon, the other men will get impatient and the best ones will be busy."

"It's the first battle for all of them?" Mai asked. When Yi laughed even louder, she wished she hadn't said anything.

"Of course not, but can you blame them? Men died today, and when you remind a man of his mortality, he remembers what he likes most in life. Good food, and the company of a good woman." Yi took a mouthful of his food and grimaced. "When all we have is women, and willing ones at that...well, why not?"

Mai could think of half a dozen answers to that, none of which she wanted to tell him. As if to illustrate her point, one woman climbed into the lap of a man sitting not far from them, pushed his chest until he lay down flat, and began riding him like a horse. "What does she think she's doing?" Mai muttered.

Yi stared at her. "You've never had a woman before."

Of course not, Mai wanted to say, but knew she couldn't. "Have you?" she asked instead.

"Of course," Yi said. "My first battle was a long time ago, and when I was younger..." He trailed off, then cleared his throat and began again. "But it is different for me. I am the Emperor's son, my children will have royal blood no matter who their mother is. A bastard child could make trouble for my family's succession. Not something you need to worry about, though. You should enjoy tonight."

"All I want to do is sleep," Mai said, watching several more couples start rutting, as if they didn't care who saw them. Perhaps they didn't.

"Mao – " Yi reached for her, but Mai shrugged away from his grasp.

"Enjoy celebrating this victory. I'm sure there will be many more," she said, loud enough for the other men to hear her. A ragged cheer rose up, the sound following her all the way back to her tent.

The sounds of celebration continued long into the night, but her heart was heavy. Men had died because of her, and because of the strange box that now sat in the camp outside her tent. As long as these things existed, there could be no victory, for too many men would die in the most horrible of ways.

By the time the sun rose, Mai had not slept, but she had thought of many ways in which the boxes might be destroyed. Most would not work, but she only needed one that would.

She staggered out of the tent. Half a dozen men, looking much like she felt, stared back at her. Including Yi and Heng.

"Good morning, Sleeping Beauty," Yi greeted her.

Mai took that to mean she looked worse than the hungover men beside him. "It will be if we have a fire lance, and someone who knows how to use it," she said.

Yi frowned. "Why?"

Mai jerked her head toward the flamethrower. "Help me take that to an empty field and I'll show you."

Eighteen

It took four fire lances before one managed to hit its target. The results were better than anything Yi could have expected, though. The explosive ball landed on top of the cart, blossoming into an orange flower that ignited the liquid pooled on the cart beneath it. Yi held his breath as the pool caught fire. A loud boom made him duck for cover as a wave of heat blasted over their hastily dug earth rampart. When Yi dared to raise his head above the rampart, there was nothing left to see except some twisted pieces of metal where the cart had once been.

Yi seized Mao's arm. "That's it! The way to break the siege. You must tell the General." He hauled the boy to his feet, and pulled him toward the General's house.

Mao resisted. "I am inexperienced in war. Surely the General knows all this already."

"If he did, he would have attacked and the siege would be over. He's a fool who might know how to train men, but he is lost when it comes to war. But you…you see things so clearly you were born for battle. To command troops in battle. To victory. More than Li, or even me."

Mao turned bright red. Evidently the boy was not used to praise. "You're mistaken. I'm not…"

"You are." Yi marched Mao to the General's house and shoved him through the open doorway.

As Yi had expected, a strategy session was underway.

"What is it?" Li asked irritably. "We are in the middle of a strategy meeting. Whatever the boy has done, it can wait. Or discipline him yourself."

"General, Mao has done nothing wrong. He says you are wrong about the city's defences. You must listen to what this boy has to say," Yi insisted.

"Who are you to criticise the General?" General Li boomed, annoyed.

"I'm Yeong Mao, sir," Mao said. "My parents were Yeong Fu and Da Ying. I have studied the art of war all my life. My mother insisted upon it."

Da Ying? Yi's ears pricked up at that name. Of all

the warrior women he'd heard of, Da Ying was the most legendary of the lot. A general's daughter, she'd married a junior officer and helped him through victory after victory until he rose to the rank of general. Then, she went into combat beside him. Yi had heard a tale about how her husband had fallen in battle, so she commanded the army in his stead, all the while carrying his unconscious body on her back. He itched to ask Mao if the story was true. And if he had any sisters. If he had to marry, a daughter of Da Ying might be his best chance of finding a woman he could tolerate.

"Well, then, Yeong Mao. Tell me what I am wrong about." There was a dangerous edge to Li's tone.

Mao evidently caught it, too. "It's not that you are wrong, sir. Those are Jun Yi's words, not mine. I merely made a remark about the fire lances and flamethrowers, and how they might be turned against the city."

General Li rose to his feet. "How?" he demanded.

For the first time, Mao seemed afraid. "Well, they are hollow, their tanks filled with explosive material. The one at the skirmish this week was a tank of liquid, which caught fire once sparked. The ones on the walls are filled with projectiles, like those you fire from a trebuchet. If you were to ignite the fuel before they could fire, then they would explode, burning away whatever fuel was inside them and rendering them harmless to us. If we took them out all at once, we might even set fire to the city, driving the people out through the gates. It would be an almost bloodless victory, sir."

General Li's eyes narrowed, but then he seemed to relax. "And how do you propose we set fire to them? We just climb over the walls and sneak into the city, hoping their troops are so poorly trained they don't see us or our flaming torches as we set their city on fire?" He laughed at his own joke.

Mao's gaze hardened. "I see no reason to fight inside the city at all. Why enter terrain so familiar to them when we can flush them out to the battle ground of our choosing? We can send flaming missiles over the walls. Your trebuchet operators will need to know their range perfectly, because they must all act at once in order to create sufficient panic in the city that the city troops will not regroup. We attack their strategy. That is how we can win."

General Li's eyes widened. "If we knew the location of all their fire weapons, that might work. But we do not."

"We would know if we could get a few men inside the city, who could then send that information back to you." Mao wet his lips. "I believe I know how to sneak in without anyone seeing me. If I can mark the locations of all the lances in the city, your men could pick them off easily."

Yi's heart jumped into his throat. "The two of us will go," he said. The thought of Mao alone in the city, where anything could happen to him...

Li slammed both hands down on the table. "Yes. Yi, you take the boy into the city. I will command our troops outside and lead them to victory."

It was on the tip of Yi's tongue to refuse. Left alone our here to his own devices, Li would surely lead his army to nothing but defeat. They were good men who didn't deserve to die in a bungled battle. But he couldn't let Mao go off alone, either.

"Yes, sir," Yi found himself saying.

The rest of the meeting passed in a blur, where Li described details that Yi knew he wouldn't remember. Not that it mattered. He and Mao would be inside the city, not preparing to attack it.

It wasn't until the General dismissed them that Yi found Mao tugging him aside. When they were out of earshot of everyone else, Mao hissed, "What were you thinking? How do you expect me to get both of us into the city? You stride around like you own the world – no one will think you are some lowly worker, if you even make it inside the walls! You should have let me go alone."

Yi glanced down, to find Mao's hand still firmly

gripping his arm. His skin tingled under the boy's fingers in a way that wasn't at all unpleasant. Why, if the boy had been a girl, Yi might almost...

Yi shook his head. He didn't want to kiss Mao. He wanted to keep him safe. "I know more about the city than you do. I have been inside, on many occasions. They weren't always hostile to the Emperor. Two of us can watch out for each other. It is no harder to get two men than one inside the city. It is not as though we were ten in full armour. Besides, your plan involves us either sneaking out of the city – much harder than sneaking in, as you've already mentioned – or shooting an arrow from the walls all the way to one of the camps. You are a formidable fighter, but you don't have the strength to draw a big enough bow. I do."

Mao's eyes bored into Yi's, weighing his soul, or so it seemed. Finally, he said, "All right, Rooster. You will watch my back, and I will watch yours. You will fire the message arrow if we must. Together, we will find the fire lances and the flamethrowers and end this war."

And then, Yi would be obedient to the Emperor's wishes. He would attend whatever court functions the Emperor chose to hold, and end in choosing one of Mao's sisters as his bride, and travel home with Mao to negotiate the marriage with the girl's father. As Mao's friend and future brother in law, the man could hardly refuse to train him. Yi truly would be the best swordsman in the kingdom. All thanks to Mao.

Nineteen

Mai tried to still the butterflies tumbling around in her belly as Heng helped her into her armour, but it was no use. The leather settled with a heavy layer of dread on her shoulders. Mai closed her eyes, forcing her breathing to become calm. This was no more difficult than taking a stroll into the village near her father's house. She would look like one of the people of Dean, not a spy come to conquer their city by stealth.

Yi, on the other hand, looked every bit the proud rooster today. He didn't share her nerves – in fact, he looked excited about the coming battle, though they might arrive too late to be a part of it.

"When we leave, I want you to ride for the capital and see that letter is delivered to my father," Yi said, pointing at scroll on the table he'd spent half the night hunched over.

"Is it a final letter to your father, in case you fall in battle?" Mai asked, suddenly wishing she had spent the night writing one, too. She could die today, and she had never said goodbye to her father. Would she ever see him again?

Yi laughed. "No. This is a stroll into the city, not a battle. I wrote to tell my father that the siege will soon be over, thanks to you, and to prepare for our triumphant return to the capital. If I know him, and I do, he will hold a ball with much dancing, so that I might choose a bride from among the girls. I daresay the girls will try to capture your heart as much as they reach for mine. After all, you will be the hero of the siege of Dean. I will make sure of it. You will have your choice of any woman you want." His gaze grew wistful.

Yi had already chosen his bride, Mai guessed, for not many daydreamed without something to inspire such dreams. She might play at being a man, but she was under no illusion that such a lie would survive the marriage bed. No woman would have her, and no man either, if her stepmother was to be believed. That left her...no one.

If she died today, no one would mourn her. But if she died with honour, the ancestors would welcome her spirit. Perhaps that was all the future Mai could hope for.

The butterflies fluttered to a halt, stilled by her sombre thoughts. Heng's arms encircled her waist, buckling on her sword. Mai closed her eyes again, imagining for a moment that the arms were Yi's. Bliss, surely, but not for her. No, she would never be a bride, let alone his. The most she could do was fight at his side and perhaps die in his arms. Not such a bad fate.

Yi could not die in the city, though. She would find a way to get him out, even if she could not. Perhaps one of his watchtower poets would sing songs about her when the war was over.

Mai threw a coarse robe over the whole ensemble, tucking her hair into a cloth cap, which turned her from a soldier girded for war into a humble peasant, collecting hay or timber to take back inside the city. They'd all seen the work parties in the no man's land between the city walls and General Li's blockade, but the besiegers paid no attention to the men who foraged for such things every other day. They were the lowest of the low in the city, and beneath the notice of superior soldiers. Except for Mai, of course, who noticed that they left the city through one of the smaller gates, where armed guards stood inside waiting, but the guards never looked at the men's faces. Their attention was for General Li's soldiers.

Today, when the peasants sallied forth from the city, then spread out across the weed-choked plain, Yi and Mai joined them, keeping their heads bowed as they collected the dried weeds and stuffed them in a sack.

The monotonous work made Yi restless, and more than once Mai noticed him losing his humble pose to survey his surroundings, like no peasant would in the presence of his betters. She hissed at him to get back to work.

Finally, she heard distant shouts and thumps from the other side of the city. The gate guards heard it, too, beckoning the cityfolk back inside, quickly, before they shut the gate. Mai broke into a run, hearing Yi's heavy footfalls hot on her heels, as she fell in with the other men. They hustled into the city, and the gate was barred behind them.

No one stopped to even look at her face, or Yi's — as Mai made her way deeper into the city. Her plan had worked. They were in.

Twenty

General Li's diversion, throwing stones over the wall with trebuchets to give his men practice for the flaming assault in the near future, lasted for a little over an hour. More than long enough for Yi and Mai to ascertain how well guarded every gate was in the city walls. They found a house a few streets in, falling down from neglect, that might do for shelter for the night, if they were forced to stay inside the city.

Several hours later, when the guards' vigilance showed no signs of lessening, Yi lay on the dirt floor beside the tiny fire, sketching a map of the city and every fire lance and flamethrower they'd found. Mao had pointed out what he thought was a fuel storage hut, for he'd glimpsed jars that resembled those the soldiers used to refuel the flamethrowers on the walls. Dutifully, Yi added that to his map as well. Destroying the fuel stores would be as helpful as destroying the weapons as well.

When he was finished, he copied the map three times, then bound each sheet of paper tightly around an arrow. Four arrows with maps – surely one would make its way back to General Li.

He took first watch while Mao slept beside him on the dirt floor. Yi resolved to do whatever it took to get the boy out of the city on the morrow. The chaos of a burning city was no place for him. No man could fight a panicked mob, and Mao would be trampled far too easily. No, they would wait for tomorrow's diversion, send the arrows toward their target, and find a way back outside.

Yi stared down tenderly at the boy. He had many brothers, but none he cared about quite as much as he did for Mao. Was it because they had fought together so much? he pondered. Perhaps. Or maybe it was something about Mao himself. For all his fighting skill, there was a softness about him that Yi did not understand.

Mao woke him at dawn, when they both knew Li would start looking for them. They stripped off their peasant garb and climbed the walls, bows in hand, when the city rang the bells to signify a call to arms. Li had placed a platoon of soldiers near the gate where they'd entered, who seemed intent on breaking through the gate, too.

Yi shook his head, not sure whether the assault was serious or yet another distraction on Li's part. Never mind. He took aim at their shields, imagining himself at target practice in camp. Each red-feathered arrow found its mark, and were embedded deeply enough in the hide not to be easily dislodged. With luck, at least one of them would make it back to camp.

After some time, the much-reduced platoon retreated back behind the blockade, dragging their injured comrades with them. Yi counted at least three red-fletched arrows among the party, and breathed a sigh of relief. Even if they couldn't make it out before the true assault on the city started, he and Mao could hole up in the falling down house until the gates opened. They had enough food for a day or two, before they would need to find some more.

On their way down from the walls, they were accosted by a hawker, who grilled skewers of meat and vegetables over a brazier. Anything was better than their rations. Yi paid for two servings of the stuff, handing one to Mao. It was the best thing he'd tasted in weeks, and it looked like Mao agreed.

No wonder Dean held out so long against the siege. When they were so well-provisioned, they had little to lose.

In the shadow of a supply hut near one of the smaller gates, he and Mao sat down to enjoy their lunch. Yi, who had taken the lion's share of the watch the previous night, dozed off.

Mao roughly shook him awake what felt like only a moment later, but must have been hours, given how much the noon shadows had lengthened in that time. The boy's eyes were wide with panic. "They're attacking again. And this time, they have fire."

Yi jumped to his feet, fully alert. "Li wasn't supposed to attack until morning. What is he thinking?"

Mao shook his head grimly. "I don't know. He surely can't mean to fight through the night. That would be – "

Something big and orange came sailing over the wall, filling the air with searing heat. Then the whole world exploded.

Twenty-One

For a rooster, Yi sure was heavy, Mai grumbled to herself as she shoved him off her. She'd slammed into the city wall, thrown by the explosion as Li's flaming missile hit the fuel storage hut that now no longer existed. The smell of scorched flesh reached her nose and Mai gagged. Only then did she notice that some of the fuel had landed on Yi's armour, where it still burned. She tried rolling him along the ground to extinguish the flames, but it was no use. Finally, she stripped his armour off him, but the damage was done. His back was a bloody mess that only the healers could take care of. She had to get him back to camp.

Another missile landed on the wall overhead, sending out a splash of orange light as it engulfed one of the fire lances. She had to move quickly, or both she and Yi might become casualties of General Li.

Mai took a deep breath. There was only one way she could get Yi out of there. It took all her strength to heave him onto her shoulders, and even then she staggered under his weight. But she had to get him out.

Step by agonising step, she made her way to the nearest gate. A small side gate, barely wide enough for one person to walk through, it had been left unguarded while men rushed around, attempting to put out the fires, even as Li's missiles lit more.

Mai kicked at the bar, knowing that if she set Yi down, she'd never manage to lift him again. She inched the bar up for what felt like an eternity until finally it rose above the brackets that held it, unlocking the gate. She managed to get the gate half open before she was nearly trampled by a platoon of Li's soldiers, who had been battering at the gate in an attempt to get in. She flattened herself against the wall as they trooped past her, ignoring both her and Yi until she recognised the soldiers who had first asked to join her and Yi in their morning sparring sessions.

"Min!" she gasped out. "The Prince of Swords is injured. Help me get him back to camp."

Min stopped and stared, but after a moment, he nodded and halted the flow of troops into the city so Mai could carry Yi out. Min led the way back to the blockade, where a temporary hospital had already been set up.

Mai cried out in relief as Yi's weight was taken from her and transferred to a bed. Healers converged on him, cutting away his clothes from his ruined back as they argued on how best to treat the burns.

"What happened?" someone asked Mai.

"We were inside the city when one of the General's thunderbolt balls hit the fuel storage hut. He shielded me from the blast, which set fire to his armour. I couldn't put out the flames, so I took his armour off," Mai said, waving her hands.

"And burned yourself in the process," the healer said. "Just look at those hands. You sit right here, and I'll fetch some salve for them. It might not help him, but those are going to hurt."

Might not…? The healers might not be able to help Yi? Mai's heart constricted in her chest. They had to save him. She'd carried him out on her back to find someone who could save him. He couldn't die now. Not after all that.

"Save him first," she blurted out, dragging her stool over to his bedside. "Nothing matters more than the prince. You have to save him."

"We will," the healer soothed, smoothing something smelly over her hands. "You just sit there and watch. We'll do everything we can for him, but we won't know how badly he is hurt until he wakes up. If he wakes up."

If?

Mai couldn't even consider the possibility that Yi wouldn't wake up. He'd been hurt trying to save her from the blast. She owed him her life. "He will," she said fiercely. "And when he does, I will be here beside him to tell him the news of our victory over Dean."

"Has the General won already?" the healer asked, as calmly as though he was asking about the weather.

"I do not know," Mai replied. "But if he is not victorious, the Emperor will not forgive his failure. For losing the prince would be too high a price for anything less than a complete victory. If you see General Li, you tell him. His strategy has put Prince Yi in hospital."

"The General never visits us here. If he is unwell, he sends for a healer to his tent, not the other way around. And speaking of healing, those hands of yours will need more than salve. I'm going to bandage them up and mix you a draught for the pain. You'll be staying here tonight."

"Until he wakes, I will stay anyway. Do what you must," Mai said, gritting her teeth as even the brush of bandages against her tender skin hurt. Nevertheless, she endured it. She drank the cup of foul-tasting tea and settled down to wait.

Twenty-Two

Yi sank into his favourite dream. The one where he was victorious from his latest battle, and he lay in the arms of his bride, a woman whose softness and curves were his alone to caress. When she moaned in pleasure, her voice was low and husky – none of the high-pitched, childish giggling so popular among court ladies. He would happily spend every night devoted to bringing her joy, if only to hear her voice. Yet she was no shy, delicate doll – oh, no. She had all the brazenness of a camp follower as she returned his attentions in equal measure. His scars earned him kisses, not disgust, like they would from court ladies who preferred their men as pretty as themselves. A real woman for a real man – that was what he craved.

Surely such a woman existed. He had to find her, because a lifetime of searching was worth it for even a single night of bliss in her arms.

A woman whose face he had never seen.

In the dream, his sight cleared, and once again, he beheld not a woman, but Mao's face.

Yi jerked awake, cursing. Why the boy had to invade his dreams like that, he did not know. If he married one of Mao's sisters, he would demand Mao leave them alone on their wedding night. And every other night, come to think of it.

Mao lay on the next pallet, fast asleep. It took Yi a moment to realise he could see far more clearly than usual, and the tent was bigger and noisier, too.

"What the − " he began, sitting up to take in his surroundings properly.

One of the big barracks tents had been turned into a hospital, which was full of wounded men. Why was he there, then? He wasn't wounded. The last thing he could remember was eating lunch with Mao inside Dean when General Li had attacked the city earlier than planned.

And the fuel storage hut had exploded.

Mao was here, in bed. Was he injured?

"Mao, wake up," Yi said urgently, reaching over to shake the boy. "Mao!"

When the boy didn't immediately wake, Yi shouted

for a healer.

A harassed-looking healer hurried over, hushing him. "You should lie right back down, or you'll make me have to bandage you again. I'll give you a sleeping draught like I did him. You're not the only patient here, you know!"

A sleeping draught. No wonder Mao wouldn't wake. Yi released him. "Is he injured?" Yi demanded.

"He burned his hands, trying to save you," the healer said. "It will hurt some, but he won't scar as bad as you. What did you do? Mistake a flamethrower for your bed?"

"I..." Yi couldn't remember. There had been the explosion, then everything went dark. "I don't know. Did he tell you?"

"He carried you in here, shouting for a healer. Looks like you took a blast to the back. That stuff even burns armour. I didn't believe it at first, until I saw the evidence with my own eyes. You two are the only burned ones, though. Seems the General has done something right this time." The healer nodded.

No, he hadn't. General Li had attacked early, Yi fumed. He and Mao should have been well out of the city before he launched the attack. Instead, they'd been caught in the middle of it and Mao...

Yi tried to swallow down the lump in his throat. The very thought that the boy had been hurt by Li's bungling cut him to the core. Li would not get away with this.

Yi rose, laying a hand on the healer's shoulder to steady myself. "I must speak with the General."

The healer shook his head. "You're not leaving this hospital in that condition. You need to get back into bed."

Yi bristled. "Who are you to give the Emperor's son orders? I will go where I wish, healer. Look to your patients."

"You are my patient," the healer pointed out drily. "If I give you one of my healing potions to improve your health, will you drink it, your Highness?"

Yi's back ached, as though he had become an old man while he slept. "If it will ease the pain in my back, yes."

He gulped down the bitter brew and handed the cup back to the healer. "Take care of our injured troops, healer. The Emperor may need them yet. For now Dean has fallen, the other northern cities may come seeking vengeance for our victory."

The healer's expression grew sombre. "Where will it end?"

"In a united empire, of course! Perhaps not in your lifetime or mine, but one day. For we are men, born to fight, and we always will." Yi grinned and strode out of the tent.

It wasn't until he was certain no one could see his face that he allowed himself to grimace at what he had to admit was a frightful pain in his back. It stung, like someone had stripped the skin from it. Yi had half a mind to strip the bandages from his torso and take a good look at the damage, but he was in too much of a hurry to bother with that now. Once he had spoken to General Li and was back in the privacy of his tent, then he could ask for Heng's help.

No, Heng should be in the capital, carrying his letter to the Emperor. The one about Mao's brilliance. Mao who had nearly died through General Li's bungled strategy. Ah, but it wasn't the General's strategy at all, but Mao's. No wonder the fool had made a mess of things. The Emperor needed more men like Mao, who were worth ten of General Li.

Yi swayed a little on his feet as he climbed the hill to the General's hut, but he put that down to not eating much since he'd left the city. Lack of food made a man weak. He would send for something directly, once he found the General.

The hut seemed unusually dark inside, but Yi stepped inside anyway, taking a moment to grab the doorframe as a strange bout of dizziness hit. "General Li!" he shouted.

"There he is now," General Li said. "The Emperor is welcome to him."

Yi blinked. The General sat at his table, holding an open scroll in his hands. Heng looked haggard, but relieved. "Did you deliver my message to the Emperor?" Yi demanded.

Heng nodded. "He sent me back with his reply." He waved at Li's scroll.

Yi saw red. "First you try to get me killed, and now you're reading my personal letters from the Emperor? Have you no honour at all?" he roared.

General Li rose, his eyes flashing. "I am victorious. The city surrendered to me. Victory is mine, and you are to be sent home to the Emperor. Immediately."

Yi snorted. "The victory is Mao's, not yours. It was his strategy. And the Emperor knows it."

Li shrugged. "No one has seen the boy since he went into the city. An unfortunate casualty of war."

Yi's fury knew no bounds. "It wasn't me you tried to kill. It was Mao. A better man, and a better general than you will ever be. You failed, Uncle. Mao lives. And he will return to the capital with me, where I will tell my father every mistake and delay in this campaign has been your doing, and without Mao, we would still be sitting here, doing nothing!" Yi couldn't seem to catch his breath. The room was growing dark again and he couldn't stop it.

Yi swayed, unable to steady himself. Before Heng could catch him, Yi toppled forward across the desk into oblivion.

Twenty-Three

Mai jerked awake, convinced her hands were afire. A quick glance told her this was not the case. In fact, her hands were bound in bandages and she was lying in a bed that also wasn't burning.

She shouldn't be in bed. Yi had been.

But the bed beside her was empty.

Mai jumped to her feet. "Where is he?" she demanded.

A healer she didn't recognise hurried toward her, making hushing sounds. "Where is who?"

Mai pointed a shaking figure at the empty bed. "Prince Yi, the Prince of Swords. He was injured in the battle."

"The Prince of Swords, lie in a soot-smeared bed,

beside a boy so covered in ash and cinders you look like one of the kitchen drudges?" The healer laughed. "The prince would not be in a tent with the common soldiers. He will be in his own tent, or with the General. But the Prince of Swords cannot have been defeated. The news would be all over the camp by now if the Emperor's favourite son was injured, and all I have heard is about the General's victory over Dean. The city surrendered before the cooks rang the breakfast gong."

The battle had raged all night? How had she slept through it?

Realisation dawned. "What was in the tea I drank? Was it a sleeping draught?"

The healer shrugged. "I gave you nothing, so I do not know. But a sleeping patient is easier to treat than one who is awake, so we help many men to sleep."

"I shall not stay here a moment longer. I must find the prince," Mai said. Whatever the healer had heard, she knew otherwise. Yi was injured, and if he had tried to rejoin the battle in his condition…

She checked their tent first, but it was cold and deserted. No one had slept there last night. The practice ground was deserted, too, so she climbed the rise to the General's house.

In the doorway, she nearly bumped straight into the healer she remembered from last night.

"You!" she exclaimed. "You drugged me, when you said you were giving me a pain draught. What did you do with Prince Yi?"

"It was a pain draught," the man said, drawing himself up. "It also relaxes a patient, so that many fall asleep. And the prince left my care, only to collapse in the General's arms. I have done what I can for him here, as he should not be moved." He glared at Mai as though she had suggested moving him.

"Will he be all right?" Mai demanded.

"He will live," the healer replied. "I shall return later, if the prince's condition changes. Until then, I have a hospital full of injured men to see to." He marched off down the hill.

Mai slipped inside. She found Yi in what looked like the General's own bedchamber, lying facedown on the bed. The General was nowhere to be seen.

"Yi, can you hear me?" she asked, her voice shaking more than she liked.

"What, did I finally manage to beat you, so you won't call me Rooster any more?" Yi turned his head and smiled weakly.

Mai breathed a sigh of relief. He could not be too badly hurt if he could make jokes. "The sun will rise in the west before you best me in a fight, Rooster. So much for watching each other's backs in the city. I had to carry you out on mine while you slept. What would the soldiers say if they knew their hero, the Prince of Swords, slept through the best part of the battle?"

"You carried me out?" Yi stared at her. "From what the healers tell me, I owe you my life. They say my armour caught fire, and if you hadn't stripped it off me, I would have burned, too. You are the hero of this battle, Mao, not me."

Mai didn't know what to say. She was no hero. She had not even fought in the battle. Much like Yi, she'd slept through it.

Yi continued, "And when we return to the capital, I will tell the Emperor so. He will give you a place at court, I am sure of it, and command you to marry, for great men like you should have sons to serve the Emperor when you go to join your ancestors." He winced. "The Emperor says I must travel to the capital immediately. But the healers tell me to wait, for I cannot ride like this. Not for a few days, at least. It feels like someone tried to flay me alive. I will be so scarred now, no woman will swoon over me. Even my bride will insist I bed her in the dark, so she doesn't have to see such scars."

"That's not true. You are still a prince, and I am certain every woman in the kingdom would be honoured to be chosen by a hero who is also the Emperor's favourite son." Bitterness welled up in Mai's belly as she said those words, for they incinerated whatever hopes she might have had, if only for a moment. But a prince – likely to be chosen as the Emperor's heir – was so far above her she would not even be allowed to sweep the floors in his bedchamber, let alone share his bed. Sharing his tent here was more than she deserved. Like the healer had said, once she returned home, she was destined to be no better than a kitchen drudge in her father's house, for if she never married, she would never be the mistress of any home at all. If only she never had to go home.

Yi grasped her hand. Despite the bandages, Mai felt his firm grip. "Promise me you will come to the capital, Mao," Yi said. "So that if I must do as the Emperor commands and choose a bride, I will have your sage advice to guide me and lift my spirits should things go wrong. I can face an enemy army with no fear, but an army of women? I will need a hero like you by my side to bolster my courage."

Mai laughed. "A rooster who runs away from a flock of hens? I wouldn't miss such a sight for all the riches in the world. I will come to the capital with you."

And watch him choose a bride, while her heart died a little inside. She had come to Dean to fight in a war. The war was won, but Mai feared she might have lost something far more important – her heart, hopelessly in love with Prince Yi.

Twenty-Four

"The Prince of Swords will not ride home in a litter," Yi grumbled when he saw the conveyance. "They are for invalids and ladies, not warriors."

Mai privately agreed, but it would not do to tell him so. "Officially, your great friend Yeong Mao, who was grievously wounded in the battle, will ride in the litter. The Prince of Swords will ride alongside it as his honour guard, and occasionally within to share his wit and wisdom with the poor invalid."

Yi dropped his voice so low only Mai could hear it. "I still cannot ride. In another few days, perhaps…"

A few days would turn into a week, and Mai knew it would be many weeks before Yi fully recovered. She had seen his bloodied back when Heng and the healers had changed his bandages that very morning. The Emperor demanded his son return home, and the Emperor must be obeyed. Especially when the General wanted Mai dead for daring to win the war, and had begun to look at Yi in the same way. Mai had found the perfect solution to prevent them both from being assassinated.

Mai sighed. "Heng will dress me in your armour, and I will ride like a rooster for as long as I need to, puffing and preening until all the men know it is you who is astride that horse. Then, when we are far enough away from camp, I will join you in the litter and do my best to stop you from getting bored."

Yi managed a faint smile. "We could take some dancing girls and musicians."

Mai felt a pang of homesickness as she remembered her sisters practicing dancing and music day and night, determined to perform well enough to catch the eye of a prince.

"And ruin the illusion? It is less than two days' journey to the capital – you said so yourself. If you truly grow bored, I will…recite poetry for you." Mai managed a wicked grin. "One of the boys on the watchtower near the gate has penned quite a pretty one. He sent you a copy to take with you to the Emperor."

Mai watched Yi try to hide how much he hated

poetry. "Must I hear it?"

"If the Emperor loves poetry as much as you say, I am sure it will be quite the favourite at court. It describes how you and the General rode side by side, leading the charge into the city, as everyone bowed low before you."

"He's too much of a coward to do any such thing," Yi declared. "Are you sure we can't have some musicians?"

Mai sighed. "Only if you want them to sing about how the Prince of Swords had to be carried home by litter after the battle, instead of riding proudly on his horse."

Yi managed a wry smile. "I think you care about my honour even more than I do, Mao. One day, when my head is not so befuddled with healing potions, remind me to thank you."

Between Heng and Mai, Yi drank enough healing potions to keep him sleeping soundly for most of the journey back to the capital, to Mai's considerable relief. No musicians needed.

As they approached the palace, Mai grew quiet, glad Yi's helmet hid her face and, more importantly, her gaping mouth. If a giant had taken her father's house, all the houses in the village, and every other noble's house in the kingdom, and piled them up harmoniously into one enormous structure, it still wouldn't convey the sheer magnitude of the Emperor's palace. It made even the city of Dean look tiny.

More than ever, Mai truly believed she did not belong here at court. Her stepmother had been right.

If it weren't for Yi, she would have left the moment he was safely home, but as he was lifted from the litter, he seized her arm and refused to let go. "You must stay with me in my apartments. My uncle has spies in court who might yet try to kill you. You will be safe with me."

Privately, Mai thought she would be safer without Yi, for she was more than a match for him, and if he was the best swordsman in the kingdom…no one else would even get close. Safer than even Yi believed. So she followed her heart and the prince inside the maze that was the imperial palace.

Twenty-Five

Though impatience ate at him, Yi waited until Heng had installed Mao in the spacious sleeping chamber beside his own before he shared his joke.

"Do you like your room?" Yi asked.

Mao nodded and thanked him.

"Just don't take any clothes from the chests in there. It belongs to my mistress," Yi told him with a grin.

Mao's jaw dropped. "Where will your mistress sleep while I am here?"

Yi was laughing too hard to answer, so Heng did it for him. "The prince has no mistress. Anything in that room belonged to the mistress of the man who had this apartment before the prince. The Emperor has many guest apartments where you might have slept, but the prince insists you stay here, in a room which cannot be reached without crossing his chambers first."

Mao nodded as if he understood. "So I am to be kept hidden here?" he asked.

"Of course not. You are free to move about the palace as you wish, as my guest," Yi said. "But a man must sleep."

"And what do I tell anyone who asks who I am?" Mao asked. "I can hardly say I am your mistress."

Both Yi and Heng laughed at that. Mao might not be a large man, but he was no beauty. Nor did he have the respectful demeanour of one of the court women. Mao might mock Yi's pride, but his was no less, Yi knew. And why not? Mao had much to be proud of.

"Tell them the truth. That you are Yeong Mao, the hero of the siege of Dean, and the Prince of Swords' closest friend." Yi smiled at Mao's blush. He was no longer a boy, but a man, yet he still blushed like a maiden.

"If I tell them the whole truth, that I am the friend of a rooster who I beat daily in every bout we fight, no one will believe me," Mao said.

"That is because all court men are roosters by your reckoning, and they won't know which one you mean," Yi replied. He wanted to laugh, but he knew all too well how true it was. "Keep your sword on you at all times, and be on your guard. They will be no match for you. After all, I, the best swordsman there is, am no match for you."

Mao smiled sadly, as though he wished things were different.

One day, Yi promised himself. When he was healed and could seek out Mao's father to train him. Then they would meet on the training ground as equals, and Mao would truly test his skill.

One day soon.

Sighing, he led the way.

Twenty-Six

Mai need not have worried. In her ordinary clothing, no one paid her much notice at all. Meals were served in the prince's quarters, and at those times she joined him, but the rest of the day was her own to do with as she wished. At first, she explored the palace, but she was terrified of wandering into the court or some place a minor country noble did not belong. For all Yi's talk of her being a hero, she didn't feel like much at all.

What she wanted most was a chance to rebalance herself, to train in the martial dances her father had taught her, but she wasn't sure which of the many courtyards and gardens in the palace would be appropriate.

Finally, she asked Heng, who directed her to the

training yard Yi usually used. When she stepped into the battleground of straw practice dummies and targets, she understood why he fought as he did. Yi had never truly trained against a worthy opponent here. Neither would she, but she did not need to. Simply performing the exercises would be enough for now.

She moved through the martial dance with her eyes closed, imagining herself home with her father. Oh, but she missed him, and her sisters. She even missed Jing, for all her complaints and commands, for they were her family. They were home. And she was…here, a tiny, insignificant bug who did not belong in the behemoth that was the imperial palace.

But she did not belong at home, either. Her father had Jing to take care of him. If she returned, he would only try to find her some sort of husband. A man who wouldn't care about the size of her feet. But she could never love him, for Yi already held her heart, and he would never know, for Mai could never tell him.

Mai kicked out at a practice dummy, and was gratified to see its head fall off and roll away. She trotted across the sand to retrieve the head, but what she found diminished her pride considerably. The straw that filled the sacking head was so old and rotten it had nearly disintegrated. A puff of wind might have carried it away, if Mai's foot had not done so.

This was Yi's favourite place to train, she reminded herself. No one had used any of this since he went to war. He would not thank her for destroying the place.

Now she felt less balanced than ever. So much for training helping her.

With a sigh of resignation, Mai returned to the prince's apartments. The chime of the palace's water clock – a wonder that took some getting used to – signalled the quarter hour. She must have been too engrossed in her training to miss the full complement of gongs and bells and the general cacophony that occurred to mark the hour. Or perhaps it was not audible in the prince's training yard – yet another reason to spend more time there.

She heard the low murmur of voices as she entered Yi's apartments, coming from his bedchamber. Not wanting to interrupt, she edged toward her own rooms to wash and change into fresh clothes for the day. She might look like a man, but she had no intention of smelling like one.

A long time passed, but Yi did not call her name. Curiosity got the better of her, so she left her room to try to discover who his visitor was.

"He is a fiercer warrior than you. I can see why you like his company," a male voice said. "In the practice yard just now, I saw him decapitating a practice dummy like you used to do. Only he didn't use a sword."

Mai's face grew hot. Yi's visitor had been watching her train?

"He would make a good captain of your personal guard when you are Emperor," the man continued. "The way he moves…he has the grace of the most skilled dancers, hypnotising you, even as he delivers a killing blow. I have never seen anything like it. And yet you tell me he devised the strategy that ended the siege, when no one believed such a thing was even possible? A strategist and a fighter. A rare combination, making him a very dangerous man. Are you sure of his loyalty?"

"He saved my life, Father," Yi said. "Carried my unconscious body through a battlefield to camp. If that is not loyalty, I don't know what is."

Realisation felled her with a flurry of blows. Yi was talking to the Emperor about her in the next room. The Emperor who had watched her train and now considered her dangerous. Questioned her loyalty. As though she would do anything to endanger the Emperor, or the man she loved.

"For that alone, I would do as you ask, but what of the man? I have never heard of him before your letters about him, and you speak of nothing else but this man. You sound like a man in love."

Yi liked men? Was that why he hadn't yet married?

Mai's eyes widened. Yet she'd shared a tent with him every night, spent so much time with him, and not once had she seen so much as a spark of lust in his eyes. Of course, there was that one night after the skirmish in one of the blockade camps, when the camp followers had tried to tempt them both into a tryst. Lust had certainly burned in Yi's eyes then, but not when he looked at her. No, his eyes had been on the woman, riding her soldier lover hard into their battle for shared pleasure. Or so it had seemed at the time.

"A superior sparring partner is easier to find than a willing bride, Father. I wager you have a hundred willing women lined up for me when I am well, but I have searched all my adult life for a man who could cross swords with me and win. I am no longer the Prince of Swords, for Mao conquers me every time we step onto the training ground." Yi laughed. "I protected your poets, giving them guard duty where they would be far from harm. All I ask in return is that you honour one man. A man who deserves your attention because of his deeds, not because of the words he might one day write."

"When you are fully healed, you may introduce him to me. See that you obey the healers and stay abed until then, boy, for I need you well. Well enough to attend the ball, choose a bride, and beget sons with her!"

"Yes, Father." Yi sounded unusually meek.

A man in purple robes swept out of the apartment, not sparing a glance for where Mai crouched behind a stone statue, for which she was grateful.

Heng, carrying the breakfast tray, was more observant. "I have the lychees you like, Mao, and peaches for the prince. The cook tells me there will be apricots tomorrow, if you wish."

Mai longed for apricots, picked fresh from her father's orchard. "Yes, please."

"I begin to think Heng likes you more than he does me," Yi called from his room. "How much did you hear?"

Mai saw no point in lying. "I did not see him watching me at training," she admitted as she pulled up a chair.

"When he was younger, my father did not know he would be Emperor. He was a younger son, and not even one of his father's favourites. He learned stealth as a way to survive at court, which served him well when a palace coup killed his father and many of his brothers. He alone survived, to become the Emperor we all know and love," Yi said.

Mai chose not to contradict him. All she knew of the Emperor was that he loved his son, cared for his health and wished him to have sons of his own.

"He is still set on finding me a bride, but he also

wants to meet you. The healers have told us in three weeks I will be well enough to leave my bed. So, in four weeks, my father will throw a ball. He has invited every noble girl eligible to be my bride, and I must choose one of them." His eyes held pain as he turned his gaze on Mai. "What if I choose wrong?"

"You won't," Mai soothed. "Listen to your heart, and follow where it leads. Think of what you want most in a bride, and watch for it. You are a prince. What woman would refuse you?"

"I don't want a woman afraid to refuse me, or one who only wishes to marry a prince!" Yi declared, slamming his hand down on the table, making the peach slices jump. "I want a woman like the ones the poets sing songs about. Their loyalty, their courage…oh, pretty, too, I supposed, and graceful. What are your sisters like?"

Mai blinked, not sure she'd heard the question correctly. "My…my sisters?"

"Yes. What are they like?"

Mai wet her lips. "Much like any other girls, I guess. At the age I started to learn the martial dance my father taught me, they began to learn court dances. With so much practice, they can't help but be good dancers." Not that she knew, because she hadn't been able to bear to watch them wince as their bound feet hurt. "They're very sweet. They deserve to marry well, to men who will care for them for the rest of their lives. Isn't that the most a girl can hope for?"

Yi opened his mouth to respond, then closed it again, as though he'd decided not to air his true answer. Finally, he said, "Perhaps."

A hope that was beyond Mai now, she knew, but at least her friend could be happy in his choice of wife. "I saw your training yard this morning. Now I know why you are such a terrible fighter. Did your weapons master never tell you that straw men cannot fight back?"

Yi laughed, and breakfast became a merry affair where the Emperor's visit was soon forgotten.

Twenty-Seven

Every day she spent in the palace, the wider Mai felt the chasm grew between palace life and hers. Here, there were hordes of servants ready to obey her every whim, but at home, she would have served Jing instead. And yet…every day she spent in Yi's company she fell deeper in love with the man.

She longed to tell him the truth, but the illusion that had allowed her to meet him in the first place was now a curse that kept her true identity a secret from the man she wished to hide nothing from. Especially when it became clear that he would be forced to choose a bride at the Emperor's ball. She knew there was little chance of him choosing her over the delicate, beautiful creatures arriving at court every day, but until he rejected her, her silly heart still held out hope that she might be the woman he chose. But as long as the illusion made her look like a man, Yi would never believe she was a woman at all.

She spent an extra hour training every morning, and another at sunset, working off her frustrations until Yi's straw dummies had no stuffing left to lose. It was never enough. Was she to remain a man for the rest of her life?

A man who could not find a bride, for she lacked the necessary parts to make a marriage fruitful, something any bride she tried to take would surely notice.

Sighing, she gave up for the day, returning to the prince's apartments by the light of the newly lit torches, for it was well past sunset now. Yi had been allowed out of bed briefly in order to be measured for splendid new clothes, but the Emperor had stationed guards outside his door to make sure he did not leave his apartment. No one stopped Mai from entering, though.

She found a lost-looking serving girl who appeared vaguely familiar standing in the middle of Yi's receiving room. The prince himself was nowhere in sight, so she addressed the girl: "What are you doing in these private chambers?"

The girl held out a basket. "I brought a gift, your

Highness. The sweetest mountain apricots you have ever tasted, as a gift from Yeong Fu in thanks for his invitation to the ball."

"Yeong Fu is at court?" Mai blurted out.

"No, your Highness, but his family has come for the ball." She shoved the basket under Mai's nose. "Take one and taste it, your Highness."

One apricot stood out, bigger and more perfect than the others. Why, it almost seemed to glow. That couldn't be right. Mai had never seen an apricot glow before.

"What magic is this?" she demanded. She would not let Jing cast a spell on the prince.

The girl's eyes dropped to her shoes. "No magic at all, your Highness. Just the rich soil, water from icy mountain streams and clean air makes fruit such as this."

"Not one I've ever seen before," Mai said grimly, reaching for the offending fruit. "I don't know what your mistress is playing at, but it stops now." Her fingers closed around the apricot, which seemed to hum happily in her hand. Definitely not normal. "Take me to your mistress, so that I can tell her myself."

The girl's horrified eyes met Mai's, before she ducked her head again. "Yes, your Highness," she said.

Mai considered telling the girl she wasn't the prince, but decided against it. She would find out the truth soon enough.

Jing's voice rang out the moment the maid walked into the guest apartment: "And? Did the prince eat his apricot?"

"No, madam. He...he..." The girl waved wordlessly at Mai.

Jing slapped the girl across her face. "Stupid country bumpkin. I knew I should have sent someone else. That is not the prince. He's just some common soldier."

Mai drew herself up. "I am no common soldier. I am Yeong Mai, the hero of the siege of Dean, stepmother. Do you not recognise the illusion you cast?" Slowly, she spun on the spot.

Jing's mouth hung open in shock. "Mai? You are still alive? You have been away from home so long. I thought you'd surely been killed, or worse. What are you doing here?"

Mai tossed the apricot into the air and caught it. "Saving the prince from your spells, it would seem."

Jing shrugged. "It is just a little help, is all. It's not like he needs the encouragement. The prince himself requested that we come to the ball. The Emperor's letter arrived weeks ago, commanding us to come to the palace." She brandished a scroll that held pride of place on the table. "See? The prince demands the daughters of Yeong Fu to present themselves at the palace, so that he might choose one of them for his bride."

Now it was Mai's turn to have trouble closing her mouth. "Lin and Lei? They are but children. Not old enough to be betrothed, let alone married to Prince Yi!"

Jing's smile was smug. "You have been away a long time. My girls have grown up." Footsteps sounded in the corridor outside. "And here they are, back from court."

The girls who minced in looked like Lin and Lei, but stretched, somehow. Thinner and taller, yet painted to look like porcelain dolls. Mai did the sums in her head, before the abacus beads clicked into place properly. She shook her head.

"They are only thirteen. You have worked some magic on them, just as you have done on me. You have turned them into grown women when they are still children!" Mai wanted to be sick at the thought of Yi taking one of these girls to bed on his wedding night. She would not let that happen. Not to him, and not to them.

"Keep your voice down!" Jing ordered. "If anyone finds a strange man in the girls' chamber, you will ruin their chances with the prince. They have been working toward this their whole lives. Perhaps they are a little young, but a young bride is a biddable one, and they have so many more fertile years ahead of them. Lin or Lei would both be perfect brides for the prince, and if I must make them a little older…why, the other court women think nothing of painting and padding their daughters. I simply made the illusion more believable."

"No." Mai shook her head. "I will not let you trick the prince into this. You must break the spell on me. Let me go in their stead. If the prince demands a daughter of Yeong Fu, I will go to the ball."

For the first time, Mai's heart soared. If she attended the ball, she would make certain Yi noticed her. Then she would have her answer, and have no need to tell him of her subterfuge in order to join the army. Why, he need never know she was Mao at all.

"You?" Jing scoffed. "A girl with the iron lotus feet of a peasant, enter the court so that she might catch the eye of the prince? I don't think so. You haven't a chance of catching a husband, let alone a prince, and you will only ruin the girls' chances if anyone learns you are associated with them. No. You shall not go to the ball."

Her heart sank, right into her mother's shoes. What was Mai thinking? Even if she went, Yi would never choose her over the hundreds of more eligible maidens.

"Perhaps if you made my feet appear as small as yours," Mai began eagerly.

"I will not!" Jing interrupted. "You cannot dance, or do any of the things expected of a court lady. The only thing you know how to hold is a sword. Go back to the army where you belong. You will never marry, and you will not go to a ball in the imperial court, where you have no place!"

Tears sprang to Mai's eyes. Tears the hero of the siege of Dean could not cry where anyone would see him. Tears Jing did not deserve to see, either.

So Mai did the only thing she could think of – she fled to the training yard from whence she'd come.

Twenty-Eight

The yard was dark, for no torches were lit there at night. Mai stumbled through the gardens, swearing as she struggled to find the path again. Had she somehow entered the wrong courtyard instead? She didn't remember there being quite so many bushes before.

She tripped over a rock, barking her shin on the way down. Instinct told her to roll, to recover, so that she might regain her feet and fight on, but Mai resisted. She barely felt the impact as she hit the ground. She had fought too long for too much that she could never have. Prince Yi would never be hers, and she could not bear to go to a ball to watch him choose someone else.

Lying facedown on the gravel path, she started to

sob in earnest. What did it matter? No one would see her here.

She should have known better. Nothing in the palace went unobserved. There were spies everywhere.

A small, feminine cough sounded from Mai's left.

Maybe if Mai ignored her, she would go away.

"Why are you crying?" a voice asked, dashing Mai's hopes.

"I am not crying," Mai snapped. "I have simply fallen and when I landed, dust irritated my eyes."

"I see no dust, Mai," the woman said, stepping forward so Mai could see her. Though there were no torches, the woman was clearly visible, as though she emitted a glow of her own. Her purple gown marked her as one of the Emperor's family, though her eyes were rounder than any Mai had seen before. And purple, the same shade as her gown, which was made in a fashion unlike any Mai had seen women wear in the palace.

If the Emperor could spy on her unseen, then this woman could only be one person.

"I am sorry, your Majesty," Mai said. "I would bow, but I am already prostrate. What dust there was has settled in my eyes."

The woman laughed. "I am no queen. No throne is worth sharing a bed with a king." She gave a delicate shudder. "I am Zuleika. Merely a lady, though not of this court, or any other."

"Are you here for the prince, too?" Mai asked. Yi would like this one, she was sure of it. Lady Zuleika had all the bearing of an empress who would bow before no one.

"In a small way, yes, but I have no wish to meet the man. I came here because of your shoes," Zuleika said.

Mai sat up, wincing. Perhaps she should have landed better. "My shoes?"

"Well, truthfully, because of my mother, and your mother's shoes," Zuleika went on. She laughed again. "You'd think I'd be better at this, given who my mother was and all, but in my defence, this is my first time."

"Your first time for what?" Now Mai was really confused. The Lady Zuleika had known her mother? She looked barely older than Mai herself.

"Why, being a proper fairy godmother, of course!"
Mai stared. "A fairy…what?"
Zuleika sighed. "Did your mother ever tell you how she came to own those shoes?"

"They were a gift," Mai began haltingly. "She was a girl in her father's camp, and the camp followers would steal her shoes and hide them, for her father had forbidden her from leaving his tent unless she was properly dressed, and she could not leave without shoes. She wished to meet with one of the young officers, the man who would later become my father, and dance for him at the victory celebration, but the other girls were jealous, and – "

"And my mother came upon her, crying, alone, much like you are now, and listened to her troubles. She gave her this pair of shoes, promising that they would grant her balance and grace for the dance of her life, and that they would never be lost," Zuleika finished with a smile. "And so your mother married your father, and they won many victories together, until they retired from war and had you."

Mai still didn't understand. "So your mother was my mother's fairy godmother, but it still does not explain to me why you are here."

Zuleika grinned. "A prince choosing a bride among hundreds of maidens from throughout the land? It sounds like a fairy tale come true. Why wouldn't a fairy godmother want to go to a ball such as this? Why wouldn't any maiden want to go?" She nodded at Mai. "Well, don't you?"

Mai found herself nodding. "Of course, but…I have nothing to wear, and my stepmother is right that no prince will want a girl who looks like a commoner when he could choose ladies raised for court life. I have no place there."

Zuleika made a derisive noise in her throat. "Your place is at the prince's side. You know it. He knows it.

Even your shoes know it."

Mai laughed. "Shoes do not think."

Zuleika winked. "Don't underestimate the power in a magical object, and you have two with you always. If you wear those shoes to the ball, I promise the prince will not leave your side. He will dance only with you, and at the end of the night, no illusion will hide what you truly are from him."

"But my stepmother – "

"Is a witch of little talent, who can only cast illusions. They look and feel real enough, but she is no enchantress. Not like I am." Zuleika held out her hand. "Mai, on the night of the ball, I shall wait here until that unbelievably noisy clock contraption strikes midnight. If you wish to have the illusion removed so that the prince can see you as you truly are, you must come to me here and I will undo Jing's spell. Or I can turn the prince into a frog, if you prefer. Not all of them are as charming as they first appear, though I'm sure your prince is the perfect gentleman. In the meantime…how about we do a little something about those shoes?"

Mai glanced down at the worn red silk. "They are the only thing I have left of my mother's," she whispered.

"But she would not mind if I made them pretty enough for court, and perhaps wove a little of my own magic into them, too?" Zuleika asked.

Mai managed a smile. "I'm sure she wouldn't mind."

Zuleika bit her lip. "How forgetful are you? Because what I have in mind would mean removing that never-lose-your-shoes spell."

"I have never lost my shoes, not forgotten them," Mai assured her.

Zuleika clapped her hands. "Good. Then I know just what to do."

Twenty-Nine

Still puzzled by her encounter with the strange Lady Zuleika, who dressed like a foreign empress yet claimed to be her fairy godmother, Mai headed back to Yi's apartments. She took longer than usual, because she kept stopping to admire her shoes, which caught the light in the most amazing ways. Zuleika had turned the faded red silk into something that shimmered partway between blue and green before covering the silk in a myriad of glass beads, which caught the light and threw it in all directions. They were ornamental shoes for court, never to be worn on a battlefield again.

Mai laughed quietly to herself. If she ever set foot on a battlefield wearing these, she would dazzle the enemy without having to unsheathe her sword.

Lady Zuleika had known her name, and seen through Jing's illusion.

The realisation stopped her dead. Perhaps the woman truly was her fairy godmother, despite her youth. But she had said her mother was Da Ying's fairy godmother, so perhaps these things were passed down from mother to daughter. Had Zuleika inherited her mother's responsibilities? If she had, that mean that her mother walked the spirit world now, just like Da Ying.

More confident in Zuleika's predictions now, Mai couldn't keep the smile off her face as she walked into Yi's sitting room.

"So you have already heard," Yi greeted her. "Who told you? Was it Heng?"

Mai stumbled to a halt. "Heard what? I was training, and then I saw my sisters, and I have only just arrived back here. I have not seen Heng since this morning."

"Good," Yi beamed. "Your sisters are here, and so are your court clothes. My new ones, too, but they are of little consequence – just something to wear to the ball. My mother said you would need court clothes, so Heng took care of it. What do you think?"

Mai surveyed the piles of neatly folded blue silk that seemed to cover every surface. "Do men really wear such bright colours at court?" she asked carefully. She already knew the ladies dressed so brightly they looked like exotic butterflies, but most of the noblemen she'd seen wore robes in dark shades of purple, red, black and green. Not until today had she seen men's clothing in this azure blue that reminded her of the mountain lakes at home on a sunny day. Or the colour of her shoes.

Yi laughed. "Men are much like peacocks in court. You have spent weeks in the palace, yet you have never attended court. Once the ball is over, that will change. I will introduce you to the Emperor, and you will spend as much time in court as you desire. Let's hope for another war before your enthusiasm wanes."

War. Would that be her life now, if Jing would not allow her to go home? It would be a lonely life, but at least it was an honourable one. "Perhaps," Mai agreed.

"This is what you will wear to the ball," Yi said eagerly, pointing at a particularly bright robe the exact same shade as Mai's shoes. "As the crown prince, I must wear a hideous shade of yellow that makes me look like an apricot." He gestured at his own gold silk robes, which were much more richly embroidered than Mai's.

Mai laid the two robes side by side. "You will be the sun, blinding everyone, while I stand at your shoulder, the azure sky in the background."

"I would rather be back at the siege of Dean than walk into that ballroom tomorrow night to select my bride," Yi admitted. "But if you are there, all eyes will be on you as the war hero. I daresay more girls will look to you as a suitable husband than me. We will choose brides together, you and I."

There was only one way they could both choose their life partners together, and even though Mai's fairy godmother had foretold it, she still didn't believe it was possible. "I will take no bride, but I will help you choose yours. I hope you choose a girl who will make you happy all your days."

"I'll settle for one who does not make me rue my decision before the week is out," Yi said, so low Mai didn't think she was supposed to hear it.

She fervently hoped he would get his wish.

Thirty

The peacock dance. Why did they always have to perform the peacock dance? It was true what his old teacher said about all colours being blinding, Yi realised now. With so much brightness, the dancing women became a blur. How could a man choose one bride when they all looked the same?

He spared a glance for Mao, who seemed too intent on the contents of his cup to care about the dancers, either. But then, Mao had never cared much for music and dancing girls.

"Which girl do you think is the most beautiful?" Yi asked, nudging him.

Mao took a long time before he answered, "I would have to say my sisters. I haven't seen them in so long, that they would hold my attention even if they were dressed in rags."

Yi's curiosity burned to see the sisters he had not yet met. "Where are they?"

Mao pointed at two girls who wore layered robes in shades of purple and gold. The Emperor's colours, which no other girls had dared to wear.

Yi stared at them hungrily. One of them held the key to his happiness, he was sure of it, but even as he focussed on one and then the other, he felt nothing. Oh, they were graceful enough dancers, and as pretty as any of the other dancing dolls, but Yi had felt more while watching camp followers capering around the campfire with common soldiers at one of the victory celebrations. He didn't understand why these girls should leave him so unmoved.

"Which do you think would make a better bride?" he asked.

Mao laughed uncertainly. "I could not answer that. Lin and Lei are my sisters. The last time I saw them, they were children, and even now they are only twelve or thirteen years old. Too young to be brides, if you ask me."

"My father has decreed that girls can marry as young as fourteen now," Yi said.

Mao frowned. "Just because they can, doesn't mean they should. Do you want a bride who is still a child, or a woman grown? You said you wanted a woman of loyalty and courage, who does not fear you. If you bed a child and hurt her, she will fear you all her days."

As always, Mao was right. He didn't want one of Da Ying's daughters to fear him. Who knew what she might do if she regarded her husband as her enemy?

An idea began to grow in the back of his mind. His father had insisted he choose a bride tonight, but he'd never said he needed to marry the girl immediately. It would give him the perfect excuse to meet with Yeong Fu in the morning to discuss a betrothal for a marriage some time in the future…and in the meantime, he would be a willing pupil to his future father-in-law.

"Doesn't watching all this make you want to dance?" Yi asked Mao.

Mao shook his head. "I only know one dance, Rooster, and it is a martial one. This is hardly the place."

Yi grinned. "I know just the place, and I will show you. I shall speak to my father for a moment, and then we will be free."

He took a moment to compose himself before he approached his father.

"Excuse me, your Majesty," Yi said, bowing. "I have made my decision."

His father's eyebrows rose. "I hope it is a wise one."

Yi prayed that it would be.

Thirty-One

Yi kept his voice low so that only those closest to him would hear. That included the Emperor, the Empress and Mai herself, for there was not even a servant within earshot, Mai noticed with relief.

"I wish to take Yeong Fu's daughter as my bride," Yi said.

Mao smothered a gasp. After all she had said, he still wanted one of the girls?

"Which one? I understand he has several," the Emperor said.

"I'm not certain," Yi admitted. "But they are too young yet, so I will negotiate the betrothal with Fu, and make my decision then. When I have his agreement, then we can set a wedding date."

Mai breathed again. So he had not made a decision after all. And when Yi spoke to her father, he would suggest Yi marry his oldest daughter, and not Lin or Lei. Perhaps she still stood a chance with the prince, however slim.

"Very well," the Emperor said.

Mai felt the uncanny sensation that someone was staring at her. She glanced around, only to meet the eyes of the Empress herself. Flustered, Mai bowed deeply. She had heard that General Li was the Empress' brother, which surely meant the woman wanted her dead as much as the General did.

"Come, we are free," Yi said, grabbing Mai's arm.

Willingly, she let herself be led out of the ballroom and into a corridor full of surprised servants. Amid a flurry of bowing, Yi dragged her through the throng to a courtyard where all was still and dark.

Yi was having none of it, though. He seized a torch and used it to light several more, before thrusting the first into the sand that marked a sparring ring surrounded by garden. This was not his usual practice yard, but another part of the palace entirely.

Yi fanned out the hem of his robe like a tail and lifted his hand in imitation of a peacock head, much like the girls in the ballroom had done. "Will you dance with me, Mao?" He nodded at the wooden practice swords stuck point first into the sand at the end of the ring.

"A rooster in the field, and a peacock at court. Are you sure you are recovered enough to dance, Rooster?" Mai asked, smiling to ease the sting of her words.

Yi snatched up one of the swords, swinging it experimentally. "We shall see, but you don't know how much I've missed dancing with you. The mornings when it was just you and me, against a whole army. No one else at court understands. Only you."

Mai selected a wooden sword, testing its balance. It would do. "You have missed the mouthfuls of sand I made you eat, every time you fell on your face in the ring? Perhaps your illness has addled your wits. The last time we sparred, I distinctly recall you cursing my ancestors for begetting children with barbarian war gods." She lifted the blade in a relaxed fighting pose.

"I really said that?" Yi's gaze sank from Mai's face to her feet. "You're going to fight me in your court shoes? Those?"

In the light of the torch, her shoes seemed to glow gold, reflecting the flames in all directions. Mai's mother's shoes had never looked so splendid.

She shrugged. "I will still beat you, no matter what I wear. Court robes or armour, army boots or my mother's shoes. But if you think they will distract you, I shall remove them." Mai slipped off her shoes and set them on the grass beside the ring.

"Court clothes are hardly good for dancing," Yi said, stripping off his outer robes so he stood in only his trousers.

Mai's mouth suddenly grew dry. The way the firelight seemed to glow as it caressed the muscles of his chest…her hands itched to trace each of them in turn, from his taut belly up to his shoulders, before cupping his face for a kiss.

Where had that thought come from? she wondered, muttering something about following suit as she shrugged out of her blue outer robe. She kept the rest of her clothes, though, not wanting to be nearly naked with him here, where anyone could see them. By the ancestors, she still looked like a man!

"Tell me when you tire," she said. "You are out of practice, after all."

They crossed swords lightly, focussing on their footwork more than the clash of blades. They danced in a circle, never taking their eyes from one another, as the balance seemed to flow from one to the other as never before. For all that he was out of practice, Yi had learned much in their time together.

Mai darted in, tapping his shoulder with her blade, and Yi laughed.

"By the ancestors, that feels good," he said.

It was Mai's turn to laugh. "You will not say that in

the morning, when your bruises start to show."

"Yes, I will!" he declared. "For in the morning, we shall dance again. I have lain abed long enough!"

She smiled. "If you wish." If she had her way, the illusion that made her a man would be gone by morning. What would Yi say to sparring with her then?

The chiming water clock bells began to ring, signifying the changing of the hour. "What time is it?" Mai asked.

Yi cocked his head to one side, listening. "Midnight, I think. Yes, that's twelve."

The sword fell from Mai's suddenly nerveless fingers. "Midnight already? No! I have to meet...I must..." Without even pausing to finish her sentence, she took to her heels, running through the corridors until she reached the practice yard where she'd first met her fairy godmother.

"Lady Zuleika?" she called, then repeated it, louder still.

No response.

"Lady Zuleika!"

No matter how many times Mai said the woman's name, she did not appear.

Mai would be forced to remain a man forever, as she watched the man she loved marry one of her sisters.

Mai fell to her knees and burst into tears.

DANCE: CINDERELLA RETOLD

Thirty-Two

So Mao had a midnight tryst? The sly fox. All that talk of never taking a bride and he'd arranged to meet some girl in the middle of the night. Laughing quietly to himself, Yi sat down on a bench to wait. If Mao wasn't back soon, he'd head off to bed. Prince or not, he still wanted to look well-rested when he asked Mao's father for one of his daughters' hands on the morrow.

When he started to feel the chill of the night air, he pulled on his court clothes again. When he picked up the gaudy gold robe, he was surprised to see Mao's shoes underneath. He'd been in such a hurry, he'd left without his shoes. Yi picked them up and set them on the bench beside him. For shoes, they were quite remarkable, catching whatever light there was and holding tight to it in the strangely angular glass beads sewn all over them. Any woman in court would gladly give her eyeteeth to own shoes that sparkled like the sun in the light of a torch – and yet they belonged to Mao. He'd never seen them before, Yi was certain – if he had, he would have remembered. And they were so small, too. Yi could not fit his foot inside one of the shoes. He knew Mao was smaller than him, but he'd never thought he had small feet before. If Yi didn't know better, he would have sworn he held a pair of women's shoes.

Heng would know. He must have commissioned these for Mao along with the rest of his court clothes.

Deciding that Mao was probably too busy with his girl friend to return any time soon, Yi rose and made his way back to his apartment, carrying Mao's shoes. He set them on the table in the sitting room, then proceeded to remove his uncomfortable court clothes.

"Those are pretty," Heng said when he walked in. "Are they a gift for your new bride?"

Yi frowned. "No. They're Mao's. Don't you recognise them? He wore them to the ball tonight."

Heng circled the table, admiring them from every angle. "They can't be his. Those are much too small." He lifted a pair of brand-new silk shoes on the table, made in the same style as the ones Yi had just kicked off. "These are the shoes Mao was supposed to wear tonight. See? Much larger."

Yi shook his head. "But he was wearing these. I saw him wearing them, then take them off, with my own eyes." He waved at Heng. "Find me another pair of his shoes from his sleeping cubicle."

Heng nodded and did as he was bid, but he came back a few minutes later, empty handed. "There aren't any. I've only ever seen him wear one pair of shoes, and they're not there."

Mao would explain things on his return, Yi was certain. He wasn't a man to keep secrets. Perhaps the shoes Heng had commissioned were too big, and he'd been forced to take whatever the tailor had spare. That something like this would be spare, though…

Yi found the jug of baijiu he and Mao had been drinking before the ball, and poured himself a cup. The strong spirit seared his throat on the way down, a potent reminder not to drink too much of the stuff. He settled down to wait for Mao.

He was woken from a doze by quiet footsteps. A girl wearing the colourless clothing of a drudge entered the room, glanced about, then headed for the table where Mao's shoes lay. Without hesitation, she snatched them up.

"Put those down!" Yi roared, leaping to his feet. "Get out!"

Startled, the girl stared at him for a moment before she remembered herself and bowed. "I must…"

"Do you know who I am?" he demanded.

Without raising her eyes to his face, the girl nodded.

"Who am I?"

"His Highness, the Prince of Swords," she whispered.

"And you would dare to steal from me?" he thundered.

"I wasn't – " she began.

"Not another word, or I shall call the palace guards and have you thrown out. Tell whatever woman who sent you that I have chosen my bride and no trick or spell will change my mind. Now get out!"

The girl hesitated for a moment, then she bowed even lower than before and scurried out.

Yi checked Mao's room, but the man had not yet returned. Perhaps he was spending the night with his mistress. A sly dog indeed. Shaking his head, Yi headed to his bed. Answers could wait until morning.

Thirty-Three

Her fairy godmother wasn't the only one who could remove the illusion. Jing could, too, Mai realised, wiping her eyes. The ball was finished and Yi had made his decision. Jing had won. Which meant Mai had nothing left to lose if she demanded her stepmother release her from the spell.

She had fought hardened army veterans on a daily basis, many of whom feared to look her in the eye. What was Jing to her? A woman, and a weak one at that. If Mai had to threaten her, then she would. Mai refused to fool the prince a minute longer.

She rose, straightening her spine so she stood at her full height. She was the hero of the siege of Dean, Mai reminded herself. She had served her Emperor with honour, and the Emperor himself had agreed to meet her. She would not be cowed by someone as insignificant as Jing.

Mai marched to her stepmother's apartment, which she now noticed was a fraction of the size of the one she shared with Yi. She found the place in a flurry of activity, with clothing flung everywhere before being packed into chests.

"You're leaving?" Mai blurted out.

"What are you doing here?" Jing asked irritably, glaring. "Have you come to gloat?"

Gloat? Mai faltered. What could she possibly have to gloat about? Jing had gotten her wish, that one of her girls would marry a prince.

"Save your breath," Jing advised. "There is no chance of the girls marrying now. Instead, we must go home and mourn."

Mai's breath caught in her throat. "Mourn who?"

"The great Yeong Fu, who surely could have held on another week so that he might see his daughters secure in marriage. Now...they will have nothing." Jing paused to bark instructions to Jia, who hurried off to fetch whatever it was Jing had asked for. "First the ancestors take my son, then they take my husband. Ah, I am cursed!"

Mai could scarcely believe it. "My...my father is dead?"

"Yes, your father is dead. It's your fault for not being there to take care of him. He talked of nothing but you the week before we left," Jing snapped. "While you were off pretending to be some hero, your father was dying. Alone."

Mai didn't know what to say. All her fierce words and thoughts had dried up. Her father couldn't be gone. He couldn't be. She had promised her mother she'd take care of him, but she'd failed. Now, all she could do was burn incense in the shrine every day and beg both her mother and father to forgive her.

"I must go home," Mai found herself saying.

Jing gave a most unladylike snort. "Another useless mouth to feed that we can ill afford? What for?"

"I will come home for my father's funeral, as is proper," Mai said, finding strength in her sorrow. "I will honour his memory. And you cannot stop me." She drew herself up and returned Jing's glare with one of her own.

"Oh, by all that is holy…I refuse to be intimidated by a girl who thinks that because she looks like a man, she is better than me!" Jing bit down hard on her lip and waved her hand at Mai.

Mai felt a faint tingle run across her skin, and then the weight of her robes dragging on the ground because – she glanced down – all of a sudden, they did. She yanked up one sleeve, then the other, seeing her own arms for the first time in too long, instead of the muscled appendages she'd grown used to. Impetuously, she threw her arms around Jing. "Thank you!"

"Quickly, take those off. You must wear women's clothes, but not too fine, or someone will question why they did not see you before." Jing surveyed the room. "Jia! Find her something of yours."

What Mai suspected were Jia's only set of spare clothes were brought, and Mai put them on. The rough cloth was strange against her skin after the smooth silk of her court clothes, but Mai knew she would not wear the maid's clothes for long.

"I will go get my things," Mai said. "I won't be long."

"Be quick about it. We won't wait for you," Jing snapped.

Mai nodded and hurried off to the prince's apartments. Hopefully, he would be fast asleep and not notice a lowly maid going about her business.

Thirty-Four

Mai hesitated in the doorway to the prince's apartments. They seemed bigger somehow, though she knew they had not changed. Only she had changed.

No, she scolded herself. She had not changed at all. She had merely lost the illusion that made her appear to be something she wasn't.

A small part of her wanted the prince to be awake, to recognise her for who she was, and claim her as his bride, like Lady Zuleika had said. But she was too mired in her grief to let even that tiny ray of hope lighten her mood. Her father was dead, and she must return home to mourn him. She would never dance with him in the courtyard again, nor bring him his tea, nor pray with him in the shrine as they laid out her mother's favourite incense. She could never thank him for all that he had taught her, the invaluable skills which had kept her alive at the siege of Dean.

A light still burned in the prince's sitting room, as though he was not yet back from the ball. The light was more than enough to set her mother's shoes sparkling where they sat in pride of place on the table. Despite herself, Mai smiled. Sweet prince. He must have seen that she'd forgotten her shoes and brought them back here for her before rejoining the festivities.

With trembling hands, she reached for her mother's shoes, magically transformed into a dream she could no longer indulge in. But she could treasure the shoes, and the memories that came with them. Mai scooped up the slippers, cradling them like the precious heirlooms they were.

"Put those down!" Yi roared. "Get out!"

Startled, she dropped the shoes back on the table. Had he looked so big and fierce before? It did not matter – he was still Yi, the man she loved. A man she must say goodbye to, for even if he had offered to marry her, no wedding could take place until the mourning period for her father was over. Not even the Emperor himself would stop her from returning home for her father's funeral.

She sighed. "I must – " she began.

"Do you know who I am?" he interrupted.

What a peculiar question. Had Yi drunk too much baijiu, or was this some strange joke? Slowly, she nodded.

"Who am I?" he demanded.

It was on the tip of her tongue to tell him he was a puffed-up rooster who couldn't fight, but realisation dawned on her that he did not know who she was. Dressed like a maid, and a girl again, she would appear as a stranger to him.

Her mouth was dry as she replied, "His Highness, the Prince of Swords." As any palace servant would.

"And you would dare to steal from me?" he thundered.

"I wasn't!" she protested hotly, opening her mouth to tell him that they were not his shoes, but hers.

He seemed to read her mind. "Not another word, or I shall call the palace guards and have you thrown out."

Mai longed to tell him the truth, but she knew he meant what he said. If he summoned the palace guards, she would either end up in a fight where someone would get hurt, or she would have to let them throw her out. And Jing would leave without her.

Angrily, Mai met his gaze, determined to make him recognise her.

Recognition sparked in his eyes for a moment before Yi turned away. "Tell whatever woman who sent you that I have chosen my bride and no trick or spell will change my mind. Now get out!"

Mai's heart broke. She was too late. Yi had chosen someone else. She had nowhere else to go but home. Tears sprang to her eyes – tears she refused to shed in front of Yi – so she turned away before he could see her heartbreak. What was losing a pair of shoes to losing the man she loved? Mai had nothing left, now, for as she departed from the prince's apartments for the final time, she left her bleeding heart on the table, beside her mother's shoes.

Thirty-Five

The next morning, Yi sent Heng to Yeong Fu's apartment to ask whether he might meet with the man over the course of the morning. Heng came hurrying back, wide-eyed. "The whole family has packed up and left. Apparently, Yeong Fu died suddenly and they all returned home for the funeral first thing this morning."

Yi's hand closed around the shoes on the table. So that was why Mao had not returned last night. He must have been with his family, and returned home with them for his father's funeral. As any dutiful son would do.

Surely he would have taken a moment to return here to pack his belongings, and say farewell. Yet all of

Mao's clothes were still in his room, and the shoes sat where he'd left them last night.

Now Yi remembered the maid from last night. Had she been sent to collect Mao's things, and give him a message from Mao? The more he thought about it, the more Yi decided it must be true. He shouldn't have frightened the girl away.

Mao was right. He should wait before he married one of Mao's sisters. Life in the army had left him with absolutely no idea how to deal with women.

Thinking about Mao, though, made him remember another important appointment. One he must keep, though Mao wouldn't.

His parents were breaking their fast when Yi entered their private courtyard, but his mother waved him in.

"Mother. Father." Yi bowed. "I have come to convey my deepest apologies for my friend, Yeong Mao. His father has died and he has returned home for the funeral."

"Your friend, the war hero?" Father asked.

"Yes."

"Who was his father again?" The Emperor reached for another slice of peach.

"Yeong Fu, the great general. His mother was Da Ying, the military strategist." Yi couldn't keep the grin off his face at those words.

Mother frowned. "Yeong Fu had no sons. Unless he fathered some on that girl…what was her name again? Jing?" She turned to her husband. "That witch girl you made him marry…oh, it must have been fourteen years ago now. He had no sons, so you commanded that he marry again. I saw her at court last night at the ball, with her two girls. She'd magicked them to look older, and dressed them in purple and gold, the imperial colours, as if they were already members of our household." Delicately, she bit into an egg.

Yi found himself shaking his head. "No, that's not possible. I've seen him fight. His military tactics and strategies are second to none. He makes me look like an idiot, and he can beat me in a fight before I can blink. He carried me out of Dean on his own back when I was wounded. He told me who his parents were, and his father trained him in war since he was a child. His mother is Da Ying, I swear it, not some witch. I have shared a tent with the man for the whole of the siege, and my apartments here since we arrived at the palace. I know him, and he cannot be anything except who he says he is!"

"Calm yourself," Mother said. She nodded at Yi. "What is that in your hand? Is that a token from your bride, so that you do not forget her?"

Yi glanced down. In his hand, he still clutched

Mao's shoes. He could not even remember picking them up. "No," he said slowly. "I picked these up in the garden, after we finished sparring. I thought they were Mao's, but…"

Mother held out her hand and Yi wordlessly gave her the shoes.

"Beautiful," she purred. "Very well made. I have never seen any of our shoemakers do work like this, though they are silk. And the glass beads! Why, every one of them looks like it has been cut by a knife, so sharply that they shatter the very light that touches them. Whoever makes your friend's shoes would have an honoured place in court, if they so wished it."

"They're not…" Yi began, but then he stopped. He had seen Mao wearing these shoes. His mother's eyes were knowing. "Did you see Mao wear these to the ball, too?"

Mother inclined her head. "Indeed I did. I wanted to ask who made them, for they look better suited for a woman than a man, and perhaps now we will never know." She eyed them. "But if your friend no longer wants them, I would like them."

"No!" Yi snatched the shoes back and hugged them to his chest. "He left them behind in his hurry to attend his father's funeral. I must return them to him."

"Convey our condolences to your friend, and to Yeong Fu's widow," Mother said. "They were married for fourteen years. I am sure she is quite bereft without him, even if their story was not the stuff of legends, like the tales of Fu and Da Ying."

Fourteen years. Mao had said his sisters were younger than that. Ordinary girls who danced and…were not Da Ying's daughters. His heart sank. So much for finding a bride with Mao's help.

"The stories say they fell in love during a campaign, but the General forbade them to see one another. She dressed in armour and marched into battle at Fu's side anyway, and when he fell in battle, she took command of his troops and won a great victory." Mother smiled. "What the stories do not say is that she was pregnant with his child at the time, and that night she went into labour early, and gave birth to a daughter. Born in the heart of battle. What an empress she would make."

Yi stared at his mother in confusion. "You mean…Mao has another sister? One who did not dance at the ball last night?"

Mother shrugged "Did she not? I did not notice every girl there. There were so many. But when you said you chose one of Fu's daughters for your bride, of course I assumed it was Da Ying's girl. The others are merely children."

Yi's head whirled. Women's shoes. No sons. Born in battle. Another sister.

Only one thing he knew for certain: the answers to

all his questions lay with Mao, and Mao alone. If he wanted to know the truth, he must ask Mao.

Yi bowed to his mother and father, thanking them for their time, before heading back to his apartments.

If Mao had left the palace, Yi would go after him. One way or the other, he would know the truth. Either Mao had not been honest about whose son he was…or Mao was no one's son at all, but a daughter.

Yi would journey to Mao's house and find the daughter born in battle, and make her put on Mao's shoes. If they fit, he would ask her to dance for him, just like the other girls had last night.

If the girl truly was Mao, he would know.

And if she was…Yi swore he would make Da Ying's daughter his bride.

Thirty-Six

When Yeong Fu's funeral was ended, Mai busied herself in the kitchen, doing the dishes to keep herself busy. After her father's death, many of his loyal servants had left, for they weren't as fond of Jing and there was plenty of work to do on the farms of the village. With all the men who had gone to war and not yet returned, every pair of hands were needed to till and seed the fields in the hope of a summer harvest.

Like most soldiers, she had learned the use of a cookfire and the kitchen here was no different, if a little more civilised. On the days when the cook didn't come, Mai had to use her cooking skills, to Jing's loud complaints. Mai closed her ears to them. She had eaten worse food prepared by the army cooks, and though it was nowhere near as palatable as palace fare, it was edible enough. As long as they had food, her family would not starve.

On laundry day, Mai found herself alone, without a single servant to help, as a plague of birds had descended on the fields and they needed every spare person to either scare the birds away or replant the seeds they had eaten. She worked all day and into the night, washing clothes and linen, before hanging it all out to dry in the yard. She might have returned Jia's clothes, but she had taken the girl's place in what had increasingly become Jing's house. The only place Mai truly felt her mother and father's presence was the shrine, now, where she had barely a moment to light a stick of incense for each of them before she had to start her chores for the day.

The one thing from her earlier life she did not relinquish was her predawn dance, though now she performed it alone. There was no one to fight or spar with, and there never would be again. The baby brother who had died shortly before his father would never grow to adulthood, so Mai was the closest thing their household of women had to a protector. She might no longer look like a man, but she was most certainly a match for one.

So every day she kept herself in readiness for an army she never expected to arrive.

But as fate would have it, the morning after laundry day, it did.

Thirty-Seven

The further away they travelled from the capital, the more each mountain lake reminded Yi of Mao. At first, it was just because they all seemed to be the same shade of blue green as Mao's court clothes in one of the saddlebags, until he found himself thinking almost constantly of his former roommate. Could the man he'd known truly have been a woman all this time?

The erotic dreams had returned, featuring a woman whose face he still could not see, but Yi no longer woke up in horror when he saw Mao's face or heard his voice in his dreams. Instead, he wondered whether Mao was simply a particularly muscular girl with a deep voice and a homely face who had chosen to join the army because she feared she would never be beautiful enough to attract a husband.

There were days he did not want to believe that Mao could be a woman, too. They were becoming fewer and fewer, though, especially when he remembered the knowing look in his mother's eyes as she'd held Mao's shoes. She had also mentioned Mao's stepmother being a witch. Yi hadn't met one before, though he had heard of them. Perhaps she had cursed her beautiful stepdaughter so that she merely looked like a man. If so, Yi would demand she break the curse as part of the marriage agreement, for he would not take a cursed bride.

Yi rode through the gates of the house, entering a courtyard filled with linens blowing in the wind as they dried, but no one was in sight. He dismounted, handing the reins of his horse to Heng, and telling his men to wait in the yard. If his mother was right, this was now a household of women, and women in mourning. He had no wish to frighten them by bringing an invading army into their home.

Someone emerged from the house and stood on the veranda, clad in white. From the quality of her mourning robes as well as her age, Yi judged her to be Fu's widow.

"Mistress Yeong," he said, bowing. "I have come to see your son, Yeong Mao, and to return his things, which he left at the palace."

"I am Mistress Yeong," the woman said weakly. "But I no longer have a son." She buried her face in her hands and burst into noisy tears.

A crying woman. What in the ancestors' name was he supposed to do with one of those?

Heng slid down from his horse and advanced to stand at Yi's shoulder. "Mistress Yeong, may we come inside to speak with you? We have travelled a long way and would like some refreshment."

"Yes…yes." She seemed to collect herself at Heng's words, and beckoned them inside.

Heng grabbed Yi's arm before he could follow her inside. "She's a witch," Heng said softly. "She has an illusion about her, making her look younger and prettier than she is. Watch her if she bites her lip, or otherwise does something to draw blood, for blood fuels her spells."

One day, Yi intended to ask Heng how he knew all this. For now, though, he simply nodded, before heading inside the house.

Thirty-Eight

The sound of hooves on the stone gateway woke Mai from her uncomfortable sleep. She had spent so long dealing with the laundry last night that she'd laid down by the embers of the fireplace, with a rice bag as her pillow, to get a little sleep before dawn. Somehow the rice bag had come open as she slept, though, and the ashes were full of rice grains. With the last harvest as poor as it had been, Mai had shared much of their spare food with the villagers, and this was their last bag of rice. Every grain was valuable.

Sighing at her own stupidity for spilling the stuff, she began sifting through the ashes for the grains of rice so she could return them to the bag. She soon forgot about horses, visitors or anything outside the fireplace until Lei burst into the kitchen.

"Mai, Mai! You must make tea. The prince is here, and he is looking for a boy. Mother keeps telling him our brother is dead, but he does not believe her. He goes on and on about how our brother bought one of his sisters a gift, but how it belonged to a girl with big feet. He keeps holding up his hands to show how big." Lei held her hands apart, much wider than her own bound feet. "You must make tea, and when you serve it, he shall see your feet and stop hounding Mother. Every time she tells him her son is dead, she cries, but he only grows angrier. The courtyard is full of men. I am afraid he will hurt Mother."

The rice could wait. Mai had not gone to war so that some lackey from the Emperor could torment her family. She still seethed at how rude Yi had been to her when she'd come to his apartments to collect her shoes. She'd teach him a lesson in manners no matter how many men he'd brought. How dare he!

She clambered to her feet, brushing the ashes from her white robe. Not so white now, but it mattered little. She could still best Yi in rags or court robes.

"But the tea!" Lei hissed.

"Men who invade a house of mourning without an invitation do not deserve tea," Mai said, striding through the home where she had once been happy. Jing's sitting room had grown shabby, but today she barely noticed it. Mai stood as tall and proud as the Empress herself at the entrance to Jing's sitting room and set her hands on her hips. "Who demands to see Yeong Mao?"

Heng shot to his feet, bowing before his knees had fully straightened, but Yi was slower to move, letting his gaze rake over Mai's body as he rose. His eyebrows rose a little, as if in surprise, but his slight smile said he liked what he saw.

Mai didn't give a rat's arse what he thought.

"Yeong Mao died on the road home from the capital. He broke his neck when his horse threw him. There was nothing anyone could do to save him. He walks with the ancestors now, including his father, and if you wish to see him, you are welcome to join them."

Yi looked stunned, but he recovered quickly.

Rooster, Mai thought, as she saw that arrogant look in his eye again. She longed to spar with him and throw him in the dust until that's all he could taste.

"Do you know who I am, girl?" he asked.

Mai could have kissed him for repeating the line he'd used the night of the ball. She'd relived that night so many times in her head, the correct response tripped off her tongue.

"Many call you the Prince of Swords, but Yeong Mao called you a rooster, with good reason, I think," Mai replied, ignoring Jing's horrified gasp. "Do you know who I am?"

The surprise took longer to leave his face this time. "The Empress spoke of a girl born in battle, the daughter of Yeong Fu and Da Ying. I believe she might be you, and if that's true, then I have something which belongs to you."

Mai folded her arms. "A gift from my brother?" She had fought in a war, not bought gifts for her sisters, let alone herself. She itched to catch Yi in a lie so she could ask him his true purpose here.

"Perhaps," he said. "I left it in my saddlebag."

Outside, where he had reinforcements, Mai added in her head. As if Yi suspected he might need them. That brought her up short. Did he truly know who she was?

She shot him a startled glance, but he wore an enigmatic smile that revealed nothing.

"Then lead the way," she said, gesturing, and he did.

She counted a dozen men and horses in the courtyard, their hooves leaving divots in her training circle that she would need to smooth over before tomorrow morning's dancing session. Mai bet Yi never let horses muck up his training yard.

Yi reached into his saddlebag and pulled out a parcel shrouded in purple silk. He unwrapped it slowly, drawing out every moment as though he enjoyed having her eyes on him. From the first glimpse, she knew what he held, though, so that when he finally held up her shoes in all their dazzling splendour, she could feign indifference despite the awed gasps from his men. Only Heng and Yi seemed immune – for both had seen them before.

"What do you think?" Yi asked.

"I think those are my mother's shoes," Mai replied. She suppressed a grin at Yi's shock. "I would need to see them more closely to be sure, but I am almost certain they are the same."

"You will! You must try them on. I insist!"

Mai waited while Heng brought her a bench to sit on, before Yi knelt at her feet.

"Your Highness, let me – " Heng began, but Yi waved him away.

"I must know that they fit!" Yi hissed. "I must know!" He took hold of her foot, and slipped on one shoe.

As Mai knew it would, the shoe fitted as though it was made for her, as indeed it was.

Yi gazed up at her searchingly. "Is it true?" he asked, half under his breath. The longing in his eyes made her wonder if he was going to kiss her.

Mai met his gaze and said nothing.

He cupped her other foot in his hand. For a long moment, he hesitated, before he finally slid on the second shoe.

"A perfect fit," he breathed. He pointed a shaking finger in Jing's direction. "Is that your mother?"

Mai laughed. "No, Jing is my stepmother, foisted on my father by the Emperor, who likes to breed more good men from the ones he has. I am the daughter of Da Ying." She dropped her voice so low only Yi would hear it. "But I think you already knew that."

She fancied that he nodded slightly, but she could not be certain.

"It is not enough that the shoes fit you," Yi announced. "Before I make my decision, you must dance."

Mai didn't like the sound of that. "What decision?"

He gave a slight shake of his head.

By the ancestors, he was putting on a show. Mai would not stand for it. "What decision?" she demanded.

He grabbed her arm and pulled her forward, until she dropped to her knees in the dirt. Mai heard the sound of steel scraping its way out of a scabbard. The touch of his sword was cold against her throat.

"Whether you should live or die," Yi said.

Thirty-Nine

She was so pretty, Yi's heart sang when he first beheld her. Maybe even beautiful, though it was hard to tell with her face smudged in soot. Her white robes were every bit as fine as those worn by the mistress of the house, though Yi fancied hers curved more at the chest than the older woman's did.

If this was Mao's sister, he would knock Yi down for thinking of her breasts. If the girl was Mao herself…would she knock him down or let him touch them? He caught himself smiling at the thought, and tried to smother it quickly. Not soon enough, though – the girl had seen, and it lit a furious fire in her eyes.

She repeated the same story the other woman – Jing? – had told him, of Mao breaking his neck in a fall. That Yi could not believe. No one could recover from a fall quite as well as Mao. But if he was not here, then the girl had to be one and the same.

She knew him, that was certain, and she knew Mao's nickname for him, too. That meant nothing, though – if he was her brother, he might have told her that and many things about his life in the army and at court.

The shoes would give him his answer. If they fitted her, then she must be Mao, just as his mother had hinted.

A bench was brought, and Yi knelt at the girl's feet, longing for the shoes to fit and yet dreading what it would mean if they did.

He'd never felt so nervous in his life. With Mao, everything had been easy. As friends and brothers in arms, he'd always spoken freely. Yet this woman regarded him with barely concealed contempt.

Heng stepped forward, offering to help, but Yi waved him away. He had to do this. He had to fit the shoes to her feet with his own hands, so that he would know if they were hers. If she had sat on the dais beside him at the ball, fought with him every day, slept beside him at night...

Ancestors. Had he been dreaming of her while he slept beside her?

Yi swallowed and looked down. Somehow, without

realising it, he'd put the shoes on her feet.

"A perfect fit," he breathed. He didn't want to believe it.

Perhaps she wasn't Da Ying's daughter. Or she wasn't Mao. Even as he voiced his doubts, she put them to rest. She was everything he could ever want in a bride, and more.

Except he had not seen her fight. That would be the final proof. Surely no woman could fight like Mao. No man alive could fight like Mao, and definitely no woman could.

He pulled her to her feet and she didn't resist. Did that mean she trusted him, or simply that she was docile? Yi couldn't be sure. He released her, and she landed neatly on her knees. Coincidence, perhaps. Or design.

He wanted to challenge her to a fight, but he would only look foolish in front of his men. The Prince of Swords, challenge a girl on her knees? But if he closed his eyes and imagined the kneeling figure was Mao…

Yi dragged his sword out of its scabbard, his hand resisting every inch of the way. Drawing his sword on a defenceless, unarmed, kneeling woman was dishonourable. She had done nothing wrong, except maybe lie to him. Either she was Mao, and she would laugh at him for daring to draw his sword, or she was Mao's sister, and threatening her would bring the man himself out of hiding. Yi prayed that he was right as he held the blade to her silky throat and threatened her life.

He thought he heard her sigh, and her shoulders slumped the slightest bit. That was all the warning he had before she swept his legs out from under him and snatched the sword out of his hand.

His men drew their weapons, forming a circle that closed in slowly. Uncertainty showed on their faces — none of them wanted to go up against an opponent who could best the Prince of Swords. Why, he was the best swordsman in the kingdom, or so they said.

They were wrong. The best was Mao.

"You wish to dance with me, Prince of Swords?" she asked. "I will dance with you, but on one condition. We dance alone."

A victory, of sorts, thought Yi, as he clambered to his feet. He nodded. "Yes. All of you, sheathe your weapons. Except you. " He pointed at the nearest man. "Hand me your sword. She's going to borrow mine for a moment."

One man sniggered, and the others followed suit. Tension ebbed away from the circle as his men realised what their eyes could already see: their prince in a sparring circle with a girl holding a sword. She was not Mao to them. As for Yi...he wasn't sure what she was to him. His best friend. His best friend's sister. Maybe his bride. If she'd have him.

Doubt crept in. What if she wouldn't?

Weapons slid back into scabbards until the only two naked blades were the one in his hand and the one in hers.

"Shall we dance?" he asked, bowing slightly as he held his sword in readiness.

Her whole face lit up with a smile so dazzling Yi's heart stopped. There was no woman in the world he wanted more.

"We shall," she said, taking a fighting stance.

Forty

It had been weeks since Mai had sparred properly with anyone, so it was impossible to keep the smile from her face as she crossed swords with Yi. Though they carried true steel and not wooden practice swords this time, she was reminded of the night of the ball, when they had circled and danced for what might have been hours as they lost track of the time. Then as now, they had matched one another perfectly. This was neither a fight nor a battle. It truly was a dance.

A dance she wanted to continue forever.

Mai faltered at the thought. She did not dare lift her hopes so high — she knew better now. She might not know why the prince was here, but it could not be to claim her as his bride. Why, he had seen her feet —

shod them himself. He knew she did not have proper lotus feet like a court lady.

So this dance must end, she told herself. Much like the siege of Dean, it would only end when there was a victor. But first, they must fight.

"What will you give me if I win this fight?" she asked suddenly.

Several of Yi's men laughed. Mai did not blame them. After all, they were loyal to their prince, and she was a girl they did not know. Of course they believed his victory was assured.

Yi stared at her for a moment. "I will give you whatever you wish," he said finally.

Your heart, her own heart screamed in her chest, but Mai ignored it. The prince could not be hers. "I wish that you would place my family under your protection, so that they do not fear the Emperor's armies or that of our neighbours. And return the men who left for the siege of Dean, for the siege is over now, yet they have not returned."

He nodded once.

"And when the prince wins?" one of the onlookers called. "What will you give him, girl?"

Mai had already given him her heart. She had nothing else left to give. "If you win, what would you ask of me?" she asked Yi.

His dark eyes regarded hers for a moment that

stretched for far too long.

Then he moved, advancing in a flurry of blows, just as he had on the day they met.

Mai blocked every blow, letting him get closer to her with each one until he was near enough to lean over and whisper into her ear, "I would ask you to be my bride, daughter of Da Ying."

His answer surprised her. Surely she could not have heard right. Yet even as she watched him, he nodded and mouthed one more word: "Mine."

There were many paths to victory, as Mai well knew.

Mai looked deep into his eyes, though two swords separated them, and chose her path.

Forty-One

It was as though time stood still, ready to repeat itself. Yi stood in this courtyard, fighting the woman in white, yet at the same time, he stood in the dust outside Dean, expecting to beat Mao, only to find himself defeated. He lunged, leaving himself open to whatever rapid defence Mao had used on him that first time. Now he would know for sure whether this woman was Mao or someone else entirely.

Her eyes met his, as if she could read his thoughts. She twisted, just as Mao had done, but instead of throwing him to the ground, the girl slipped and landed flat on her back. Defeated, as Yi brought the tip of his sword to her throat.

Her gaze was as tranquil as one of the mountain

lakes he'd passed to reach her home. "Victory is yours, my prince," she murmured.

His heart sank like a stone. No. He didn't want to be victorious. He wanted Mao. This had to be him…her. But he had never beaten Mao in a fight. Never. So this girl with Mao's eyes couldn't be…

"Leave us," he said. When no one obeyed, he repeated, much louder this time, "Leave us!"

His men retreated out the gate while the Yeong household headed back into the house. Where they could all spy on him and the girl, Yi presumed. He hoisted the girl to her feet and dragged her into the nearest building – her ancestral shrine, he realised, once they were inside. A fitting place to execute her, if that was his wish, but if he killed her, any answers she might have died with her.

The strange girl didn't struggle in the slightest, letting him manhandle her into the place without a murmur. Did she want to die?

He released her, expecting her to stumble, but she merely straightened her spine, then remembered herself and bowed her head.

"You're not Mao," Yi said bitterly.

"I told you, Yeong Mao died on the road between the palace and home," she said.

"Then where is his funeral tablet, so that I might burn some incense for his spirit?" Yi demanded. "I owe him my life, and if he is dead, I cannot repay my debt."

The girl swallowed, looking uncomfortable for the first time. "He has none. Nor will he, while I yet live."

"But you are not Mao!" Yi repeated.

She smiled sadly. "No, I am not. I am Yeong Mai, the daughter of Yeong Fu and Da Ying. Victor of the siege of Dean and every bout I have fought against you. Mao was an illusion cast to allow a woman to join the army in her father's place, to save her family. This I have done with honour. I should be content."

"You didn't win that fight out there, and that is why I know you can't be Mao!" Yi said. Mao had perfect balance. Mao would never have slipped…especially not in those magical shoes.

"Because I did not tip you on your royal behind as I did during our first sparring match, and countless times after? You'll never be a good fighter, Rooster, unless you truly master the art of war. I have already won a victory that way. Once I have won, I do not repeat my tactics but respond to circumstances in a variety of ways. A good general is not a predictable one." She stepped close so he could feel her breath on his face as she looked up at him. "Who says I did not win?"

Ancestors help him, Yi wanted to kiss her. To grab this woman with both hands and plunder those lecturing lips until he forgot what she'd said. Until she forgot, too. He forced himself to step back. "Me. I mean, you didn't win. You slipped. I saw you."

"I lay down, with my sword in hand," she corrected, showing him her sheathed blade. Huh. She must have put her sword away as he dragged her across the yard. "It does not follow that because I am victorious, you are not." She gestured toward the courtyard. "And it is not seemly that a prince should be defeated by a girl in front of his own men. You offered a victory more tempting than the one I had planned for, which I choose to accept."

"You choose to…" Nothing made sense any more. Least of all the thoughts in Yi's head. "What do you accept?"

The girl – Mai, Yi reminded himself – licked her lips nervously. "You said if you won, you would take me for your bride. My sisters would consider a prince for a husband to be the ultimate victory. Though I don't often agree with them, this time…I might." Her eyes seemed to dance, though the rest of her stood still, anticipating…something.

Mai or Mao or whoever she was had more pride than the Emperor himself. Yi laughed. "You might consider me a suitable victory prize?"

Mai tilted her head as she scrutinised him. "Your body is sound, and your mind is mostly so. Your sense of humour and manners are charming enough. But you are a terrible fighter. A girl could beat you, Rooster." When she smiled like that, so full of mischief, Yi almost saw Mao in her face…but…she was much prettier than Mao.

"You could beat me?" he asked, assuming a fighting stance. "If you wish to spar again, we will, but the outcome will be the same."

Her smile didn't fade. "I will still win, but without witnesses, you might not." She beckoned him to attack.

Yi strode forward and…

…somehow found himself lying on the cold tiles, gasping for the breath his fall had knocked out of him as his sword clattered against the far wall, out of reach.

Gentle feminine laughter greeted him and he glared up at Mai's joyful face. "Are you happy now, my prince? I can teach you how to fight as I do, you know. My father taught me everything he knew, and I will share it with you. You only have to ask. I know a courtyard in the palace where we can dance together daily, if that is your wish." She held out a delicate hand to help him to his feet.

She couldn't lift him, so Yi waved away her offer of assistance and clambered to his feet on his own. "Mao…"

"Mai," she corrected.

"Mai," he repeated. Even her name on his tongue tasted sweet. "All those nights we shared a tent, I dreamed of a woman I could not see. A woman who held my heart in her hands every moment I was with her. Yet when I tried to see her, all I saw was my roommate, Mao. His face would shock me awake, every time, because when I looked upon him, I felt no desire at all. And now I look at you…and I wonder…"

"I did not dream of you," she admitted slowly. "But when Heng helped me into my armour, I wished it was you." She blushed. "And when we fought together, melee style, I often stood closer to you than necessary, so that I might brush against you during the fight."

"I did not want a bride," he began.

"And I never wished to be one," she finished. "Yet when you offered…" Her eyes grew very wide and dark. Mountain lakes a man could get lost in, if he wasn't careful.

What was he saying? Yi was already lost, a long time ago. "Be mine, Yeong Mai," he said softly. "I cannot send a matchmaker to ask your father for your hand, so I must ask you here, before your ancestral spirits. Will you be my bride, though I am such a terrible fighter, even an orphan girl could beat me? I will endeavour to protect you, and your family, as best I can. Mao was the best friend a man could ever have, but I would ask for more from you, Mai. I want you to be my friend and my lover, as I will be yours. I owe you my life, and I will give it to you freely, one day at a time, every day I have, until we join our ancestors in the spirit realm."

Her eyes held wonder, but also warmth. "I will." A tiny smile teased him. "But first give me a taste of what to expect. I know the quality of your friendship, and what kind of dancer you are, but I am new to love."

She wanted him to make love to her here, in her ancestral shrine? Yi swallowed. "Would a kiss do? A taste?"

She nodded once. "Perhaps." Mai stood calmly with her hands by her sides, waiting.

For him, Yi realised. She had always insisted he attack first, and this was no different. She would judge his kiss the way she judged his fighting. His heart grew cold. What if she found him wanting?

"Are you as experienced at kissing as you are at fighting?" he blurted out.

Her calm evaporated. "I…have never…"

A girl who could put a grown man on his arse as easily as breathing wouldn't have been the victim of stolen kisses, Yi realised. It was a lucky man who could touch her at all.

The thought gave him courage, bolstered by the panic in her eyes. He would protect her and take care of her.

Yi raised his hands to show he was unarmed, then closed the distance between them in two strides. One hand grasped her shoulder – gently, for she was far more delicate than Mao – as he lifted his other hand to her face. Still he hesitated. He didn't want to mess this up, not least because he'd end up flat on his back on the floor if he did.

He traced her lips with his thumb. They were softer and plumper than he'd imagined, even in his dreams. Kissing her would be…

She bit his thumb. Gently, but just enough to sting.

"When campaigning, be swift as the wind," Mai whispered. "Do you wish to fight for my heart, or not, Rooster?"

He remembered the words, for he had heard her say them before the start of every fight. "Plunder like fire, stand as firm as the mountains, and move like a thunderbolt."

His fingers tangled in her hair as he pressed his mouth to hers, lightning-fast. Swift enough to steal the breeze of her breath as she gasped, parting her lips just wide enough to let his tongue plunder her mouth. Desire blazed inside him as her arms wrapped around him, so that her body pressed against his so firmly he wanted to topple them both to the tiles and make love to her then and there. He didn't want just her heart, he wanted her whole body, too, for she had ensnared his spirit so completely he was bound to her already.

After an eternity that was still too short, Mai broke the kiss, laying her head against his heaving chest. "I like your fire, my prince. And you are…quite firm." She was pressed so tightly against him, she couldn't help but feel his arousal.

Yi reddened. "I will control myself until you are no longer in mourning, and we are married," he said.

Mai laughed. "I meant the muscles of your chest, but yes, that one feels firm, too. Like you desire me, even though…I am like this." She gestured at her body.

His gaze followed her waving hand and his desire burned brighter still. "How could I feel anything else? You are not just the most beautiful woman I have ever seen. I have fought at your side, when I should have spent every day fighting for you. You hold my heart, Mai, and you always will." He inhaled some of the incense smoke which made him cough, spoiling the effect of his words.

"It seems my mother's spirit approves," Mai said, pointing at the offending incense. "My father knows better than to go against her wishes. My heart is yours, when you choose to claim it."

Now, his heart urged, but Yi resisted. The girl was still mourning her father, and they could not marry until her mourning period was past. "I choose to claim it now with a kiss, and a promise that the day your mourning ends, I shall have the rest of you, too."

As his arms slipped around her waist, pulling her in close, she said, "You will, my prince," before he silenced her with a soul-consuming kiss.

Forty-Two

The wedding formalities seemed to take an eternity. When Yi escorted her to yet another chamber, Mai swore that if she was forced to drink another cup of tea, she was going to accidentally spill it down her robes so that she could excuse herself to change clothes. If it weren't for Yi at her side, she would have heartily refused to marry at all by the end of the first hour. As it was, she gritted her teeth, kept her eyes lowered and imagined the calm mountain lake beside her family home.

Yi closed the doors behind them. "Would you like some tea?" he offered.

Mai whirled, ready to tell him exactly what she thought of tea, only to discover him grinning with a bottle in his hand.

"Because my family or the servants have only left us this fine bottle of baijiu to drink. No tea at all," Yi finished.

Mai relaxed enough to laugh a little. "If that is anywhere near as good as what we were drinking on the night of the ball, then yes."

Yi unstoppered the bottle with a satisfying pop. He held it to his nose and inhaled deeply. "As I suspected. My father has given us a bottle of his best, to celebrate."

He found two cups and poured the clear liquor into them. Mai reached for the nearest one, but Yi stopped her. "Wait. This is strong stuff. Before we have any, I must make certain I married a woman, and not a man."

Mai raised her hands to remove her veil, but Yi stopped her again.

"Please. I have dreamed about this moment." He laughed nervously. "Usually it's good, and you are a beautiful woman, but sometimes I see the man who knocked me to the ground so many times in training."

"I did not knock you down," Mai replied. "You lost your balance and fell, more often than not because you did not see a blow coming. You should be more observant."

"Tonight, I will be," he promised, reaching for her.

Carefully, he lifted the veil from her head. "Such beautiful hair. I must see it free, as it was the day you bested me in the courtyard of your ancestral home."

She helped him unpin her hair, so that it cascaded down her back.

"So beautiful," he breathed, stroking her hair.

No one had ever touched her like this before. Mai closed her eyes, finally understanding why her stepmother's cat purred when she stroked it. If Mai could purr, she would definitely do so when Yi stroked her like this.

She wanted to protest when he stopped, but his hands had moved to her front, untying her robe, so he could slip it off her shoulders, leaving her clad only in her underskirt.

Yi's eyes shone with admiration. "To think I bathed beside you a thousand times, and shared a tent with you for countless nights, and yet I never saw these sweet breasts. You are right. I should have been more observant."

Mai felt her cheeks grow hot as he continued to stare at her chest. "You definitely did not bathe with me a thousand times. A hundred, or maybe two, but you avoided bathing for days at a time. I bathed a thousand times, morning and night, and sometimes after a hard training session. I may have pretended to be a man, but I could not tolerate smelling like one."

"You have always smelled like paradise," Yi admitted. "Sometimes, I wondered what was wrong with me, for I would wake many a morning filled with desire, and yet when I opened my eyes I would see Mao, a man I did not desire at all. Yet now, it all makes sense, and I cannot resist." He cupped her breasts reverently, bowing to kiss each one.

Mai gasped at his touch, wanting to beg for more but too nervous to say a word. She swallowed, and made her decision. She unfastened her underskirt and let that fall, stepping out of her shoes so she stood naked before him. "This is the body you bathed with, and lay on the pallet beside you when we shared a tent. I am smaller than Mao, and softer, but I wear the same scars. I – "

Yi trailed a line of kisses down her shoulder. "I fought at your side as you gained every one of them. And to think I allowed Heng to dress you in your armour, when it could have been my hands on you every day. I only wish I could have protected you from war the way a man is supposed to protect his wife. I promise you will never have to fight another battle for as long as I live."

"Only if you do not fight any, either," she countered. "For the best swordsman in the empire, you have needed to be saved a lot." She smiled. "But if I go to war again at your side, your hands alone will help me with my armour. You don't know how many times I wished it was you instead of Heng."

Yi bowed. "As my lady wishes, if duty and the Emperor allow."

Duty. It was their duty to consummate this marriage, and Mai had longed for this for…longer than she liked to admit. "Right now, your duty is to disrobe for your wife," Mai said, more nervous than she expected.

She had seen him naked so many times, she could trace every scar from memory. Yet now he was her husband, and that fierce warrior body would join with hers, her heart danced in her chest in anticipation. Eager anticipation.

Now he was the one who hesitated. "I have more scars than you. Some from our last battle which have not completely healed. If you expected a husband who is handsome and whole, I am no longer that man. The scars on my back…"

"My prince, I will know and love every scar, for as you say, I fought at your side as you gained every one of them," Mai said. She unfastened Yi's robes, baring him to the waist as they fell to the floor. She moistened her lips nervously, then reached for the cord holding his pants up and untied that, too. Trying not to think about how they were both naked, she forced herself to walk around him, taking note of every scar from the faded lines on his shins through to the badly-healed burns on his back. She couldn't help laying her hand on the shiny skin. "Does it still hurt?" she murmured.

"No, and with your hands on me like that, I would burn again, just to feel your touch," Yi said.

"My hands are yours to command, my prince," she replied. "After all, you won the fight, and you have yet to claim your prize."

"I want to claim you, but you are no prize," he said, pulling her hard against him when she opened her mouth to protest. "You are the reason I will fight my whole life long, so that I can keep you, and keep you safe. For I could stand losing each and every city in the kingdom, and even the throne itself, but I would not survive losing you. I love you, Mai, my dancer, my balance, and all the honour and glory a man could hope for. All I can offer in return is myself, as your prince."

Her prince. Yes. Holding tight to him, she backed him toward the bed until she tripped him and he tipped backward onto the mattress. Yi didn't let go of her, so she landed on top of him, blissfully aware of his hard, naked body beneath her.

Remembering the bold camp followers she'd envied so long ago, Mai sat up, straddling Yi's hips. She drew in a deep breath and drove her hips down, taking his length inside her. She gasped at the strange fullness, but it felt so right that it was but a moment before she started to move, riding him like she'd wanted to for so long.

"Mai…oh, ancestors, Mai!" he cried, grasping her hips as he thrust into her, matching her rhythm perfectly.

Balance. This was balance, the transcendental dance of two lovers so perfect for each other that when they joined, the rest of the world fell away.

And then the balance tipped, sending Mai's very soul flying to the heavens as she cried out for joy. Yet as she flew, Yi's arms held her securely, as his matching cry rang out across the sky. They flew together as one.

Mingled, joyous sounds that would ring in her ears for ever after, as Yi made her happy, again and again. Finally, Mai understood the fairy tales, knowing that if anyone got to live as happily ever after as her and her prince, then they were fortunate indeed.

451

Fly:
Goose Girl
Retold

DEMELZA CARLTON

Book 3 in the Romance a Medieval Fairy Tale series

cdlii

One

"Hurry up, you goose! If the guard returns, you'll get us all into trouble!" Lagle hissed.

Ava bent to retrieve the towel she'd dropped, then, obedient to her sister's order, broke into a run as she fancied she heard footsteps. If the guards caught the princesses out of the harem, they'd only lock the girls back in, but then they wouldn't get to swim.

And Lagle would definitely blame her. The guards might not punish princesses, but Lagle was the Queen's daughter, making her the highest ranking princess among the myriad daughters of minor wives and concubines, and she would be certain to make Ava's life hell.

So Bianca led the way to the pool, swearing she'd gotten directions from one of the young princes who'd watched soldiers learning to swim there. Lagle strode behind her with her proud head held high, and Ava brought up the rear with a bundle of towels that was too heavy for her to carry without dropping them along the way. When yet another towel slipped from her grasp, earning her a glare from Lagle, Ava was almost ready to give up and head back to the harem. The only thing that kept her putting one foot in front of the other was the thought of the tantalising coolness of immersing her whole body in water, while the rest of the palace sweltered in the unseasonable spring heat. To stop being sweaty and sticky for just a few hours would be bliss, and well worth the walk even with a load of towels.

And Bianca would be there, Ava consoled

herself. The expedition might be Lagle's idea, but without Bianca, it could not have happened. Bianca was the only one of her sisters who seemed to see Ava at all. To the rest, she was invisible, a princess so low in the pecking order that they rarely remembered her name. Most of them didn't remember her mother's name, either, for Sumi had died giving birth to Ava, a scant seven months after entering the harem. A captured prize from one of the King's many battles, Ava had heard, who the King had favoured for a few short weeks until some other jewel of his harem caught his eye. A harem Ava had left only a handful of times, because the King protected his daughters fiercely, whether they were as highborn as Lagle or as insignificant as Ava.

If he knew three of them had sneaked out of the harem, heading for the soldiers' barracks...Ava shivered.

Moonlight sparkled on the pool surface, making it look almost magical. Two towels escaped from her arms, which made her deliberately drop the rest in a pile on the tiles. Bianca and Lagle had already started to shed their robes, so Ava shyly followed suit.

Bianca entered the water silently, slipping under the surface before swimming away from the edge. Ava was impressed, and she began to wonder how often Bianca had visited this pool before. She couldn't have learned such swimming skills in the harem.

Lagle jumped into the water with a splash and a squeal. Ava opened her mouth to beg her to be quieter, but she knew it was no use. When had Lagle ever listened to anyone, let alone Ava?

Ava crept across the tiles to the pool edge. The stone was surprisingly warm underfoot, perhaps from lying in the sun all day, and it was with considerable relief that she dipped her toes into the water. "It's cold!" she exclaimed.

"It's best to get in all at once. You'll soon grow used to it," Bianca advised.

Ava pulled her foot out of the water, and a

breezy gust chilled her wet skin. If one foot could be this cold, what would it be like when she hoisted her whole body out of the water, soaking wet? Why, she would freeze.

"I've changed my mind," she murmured, backing away from the water.

Lagle sent a wave of water in her direction. "Coward! Swelter, then. See if I care."

Ava reached her clothes and struggled back into them. She couldn't be sure if she'd tied everything correctly, in the dark without a mirror and all, but she did the best she could.

She sat beside the towels, drowsing in the heat while her sisters splashed. None of them had slept well with the heat these last few nights, but her airless cubicle was flush against the western wall of the women's palace, turning it into a veritable oven. Perhaps if she lay here for a few moments until the other girls were finished in the water…

Ava stretched out on the towels and slipped into a dream.

Two

Not for the first time, Yun wondered when this nightmare would end. Certainly not today, or tomorrow, for there were too many corpses to bury after this latest battle. Not that he'd be doing it – burying the dead was work for common soldiers, not princes.

Princes were supposed to take pleasure in sights like this, or so his older brothers told him. Then again, his brothers took pleasure in a great many things that turned Yun's stomach.

Take Gang, the heir to the throne and their

illustrious general, and Chao, second in line on both counts. They had set up camp just outside of town, and the pen where their horses should have been was now filled with sobbing women. The wives and daughters of the men who had died on the battlefield, defending the village, Yun assumed from their clothing.

He didn't need to follow the grunts, whimpers and screams to know his brothers had already started celebrating their victory. He wished he didn't have to witness it, but their father would not wait.

Shoving his way into Gang's tent, he averted his eyes from his rutting brother and the girl who squirmed and sobbed beneath him.

"What word shall I send to Father about the battle?" Yun asked.

"Can't it wait?" Gang grunted. He backhanded the girl across the face. "Silence! I can't hear a thing over your whining!"

"I wish it could, but Father must know our losses, and how many – "

"Enough!" Gang roared, drawing his dagger. He plunged the blade into the girl's throat, then yanked it out again. While the girl choked on her own blood, he rose to his feet and tugged down his robe. "What did you say? I couldn't hear you over that bitch's complaints. I told her to shut her mouth, but like all women, she wouldn't listen. She would have made a terrible wife. I did the world a favour." He grinned, wiping his dagger on the dead girl's ripped garments before sheathing it at his waist.

Yun fought down the bile rising up in his throat. How he'd grown up in the same household with Gang, he did not know. "I said, Father will want to know how many of our men died, and how many of the enemy. We must send a rider today."

Gang shrugged. "I don't know. Ask Chao. He keeps track of such things. Can't you see I'm busy?" He ambled out to the pen and seized the nearest girl by her hair. When she screamed in pain, Gang drew his dagger and sliced off her tongue. Then he dragged the gurgling girl to his tent.

Judging by the screams coming from Chao's tent, Yun wouldn't like what he found there, either. But, unlike his brothers, he was an obedient son.

Yun was gratified to find Chao still had his clothes on, though he had a girl in his tent, too. He'd tied her to the tent pole in the centre and chosen to amuse himself with one of the whips the enemy troops used on their horses. He must have been at it for some time, because the short lash had already turned the girl's clothes to ribbons and her exposed skin was a mess of bloody stripes.

"What do you want?" Chao snapped.

To stop this, Yun thought but didn't say. "Numbers for Father. How many dead?"

Chao tucked the whip under his arm and headed for the tiny table in the corner that was already covered in scrolls. He unrolled three before he found the one he wanted, and thrust it at Yun. "Here. Go. If you come back quickly, there might be some girls left for you, too, if we're not through with them yet."

Struggling to keep his expression blank instead of revealing his horror, Yun thanked his brother and hurried out.

For a moment, he stopped beside the pen. The women shrank away from him, as though they'd heard Chao's offer. Perhaps they had.

He glanced around. No one was in view, and his brothers were busy. Yun approached the gate. Any of them could have opened it, for it was latched to keep horses from escaping, not humans. Yet none had.

"Run," he told them, flinging open the gate. "If they catch you, they will kill you."

One woman lifted her head. "We have nowhere to go. They killed everyone else, rounded up us women and…some of us were sent here, while the rest are in the main camp. Entertaining the army." Her accusing eyes told him she knew exactly what that entailed.

"Then die here, or fly and hope to live. The choice is yours, but you are fools if you stay here," Yun said. He turned on his heel and headed deeper into the camp in search of a messenger to carry word home of their victory.

Behind him, a dozen frightened birds flew from their coop. Yun hoped that the ancestors would watch over the escaped girls, even if they weren't his people. They deserved to fly free and not die slaves.

The sounds of revelry drifted through the camp. It seems that the soldiers had discovered the other girls, the ones his brothers had rejected. No doubt all the messengers were taking their turns along with the other men.

Was there something wrong with Yun that he liked his women willing, he wondered. For if the rest of the army derived so much pleasure from striking fear into feminine hearts, surely the fault lay with him.

He did not belong here.

Yun himself would carry word to his father. Leave this stinking battlefield and its sickening pleasures to those who enjoyed such things. Yun would ride for home, and do everything in his power to persuade his father to call off this war.

And as Yun rode off, startling clouds of crows which had already begun to feast on the bloated corpses, he swore that he would rather be among them than become like his brothers.

Three

Bright light beat at Ava's eyelids. She groaned softly. She must have overslept, and now someone had come to fetch her to breakfast.

"Who is she?" a male voice asked.

Ava jerked awake. Men didn't belong in the harem. She sat up, pulling her robes tight around her, and found she was the focus of a dozen pairs of staring eyes.

"Ava," she managed to say, in a voice so small a mouse would be ashamed to own it.

"Look at the cloth. That's silk. She must be

a maid to some great lady, if she gets to wear silk." The speaker thrust his face close to Ava's. "What are you doing here, serving maid? Don't you know a soldiers' camp is dangerous? Or did you meet your sweetheart here last night?"

Loud laughter rang out.

Ava tucked herself up smaller. If she could have magicked herself invisible, she would have.

"Who were you meeting, girl?" an authoritative voice demanded, and the laughter died. A soldier more richly dressed than the others stepped forward. "Tell me his name!"

"I wasn't meeting anyone," she whispered, feeling tears form. She wasn't used to being shouted at.

"Then tell me the name of your mistress. She will get his name out of you, I have no doubt."

Ava shook her head. "I am no one's mistress. I am a maiden, sir." Her cheeks grew hot. A maiden among so many men — this was why she should have stayed in the harem. "My sisters…" She stopped, not willing to draw Lagle and Bianca into her predicament. Perhaps they had made it back to the harem already, missing her in the dark, thinking she had already left.

"What about your sisters?" the man in charge asked.

"They will miss me at breakfast," she admitted. "They will search the harem for me. Perhaps they are already. It is past breakfast, I think."

The man muttered a curse, then pointed at two men. "Batu, Esen. Take her to the harem, and find out who her mistress is. When she is safely inside, return with names."

Both men bowed. "Yes, General."

Batu offered his arm to help Ava to her feet. At first, she hesitated, then realised if she didn't accept his assistance, these men might take hold of her and carry her back. She rested her fingers lightly on his arm and leaped to her feet, breaking the contact before she was burned by it. For she would be, she was certain of it – to touch a man or be touched by him was to be changed forever.

She rubbed her tainted fingertips against her skirt, hoping that such a tiny, brief contact wouldn't be enough to change her. She scarcely had any place in the harem as it was. Where would she go if they threw her out?

The doors to the women's palace loomed like they never had before. Two guards stood sentinel, relaxing in relief when they spotted Ava.

"You found her!" the guard on the left said.

The soldiers exchanged glances. "We did."

"Where?" Right asked eagerly.

Batu said, "By the barracks pool."

The guards bowed low. "Princess, how did you get to the barracks?"

She could not betray her sisters. Ava shook her head. "I do not know. I woke up and there were men..." She shuddered and her voice died.

"Tell the Queen she is found. Summon

servants to help the Princess. Quickly!" Left said to someone inside the palace.

"Princess." The soldiers seemed to realise it at the same moment, sinking to their knees and touching their foreheads to the tiles.

Ava wanted to sink through the floor. "I'm tired. I want to sleep," she lied. Anything to get her out of their sight.

"Come, Princess," said a female voice. Two wide-eyed maids took her arms and led her into the palace.

Ava was too weak to protest as she was taken to her chamber, undressed, and put into bed.

She wasn't changed, she told herself. She wasn't.

But she couldn't help thinking of the soldier she'd touched, however briefly. Batu, that was his name. He'd rubbed his arm as he walked away, with a stunned look of something like awe on his face. She might not be changed, but Batu would not forget this day. She lay back and wished she could forget.

Four

Dirty from long days of travel, Yun knew he could not bathe until he had delivered his report. So he made his weary way to the throne room and prostrated himself at his father's feet.

The petitioner who Yun had interrupted nudged Yun's leg with his foot. "What is the meaning of this? Who is this ruffian?" he demanded.

A country baron who had never been to court before, Yun guessed.

"I am Prince Yun Bataar, your youngest son, Divine Emperor," Yun said. "Please forgive my dishevelled state. I bring news of the battle on our southern borders. Our armies were victorious once more, with numerous enemy slain." He proffered the scroll Chao had given him. "A report from Prince Chao."

"Get up and give it to me," Father said wearily, holding out his hand.

Yun jumped to his feet and ascended the dais to his father's side. "It was a slaughter," Yun said. "I'd be surprised if Chinggis can field a proper army after that, we've killed so many of them. If it were up to me, we'd call off the war here and now. No more fighting."

"And what about their attacks in the south-eastern villages? Baron Dong tells me he has no one left to plant next season's crops, for they are all dead. Chinggis has an army, and they outnumber us. If we stop fighting, their victory is assured, which is why this war will continue as long as I or Chinggis lives. Only a fool would think of stopping." Father eyed

Yun darkly. "But you have always been a fool, writing songs and poems when your brothers were learning to rule. Good thing you are the youngest son and you will never be Emperor. If you were to rule in my place, the empire would fall." He laughed, and was echoed a moment later by the rest of the court.

When the empire's army was too busy raping the women of one village to save their own people, perhaps it deserved to fall.

Yun gritted his teeth, biting back the retort he wanted to make. He'd learned everything his brothers had, and he was far from a fool. Which was why he held his tongue.

"You may return to the army and tell your brothers they have done well, but they need to march for the south-east at once."

Where his brothers would find no sign of Chinggis' army, so they would cross the border to slaughter another village in the name of retribution. And procure more women…

Yun tasted bile in the back of his throat. He had no desire to watch his brothers torment people who had done nothing to deserve it. Better to be a court fool than a dishonourable soldier.

But his father wouldn't want to hear a word against his favourite sons.

"Oh, but I couldn't!" Yun exclaimed in feigned horror. "Not after my first campaign. I must compose an epic poem about our most recent victory while it is still clear in my mind!" He wanted to cringe at how foolish he sounded. Surely his father wouldn't believe…

The Emperor clapped his hands. "That's my boy! After their first battle, your brothers all wanted another one, but you want a poem, and you shall have it! Never let it be said that I don't treasure my sons. You write what you will, and you may perform it when your brothers return victorious." He waved at a nearby servant. "Go with the prince, and make sure my boy has everything he needs."

Yun muttered his thanks and bowed briefly before he fled the court, with the servant close behind.

More than ever, he wanted to vomit. How could he create something that glorified torture and slaughter, when he wanted to stop it?

Perhaps he was a fool after all.

Five

Ava expected to be summoned to her father's throne room at any moment, but as the day dragged on, boredom overtook fear in her mind. There was nothing in her sleeping cubicle but the bed, and lying on it didn't bring her any rest. Curse her for falling asleep last night.

What would her punishment be? If it involved incarceration in a chamber as small as this one, she would lose her wits within the week. She could feel them slipping even now…

Someone threw open the door and Ava blinked in the light, trying to focus on the person who stood in the doorway. "You are to come with me," a female voice said, gesturing imperiously.

Ava clambered to her feet and followed the woman she did not know to a part of the women's palace that was forbidden to her, and, in fact, most of the other princesses: the Queen's apartments.

As the King's principal wife, her apartments were as big as the rest of the harem the other women shared, and the two were separated by a set of double doors that looked gold, or gold-skinned, at least. Her father had conquered enough territory to own solid gold doors, if he so chose, Ava knew, but she wasn't sure why he would want them here, where few people would see them. Why, only the Queen, and the Queen's servants ever entered these chambers. If the King wanted any of his wives or concubines, he summoned them to his own chambers.

"She awaits you inside," the serving woman said.

Ava took a deep breath and pushed open those gleaming doors, then stepped through. Rich carpets covered the floors here, all the way up to a dais where the Queen lounged on a pile of cushions. A throne room without a throne, for the Queen's power came not from a chair but a bed.

Ava shivered. The most powerful woman she knew only had power because she opened her legs to a powerful man, so that she might bear his children. Was that the best destiny she could aspire to? If importance came at the price of letting some man paw her, then Ava didn't want to be significant. Men could keep their hands and all their other parts to themselves, as far as she was concerned. At least her body would be her own.

Unless the man were one who was so awed by her, like Batu had been, that his every touch, his every caress, was like a paean of worship to a goddess.

Ava almost laughed aloud at the thought. She was no goddess. She was barely even a princess, for her mother had been only a concubine, and the King could have chosen not to acknowledge her as his daughter. If she was the goddess of anything, it was shyness. A deity so minor, no one ever noticed her to pray to her, which was probably a good thing.

Ava reached the foot of the dais and bowed low, touching her forehead to the floor, then waited.

"So you are the girl who escaped the harem to seduce some common soldier," the Queen said.

It was on the tip of Ava's tongue to tell her the whole expedition had been Lagle's idea, but she kept her mouth firmly shut. The Queen hadn't asked her to speak, let alone rise, yet.

"But what more could one expect? Your mother was little more than a common whore when she seduced my husband on the battlefield. That he brought her here to the harem was an insult to all the noble-born wives who had to share it with her. And you!" The Queen surveyed Ava, her lip curled in disgust. "Running off to the barracks at the first opportunity! You can't be kept in the harem with the other, more virtuous princesses."

"Like Lagle?" Ava retorted before she could think to close her mouth.

The Queen pounced. "Exactly! You should be trying to emulate my daughter. In fact, that is exactly what you will do. Henceforth, you shall be her lady-in-waiting so that you learn how a proper princess behaves."

Like a spoiled brat, Ava thought darkly but mercifully managed not to say. At least she wouldn't be forced to serve Lagle for long. Her sister's upcoming nuptials were common knowledge. The Queen wouldn't want her…

The Queen continued, "You will accompany Lagle to her husband's palace when she marries, for she must have attendants. That should keep you out of trouble, and far from the young princesses who might be corrupted by your bad example. Lagle is too far above you to sully herself in such things."

Ava's mouth dropped open and she couldn't seem to close it. Leave the harem as Lagle's servant? Did the Queen not know her daughter at all?

Evidently not.

"You had best pack your belongings. Lagle leaves within the week."

Coldness settled over Ava. Exile. She had thought the Queen would send her to the Summer Palace, as rumour said she did with any other princess who irritated her. But sending her to a foreign court with Lagle would be much worse.

"Consider yourself lucky, girl. There are dozens of other highborn girls who would be honoured to serve Lagle when she becomes a queen in her own right. If you do not thank me, I will think you terribly ungrateful."

"I thank you, Your Majesty," Ava said dully.

"You may go."

Ava backed out of the Queen's presence with all haste. It was only when the golden doors closed behind her that Ava dared to breathe again. Her shoulders drooped as her heavy fate settled on them.

Exile with Lagle. Horrors.

Perhaps life imprisonment wouldn't have been so bad. Too late now.

Ava sighed, and accepted her fate. What choice did she have?

She hurried back to the harem to find Bianca, her only friend, and tell the other girl what had happened.

Six

Yun stared at the blank piece of parchment, but he didn't see it. Instead, he saw the pale faces of the girls shut in that horse enclosure, blank and awaiting their fate. Or the corpses of their dead men, who died fighting to save them. Died, and failed.

Farmers. Peasants. Not fighters.

Their daughters and wives. Dead now, like their menfolk, he had no doubt.

He rose from his stool and paced the room.

He wished he'd never gone to war. Never

killed, never seen the aftermath. Never seen the monsters his brothers became. But it was too late for wishes now. Wishes could not bring back the dead whose vengeful spirits would haunt him until the day he died, and maybe afterwards in hell, too.

How could he glorify the slaughter he'd seen?

Yun didn't have words to describe it, and the pictures in his head would not let him rest.

He plunged the brush into the ink and yanked it out again, splattering the table with black spots. Dried blood, he thought, as he swiped the brush across the page. Dead faces with eyes that stared, dead eyes in living faces, and still he heard their screams. He drew their essence on the paper in stark black lines until there was no pristine paper to soil with the people of his nightmares.

And still it was not enough.

Yun sank to the floor, cradling his head in his hands.

He was a fool, like his father said. A fool to

have gone to war, a fool to have come home again.

For one heartsick moment, he wished he was more like his brothers. Capable of revelling in the suffering of others, taking pleasure in causing it.

Then sanity returned.

Yun grabbed the sheets littering the table, crumpling them into a ball against his chest. He pitched the papers into the fire, watching the flames flare up and consume his creations. If only the fire could consume his visions as well. He would welcome hell after death if it could make him forget.

Seven

"You're going where?" Bianca exclaimed.

"To the nether hells, where I'll have to serve Queen Lagle," Ava repeated.

Bianca shook her head. "I don't understand. Why? Lagle doesn't even like you. Why would she ask for you to accompany her to her new court?"

"Because of last night," Ava admitted.

Bianca clapped her hands to her mouth. "You mean you were caught coming back? Is that why no one could find you this morning?

Last night, when we finished swimming, Lagle said she saw you leave, so we should hurry back before we were caught."

"I fell asleep in the garden and when I woke up this morning, the courtyard was full of soldiers."

Bianca paled – quite a feat, seeing as her skin was the palest of any of the princesses already. "Surrounded by men? What did you do?"

Not wanting to admit the embarrassing truth, Ava asked, "What would you have done?"

"I would have done my best to disappear," Bianca began, then stopped. "Run, of course. What did you do?"

"I…" Ava reddened. "I tried to disappear, but there were so many of them. I'm no witch, who can make myself invisible at will." From the way Bianca avoided her eyes, Ava suspected her sister knew more of such things than she did. More than once, she'd seen a shimmer of magic around Bianca. "I did what I always do. I fell to pieces. I'm not brave like you, or even Lagle. They marched me back here until the Queen summoned me to tell me my punishment. Hell serving Lagle."

"How many soldiers were there?" Bianca demanded.

"Dozens. I didn't think to count them."

Bianca waved her hand in dismissal. "Any girl surrounded by a dozen men, let alone more than that, would be crazy not to be afraid. Yet you must have done the right thing, for they didn't hurt you, did they? Against a dozen men, I'm sure I wouldn't have your presence of mind. You are as brave as you need to be. As brave as Lagle, or me, or any one of us. You are our father's daughter, and he fears nothing."

Ava managed a watery smile. "Sometimes I wonder."

Bianca shook her head. "Don't. You were born here, which makes you one of us. The daughter of a slave, a concubine, a wife or a queen, it doesn't matter – you are the daughter of the King. A princess in your own right. In any foreign court, that makes you Lagle's equal, and don't let her airs and graces fool you. She is no better than any of us." She grasped Ava's hand. "Once you leave here, forget everything you thought you knew of harem politics. You are a princess, and you bow to no one but your king and your husband. And who knows? Maybe a husband awaits you, too – Lagle might marry the king, but he could have brothers or sons who are worthy of you. They will not notice a servant…but they will notice a princess who stands proud. The Queen might think this a punishment, but she is wrong. This is freedom for you. I only wish I could be so lucky."

Ava's fingers tightened around Bianca's. "Come with me. Please."

Bianca bowed her head. "I cannot. The Queen's attention fell on me today while we searched for you, and she chose to send me away, too. I leave for the Summer Palace."

"No!"

Bianca smiled sadly. "Yes. It is not so bad. Without you here, I should be lonely. At least at the Summer Palace, I will have the company of other banished sisters. Hazel was sent there, I believe. And Brenna. There is a lake there, I have heard, where we may swim in summer."

Swimming. Not something Ava ever wanted to do. "You will like that," she said grudgingly.

"Only if you promise to make the most of this wondrous opportunity, too. Swear to me that you will not be a mouse any more. Once you leave this palace, you will have the courage and strength of a koi, swimming upstream. No matter how high the waterfall, you will leap to the top. Promise me!" Bianca insisted.

Ava choked out a laugh. "You want me to promise to be a fish?"

"The bravest, most determined fish, who will one day become a dragon, while the rest of us must swim in the stream. Sumi would want this for you, though she is among the ancestors now. Be the fish who flies, Ava." The entreaty in Bianca's eyes brought Ava to tears.

"I will," Ava swore. "By our shared ancestors, and my mother, I swear to you that I will do everything in my power to leave the mouse behind. For you, I will be a leaping koi."

She only hoped she would have the strength to keep her promise.

Eight

"What ails you, Little Fish?"

Yun turned in surprise to find his mother standing in the doorway to his apartment. She hadn't called him that name for a very long time.

He dropped his brush on the table. "It seems I cannot write poetry any more."

The Empress waved her hand airily. "Who can? It is a fine thing for a boy to play with, but you are a man now. A man who has been to war, and come back alive. Not many can say that." She eyed the drawings scattered across the table.

Yun rushed to cover the corpses, but it was too late. His mother had seen all. "Forgive me, Mother. These are not something an empress should see."

"It's not something anyone should see," she said. "What you need is a distraction."

Yun wasn't sure whether he wanted to laugh or cry. What in the world had he not yet tried that could possibly take the battlefield out of his brain?

"A wife would keep you busy."

Yun stared. "A what?"

The Empress's eyes were calculating. "A wife. There are plenty of unwed girls in the palace, daughters to members of the court. Your father gets a dozen petitions every week to let you wed one of them. He thinks you are a boy still."

"No one who has survived a battle like that one is a child. The things I have seen…" Yun shuddered. "Mother, I am a man, but a broken one. What use would I be to a wife? How could I look at her without seeing..." He swallowed. He couldn't tell her about the girls his brothers raped. There were some things no empress should know.

"You are not your brothers," Mother said sharply. "If you treat your wife as they have done theirs, you will no longer be welcome to visit me."

His mother's apartments and pleasure garden were the only place he could find peace, if for a few moments, and she knew it.

"Is there anything you do not know about what goes on in the palace, Mother?" Yun asked.

Mother sniffed. "I am the Empress. There had better not be, or my spies are remiss in their duties. What do you want in a wife? Young? Or closer to your age? Court raised, or from one of the provinces? Pretty, of course, to please your artist's eye. What of her disposition? You are not likely to frighten a girl into obedience, like your brothers, so I suppose you will want one who is already quite docile. Perhaps one with skill in healing, who can help you sleep. Or would you prefer her to be able to sing you to sleep?"

Dizzied by details, Yun shook his head. "Mother, you ask too much. If I must have a wife, my only measure of feminine perfection is yourself, and there can only be one Empress."

Mother narrowed her eyes. "Don't be foolish. A girl fit to be the next empress after me would never be content to marry a youngest son. She would push you to be more ambitious, to make your father name you heir instead of your brothers. She would twist you into a man who is not my son."

"Ancestors forbid any woman try to take me away from you, Mother," Yun said. "So it is best if I do not take a wife at all. What would I need one for, anyway? Father would only send my sons to war and my daughters to marry men he wishes to honour. My brothers can sire such children on their wives. No need for me to get involved."

"No, I should find a girl for you. You will choose wrong. My spies tell me things you will never know until it is too late," Mother declared. "It is settled, then. I will find you a wife, and you will marry her."

Yun sighed. There was no point arguing with the Empress. "Yes, Mother."

Nine

On the morning of her departure, Ava was surprised to find both Bianca and Bianca's mother, Militsa, in the courtyard, among the milling horses and men.

"What are you doing here?" Ava asked.

Militsa smiled indulgently. "On the day both my daughters leave the shelter of the palace for the wide world, I wouldn't be anywhere else."

Ava ducked her head. She wasn't Militsa's daughter, not truly, and no one could mistake them for kin. Militsa's ice-pale hair, only a shade lighter than Bianca's, marked her for what she was: a daughter of a chief from one of the tribes in the far north, taken as a hostage to ensure her father's good behaviour. With a courage Ava found hard to emulate, Militsa had turned her captivity to her advantage, becoming one of the King's concubines. She had been friends with Ava's own mother, Sumi, during the brief time Sumi lived in the harem, and when Sumi lay in a welter of blood on her birthing bed, she had placed Ava in Militsa's arms and begged her friend to take care of the baby. If it weren't for Militsa's kindness, Ava might have died alongside her mother.

"I'm going, too," Bianca said cheerfully, interrupting Ava's reverie. "Our father's guards will escort us to the border, which you and Lagle will cross alone, for the city is not far, and while the Emperor's troops might attack a party of fighting men, they would not harm two highborn women, travelling alone. The guards will take me to the Summer Palace, for there are tales of discharged soldiers and other disreputable men who prey on travellers who take the army roads, as we must. No common soldier shall have me!" She waved her hand and it seemed to Ava that a silvery glow enveloped her fingers.

A glow Ava had seen before, though others had not. Sometimes, when Bianca sneaked through the harem unseen, such a glow had encompassed her whole body. Magic, somehow enhancing her ability to hide. Bianca had never spoken of it, and Ava had never been brave enough to ask, but Bianca's mother's eyes missed nothing.

Militsa embraced Ava, in the fashion of the northern tribes, for such things were foreign to Ava's own people. Yet she endured it, because she knew it was Militsa's way of showing her love. "Watch for evil magic," Militsa whispered. "The Queen's daughter has no magic of her own, but the Queen will not send her to a foreign court without a spell or two to protect her, and possibly more besides. For all this talk of a marriage alliance bringing peace, I fear this one will only escalate the war."

Ava opened her mouth to ask what Militsa meant, but the woman pulled away and nodded toward Lagle and her mother, who had finally deigned to join the travelling party.

The guardsmen bowed as the two ladies passed, before returning to the business of readying the horses for the ride. So it was only the three women who noticed the exchange between the Queen and her daughter.

Lagle struggled into the saddle, even with the aid of a mounting block. She was no horsewoman, thought Ava as she stroked her own mount's flank. The women's palace had included a small stable and a park in which they might ride. Granted, the park was too small for the ponies to move faster than a sedate walk, but Lagle had not set foot in there for as long as Ava could remember. As she and Bianca rode every day the weather was fine, Ava guessed this meant Lagle had not sat astride a horse before. Falada, a great grey horse that contrasted strongly with the others' much darker mounts, shifted from foot to foot under Lagle's weight, as though trying to decide whether she could be bucked off.

A groom caught the beast's bridle, forcing it to stand still.

"A gift for you, which you must wear always," the Queen said, handing something up to Lagle. It appeared to be a necklace, for the girl slipped it over her head and the pendant sat on her breast, glowing red. "As long as you wear it, you will never forget who you are, where you came from, and what you must do." At her words, it flared brighter.

"I will never forget," Lagle said, tossing her head. The horse copied her, nearly unseating her, if it weren't for the groom's grip on the animal. When Lagle regained her balance, she tugged her cloak forward, hiding the necklace from sight.

Ava turned to ask Militsa and Bianca whether they'd seen the strange glow, but they had moved across the courtyard to stand beside Bianca's horse. As she watched, the mother and daughter embraced before Bianca leaped lightly into her saddle. Her horse danced beneath her, but Bianca merely patted the mare's neck and it settled.

Ava's turn. She leaned into her horse's flank, breathing in the animal's warm scent to reassure her. She wasn't afraid, she told herself. She wasn't. Ava swung into the saddle, taking courage from the mare's steady strength. She would be brave, just like she'd promised.

Bianca brought her mount beside her. "Thinking fishy thoughts, sister?" she asked.

Brave, fishy thoughts. "Indeed," Ava said.

"Form up!" the guard captain bellowed. "We're heading out!"

Ava obediently nudged her horse to walk in step with Bianca's as the troop moved out.

"Time for a new adventure," Bianca said, grinning. She always did like listening to tales, though some of them terrified Ava. Heroes and battles and monsters and...

Ava shuddered.

"Fishy thoughts," Bianca reminded her.

"Fishy thoughts," Ava echoed. She managed a wan smile. "Bring on the adventure."

Ten

"You should choose her, Little Fish," Gang said, nodding at a girl who didn't look more than six years old. He chortled. "She's probably all you can handle."

"No, that one!" Chao said, pointing at the child's nursemaid, who looked older than Mother. "Much more obedient. Our Little Fish needs a docile bride, for he is not used to command."

Yun glowered at his older brothers before a quelling look from the Emperor silenced them for a moment as they lined up on either side of him.

Then Gang said, "Hurry up and choose one, Little Fish. Mine is barren, and I want to pick her replacement. I will never hear the end of it from Mother if I steal the toy my baby brother wants, so make your choice!"

Oh, as if the pressure from his mother wasn't bad enough. Now he had to worry about what his brothers might do to the girls he hadn't chosen. They could take them as concubines, or discard their wives to take new ones. Whereas Yun could only save one from their clutches. Letting his mother select the girl seemed like a coward's way out.

Their father held court, shooting them occasional glances to quiet them, but his brothers teased him mercilessly. By the end of the day, Yun was thoroughly sick of the very thought of marriage. His brothers had given their verdict on every woman in court and Yun had begun to wonder if there might be a monastery he could retreat to. One where he did not have to marry anyone. He'd be a useless husband, anyway.

Perhaps if he waited long enough, his mother would arrive at that conclusion on her own, and not make him marry anyone.

The thought cheered Yun considerably.

"What are you smiling about, Little Fish?" Chao hissed. "Did you decide on the one with the big boobs? I think I've had her already. No virgin bride, that girl."

Yun prayed that his brother was lying. Deflowering the daughters of their father's courtiers without even taking them as concubines was the height of dishonour.

He almost wished himself back on the battlefield, where he wouldn't have to endure his brothers' taunting.

Almost, but not quite, Yun reminded himself. He was sleeping better now, for the visions of war were fading a little, but he was still no closer to the epic poem he'd promised his father.

No wife, no poem…was his life destined to

hold anything important? Yun doubted it. After all, the eighth son of the Emperor was so far from the throne, he was nobody, really. A nobody in nice clothes. Fate had been so generous to his brothers, she'd had little left for him. Perhaps he should just be grateful for the crumbs he had. Paper to write his poetry on. Perhaps one day he would write something worth keeping.

Eleven

Ava's horse settled into a fluid canter that at first had her hanging on for dear life, before she realised that the mare knew what she was doing and had no intention of losing her rider. Only then did Ava relax and enjoy it, as Bianca seemed to do, judging by her wide smiles.

For the first time in her life, Ava felt free. Free of fear and free of the harem that had imprisoned her so completely without her even realising it. If only she could ride like this forever, like her chestnut mare wanted to.

All too soon, the captain called a halt. Ava couldn't see past all the mounted men in front of her, so it came as a surprise when Bianca grabbed her round the middle in a hug.

"Stay safe, and be brave. Today you fly free. Fishy thoughts, Ava," Bianca murmured before she released her.

A lump formed in Ava's throat. "You, too," she whispered.

Would she ever see Bianca again?

"This way, Princess," the captain said, beckoning for Ava to follow him.

Yes, she was a princess. Lagle's equal, now she had left the harem. Ava straightened her spine and held her head high.

The path the captain indicated might once have been a road as wide as the one they now travelled, but it was now so overgrown it seemed little more than a track, and a narrow one at that. Ava started forward.

"I must go first," Lagle said haughtily, shoving past Ava.

Ava's mare moved out of Falada's way,

allowing the larger animal to pass. The captain lined up four packhorses behind Ava, all roped together, before he fastened their lead rope to Ava's saddle. At the captain's nod, Ava nudged her mount along the path Lagle had taken, and she heard the captain order the packhorses to follow.

She hoped Lagle knew the way, and that it would not be too long, for the wooded path was surprisingly dark and cool on what had seemed such a hot day. Ava longed for a drink, but she did not know where to find one. Perhaps there would be a stream, or the city would be close. In the harem, it would have been a simple matter of summoning a servant, but there would be no servants until they reached their destination, so Ava plodded on in Lagle's wake.

Finally, Lagle came to a stop at the edge of a river. The current ran fast, but it appeared to be shallow enough at this point to be forded, what with the track ending here and starting up again on the far bank.

Ava looked longingly at the water, and her horse seemed to share her thoughts, for the mare ambled up to the riverbank and stuck her nose in the river.

Thinking the other horses would need a drink, too, Ava slid to the ground and untied them. They lined up alongside hers, slaking their thirst, and she envied them. But not for long.

Ava rummaged through her saddlebags and found the silver cup Militsa had given her for a parting gift. She found a spot upstream of the horses, and dipped her cup. The water was so cold she cried out as it froze her fingers, but that didn't stop her from lifting the brimming cup to her lips and drinking deep. Then refilling it for another drink.

"Fetch me some water," Lagle ordered.

Ava considered offering the full cup to her sister, but another sister's words came to mind, that she and Lagle were equals now, so she drank instead. And a third time. Only then did she fill the cup for Lagle. As she held up the glittering goblet, Lagle's blow struck it out of her hand, spilling the contents at her feet.

"Not in your plain cup, you fool! In my golden one," Lagle insisted.

Ava stooped to pick up her precious cup, pausing to check that its fall hadn't dented the soft metal, before she answered, "And where is your cup?"

Lagle waved languorously at the pack horses. "With my things."

"Then you can get it, and fetch your own water," Ava said slowly. Oh, it almost hurt to force such words out. But she'd promised Bianca to be brave, and here she was. "If you don't want mine, I shall go back to quenching my own thirst."

Deliberately, Ava returned to the riverbank and refilled her cup once more, though she didn't really want another drink. She sipped slowly, all the same, knowing it would goad Lagle into action.

Lagle let out a furious shriek, followed by a string of insults that grew louder with each word she uttered. Ava had never heard such foul language, and neither had the packhorses, it seemed, which bolted in fright.

"Get me a DRINK!" Lagle screamed over the thunder of hooves, stabbing a finger in the direction that the horses had fled. Like a tantruming child, she flailed her arms and drummed her heels against the sides of her horse. Falada leaped into action, like any well-trained warhorse, and charged across the river. Lagle shrieked again and yanked hard on the reins, bringing Falada up short. Lagle kept going, though, right over the horse's head and face-first into the river.

For a moment, Ava froze, not sure whether to laugh or ask Lagle if she was all right. When the girl didn't surface, Ava had her answer, and she waded into the river, careless of the water seeping into her boots. She might not like Lagle, but she wasn't about to let the girl drown.

Ava dragged Lagle to shore, where her sister coughed up a great deal of water, but she didn't wake. A trickle of blood ran down Lagle's face from under her hair, so she must have hit her head when she fell, Ava decided. The pendant around her neck had smashed in the fall, too, leaving little more than a few shards of broken glass tangled in the ribbon. A drop of what looked like blood remained on the stopper, glowing red like the whole thing had before. Ava knew little about magic, but one thing she knew for sure: magic was fuelled by blood, and a single drop was enough to cast a powerful spell. If the bottle had been full of a witch's blood, the spell it cast could have untold consequences.

Or it could simply have been a protection spell to keep her daughter safe. Everyone knew that the Queen doted on her daughter as much as she spoiled her.

But if the spell was evil instead…it could risk the very peace she and Lagle were supposed to secure for their people.

Ava closed her eyes and made a decision. Pulling the necklace over Lagle's head, she pitched it into the river.

She tried shaking her sister awake, but Lagle just lay there, lifeless. Or as lifeless as she could be when she still drew breath.

Finally, Ava persuaded Falada to lie down beside his rider, so that Ava could shove her unconscious sister onto the animal's back. Using the rope the packhorses had left behind, she tied her sister into the saddle as best she could so the girl wouldn't fall off, and tethered Falada's reins to her own mount.

Facing the river, Ava took a deep breath. Fishy thoughts, she told herself. It was her turn to lead.

So Ava led the way into the water.

Twelve

Between his brothers and the words that just wouldn't come, Yun needed an escape. So in a fit of frustration, he begged his father to allow him to do guard duty with the rest of the palace garrison. Marching up and down the walls would make him feel more martial, he'd said, or some such nonsense. Yet, to his surprise, his father had agreed.

Which was why Yun was the first man to spot the strange packhorses.

They came galloping up to the walls as

though all the demons in hell pursued them, lathered like they'd been running for some time. Eyes rolling in panic, they'd been too tired to do more than stand by the bridge, their sides heaving beneath their panniers. When no one appeared to take charge of them after several minutes, Yun headed down to investigate.

It took him some time to calm the beasts enough to take the bridle of the nearest, but as his fingers closed on the leather he froze. The bridle he held wasn't the sort of craftsmanship he normally saw in the empire. The intricate braiding proclaimed it the work of the Horse People. He'd seen enough of it at war. So what were some of their pack beasts doing here now?

Yun unfastened the nearest bag. It was full of silks – women's clothes, and finery, at that. He checked them all, but he found nothing more aside from some jewels stowed beneath the silk, and other such trinkets. But where were the women who owned them? Fine ladies didn't travel without an armed escort. Especially in times of war.

He left the horses in the care of some stablehands, and carried the bags up to his mother's chambers, where he left them to go and search for her. He didn't need to look for long – she was feeding the birds in her private garden.

The brilliant coloured songbirds descended into anarchy like a flock of common sparrows when they spotted a particularly tasty morsel. Mother chided them, but her voice was drowned out by the chorus of squawks as they fought for a piece of fruit.

"Mother, I must ask your advice on a strange matter," Yun began, not sure how to continue.

"Is it about a strange girl?" Mother's smile made him wonder if she could read his mind.

Yun bowed his head. "I fear if there is a girl, something terrible has befallen her. I found her belongings on the backs of horses that came from the Horse People. Highborn, certainly, but nowhere to be found. Mother, has anyone fled the city of late that you know of?"

Mother's eyes narrowed. "One of your brothers' wives, perhaps? I know of no other who would want to. But I know of none who have been missed, either. Let me see the girl's things."

Yun led her to the pile of bags, and Mother summoned a servant to unpack their contents. Gown after gown was held up for the Empress's inspection, but she only shook her head.

"I have never seen a girl wear such gowns, in court or elsewhere," Mother said. "She is not one of your brothers' brides, or one of the girls at court. Perhaps someone's wife as they fled the borderlands for the safety of the city, but were attacked on the way."

"But if they were attacked by Horse People, they could not have been but a few miles from the city. How could they come so far within our borders without us knowing?" Yun asked.

"And if the horses belong to Horse People, where are the people now?"

Mother bit her lip. "Your father is a fool to dismiss you, for you have more wits than he will ever know. Yet I cannot answer your questions, any more than you can. Leave these things with me, for if their owner arrives, I will no doubt hear of it before you do. Return to the wall, and be vigilant. If there truly are Horse People so close to the city, we cannot be too careful."

Yun rose. "I should tell the Emperor."

Mother shook her head. "Tell him what? You have found some horses and gowns with no owner? He will dismiss them as easily as he dismisses you. Find one of the Horse People and then you will have something to show him. Until then, I fear we are as blind as birds flying in a snow storm. And I do fear for us all."

Yun bowed reverently. "Thank you, Mother. I will do as you say."

"Have you given any more thought to

finding a bride?" she asked wryly.

He bowed lower still. "No, Mother."

"When we have solved the mystery of the missing lady, I will find you a bride."

"As my Empress wishes." Yun touched his forehead to the floor at her feet before rising to go. "In the meantime, I must return to my post on the walls."

Thirteen

Onward Ava plodded, pausing every dozen steps to push Lagle higher onto her horse's back so she would not slip off. She would have given everything she owned to be riding full tilt along the dusty army road with Bianca to the Summer Palace.

The thirst she thought she'd quenched raged again, but she could do nothing about it except hope that the journey would be over soon.

The forest ended as abruptly as it had begun — on the banks of another river, or so it seemed, for this one was wider and deeper than the one they had forded several hours back. There would be no fording this river, so it was a mercy that a wooden bridge spanned the watery barrier that would otherwise keep them from the city.

Until they emerged fully from the forest, trees had hidden the city walls, which rose up higher than those of Ava's father's palace. Why, she could see men marching atop them, armed with bows and spears. Whispering a prayer to the ancestors that the men would not see two women as invaders to shoot at, Ava led the horses onto the old bridge. The paint had long since faded and cracked. Much like the road that led to it, the bridge had fallen into disuse. Perhaps Ava should have prayed for the bridge to hold them so that they might reach the city – never mind the men on the walls.

Falada turned skittish, having to be coaxed over the bridge with soothing words and repeated tugs on the reins before the warhorse would follow Ava to the open city gates. She was so preoccupied with the horses that Ava didn't see the approaching guard.

"HALT!"

The authoritative shout undid all Ava's efforts to calm Falada. The horse reared, throwing Lagle to the cobbles.

The guard who'd presumably shouted jumped clumsily out of the way of the horse's flailing hooves – no mean feat, given he was covered head to toe in armour.

"Get your animal under control!" he growled.

Ava wanted to say that she'd had them under control until he startled them. What kind of barbarians were these people, causing trouble and then blaming her for it? Surely it was a man's job to protect women, not frighten their horses and shout at them.

Unless he was a true barbarian, the kind that would ignore the fact that Lagle lay on the ground, more injured than before.

Ava slid to the ground, keeping a firm grip

on the reins of both horses as her lifeline to the civilisation of home, as she went to where Lagle lay in a crumpled heap. Her head wound had resumed bleeding.

"Look what you've done!" Ava cried, lifting her bloodied hand so he could see it. Tears trickled down Ava's cheeks and she was helpless to stem the flow. Would he throw her to the cobbles next?

"This is a city gate, and it's my job to guard it, mistress, letting no enemies inside," the man said. "Be you friend or enemy?"

"We have done nothing to you. Nothing. And you...she...do you have someone who can help her? If you fetch a physician, someone who knows how to care for her..." Ava dissolved into tears again. She might not like Lagle, but she had no desire to see her sister die.

"Mistress, I am a guard. I can't leave the gate unguarded. My captain would – "

"Berate you if he knew you'd let a woman die while you argued with a girl at the gate," another voice finished for him. The second man wore similar armour to the first, though his seemed to fit him better, with a shine to the leather that caught the sun. "Fetch a physician. I will find out what kind of threat a two-woman army presents to the city." None whatsoever, the dark eye slits of his helm seemed to say.

"Begging your pardon, sir, but if one of the women was Da Ying, she could take the city single-handedly, or so the stories say." The first man hesitated, then bowed. "I will get that physician." He hurried away.

The new man cocked his head as he surveyed Ava. "You're smaller and younger than I'd expect of the legendary Da Ying. But I am told appearances can be deceiving. Is that who you are?"

Ava peered up at the man through the veil of her tears. "I've never heard of her. I am Princess Ava, the daughter of King Chinggis, and we've been sent to forge an alliance with your king." She struggled to lift Lagle off the ground, but she wasn't strong enough. "If she dies, my father is likely to consider this as an act of war if you don't help her!" Her words ended in a sob.

"I think we have more than enough war for two kingdoms right now. Though you might want to remember we have an emperor, not a king, when you meet him." The man crouched beside her, slid his hands under Lagle and lifted her effortlessly into his arms as he straightened. Covered in mud and blood, her clothes torn from two falls, Lagle looked more like a beggar than a princess against the leaping fish tooled across the front of his breastplate. "I will see that your maidservant is cared for. Is there anything else you desire, Princess? Or do you wish to be presented to the Emperor immediately?"

Ava's mouth dropped open. Why would she be presented to the Emperor when Lagle was…was…

She swallowed. Lagle was unconscious, injured, and in no fit state to be presented as an emperor's bride.

"I would like to freshen up, and make myself presentable," she managed to say. If she took long enough, perhaps Lagle would wake and recover sufficiently for an audience with the Emperor.

He nodded. "I'll have some of my men form an honour guard to escort you to the palace, where apartments will be prepared for you." He gestured toward another guardsman, issued his orders, and marched off with Lagle still in his arms.

Ava opened her mouth to protest, but a crowd of men surrounded her, taking the reins from her nerveless fingers. The memory of waking up beside the pool silenced any urge she had to speak. Meekly, she went with them without saying a word.

Fourteen

Yun's favourite part of guard duty was walking the walls, even before his mother had ordered him to do so. Officially, he was watching for invaders, and from that high vantage point he could see so far, some days he could see clear to the mountains, on the rare occasions when they weren't shrouded in cloud. Striding along the walls gave him a sense of purpose, for if war came here, he would happily fight to protect his home.

Today, the mountains hid their crowns, and

the people of the city went about their normal business. All except one woman, by the sound of things, whose shrill voice rang through the streets like a warning bell. Curiosity drove Yun to investigate.

The woman – scarcely more than a girl, judging by her diminutive size – struggled to keep two horses under control while she tried to lift a woman from the ground. A guardsman stood by, speaking to her but not offering her any assistance. Yun hurried down to the gate, shaking his head in an attempt to banish the image that suddenly plagued his mind – one of the women penned up in his brothers' camp. These two were nothing like them, judging by the richness of their clothing under the dust.

Why would two women travel alone? They had not even a single guard to see to their safety. Perhaps they, like Baron Dong, were the sole survivors of an enemy incursion.

The same incursion that had killed the owner of the silk gowns? Yun's blood ran cold. These women still had their saddlebags, so they could not be one and the same.

As Yun approached, it quickly became apparent that the larger girl was unconscious and injured. Sending the guardsman for a physician also gave him the excuse of questioning the girl to assuage his curiosity.

He knelt to lift up the injured girl as he asked the younger one what her name was. If he knew where she was from, Father might be able to send troops there to prevent further bloodshed.

He almost dropped her companion when he heard the girl's name.

"I am Princess Ava, the daughter of King Chinggis." She stood tall and proud, as Yun would expect of his enemy's daughter, and she surprised him again by insisting she came in peace.

Yun was lost for words. He managed to babble something about how he would take care of the unconscious girl, before he remembered himself and asked the princess if there was anything she wished of him. He prayed silently that she would not ask for anything that he, as the Emperor's youngest son, could not deliver.

He breathed a sigh of relief when all she asked for was a place to wash, and an audience with the Emperor.

Yun rounded up a squad of guardsmen to act as her honour guard, sending a runner ahead to make sure an apartment would be prepared for her. He carried the unconscious girl to the palace gates, before passing her to some servants. They could find suitable accommodation for her and see that a physician tended to her injuries, whatever they might be.

He had one last task to complete to keep his promises to the foreign princess. He strode into his father's throne room, whistling a folk song about geese.

The crowd of petitioners parted for him, some more willingly than others. Yun didn't stop whistling until he'd reached the foot of his father's dais, where he sketched a quick bow that he knew would scandalise the courtiers even more.

"Chinggis sent you a gift, Father," Yun said.

The Emperor's tolerant smile turned into an expression of thunderous anger. "More heads? Or hands? If he thinks to butcher my people, he will pay dearly for it."

"Two heads, four hands, attached to two lovely young women, actually," Yun said. "One of them claims to be his daughter."

"And the other?" Father demanded.

Yun shrugged. "Unconscious, and not saying much. I think she might be the Princess's maid."

This only seemed to darken Father's mood. "Keep them apart. Send their belonging to the Empress, and make sure she knows to search them. The Horse People are treacherous by nature and the women are worse than the men. Especially the witches. Did she cast a spell on you? Or touch you at all?"

Yun burst out laughing. "If she'd cast a spell on me, how would I know? And of course I touched the maid. I carried her into the palace, for the unconscious girl couldn't walk, and the Princess was too small to carry her." He sobered when he remembered the Princess. "The Princess seeks an audience with you. I had her shown to a guest chamber so that she might bathe before she comes before you. What am I to say to her when she asks for her clothes? You cannot think to invite her to come to court naked."

Several men laughed, but the Emperor did not.

"Have your mother send something suitable," Father said, waving his hand in dismissal.

Yun considered sending a servant, but his father's attitude toward the Princess and the Empress nettled him. An empress was not some common maid, to paw through a guest's clothing or source a gown for a girl. And the Princess was no witch, he was certain of it. If she was, she would have enchanted the guard and sneaked into the town unseen instead of causing the scene where he'd been forced to intervene.

Yun executed a mocking bow. "As the Divine Emperor wishes, for his smallest whim must be obeyed."

He heard his father's snort as he marched out of the throne room, toward his mother's apartments.

The Empress was waiting, as though her spies had already told her the news. Yun didn't doubt that they had – his mother knew everything that went on in the palace.

"I thought you would be too busy to visit me," Mother said before Yun could even offer a greeting. "Carrying a girl through the city streets into the palace, getting bespelled by witches, and upsetting your father." Mother set down her embroidery. "Are you in love with the girl?"

It was Yun's turn to snort. "The Princess's maid? No."

Mother's eyebrows rose. "So you believe that the girl is a princess, the daughter of

Chinggis?"

Yun considered for a moment. "She didn't bow or lower her eyes or any of the things I'd expect from a lower born woman. And the way she said it…I believed her. If she'd wanted to lie, she would have said she was the daughter of one of our allies, not the daughter of such an enemy. Why, my brothers would have killed her on the spot once they heard her father's name."

"Does this princess know who you are?"

"Everyone knows my armour. Who else carries the leaping fish?"

Mother shook her head. "Everyone in the palace, maybe, but not all of the common people know it. How would a foreign princess know that you are a poor fisherman?"

"I'm not a poor fisherman," Yun protested. "I fished that koi out of the ponds myself, with no help from my brothers. I lay there for hours, waiting for it to take the bait. It was only when I tried to pull it from the hook that it leaped, flying so high it reached the top of the waterfall. It must have swum upstream to the river, for I never saw its like in the palace gardens again."

"None of your brothers would have borne the insult, armour made to immortalise your defeat. Yet you…"

"It's good armour," Yun said. "Chao intended to shame me, I am sure, but the joke was on him when I wore the breastplate anyway. What use is a youngest son but to make his elders laugh? Perhaps I should sharpen my singing skills so that I might entertain you all at dinner." He didn't mean to sound so bitter, but that's the way the words came out.

Mother laid a hand on his arm. Such small fingers were surprisingly heavy when they carried the weight of a mother's love. "You are not useless, Yun. Perhaps you have yet to find your purpose, but I pray it shall reveal itself in time. How goes your poetry?"

"It goes poorly. All I can see is carnage, Mother. The blood on the battlefield. The honour and glory and all the things that go with victory elude me." Despair welled up. He would never be a poet.

"Describe the Princess for me."

Yun hadn't heard right. "What?"

Mother repeated patiently, "Describe the Princess for me. What manner of beast does she remind you of?"

A beast? She was a girl, a woman, not some coarse creature. And yet the idea took root, spreading through his thoughts. "A bird of a girl, small and light and delicate, but with a sharp tongue and a shrill voice." Yun smiled at the memory.

"What kind of bird?" Mother demanded.

"Not an eagle. She is no hunting bird of prey. Yet she is no seed-eating sparrow, either. She is a caged songbird, I think. Her colours do not blaze the brightest, and her song is not the sweetest, but she belongs. Yet from looking into her bright eye, you know she is watching the door, waiting for something to change so that she might be free."

Was she? The vision of the Princess as a bird flying from her cage felt so right, it was hard to doubt it. Yet he did not doubt the vision had leaped fully-formed from his own imagination.

Mother's eyes were upon him, searching his soul, it seemed. "When your father meets this girl, I shall be in court. And so will you."

Yun knew better than to protest. Besides, he'd get to see the Princess again, and see how she compared to the songbird in his imagination.

Fifteen

Ava was led to a sumptuous apartment that would have satisfied the Queen — much too grand for her, Ava wanted to say, but perhaps this kingdom was richer than her father's. This might be an ordinary chamber in an emperor's palace. Lagle was surely just as well accommodated. If not, Ava would soon hear of it, the moment Lagle awoke. For she would wake. She must.

"Do you wish to wash, mistress?" a female voice asked.

Ava whirled, to find a half dozen maids bowing low, each bearing a bundle of fabric. They bowed again in unison.

"Ah…yes," Ava said, looking for a jug and a bowl.

"Follow me to the bath house, mistress," the same voice said, and one of the maids turned and led the way out of the chamber.

When Ava entered the bath house, she wished she hadn't. The ornate bath inside was big enough to swim across, or to hold at least a dozen people. Lagle would love it, Ava was certain. As for Ava herself, she felt the maid's eyes upon her as she forced herself to undress and enter the bath as if she was used to this kind of luxury. To her relief, the water was warmer than the pool outside her father's barracks, so she managed to slip beneath the surface without showing too much of the un-princess-like panic welling up inside her.

At least fishy thoughts seemed more natural in water, she thought to herself as she scrubbed away the dust from the journey.

All too soon, she was clean, and she surrendered her body to the army of maids who had returned. They dried, patted, perfumed and dressed her in finery that she definitely didn't recognise. Judging from the way the maids fluttered around her, up to and including three of them dropping to the floor with needles and thread to raise the hem of her gown, Ava assumed the clothes were new garments made especially for Lagle, who was almost a head taller than Ava and somewhat stouter, too.

Ava considered telling them that they would have to unpick their work when Lagle awoke and demanded her dress back, but she decided against it. Let Lagle give them the bad news. Ava had enough to worry about, being presented to the Emperor and all. Being presented as his possible bride, if Lagle didn't recover.

A shiver ran through her at the thought, one that wasn't entirely unpleasant. What if she was like the heroine in one of Bianca's stories, and the king fell in love with her, naming Ava as his bride instead of Lagle? For one thrilling moment, Ava imagined herself as a queen, no, an empress, seated upon a throne with a crown on her head. Were crowns heavy? With so much gold and jewels, surely it would be a heavy burden on one's head. She had heard that her father preferred a military helmet because it did not weigh so heavily on him as a crown.

If even her father complained of it, then wearing a crown must be a heavy burden indeed. Far too heavy for Ava, a princess so insignificant she would live out her days in service to Lagle.

The weight of this thought brought Ava rapidly out of her reverie. She shook her head, resolving to think braver thoughts, as Bianca had advised her. Lagle might marry the king, but there were surely princes and noblemen who might marry her and whisk her away from her miserable fate as Lagle's maid.

"Does the gown not please you, mistress?"

one of the maids asked, frowning deeply. She gestured imperiously and two maids stepped forward, carrying a mirror between them that was almost as big as Ava herself. "This is the fashion worn by all the great ladies at the Emperor's court, but if you wish to change, we are here to serve, mistress."

Ava scarcely recognised her own reflection. Even in the muted lighting in the bath house, the gold embroidery on her gown glittered, drawing her eye away from the layers of shining silk beneath it. Her hair had been tamed into an elaborate coiffure atop her head, the curlicues reminiscent of a flower opening its petals to greet the dawn. Beneath it all, the maids had painted her face so that her unnaturally pale cheeks resembled Bianca's, while her carmined lips made her think of rosebuds. Yet it was her own eyes that drew her in. Dark and mysterious, the maids had applied layers of powder and paint until her eyes seemed to draw in the spirit of anyone who dared to meet her gaze. Even as her eyes widened in fright, they only appeared deeper and more dangerous. The eyes of a queen, Ava thought uneasily.

Ava assured the maids that everything about her toilette pleased her, for she now looked every bit a queen.

She received a flurry of bowing for the compliment before the maids hustled her back to her apartment, where two impatient guardsmen waited. Not that she could see their expressions or even their faces under their helmets, of course, but the way they hurried her off in a new direction, muttering about how long ago the Emperor had summoned her and how angry he would be at the wait, certainly confirmed it. Ava had to take two steps to every one these guardsmen took, so small was she, but they never slowed, so by the time they reached the ornate bronze doors to the throne room, Ava was out of breath from running to keep up. She would have crashed into the doors when her guards stopped abruptly, if it wasn't for the doors themselves swinging open before her, almost as if by magic. Ava didn't see the telltale glow of a spell, though, and the mystery was solved by the presence of two more guardsmen, standing behind each door.

She stumbled inside, flustered and wishing herself back in the relative peace of the bath house, even before the crowd turned to stare at her. Men and women both, far more richly dressed than she was, their dark eyes seeming to suck at her spirit as she passed them.

Fish had dark eyes, Ava reminded herself, and so did she. She drew herself up, remembering her promise to Bianca, and waited for her name to be announced.

The herald's sonorous shout made her sound far more important than she felt, even if most of the titles he described were her father's and not her own. He made no mention of her mother, which Ava supposed was better than being described as kin to the Queen.

As the herald's words rang out, the stares that had been directed at her now lowered to the floor, as the entire court bowed to a foreign princess. Feeling herself invisible in a hall full of people gave Ava the courage to move forward, something she wouldn't have thought possible a moment before, with all those eyes upon her.

On a dais at the far end of the hall sat the Emperor on his throne, flanked by other people on lesser chairs. Reminded of her father's throne room, which was much smaller, Ava kept her eyes on the floor so that she wouldn't trip on her stately skirts and embarrass herself. When she reached the foot of the dais, she dropped gracefully to her knees, allowing her skirts to fan out around her, before bowing so low her forehead touched the floor.

Princesses bow only to their king and their husband, no one else. Bianca's warning rang in her head, too late.

Ava struggled to rise, but the damage was done. She had subjugated herself before a foreign king. Her face red with shame, she stayed on her knees to hide her embarrassment.

"So, Chinggis sent a witch to bespell me. He thinks I am a coward, to be frightened by a mere child!" the Emperor roared. "Or maybe she is not really a child. The stories say his witch queen casts spells to make her appear more youthful. Perhaps Chinggis is a defiler of children, who likes his girls so young!"

Laughter erupted around the hall, echoing off the walls. Ava's blood simmered.

"Try to cast your spell, witch! My guards will cut you down before you can spread any evil here!" the Emperor continued.

Ava wet her lips. "I'm no witch."

"You lie! Why else are you here? I agreed to meet no envoy of Chinggis!"

It began to dawn on Ava why she and Lagle had been sent across the border without an escort.

"I am here to make peace through an alliance. A marriage alliance," she said carefully.

The Emperor snorted. "An alliance with who?"

"With you." It was on the tip of her tongue to add, "Your Majesty," as she might when speaking to a king, but she wasn't sure what to call an emperor. Lagle would know. That's why she should be here, not Ava.

An ominous silence stretched between them. Ava dared to raise her head, to find the Emperor staring at her.

"I don't need another wife," he said coldly. "My Empress has given me many sons, who have wives and children of their own. Go back where you came from, girl, and tell your witch mother we want none of her kind here."

"I cannot return without..." Lagle, she wanted to say, but instead she said, "without an alliance and a promise for peace."

"Your kind want nothing but war."

Muttering rumbled around the hall as many of the courtiers agreed with the Emperor.

Ava swallowed. "I don't. I want peace. My father wants peace. That's why he sent his daughter here to marry…marry into your family." She didn't dare say that Lagle was here to marry him. Lagle would never agree to be his wife if she couldn't be queen. "If not you, then perhaps one of your sons…?"

Lagle might settle for the crown prince as a husband. Maybe.

Another snort. "Only the child of Chinggis would dare to demand one of my sons in marriage. None of my sons would take you for a wife, or even a concubine. What man wants a viper in his bed?"

Titters came from the crowd, which quickly silenced as footsteps sounded on the stone floor.

"I might. If I survived the night, it would make a wonderful tale to sing at feasts," a familiar voice drawled.

Ava turned her head in time to see an armoured man leap down from the dais. No one, not even the guards beside her, moved to stop him.

"She looks so lovely down there on her

knees. No wonder you're drawing this audience out, Father. When you're done, I'd like her." The man pulled off his helmet, revealing quite a handsome face. He winked at Ava.

The Emperor's eyebrows bunched together. "Better to send her home to her father than risk war or worse."

More muttering came from the crowd.

"But look at her, Father. As pretty as a poem. Just what I want in a wife."

Wife? No, Lagle was the one who was supposed to get married, not Ava, and surely not to this strange prince who spoke of songs and tales and poetry. Surely the Emperor wouldn't change his mind on the whim of his son.

"Are you a virgin?" the Emperor demanded.

Ava blushed scarlet. "Of…of course."

The Emperor turned to his son. "See if she lies, and if she bears a witch mark."

"When I have her alone in my chambers, I will make a thorough investigation," the prince said gravely.

The Emperor gave a curt nod. "Be it on your head, then." He clapped his hands. "Summon a matchmaker. This marriage will happen now or not at all."

Ava's mouth dropped open. Now? But Lagle...

The Emperor's gaze was fixed on her. "Have you changed your mind, daughter of Chinggis?"

Slowly, Ava shook her head. "If a marriage alliance is the price of peace, then I will play my part in it. I will marry the prince...the prince..."

"Yun Bataar," the prince supplied with a sweeping bow. "The eighth son of our Blessed Emperor. Delighted to meet you, Princess Ava."

Lagle would never agree to marry an eighth son. A king, or the heir to the throne, were all she would agree to. Of course, Lagle would probably not permit Ava to marry a prince before she herself was married.

All the more reason to do this now.

"I will marry Prince Yun Bataar as soon as the ceremony can be arranged," Ava said, trying and failing to still the shaking in her voice.

She was about to discover just how quickly that could be.

Sixteen

When the Princess entered the room, her face froze in terror. Yun wanted to get up and tell her everything would be all right, but as he rose from his chair, his mother's hand landed on his arm.

"Don't," she whispered.

While Yun might disagree with his father, he never disobeyed his mother. Reluctantly, he subsided.

When the Princess reached the foot of the dais, she fell to her knees, as though they would no longer carry her. Again, Yun felt his mother's restraining hand on his arm, and again he resisted going to the girl's assistance.

Yun's blood simmered as his father tormented the girl, calling her names while the court laughed. He charged her with crimes that should rightly be laid at Chinggis' door, not his daughter's, but no one else seemed to care.

And then his father called her a witch.

The girl's head jerked up, just enough for Yun to see her eyes flash with fury. "I'm no witch."

Yun almost laughed. If she was a witch, she would have cast a spell then and there on the Emperor. That she didn't was proof of her honesty.

Then she uttered six words that made Yun sit up and listen: "I am here to make peace."

His mouth grew as dry as the desert, while his heart beat faster. Could this girl persuade his father to accept a peace alliance where he had failed?

Suddenly the girl on her knees no longer

looked so subservient. She looked like a snake ready to strike, but choosing to spare him. Because she wanted peace.

Marriage. Why were they talking about marriage? Yun must have missed something. She wanted to marry one of the Emperor's sons?

His belly twisted within him. If any of his brothers got hold of her, they would make her suffer. The pain of the girls they'd tortured to death in that village would be nothing compared to what they'd do to Chinggis' daughter.

"Save her," Mother hissed. "Ask for her."

Yun stared at the Empress, but she only stared implacably back. She had given him an order. One that he must obey.

"What man wants a viper in his bed?" Father demanded.

This time, Mother didn't stop him when Yun rose. Of course not. "I might," he said with forced nonchalance as he strode to his father's side. "If I survived the night, it would make a wonderful tale to sing at feasts."

The Emperor stared at him, lost for words.

But Yun detected a wavering. If his father gave him the girl, perhaps peace would be possible.

Yun continued in the same vein, talking of poetry and nonsense until his father's patience wore thin. Thin enough to concede to what Yun wanted.

"Be it on your head, then," the Emperor grumbled.

Yun held out his hand for the girl's, and for the first time felt the tremors running through her. She truly was terrified, but she had stood up to his father all the same. More than ever, he wanted to save this princess from the rest of his family.

"I am Yun Bataar, eighth son of our Blessed Emperor," he told her. Her face fell, and he stumbled over his polite words about how pleased he was to meet her.

The proud Princess didn't want an eighth son, and who could blame her? But if she knew what the other seven would do to her…

No. Yun would not let his brothers harm her.

"I will marry Prince Yun Bataar," the Princess said, the proud tilt of her chin announcing that she would accept nothing less.

Yun's mind whirled. Hadn't his father offered her as a concubine, a mistress? When had he agreed to make her his wife?

He directed a silent entreaty to his mother, begging her with his eyes to tell him what to do.

The Empress's eyes blazed. She nodded once, a jerk of her head that left Yun with no other choice.

"The sooner I get her alone in my chambers, the better. Thank you, Father," Yun said.

The girl trembled, and Yun wished he could reassure her, tell her she had nothing to fear from him. Not tonight, not ever. But as the Emperor's joke of a youngest son, he had a role to play. So he smiled, and joked, and generally made light of his marriage, even as they said their vows. It wasn't until they reached the privacy of his chamber that he allowed the façade to slip.

He poured himself a drink and downed it in one gulp, before pouring another. Only then did he have the courage to speak to her. His wife.

He turned and opened his mouth, but what he saw left him speechless.

Seventeen

For all the talk in the women's palace about how grand Lagle's wedding would be, with many changes of clothing, complicated ceremonies and public spectacles that Lagle had boasted about endlessly, Ava's wedding to Yun was surprisingly simple. No clothing changes, and the ceremony was so fast she had trouble following it. Surely all she'd done was serve a few cups of tea and sipped at her own before she was bundled out of the throne room for what she thought would be the first change of clothes. It wasn't until the last maid had left that she realised she was alone in a room with Yun and, to her gut-churning consternation, a bed.

Yun poured himself a drink of something that smelled far stronger than the traitorous tea she'd been too busy drinking to notice her own marriage ceremony until it was over. He offered Ava a cup of the pungent liquid, but she shook her head. If she drank a single mouthful, it would only come right back up again. She'd left the only mother and home she'd ever known, with the prospect of a lifetime of servitude to her least favourite sister, and before she'd had time to mourn her loss, her fate had twisted so inexplicably to give her a husband.

Which made her a wife with wifely duties, Ava reminded herself.

Though she was one of the King's daughters, sex was no secret in the women's palace. She knew very well what was expected of her, though she had never expected to need that knowledge until now. Methodically, she removed her clothing, layer by layer, until she was down to her thin shift. She considered removing that, too, but she'd heard that some men preferred to do their own unveiling, especially the first time.

Ava swallowed, climbed onto the bed, lay down, and spread her legs. Closing her eyes, she prayed to the ancestors that Yun's attentions would be over quickly.

"No drink, and straight to business? Are you sure you are Chinggis' daughter?" Yun asked, laughing.

Ava's eyes snapped open. Not a day passed that Lagle hadn't made some scathing comment about her legitimacy. All Ava knew what that her father would never have kept her if he was in any doubt that she was his child.

If Yun doubted it, why had he agreed to marry her?

"I am Chinggis' daughter," Ava said slowly. "And your wife."

The word sounded so strange.

Yun's laughter died. "Yes, which means I have a duty to perform." He began to disrobe, and Ava closed her eyes again. The more she saw of him, the more he would frighten her.

She felt his weight compress the mattress near her feet. Ava risked opening her eyes.

The man who knelt between her legs was magnificent, and with every bit of him on display, she could look her fill. Perhaps she might enjoy a little of her marriage bed, if she could look upon a man like this while he did whatever he wanted with her. Bianca would have loved to marry such a handsome prince.

Bianca would also be braver about her wedding night than Ava, who began to shiver as she remembered what would happen.

Yun lifted his arm, looking determined, and light glinted off metal. The metal of a dagger blade he held poised, ready to stab into her flesh.

Ava screamed.

Yun grunted, then said, "There."

Ava dared to open her eyes. He'd sliced his

hand, and now he held it between her legs, so close the blood almost dripped on her instead of the sheet beneath her. Wide-eyed, all she could do was stare as he let his hand bleed for a long moment, before wiping it on the sheet. His fingers brushed her thigh and she shivered again, but not entirely out of fear this time.

"Go up to the top of the bed, and cover yourself," Yun advised.

Ava scrambled to obey, too confused to do anything else.

Yun ripped the bloodied sheet off the bed and gave a shout of triumph. He threw open the room door and flapped the sheet at the crowd of courtiers waiting outside. "She fought fiercely to start with, but I tamed her. See?" He pointed at Ava, who curled up into a tiny ball at the head of the bed, as far away from the door as possible, then flapped the sheet again. "I should thank Chinggis for his gift of a sweet virgin bride."

The courtiers tittered and the crowd slowly dispersed until only Yun stood in the doorway, no longer holding the sheet.

"Get some sleep," Yun ordered. He wrapped a robe around himself, then left, closing the door after him.

Ava waited, but he didn't return. After a while, she uncurled and allowed herself to relax. Evidently her husband didn't want to share her bed tonight. She would summon up the courage to ask him why later. For now, she stretched out on the bed and fell asleep.

Eighteen

Yun paced the walls, unable to get the image out of his head. Of her, his wife, the pretty princess stretched out on his bed in a shift so thin he could see every delicious detail of her body through it, which should have aroused him beyond belief, if it wasn't for her expression.

Her squeezed shut eyes, her wobbling lip, her clenched fists on either side of her throat...as though she expected to be punished.

What had she done to deserve punishment?

Nothing, he told himself. She wanted peace, the same as he did. She had consented to the marriage, and shown courage when his father had humiliated her before the court. She had even spread her body out on the bed, a sacrifice to this marriage alliance she wanted…but not with him.

I am not my brothers, Yun raged inwardly, wishing he could shout it at the top of his lungs. Everyone already believed he was mad, but until today, they'd have been wrong.

And he didn't dare tell anyone what he'd done. He was a man, and it was his job to shed blood in the name of war and peace. As a woman, she shouldn't need to. So he'd turned his dagger on himself because he couldn't bear to hurt her…and he refused to let anyone suggest the marriage hadn't been consummated. If their marriage dissolved, there would be nothing to stop his brothers from hurting her. As it was…it was only their love for their youngest brother that kept her safe. He prayed that would not change.

As a cold wind started to blow, Yun warmed himself by imagining what it might be like if Ava was willing. If one night he entered his bedchamber and found her with her legs and her eyes open, wearing a welcoming smile. How he would cradle her delicate, birdlike body as he made love to her, eliciting gasps of pleasure from her, not pain. Not just once, but all night, or until she lay in his arms, spent, with a smile on her lips that not even sleep could wipe away.

Bliss, surely.

But not tonight.

So Yun continued to march along the walls, staring out into the darkness for an enemy he could not see, wishing he was in his bedchamber with the lovely woman who had somehow bewitched him without one whit of magic.

Ava, the wind seemed to whisper, but Yun closed his ears to it.

Nineteen

When Ava woke in the morning, she was still alone in the bed. The same maids from yesterday ushered her to the bath house, but today none of them would meet her eyes. In fact, they seemed hesitant to touch her now.

Finally, she couldn't bear it any longer. "What have I done wrong?" she asked. "Yesterday, you were all happy to help me bathe and dress. Today, you act as though Prince Yun's wife is unclean."

The maids exchanged glances for a long

moment, before one of them stepped forward and spoke up.

"A thousand apologies, mistress, but the Emperor's sons are known for their rough use of women, especially their wives. Most new brides in the palace do not wish to be touched the morning after their wedding night, and many of them have ordered us to look away instead of staring at their hurts. After so many new wives screaming at us not to be touched or stared at, we now do this as a matter of course, in order to better serve you. My deepest apologies if this offends, mistress. If you will tell me where your hurts are greatest, we have salves that may help, if you will permit us to apply them."

Ava's mouth dropped open. So it was true and this was a barbarian kingdom. Men who hurt their women instead of protecting them. Her father had never done such a thing to any of his wives or concubines. Oh, she'd heard that a girl's first time could be a little painful, but no new resident to the women's palace ever appeared to have been beaten.

"I have none," Ava said slowly. "Prince Yun was…" Inexplicably merciful? Not attracted to her in the slightest? Unwilling to consummate the marriage while willing to go to great lengths to hide this? Ava settled for, "He was kind."

"His Royal Highness Prince Yun is different to his brothers," the maid who'd spoken admitted. The other girls tittered and some even blushed.

"I must dress to please him better today," Ava said, not realising she'd spoken aloud until the maids brought her another new gown.

"Very good, mistress."

Lagle would not want to marry the crown prince or any of his brothers if they beat women. Why, her head injury from her fall from her horse might be the least of her hurts if she did.

"Where is Lagle?" Ava asked.

"Who, mistress?"

"Lagle, the girl who arrived with me. She

was thrown from her horse and hurt."

More glances were exchanged. "Do we not serve you well enough, mistress, that you wish for your foreign maid?"

Lagle, a maid? Ava hoped no one had said that to Lagle. "I must see her, and know she is well."

"The Emperor commanded that we must serve you, not your foreign maid, in case you mean the empire ill, but he did not say you could not see her," the maid began. "When you are dressed, I will take you to her."

Ava nodded her thanks and submitted meekly to the maids' ministrations. Perhaps if she looked beautiful enough today, Prince Yun would take Ava as his wife properly tonight.

Twenty

Lagle's chamber was as spare and small as Ava's old one at the women's palace. More so, perhaps, as she had no spare clothing or even any belongings to personalise the space. Ava dreaded what Lagle would say when she discovered she'd slept upon a pallet and not the golden feather bed she'd boasted about so many times in the harem.

"Has she awoken?" Ava asked, though she knew the answer before the words had left her lips. If Lagle had awoken before this, the whole palace would have heard what she thought about being made to lie on a pallet. As the girl who crouched on the floor beside Lagle shook her head, Ava said, "Very well. Have my old chamber prepared – the one where I was taken before I wed the prince – and see that she is moved there. She must be cared for as though she was the Queen herself, or…" Or Lagle would scream the very roof tiles off the place, Ava thought but didn't say. She swallowed. "Or you will answer to me," she finished instead.

"No, mistress, we cannot. Perhaps things are different where you are from, but here…we could never allow a girl of a lower caste taint the guest chambers of the very highest. She must stay here, as the Emperor commands." The maid shook her head furiously. "If the Emperor should hear of it, he will take all of our heads for allowing such a thing. Even if he does not take yours, he will make the prince punish you, for it is a husband's duty to discipline his wife. Better to let this girl die of her injuries than be injured yourself, mistress, for you surely would be. Prince Yun is as strong a warrior as any of his brothers."

Ava wished she could trade something, anything, for the courage to say that a girl's life was worth a little pain, but if her maids would have to die to give Lagle her golden bed, then a pallet wouldn't hurt her. Lagle would make her wishes and her position known the moment she woke.

"She wakes, mistress," the crouching girl said, nodding at Lagle.

Sure enough, Lagle's eyelids fluttered again as she screwed her face up. "My head hurts," she whimpered.

"Fetch her something for the pain," Ava ordered. "Quickly."

"Who are you?" Lagle asked, blinking. She gazed straight at Ava.

Before Ava could respond, one of the maids cut in, "This is your mistress, Princess Ava, wife to Prince Yun, eighth son of His Imperial

Highness, the Emperor himself. Show respect!"

Lagle lowered her gaze. "I seem to have forgotten. A thousand apologies, mistress. Have I overslept?"

This didn't sound like Lagle at all. "You took a blow to the head when your horse threw you," Ava said slowly, her heart sinking at Lagle's blank expression. "Don't you remember?"

Lagle shook her head. "No, mistress. I only feel fear when you speak of horses, and a desire to avoid them as much as I can. Yet you say I climbed upon one's back?"

Ava didn't know what to say. Could the bump to her head have scattered Lagle's wits and her memories, too? Bianca had told her tales of such things happening to soldiers in battle, but Ava had never imagined she'd see such a thing happen to Lagle, of all people.

"How dare you ask questions of your mistress! Show more respect!" a maid scolded.

Lagle cast her eyes down once more.

"Apologies, mistress. I forgot myself." She struggled to sit up. "Please forgive...augh!" Her voice died in an exclamation of pain and she flopped back to the pallet, lifeless, or seemingly so. She still drew breath, to Ava's relief.

"You should not be here, Princess," one of the maids said. "Permit me to take you to the pleasure gardens, where the other wives will be at this time of the day."

Ava nodded. There was little more she could do for Lagle until the girl woke again or regained her memory. Perhaps one of the other princesses would be willing to talk to her. It would be nice to have a friend, if such a thing were possible.

When they reached the garden, though, all thought of princesses or even people flew out of her head. Ava had never seen such a beautiful place. It was as lush as the forest she and Lagle had travelled through only yesterday, but far more beautiful. Flowers and scents assailed her on all sides, as she followed the path curving gently through what could only be paradise.

"That's Prince Chao's wife, Fang," the maid said softly, inclining her head. "She has not spoken since her wedding night, a year ago. He is the second son, and it is said that if Prince Gang, the crown prince, does not beget a son on his wife, Lan, that the Emperor will declare Chao his heir instead, for Fang has borne him a boy and she is already carrying a second, or so her maids say."

Ava tried not to stare at Princess Fang. Her silk robes draped around her in such a way that she could not tell if the woman was eight months pregnant or not carrying a child at all. Between her pale face and haunted eyes, Ava had the impression that the woman was more spirit than human. The shadows beneath the princess's eyes looked like bruises, instead of the evidence of sleepless nights. Perhaps they were both, Ava realised with alarm as she remembered what her maids had said in the bath house that morning.

A woman swathed in red silk moved slowly past, bent over with what Ava thought was age. Ava and her entourage halted to permit the dowager to pass.

It wasn't until the woman sank onto a bench, her attendants settling like a flock of birds around her, that Ava realised she wasn't elderly at all — the woman couldn't be more than twenty, if that. Her face screwed up in pain before she smoothed it into a blank look much like that of Princess Fang.

"I didn't think Princess Lan would be able to leave her bed for three days, at least," the maid said in a low voice.

"Is she ill?" Ava asked, taking a step toward her. If she couldn't help Lagle, perhaps she could be of service to someone else.

"If she were, she would not be here. The crown prince often speaks of setting her aside for a more fertile wife. As if three daughters in as many years is not fertile. No, her husband punishes her soundly after the birth of each girl. Half the palace hears him shout at her for failing to give him a son. The prince announced the birth of his daughter yesterday morning, vowing to beget a son that very day. Judging by how slowly she moves today, he's had her in his bed all day and all night, though the new babe is barely out of her belly. No wonder there was no salve left in the bath house this morning for you."

Ava gasped. What kind of prince would beat and bed his wife repeatedly for a day and a night? A monster, not a prince at all, she resolved angrily. "The men of this kingdom sound like monsters," Ava declared.

The maids gasped.

"Please, do not say that, mistress," one begged.

"They are merely men," the gossiping maid added. "They have wants and appetites that women must satisfy, without ever understanding why. All men want sons to send to war, to rule their lands and light incense in the shrines for them when they are gone. What else are women for, but to serve?"

This was not the way of things in the women's palace back home. True, the wives and concubines who lived there served her father, but not in such a way that interfered with their own pleasures. Occasionally a girl might not go horseriding for a few days after birth or after several nights with the King, but she would always say so with a sly smile, which the other wives and concubines shared. None of this haunted, pained expression shared by the princesses in this barbarian palace.

More than ever, Ava wanted to thank Prince Yun for his kindness last night. If not for him, she might be a quivering shadow of herself like the other girls.

"Will this suit you, mistress?" a maid asked, gesturing toward an empty bench.

Ava nodded, accepting their assistance to arrange her skirts as she settled onto her seat. While her maids gossiped about the other princesses in the palace, occasionally breaking off to bring Ava refreshments, Ava's mind wandered back to her home, and the Summer

Palace where Bianca had been taken. She wondered whether anyone missed her, and what they would say if they knew what was happening here. She thought about sending the Queen a note about her daughter's fall, but decided against it. Ava didn't want to fall afoul of the Queen's wrath ever again. Let Lagle write a letter to her mother when she recovered. Lagle wouldn't allow one of these barbarians to touch her, let alone wed her, and she'd want to go home. Leaving Ava alone among them. Ava wasn't sure whether she wanted that or not.

Now that she had flown from the harem, Ava wanted to see what this adventure had in store for her. A handsome prince for a husband might be just the start.

Twenty-One

Yun woke to birdsong. A screeching chorus that no man could withstand. He cracked open one eye and wished he hadn't, for the sunlight beat down on him mercilessly.

"I thought you would sleep all day," Mother's voice remarked.

He could not ignore the Empress.

Yun levered himself up into a sitting position, rolling his shoulders to rid them of stiffness. He should not have slept on a bench in his mother's private garden. Yet where else in the palace could he find peace?

"Did you make a poor choice of wife?" Mother asked.

Yun wanted to argue that both she and his father had pushed him into the marriage, but he knew that the decision had still been his own. He thought of the lovely Princess Ava, probably still asleep in his bed.

"No." He sighed. "She is lovely and obedient and everything I could want. A worthy wife, in all the ways I could name. I simply could not sleep, so I walked the walls for a while, and then I think I came here." He frowned. "I did not mean to fall asleep."

Mother laughed softly. "Your father came here looking for you, but I told him not to wake you. He made me promise to remind you that it is her duty to bear sons, and yours to beget them."

More fools for the court, to take after their father, Yun thought sadly but didn't say. With his seven older brothers, his sons would never be heirs to his father's throne.

"You may rest a little here, first, though," Mother continued. "I will send for some food and drink. Is there something you wish to ask me?"

For a moment, Yun considered confessing last night's subterfuge to his mother. But he banished the idea as quickly as it had come. No, he could tell no one. There were few secrets in the palace, and anything said aloud could be overheard.

He rose and headed for the cage of birds. A flurry of bright wings warned him he had come too close for the comfort of some. Did Ava long to flee from him, too?

Amid the bright parrots and orioles, there was a plain-looking bird in brown and white. "Mother, what is that bird? I don't think I've seen it before."

The Empress approached. "I thought you'd ask me questions about women, or pleasing your wife, not birds. If you mean my newest pet, she is a lark. One of your brothers brought her back for me from the Horse People's lands, thinking I might enjoy her song. But she has not sung yet." Mother stared intently at the bird. "Perhaps she is not yet comfortable in her new home. Or maybe her heart does not hold enough joy to raise her voice in song."

"It is a hard thing to abandon the life you knew, and make your home anew," Yun said slowly, thinking of Ava. Her courage was greater than even he'd known. What, and who, had she left behind?

Refreshments arrived, and he made small talk with his mother for as long as politeness required. Yet his restless mind wandered, from Ava to the birds before darting back to Ava again.

"Where is Ava, Mother?" he asked suddenly.

She laughed. "I'm surprised it's taken you so long to ask. She is in the pleasure garden, with the other princesses."

Yun's heart sank. The other princesses were his brothers' wives. If they talked to her, they were bound to tell her about his brothers. Girls gossiped, and they would welcome another who was their equal. Even now, they could be frightening her with stories of their wedding nights, or of any night since, knowing his brothers and their tastes.

If she suspected him of being like his brothers, she would run screaming at the sight of him, he was sure of it.

Then he would be forced to give up all hope of ever having a willing wife.

No, he did not want that. He wanted her, one day, even if that day was far into the future.

One day he would hear his lovely lark sing.

Yun bade his mother farewell and headed off to find his wife.

Twenty-Two

What sounded like a smothered scream jolted Ava out of her daydream about swimming with Bianca at the Summer Palace. Ava scanned the garden, just in time to see Princess Lan fall off her chair, to the consternation of her attendants. Together, they carried her inside the palace.

Ava prepared to return to her thoughts, when another sound caught her attention — this time, a male voice.

"Have you seen her?" the man asked.

Princess Fang dropped to her knees on the grass, extending her hand in Ava's direction.

The man turned and a grin lit his face. "There's my little wife! My illustrious father reminded me that a marriage is not successful without sons, so it's off to bed for you. I hope you're well rested after last night, for there'll be very little sleep for you tonight, either."

Behind him, Princess Fang fainted.

Prince Yun didn't seem to notice as he marched across the grass toward Ava, beckoning imperiously. "Come along, bed! The Emperor commands it!"

Numbly, Ava obeyed his summons, following him on leaden feet back into the cold darkness of the palace.

He led her to the bedroom they'd shared after the wedding ceremony, and waited for her to enter before closing the door firmly behind her. Then he set his back to the oak door and just grinned.

Silence stretched for a long moment before Ava ventured, "Would you like me to disrobe for you, Your Highness?"

His eyes burned with desire, answering for him.

Swallowing, Ava fumbled with the ties of her gown.

His large hand closed over both of hers, making undressing impossible. Prince Yun's eyes softened as they met hers. "My body would have me say yes, and make you a proper, dutiful wife, like it wanted to do last night." He sighed. "But my spirit refuses, insisting that you are more than a simple vessel to hold children."

Remembering the words of her gossiping maids in the garden, Ava said, "It seems that is all your people believe women are for." She winced at the accusation in her tone.

Yun clapped his hands. "So you have heard the other princesses' stories, yet you are not afraid. There is the spirit I saw yesterday! Such courage."

Ava couldn't help it. She laughed. "I have no courage, Your Highness. What you mistake for courage is pure terror, stopping me from running away from what frightens me, as a sensible person should."

Yun shook his head. "No. I saw terror, too, but I saw more courage in you yesterday than on a battlefield full of men. You sat there, on your knees in his throne room, and defied the Emperor himself to his face. I couldn't let my brothers break such a spirit. You are a treasure. And so, here we are. Keep your clothes on, if you wish. Amuse yourself as you please. I have a poem that burns to be released, if I have but the wit to write it." He headed for the table in the corner of the room by the window, and searched among the papers that covered it until he unearthed a brush.

Ava didn't know what to do. "So you don't want me, Your Highness?" The words came out sounding forlorn.

"Weren't you listening to a word I said?" he asked without looking up.

"I listened, but I still don't understand."

He sighed. "Did you not hear me call you a

treasure?"

"Yes, but –"

"What does one normally do with treasures?" he asked calmly.

"Keep them safe," Ava whispered. "Like you kept me safe from your brothers by marrying me yesterday."

"And from me," he added.

"But the…but they say you are different to your brothers. Not like them," Ava began, fearful all over again. If he never bedded her, she'd never bear him a son. If there were no sons, the Emperor would order him to punish her and…Ava shivered at the thought of being beaten so badly that she hobbled around like Princess Lan or that she might faint at the sound of a man's voice, like Princess Fang.

He laughed softly. "Barely here a day and you already know the palace gossip. If your father sent you here as a spy, we are all doomed."

"My father didn't – "

He hushed her. "No need to protest,

Princess. No one can feign terror like you showed yesterday. My father already believes you to be a spy, and whether you are or not, he will not allow you to get a message out to your father, no matter what you discover. Other than that, you are my wife, entitled to all the honour and privilege due to a princess in the palace. Enjoy it. I doubt many of the others do." He dipped his brush in a jar of ink and began to write.

So he had seen the state of the other princesses, and still done nothing. "When will you break me like your brothers have done with their wives?"

Yun set his brush down. "I am not my brothers."

Ava wet her lips. "But you are still a man, and I am your wife. Those poor girls in the garden – when will that be my fate? I deserve to know."

He rose and strode toward her until barely a breath separated them. "What if I say now? What if I tell you to take off your clothes, lie on the bed and spread your legs, like a good wife?"

Ava's hands went to untie her lacings once more. "Then I will be a good wife, like I should."

Again, Yun stopped her. "Enough with the undressing! I will not have an unwilling wife!"

"I married you willingly," Ava said steadily. "And I am willing to give my body to you, to do with as you wish, just as I was last night."

"That wasn't willing! That was grudging."

Ava took a deep breath to steady herself. She wanted to give up, but something within her wouldn't let her. "I am willing."

"No, you're not. Willing is when you want me so much, you would search through the palace to find me, drag me back to your bedchamber, tear off my clothes, and have your way with me." Yun's eyes were dark and unreadable. "Are you willing to do all of those things?"

Ava couldn't seem to close her mouth. Did women really do such things? She'd heard stories in the harem and Bianca told more tales than most. Empresses who had kept harems of men solely for their pleasure. Women who had their own desires and needs and destinies, who…

"You look lost."

Yun's amused words drew Ava out of her dream. "Only lost in thought, Your Highness," she said. "Especially as you searched for me, found me, brought me back here and…and…it would be a shame to tear such lovely clothes."

Yun tilted her chin up so her eyes met his. "There are plenty more in the palace. If you want me in your bed, say so, and you shall have me."

As Ava looked into his eyes, she felt like she'd swallowed a snake that now writhed in her belly. There was something about this man that made her want to say yes. After all, Prince Yun was not like his brothers.

The image of the two broken princesses in the garden popped into Ava's mind. If a prince could do such a thing to his wife…

Yun moved away. "Let me know if you change your mind. I'll have to share your bed for the first month of marriage, as custom demands, but I won't touch you unless you ask me. You may retire when you please. I will continue writing poetry while I still have light."

He returned to the table and his papers.

Ava sat on the edge of the bed, suddenly exhausted by the exchange. Would she ever be willing in the way he said? Was it worth a chance to find out if the tales were true, and a woman could take pleasure in her marriage bed? Could she, with Yun?

A man she barely knew, Ava scoffed, as she often had to Bianca when her sister had told her tales of couples falling madly in love on their first meeting. Bianca insisted such a thing was true, but Ava had her doubts. What happened in tales rarely occurred in real life. If she trusted Yun, perhaps she would not mind so much when he touched her. To trust him she must know him better.

"I have heard that poetry speaks of the writer's spirit," Ava said slowly. "May I read some of yours?"

"Absolutely not," Yun replied.

Defeated, Ava readied herself for sleep. When she had removed all her clothing except her shift, she climbed beneath the blankets and tried to sleep, but rest eluded her. Her thoughts swirled too fast.

"Why not?" Ava asked finally.

Yun turned to stare at her. "What?"

Ava had a strong desire to stay silent, but she'd been brave enough to ask once, and a tiny whisper of courage still remained. "Why won't you let me read your poetry?" she asked.

"Because I won't let anyone read it. It's not good enough to be shown to anyone."

Ava wasn't sure what to reply to that. "One day, I would like to read it," she said finally.

"Then you will be the first."

Yun returned to his work, and Ava decided not to disturb him further. She could ask him again later. After all, they were married now, and would be sharing a bed for a month. Surely he'd give in to her eventually.

Twenty-Three

Yun tried to concentrate on the page before him. With all his might, he strove to conjure up the image of a noble battle, an army victorious. He'd have settled for the bloody battlefield, strewn with corpses. Yet all he could see in his mind's eye was her hands, fluttering at her breast as she offered to unlace her dress.

Willing, yet wishing she could fly free. Far from fearless, for she knew about his brothers and their wives, though she did not fear him.

Laughter like chattering parrots as she described her terror.

What sort of woman laughed in the face of her own fear?

If he touched her breast, would her heart flutter beneath his fingers?

With trepidation, he lifted his brush and wrote:

My love is a bird

Bright of eye with airy wing

Fluttering high with my heart

Teaching it to sing

The moment the words were on the paper, he wanted to screw it up and throw it across the room. He would not sing, not if he couldn't compose something about his brothers' victory.

"I have heard that poetry speaks of the writer's spirit."

Yun stared at her. Why was she still awake? Had she watched him write words about her?

A faint blush coloured her cheeks. "May I read some of yours?" she continued.

Show her his feeble love poem? Then she truly would know him for a fool.

"Absolutely not," he said firmly, trying to sound as frightening as his father. If she was the obedient wife she claimed to be, she would not push further.

Yun waited, every muscle held in taut expectation as he prepared to defend his piece of paper from her sight, but she merely moved past him to lay her clothes on the chest at the end of the bed. The shift she left on was too large for her tiny frame, drifting around her like cloud, or mist, letting him see curving details that tantalised him before they disappeared beneath the linen veil.

His brush moved almost of its own accord over the page:

My love is a dream

Clothed in caressing mist

Even in silence

Her lips beg to be kissed.

"Why not?" she asked softly.

Yun dropped his brush. "What?"

"Why won't you let me read your poetry?" she asked.

Because it is about you, he thought but could not say. Because it's not good enough. And it never would be. Yun stammered an excuse, but she didn't seem to be listening. She just regarded him, dark eyes deep with thoughts she did not share.

His thoughts whispered unbidden:

My love is a mystery

I long to uncover

Wrapping her in my arms

She chooses me as her lover.

Her voice was soft, tentative, like she feared to frighten him. "One day, I would like to read it." Her dark eyes reflected her sincerity, but they also implored.

By the ancestors, when she looked at him like that, he could deny her nothing. "Then you will be the first," he promised. Trying to remember the words of those last few lines, Yun lifted his brush. To his dismay, the ink had smeared across the page, leaving most of it unreadable.

He pulled out a fresh piece of parchment and dipped the brush into the ink once more. The smooth strokes of the brush were almost hypnotic as he wrote the words out again, before adding the final lines. He blew on the page gently to dry it, not willing to bury his precious poem in sand.

It also gave him an excuse to delay showing her. Would she like it, or think him a fool? He wasn't a poet, not truly. He only had to pull out a single scroll bearing the immortal words of Li Yu – perhaps his poem about the Heavenly Woman. Li's words conjured her up perfectly, with the love he felt for his empress, for he was both wise emperor and skilled poet.

Neither of which Yun would ever be.

Yun sighed. The ink was dry – he could delay no longer. Holding the scroll before him as his shield, he turned to face Ava. Let her think of him as she would.

Her glossy hair shimmered like a cloud on the pillow, drawing his attention to the feathers of her dark lashes against her cheek as she slept. He didn't want to wake her. Not for something as inconsequential as his poem.

Yet he couldn't resist approaching for a closer look at his sleeping wife. Heedless of where he stepped, Yun brushed against her shed clothes, sending them sliding to the floor. He bent to retrieve them, and was struck by the wondrous fragrance emanating from the silk. He buried his face in the fabric and inhaled like a drowning man drawing his first gasping breath.

Ava. If her clothes smelled so lovely, what bliss it would be to feel her silken skin against his, instead of just her discarded garments? Stronger, more heady, and much harder to resist, he was certain.

He forced himself to stay back, keeping his distance from the bed where she slept. He gripped the screen by the wall, the silvery pearl-shell smooth under his fingers. Would she feel this smooth? Only not so hard and cold. Softer and warmer and…

The folding screen clacked shut, nearly making him fall over.

Yun swore. If Ava opened her eyes now, she would see him as he truly was — a bumbling fool.

Luckily, her eyes remained fast shut. One day, perhaps they would regard him with love.

In the meantime, he would attempt to write something better. Poor poetry was hardly likely to win this lady's heart.

Twenty-Four

When her maids were done dressing her the following day, Ava asked to see Lagle again. The palace was too quiet for her sister to have recovered, and she worried about what would happen to her if Lagle died. The Queen had a long reach, and Ava shivered at the thought of what the Queen might do to her here.

After considerable hesitation, the girls led her back to the room where she'd first seen Lagle, only to find it empty.

Ava stared down at the thin pallet, hope

rising in her breast. "So she is recovered, and she has been moved to a better chamber?" she asked eagerly.

The maids held a whispered conference.

Finally, one ventured, "We do not know, mistress."

"Find out, then," Ava snapped, startling herself with her imperious tone. She opened her mouth to apologise for the curt order.

"Yes, mistress," the maids chorused.

One of them added, "Would you like to go to the gardens now, mistress?"

Ava agreed – what else did she have to do here? – and followed them to the spot where she'd spent most of the previous day.

Today, she was restless, with no desire to sit around all day long until Yun came to frighten all the other wives and fetch her again. Besides, she'd only seen two of them yesterday – with seven other sons, that made at least five more wives she hadn't yet met. They couldn't all be quivering wrecks.

So Ava strolled through the gardens,

listening to her maids relate the goings-on inside the palace as Ava tried to spot the other wives. One of them was asleep on a bench, while one of her attendants fanned flying insects away from her face. Another had actually climbed partway up a tree, so that she sat on a broad branch above Ava's head. Her attendants knelt on the grass below their mistress's tree, quietly sewing.

None of the princesses looked up as Ava passed, though their attendants shot her a curious glance or two. It was like being invisible.

"Why won't they look at me?" Ava blurted out, until realisation dawned. "Never mind, I know."

She was the newest wife of the youngest son. A nobody. The lowest ranking woman in the harem, just as she had been at home. Bianca was wrong. Nothing ever changed for Ava.

"I beg your pardon, mistress. What did you say?" a maid asked.

"Nothing," Ava replied, waving away her initial concerns. "I answered my own question. The other wives won't look at me or speak to me because I am beneath them. I am the wife of the youngest son."

The maids gasped.

"Oh, no, mistress," one of them said. "They were high ranking ladies in the court before they married and became the princes' wives. You were born a princess. They lower their gazes in respect for your high rank. They would not dare speak first to a princess of royal blood. It is a wonder that Prince Gang did not set aside Lan so that he might marry you instead. If Prince Yun hadn't taken a fancy to you and insisted on marrying you immediately…but the Empress is fond of her youngest son. Perhaps the Emperor chose to honour him to please the Empress when he gave you to him."

Ava opened her mouth to say she was no prize, but words failed her. Perhaps things were different at this foreign court, after all.

Twenty-Five

"Is there good news, sir?"

Yun dragged his thoughts away from his search for the right words to describe Ava's voice. "Hmm?"

The guardsman coughed. "Beg pardon, Your Highness. But seeing as you're whistling so cheerfully and all, I thought you might have heard some good news."

He'd been whistling? Yun couldn't remember the last time he'd done that. But he couldn't think of any news, except... "I have a new wife," Yun said. He supposed that was news.

"I'd heard, sir. Congratulations. We heard she was some sort of barbarian princess. One of the Horse People." Though only his eyes were visible, his expression was uncomfortable. "Is it true that she's a witch, sir?"

She'd bewitched him, in ways Yun hadn't thought possible. Yet he found himself shaking his head. "She is the loveliest woman I ever beheld. Sweet and obedient and..." And what? He knew very little about her, aside from her courage in the face of her fears. But fearlessness was not something a man normally praised in his wife. The clouds shifted, pouring sunlight down on the battlements. It warmed him like...like her request to see his poetry, though he had yet to show her. He'd managed to avoid it so far, but perhaps tonight... "She can make sunlight sing," he finished.

The guardsman coughed again. "I've never

heard it sing. Sounds like magic to me, sir, if you don't mind me saying."

But it wasn't. It was just…Ava. "Are you married?"

"No, sir."

"Ever been in love?"

"I love my mother and my father, and my family, sir."

Yun laughed softly. "I mean with a girl. So in love with a girl, your heart would burst if she married another man?"

"I don't think so, sir."

Yun clapped the man on the shoulder. "Then consider yourself fortunate. For love can create magic so powerful, I don't believe even a witch could break the spell. When such a spell is cast on you, then we can raise a drink together and toast the magic of love."

"It would be an honour, Your Highness."

It wasn't until the guardsman was gone that Yun realised he hadn't even asked the man's name. So caught up in his thoughts of Ava…

Tonight he would show her his work, Yun

vowed. Good or bad, it would at least tell her the depth of his feelings for her. Perhaps they might even share a kiss, a prelude to something more…

He walked the walls as though wings were attached to his feet. The sunlight sparkled on the river particularly prettily today. Shun the gooseherd had a new assistant this morning, who was quite the dullard, to hear him shout at her. But the girl had been foisted on him by his superiors, so he was stuck with her, or so he said.

Yun watched, bemused. Who would give a girl to the gooseherd?

But as the girl and her hissing flock passed beneath the wall, Yun felt a jolt of recognition. She wasn't just any girl. She was Ava's maid, the girl he'd carried into the palace on the day they arrived. It was madness to make a lady's maid into a bird herder.

This was his father's doing, Yun decided. He'd talked of separating Ava from her maid, and this was how he'd accomplished it. Sheer foolishness, is what it was.

Yun descended to the courtyard and marched purposefully toward the throne room. Ava was no danger to them, he was certain of it. Where was the harm in letting her see a familiar face every day on one of the maids who helped her dress? He would speak to his father and secure the services of the new goose girl. Without her geese.

An hour later, Yun emerged from the throne room, his head full of his father's words, but he still did not have the goose girl. His father insisted she must stay where she was, for her own good, if it was to be believed, for she had some sort of brain fever, the physicians said, and she must be kept away from other people lest the disease spread.

Yun shook his head. He didn't understand it. Who had ever heard of a disease that attacked the mind? Unless this madness had infected the physicians, too…

"Your Highness!"

Yun slowed to a stop. "Yes?"

The servant halted, breathing hard. She wore silk, marking her as a lady-in-waiting to someone of importance. Yun didn't recognise her, but then he didn't know all of his mother's servants. And who else would send for him?

"Your Highness, you are needed in the pleasure garden. Your wife has gone mad!"

No. Not Ava. Yun broke into a run.

Twenty-Six

A week passed, each day much the same as the others. Every night she shared a bed with Prince Yun, who said little to her and didn't touch her at all. Each morning, the maids would serve her breakfast and help her bathe and dress before accompanying her to the pleasure garden for another day of sharing palace gossip.

Mostly, Ava just let their voices wash over her, drowsing in the sweet-scented air like the other wives did. Yet after a week, the endless stream of stories began to irritate her.

"I don't care whose wife is sleeping with which official in order to get her daughter on the list of potential brides for the crown prince!" Ava burst out. "How can you know so much about who shares whose bed when you can't tell me where Lagle is!"

The maids babbled their apologies, but today Ava would have none of it. Whenever she had been this frustrated in the women's palace, Bianca had dragged her to the stables. A day spent with the horses always helped.

"Have my horse saddled. I wish to ride," Ava said, wondering for the first time where the palace ponies were kept. None of the other wives seemed to want to do more than sit and stare into space in the garden, but that only made Ava feel useless.

One of her maids hurried away to relay her order to the grooms, while the others ushered her back to her chambers to change into suitable riding clothes. The skirt of the robe she wore today was wrapped so closely around her legs that Ava struggled to take more than the tiniest steps. Attempting to mount a horse would show a scandalous amount of her legs, or rip the fine silk asunder, neither of which Ava wanted. Especially if Lagle discovered Ava had destroyed her favourite new gown, as surely this must be.

More appropriately attired, Ava returned to the garden to wait for her horse. She didn't have to wait long – her breathless maid hurried across the grass, dropped to her knees and said, "Mistress, I asked for your horse, but the grooms say it's no longer in the stables. It's gone."

A red haze misted Ava's vision. "First Lagle, now my horse! Can you find nothing in this palace? What will I do when you lose my clothes as well? Go naked?"

Amid exclamations of horror and another round of apologies, one maid's voice quavered, "But you did not bring any clothing, mistress. The Emperor commanded that we only bring you new gowns fit for a princess in the

Emperor's palace. If we were to lose these, the imperial tailors would only make more for you."

Ava's mouth gaped. She wasn't wearing Lagle's clothes after all? Her own clothes had been in the saddlebags strapped to her own horse, so Ava knew her things had arrived with her. One of the gowns had been a gift from Bianca, embroidered by her own hand. And the cup Militsa had given her as a parting gift had been among her things. Was all she owned to be lost in this enormous, heartless palace?

Her maids cowered as Ava began to shout in earnest, venting her frustration at the top of her lungs to the very trees themselves, for it felt like no one else was listening.

"So have you truly gone mad?" a loud male voice interrupted.

Ava whirled.

Yun stood before her with his arms folded, an amused look on his face. "One of Princess Lan's attendants told me that my wife had gone mad and I had best deal with her before my father heard about it. I suspect it's too late for that. Half the palace has heard you, and that half is terrified." He gestured around the garden.

Only now did Ava realise the effect of her outburst. Lan and Fang had curled up on their benches, their hands over their ears, oblivious to the attempts of their attendants to calm them, and the other wives looked almost as frightened.

"I only wanted to know where Lagle and my horse were. And my things," Ava said. "No one will tell me."

"You never asked me," Yun said.

"No, I didn't," she said slowly. "Do you know where they are?"

He grasped her arm, firmly but without hurting her. "Come, I'll show you."

Willingly, Ava walked with him through the passageways of the palace, trying not to hold her breath. If she could just be sure Lagle was safe and she found the gifts from her family, it would be all right. Her horse and her clothes were nothing special. Not like the gowns packed for Lagle, fit for a queen, or Falada, the magnificent warhorse who had seemed intelligent enough to make his wishes known.

Ava barely managed to keep up with Yun as he took the stairs two at a time, to a level of the palace Ava was sure she hadn't seen before. Surely she had to be at the very top of the palace, she thought as she struggled to catch her breath. No one would keep horses up here. Falada would break down the door of his stall rather than be stabled so high.

"Here." Yun pulled Ava out onto a balcony where the overhanging roof hid them in its shadows. "There's your maid."

Ava scarcely recognised Lagle as the girl garbed in brown like a nun. Her clothes certainly weren't silk, for Lagle paused to itch a spot where the rough fabric evidently troubled her.

Ava started to ask why her sister was dressed so poorly, when a deafening cacophony filled the air. The honking of what appeared to be a hundred geese, which flapped and waddled around Lagle's feet, drowned out anything Ava could say.

A man emerged from among the geese, aiming a cuff at Lagle's head. Ava gasped at the thought of him striking her, but Lagle ducked aside so the blow never landed. Almost as if she'd had practice. She flapped her hands like wings at her sides, urging the geese out the gate. The birds obeyed her, rushing to put themselves between the man and Lagle.

"Who is that man?" Ava asked.

"Shun, keeper of the royal geese," Yun said. "He's the only one who was willing to take on a girl whose head is addled, but I think he heartily regrets agreeing to it."

"Addled? Her head is addled?" Ava repeated. The Queen would never forgive her if Lagle didn't recover. She would...

"When she seemed recovered, my father ordered her put to work, but not for you. He still thinks you're a spy. He sent her to the kitchens, but she burned the rice and has no skills with a knife when she was set to peeling the vegetables. They sent her to the laundry, but she ruined one of my mother's favourite gowns, so she was sent back. She cannot remember how to do anything, it seems. She can't sing or sew or cook or wash, and my father ordered one of his guards to execute her, for there is no place in the palace for a servant who has forgotten how to serve. She fell to her knees in the courtyard, begging to be allowed to live, when Shun came in with the geese. The whole great honking lot of them. The birds attacked the guards, the way geese do, and it was chaos for some time until she shouted at the birds to be silent. They did, so my father gave her to Shun to be his assistant. She doesn't even remember her name, so they all just call her the goose girl, for she's the only one who can command the geese."

"What did Lagle say about it?" Ava asked.

Yun shrugged. "I don't know. Thanked my father and the ancestors for sparing her, I suppose, and hurried off to tend the geese before he changed his mind." He nodded at Lagle. "This is as close as you'll get to her. You won't be allowed to speak to her, or give her any messages to take out of the palace. As for your horse…"

Lagle had stopped at the gates. She wiped something from her hair and looked up.

Ava gagged. Someone had suspended Falada's head from the gate. Recently, too, for blood still dripped from it – that's what Lagle had wiped off her hair.

"Why?" Ava choked out. "Why kill a perfectly good horse and do that to him?"

"That horse injured three grooms before one of my guards took his head," Yun said. "Quite uncontrollable. Didn't you say he threw your maid and nearly broke her head?"

"Yes, but…" Ava wanted to say that Lagle had been a poor rider, goading him into it. "He was spooked," she said instead.

"Well, he's a horse spirit now, and maybe he can do some good to fix the damage he did. The healers swear the best way to cure her head is to hang up the horse's head until his spirit restores her mind. I didn't quite understand the details — they spoke of humours and elements and all manner of things that are beyond the knowledge of a simple poet," Yun said.

"Not just a poet," Ava said. "A prince and a soldier, too."

"And a husband, who has his duty to perform," Yun said gravely. "Do you know the cure for a wilful wife, who asks too many questions and shouts when women should be silent?"

Ava shook her head, though she suspected she knew the answer.

"A properly masterful husband, who shows her where her place is. And yours is in bed, wife!" Yun said gleefully as he took her arm once more and escorted her back to his chambers.

Where he would abandon her to spend all evening on his poetry again, as he had every other night she spent with him, Ava knew. For all his talk of bedding her, this was the first time he'd laid a hand on her all week, and he released her the moment they were alone.

It wasn't until much later that night that Ava remembered her cup, and by then, Yun was asleep in the bed beside her, snoring softly in the dark. She hadn't the heart to wake him, so she resolved to ask in the morning. Nothing seemed to change here, so one night couldn't make a difference, surely.

Or so Ava thought.

Twenty-Seven

The goose girl felt something drip onto her face. She glanced up, expecting rain, but all she saw was the red-painted gate with a horse head hanging beneath it. As she watched, a large drop of blood detached from the head and splattered to the cobbles by her feet. Something landed in her hair and when she touched it, her fingers came away red. Nothing made sense to the goose girl; this least of all.

Herding geese, hanging horses from gates, wearing a scratchy brown robe, sleeping on a straw pallet that she was certain contained fleas…she longed for a hot bath, big enough to immerse herself in to scrub off all the filth. The thought was gone as quickly as it had come, for how would a peasant girl who tended to geese ever receive the luxury of a hot bath? She bathed with a cloth and a jug of water when she could. If she wanted to bathe her whole body at once, she had best take a dip in the river.

A gobbet of flesh landed on her shoulder, staining her robe red before she could shake it off. A dip with her clothes on, the goose girl promised herself, so that she might wash her robe along with herself. Best to find a private spot, where Shun couldn't watch her. She'd already caught him leering at her in the servants' sleeping chamber, when she washed, and he hadn't been the only man who did. The only thing that kept their hands off her was the whispered rumours of her being a foreign witch.

The goose girl had almost laughed when she

heard it – how could a girl who couldn't remember her own name be a powerful witch, capable of casting spells? Yet they saw the way the geese obeyed her and said it was witchcraft. One night, one of them would grow bold enough to do more than watch, though, and she knew she had no spell to stop him.

Best to bathe in the river, then, the goose girl resolved, chivvying her charges through the gate, toward the lake where they spent their days. Like every other day she could remember, the goose girl followed the river, then walked along the bank of the canal that led to the lake. When the lake was full, it emptied out into a little stream that rejoined the river a half mile downstream, but the hot spring days had drunk the lake water until the water level had dropped so much that the stream ran dry.

The goose girl shooed her birds into the lake, then waited for Shun to catch up. He came huffing and puffing down the hill, then flopped down under a tree. He drank deeply from the water bottle he kept tied to his belt, then threw it at the goose girl. "I'm empty. Fetch me a drink, girl."

"From the lake?" she asked. Surely it would have been easier for him to sit beside the lake, where he could drink as much as he pleased, instead of sitting under a tree ten yards away.

"Of course not, dolt. The geese and the city foul the lake so it's not safe to drink. Fill my bottle in the river."

The goose girl snatched up the bottle, darting into the dry stream bed. She jumped down the steps that had once been a pretty waterfall, following the sound of running water to the river. She found where the stream fed the river, then turned upstream. The river curved a little to go around a massive tree, and she had to fight her way through underbrush to reach the bank on the other side of the tree. When she did, she drew in a breath.

The pool before her was perfect. The tree had dammed part of the river to create a pool that had none of the river's turbulence, yet it looked deep enough for the goose girl's longed-for bath. Dappled sunlight glinted on the pool's surface, enticing her in.

First, she opened the water bottle and filled it in the pool, before jamming the stopper into the neck of the bottle. She set the bottle between two tree roots, half immersed in the pool, to keep the contents cool. The remains of a tiny broken glass bottle were caught between the roots, but the goose girl paid it no heed. Now, her time was her own.

The goose girl had no patience for getting in slowly. She simply stepped in and sank, letting the water close over her head before realising the pool was deeper than the expected. She thrashed to the surface, relieved to find it wasn't far.

Coughing and spluttering, she stayed at the surface until she had caught her breath once more, before she slipped out of her hated robe. She scrubbed it against a tree root, rinsing it until she could no longer see the blood. Then, she draped it over a branch, hoping it would dry while she washed herself.

But washing was thirsty work. The goose girl shifted to where the river fed her pool, and cupped her hands for a drink. The water was cool in her hands, but the first sip burned her tongue. Nevertheless, she drank more, sucking the drops from her fingers until they were dry.

A princess should drink from her golden cup, not her hands, her mother's voice insisted. A princess bathed only in perfumed water, brought to her by her many servants.

Knowledge blossomed in the goose girl's head.

"Where's my drink, girl?" an irate male voice demanded. Shun's head appeared over the underbrush.

"Fetch it yourself," Lagle told the fowl keeper. Princesses did not serve peasants.

"If I have to drag you out of there, I'll box your ears, girl," he threatened. "I'm not scared of no witch."

Witch. Lagle tasted the word, feeling it curl around her tongue as she drank more of the river water. It burned her throat like the finest wine. "You should be scared," she purred, stepping out of the pool. Water cascaded down her naked body, shimmering in the sunlight. "I am the most powerful witch your pitiful kingdom has ever seen. I will ensorcel your king and eat his heart."

"I'll tell the guards you said that!" Shun said, backing away.

"Do. Tell them to bring me robes fit for a queen when they come for me. I will wear nothing but silk now," Lagle said, lifting her cupped hand over her head so that more of the enchanted water trickled into her mouth. The more she drank, the more powerful she felt. "Have them deliver me to the king."

Shun disappeared out of sight.

"You forgot your water bottle!" she called, but received no answer. "My water bottle now," she said to herself, as the enchanted water within her began to whisper what she needed to do to become a queen.

Lagle listened.

Twenty-Eight

Constant worry about what the Queen would do to her nagged at Ava's mind until she could scarcely sleep. In the garden the next day, she drowsed while her maids gossiped, until she heard a voice urgently calling her name.

"Princess Ava, you are summoned to the throne room."

Ava opened her eyes to find two guards before her. She bit her lip, forcing away the memories of the guards who'd escorted her back to the harem in her father's palace, and rose. She had to almost run to keep up with the two soldiers whose strides were much longer than hers, and her racing heart wasn't helped by the panic that engulfed her.

Had the Queen discovered Lagle's injury and Ava's marriage already? Ava couldn't think of any other reason why she would be summoned to the throne room, unless the Queen or someone from her father's court was here to punish her. Unless the Emperor knew that she and Yun hadn't consummated their marriage.

Ava's feet felt heavier with each step. She didn't want to face whatever awaited her, but if she ran, where would she go? It was all very well to think brave fishy thoughts, but it was another thing entirely to take a leap into the unknown. Perhaps the Emperor wished to apologise to her for believing her to be a spy.

The guards escorted her to the foot of the Emperor's dais, where she dropped into a deep curtsey before she could be commanded to do so.

"There's the lying, traitorous slut," Lagle said.

Ava gasped, raising her head to see Lagle seated beside the Emperor on the throne normally occupied by the Empress, who was nowhere to be seen.

"Bow before royalty, peasant!" Lagle ordered.

Ava couldn't help it. She smiled. "You are well, sister," she said. "Thank the ancestors that you have recovered."

"You are no family of mine!" Lagle stormed. "Tell the king what you really are. Tell him you are my insubordinate maid who turned traitor the moment my guards were out of sight, making my horse throw me off then switching clothes with me while I was unconscious so that the king would believe you were his bride, and not me. Tell him how you stole my rightful husband, pretending to be a princess, when you were really sent here as my maid to serve me. Tell him why you're here!"

Tears sprang to Ava's eyes, but she

struggled to speak before her throat choked up. "I'm here to seek peace between my father and the Emperor through a marriage alliance between his family and mine. When you fell off your horse, I lifted you back on and led you here, making sure you were cared for before I even saw the Emperor. I did…what had to be done. As my father's daughter." She swallowed. "I am a princess, the same as you."

"You are not the same as me," Lagle spat. "Guards! Execute her!"

A hand grasped Ava's arm, dragging her to her feet. She opened her mouth to scream, only to discover that the hand belonged to Yun.

"A wife's punishment is her husband's duty," Yun said dully. "Princess Ava is my wife, and no one shall touch her but me."

He yanked Ava's arm, dragging her out of the throne room. Too late, she realised that he was enveloped in a faint red glow — a curse, and one Ava recognised. She scanned the throne room, seeing the same glow emanate from Lagle, the Emperor, and the younger crowned men who shared the dais. Yun's seven brothers, she assumed. All under the same spell.

The curse hummed with malevolence as Yun dragged her out the door, heedless of how much he hurt her. This wasn't like him – the man who'd sworn not to touch her without her asking him to. Ava tried to concentrate on the curse to distract herself from the pain.

Red, yes, and filled with hate, it was a sort of seduction curse, which drew all men to one woman, slaves to her every wish. Lagle had somehow enslaved Yun, his father and his brothers with this curse. Ava had to break it or she would die, she knew. She cast her mind deeper into the magic, looking for the key to break the curse.

She gasped when she found it, for the solution was so simple.

But would it work?

Twenty- Nine

Punish your wives for being unfaithful, the witch's voice whispered in Yun's head. Put your children to death for being bastards. Then return to me and battle with your brothers, for the victor will have me and the throne.

Over and over, the words repeated, as he tried to shake them out of his head. He felt the compulsion to obey, but the thought of a woman as spoils of war turned his stomach.

And Ava…Ava…he took one look at her and the witch's voice rose in volume, drowning out Ava's sweet tones. A wife who had not yet given him children because he had not given them to her. The throne was not his. Never would be his. Leave it for his brothers to fight over.

Punish your wife! The witch's voice rose to a shriek in his head.

Yun took Ava's arm and repeated the witch's words. He would punish his wife.

Who had never done anything wrong. Staring into her eyes, he knew this with a certainty he could not deny.

Help her to fly. Open the gate.

In his head, Ava stood in the horse pen in his brothers' war camp. But where the other girls cowered in the corner, she stood tall. Reached down of her own accord and opened the gate.

"Better to fly than die," she said, echoing his own words. "I choose to be free. You must choose, too."

"I serve the Emperor's throne, and I will never be free," Yun told her. "But I will protect you, so that you may be."

Her fingers stroked his cheeks, her dark eyes burning with a passion Yun had never seen before. Her lips were warm and sweet, everything he had imagined she might be, and more. He pulled her close, determined to kiss her properly. To show her the depths of his passion. How much he longed for her, wanted no one else but her.

She let out a little sigh, parting her lips to tease him with her tongue.

No woman had ever tasted this good. Her very breath tasted like the nectar of the gods. He could drink her in and want nothing and no one else forever.

An eternity later, Yun pulled his face away from hers, gasping for breath. "Ava, my Ava," he panted. "I love you so much. More than life itself. Please tell me you want me to kiss you again."

If she refused, he would beg. On his knees, if it would help. He would prostrate himself before her.

Her whole face lit with a shy smile. "Yes."

Thirty

Ava paused to catch her breath after yet another blissful kiss from Yun. Somehow, they'd broken the curse.

Reality intruded on her euphoria. "The curse," she said urgently. "Your brothers…the Emperor…they're still under a spell. We must fetch their wives to break the curse." Even as the words left her lips, her heart sank. She'd seen the other princesses in the garden, and their frightened reactions when any man, let alone their own husbands, entered the garden.

None of the other princes' wives held any feelings resembling love for their husbands. None of the princesses would be capable of breaking the curse. Perhaps a mistress or concubine…Ava's thoughts flashed to her mother, and she had an idea. The Empress. Surely the princes' mother held some love for her children. Perhaps even the Emperor, too.

"The Empress," Ava said. "We must go to her and tell her what has happened. Perhaps she can help."

Yun's arms tightened around her. "Perhaps she can. I shall send a servant with a message to my mother. But as long as my brothers and my father are enslaved to that woman, you are in danger. Her hatred for you burns brighter than any torch. Imagine what she will do to you if she knows you can break her spell. No, you must be kept safe. I will take you to my chambers and guard you myself while we wait for word from my mother."

Yun threw open the door to his chamber, gesturing for Ava to precede him inside. Ava took three steps into the room, then stopped dead. She dropped to her knees. "Empress."

"Mother? What are you doing here?" Yun asked, closing the door.

"He's finally done something so stupid it will cost him his throne," the Empress said, resting her elbow on the ornately carved arm of Yun's favourite chair.

Yun hastened to gather up his papers from the desk in front of her. Even his mother wasn't allowed to read his poetry, it seemed.

Ava's blood ran cold. "Who has, Majesty?"

The Empress sighed. "It's Imperial Highness, not Majesty, but it doesn't matter. Get up, girl. You won't do anyone any good down there on your knees."

Ava summoned her courage. "But you can, M...Imperial Highness. Your husband and your sons are under a terrible curse that only you can break."

"It's too late for that. His witch of a mistress is far ahead of you. Even now, the pleasure gardens are awash with blood. First, she ordered my sons to kill their children. Then, their wives. Now, they are fighting each other to the death for my husband's throne and the dubious pleasure of sharing her bed." The Empress eyed Ava. "You must be a witch, too, that you are immune to the curse."

"I'm not a witch. I only have the gift I inherited from my mother – I can see spells and how to break them. No more." Oh, how Ava wished she was more. A powerful enchantress who could cast spells at will.

"Perhaps it will be enough. Will you use your gift to protect my son, keep him from harm, and ensure him a long life?" the Empress demanded.

Ava glanced at Yun "He is my husband. I am honour bound to care for him as a good wife."

The Empress's gaze seemed to see right through Ava to her very soul. "You also vowed to bear him sons."

By the ancestors, she knew. Ava didn't know how, but the Empress knew they hadn't consummated the marriage.

"I will," Ava said, vowing that she would give herself to Yun that very night. If his lovemaking was anything like his kisses, perhaps she might even enjoy it.

"I hope that's true," the Empress said. "For while my family paints the throne room walls with royal blood, there is an army camped outside the walls. If only my stupid husband had lived to see it, for he was right. An army led by your father, girl."

Ava gasped. So much for the alliance Lagle had been sent here for. While Ava had pleaded for peace, her father had been planning war. Maybe even with Lagle as a pawn in the game. "I didn't know. The Queen told me…"

"The witch queen whose daughter commanded the slaughter of my family?" the Empress demanded.

Ava didn't know what to say, so she merely nodded. "She sent me here as a punishment, to serve Lagle, though I am my father's daughter, too. Lagle was determined to be queen here."

The Empress gave a little snort of laughter, that turned into a cough. "Yet fate has other plans. While my family lies dying in the throne room, an army waits to conquer this palace and all who live here. What will you do about it?"

Yun stepped forward. He bowed his head. "I will lead my father's army to victory. I might be the youngest, but I am still a prince. They know me, and will follow me."

"Don't be daft," the Empress snapped. "By the time the army gets here, the palace will be overrun. You can't lead an army if you're dead. You must flee to the Winter Palace, where you will be able to safely take the throne. Find a way to get him there safely, Princess. You are my son's only hope." She waved at a new chest that sat beside the table. "You will find your things in there. Two of the horses you arrived with are packed and saddled in the stables, waiting for you. Lose no time, Princess. Grandsons can wait until the throne is secure." She grimaced, lifting her hand. It was covered in blood. "Swear on the ancestors you will do everything in your power to protect him."

"Mother, we must find you a healer. Let me send for one," Yun begged, reaching for a bell to summon a servant.

As Ava watched, blood ran down the Empress's side to soak her skirt. She did not have long left.

"I swear by my ancestors and my life, I will save your son," Ava vowed.

The Empress nodded and closed her eyes.

"Mother!" Yun howled, but it was too late. The Empress was gone.

Ava fell to her knees beside the chest, rifling through the clothes until she found the gown Bianca had made for her. It was the finest she had, in the style of her father's court. As she stroked the silk, she began to have an inkling of a plan. It was risky, but it was all she had. If it worked, she could save both herself and Yun from her father's army. But it would only work if she had the courage to carry it out.

With trembling hands, Ava garbed herself

for battle.

Thirty-One

"You look like a barbarian princess," Yun remarked, his voice muffled by his guard helmet as he rode behind Ava. "I've never seen a court dress made to be worn by a lady astride a horse."

"I am a barbarian princess," Ava replied. "And you're supposed to be my bodyguard, so please keep quiet. If my father's army knew you were the Emperor's son, and the commander of the opposing army, they'd slaughter you on the spot."

Yun sounded amused. "My sword isn't just for decoration, Princess. I know how to use it. I might prefer poetry to swordsmanship, but I was a match for any man on the battlefield or in the practice ring."

"There has been enough blood spilled today," Ava whispered, fighting tears. "I won't have you killing anyone else, for there are thousands of them and only one of you. I vowed to save you, and I will, but only if you can keep your sword to yourself!"

Yun chuckled. "Yes, mistress."

Not for the first time, Ava regretted her decision to engage in this crazy scheme. But what other choice did she have, if she wanted to keep Yun alive?

None, Ava told herself, which is why she had to remind herself with every step that if her courage failed, Yun would die and his blood would be on her hands. So fishy thoughts were the uppermost in her mind as she guided her horse through the outskirts of the army camp. Though leaping to the top of a waterfall would be easy compared to her task today.

Row upon row of tents stretched as far as she could see, but they were nothing compared to the number of eyes staring at her as she passed. Her neck ached from forcing herself to hold her head high, when it felt far more natural to duck her head to whatever authority presented itself. Even her husband trailed behind her like a subordinate.

"Halt."

Ava was almost grateful for the order, though she knew it would take an even greater act of courage to start her moving again if she stopped.

Nevertheless, the two armed guards barring her way gave her no choice but to rein in her horse.

"You go no further. No camp followers allowed into the main camp before nightfall and he's not allowed in at all. He's a palace guard."

Ava's horse tossed her head, and her

mistress copied her. "I am Princess Ava, daughter of King Chinggis and wife to the Emperor's son, Prince Yun Bataar. I was sent here by my father to secure a marriage alliance with the Emperor, and now I come on behalf of my father's allies to bring him a message. A message I will only give to my father himself, so either summon him or let me pass." She hoped they didn't hear how much her voice shook. If she had to be any more overbearing to gain entrance to the camp, she wasn't sure how she would manage it.

"Princess Ava? The princess who visited the soldiers' swimming pool?" a voice asked eagerly. "Batu, is that really her?"

A soldier scrambled out of one of the tents to her left. His eyes widened and he dropped to his knees, bowing so low his forehead touched the dust. "Princess Ava! We are honoured."

The other soldiers around looked from one another to the kneeling man before bowing just as low. "Princess."

Ava wet her lips. "Please, I need to see my father."

"At once, Princess." The first man leapt to his feet, and Ava recognised him as the soldier who had returned her to the harem. "If you will follow me."

She glanced at Yun. "My escort will come with me. He is my personal bodyguard, and I go nowhere without him."

"As you wish, Princess."

Batu led her to a tent that was larger than the others, but that was all that distinguished it from the rest of the camp. He gestured for her to wait, before slipping inside.

Ava dismounted, hearing Yun doing the same behind her. A groom appeared to take her horse and Ava allowed the animal to be led to the horse line that held her father's own mounts. Beautiful creatures, all of them, just like Falada had been.

Batu backed out of the tent, and bowed low to the man who stepped into the sun. "Majesty," Batu said.

King Chinggis ignored the soldier, for his gaze was fixed on Ava. "Sumi?" he whispered. "I thought you died. Is it really you?"

Thirty-Two

Ava didn't hesitate. She strode forward with her eyes downcast before prostrating herself before the King. "Father," she said. "I am Sumi's daughter. She died giving birth to me, and I was brought up in the harem with your other wives and daughters."

"You are my daughter?" he asked, sounding bemused. "You look just like her."

"Of course, Father. I am Ava, the princess you sent with the Queen's daughter, Lagle, to marry into the Emperor's family and form an alliance, so that our peoples may live in peace." Ava did her best to keep her voice steady, so he wouldn't recognise the lie.

"The bodies in the throne room tell me there is little peace here," the King remarked.

So he already knew. The Emperor had been right about there being spies in his court.

"The Emperor would not agree to an alliance, though Lagle tried everything to persuade him. She took the only action she felt would please you." Or please the Queen, Ava thought but did not say. "With the Emperor dead, the throne falls to one of his sons. With one of them, an alliance can be made."

"My men tell me the sons are dead, too."

Ava stifled a sob. The Empress had been right. So much death. For all their faults, Yun's family didn't deserve to be slaughtered. Yun least of all. She drew in a deep breath, praying silently that her idea would work. "Not all," she said finally. "One survives, and he is a prince of peace, not war. I come to negotiate on his behalf, and all his people. He wishes to rule what lands he has left, without worrying about war. You have enough enemies, but what of an ally, a neighbouring emperor, who swears never to take up arms against you or yours, so that he might build a refined court the like of which the world has never seen before. A court that your grandsons will inherit."

"My grandsons, eh? Which one did you have in mind?"

She fought to keep her voice from shaking. "Why, the one I carry now. Son to the prince, my husband, who seeks an alliance with you for a lasting peace."

"Some husband this prince is, sending a woman as his envoy. Such a coward should not be emperor of anything, let alone husband to one of my daughters."

"I am no coward, sir," Yun said, his boots crunching as he strode to Ava's side. She could see the dusty toes of them, though she didn't dare raise her head. "I am Prince Yun Bataar, the Emperor's son and heir, and husband to

Princess Ava. She begged to be allowed to speak to you first, and I granted her wish, for she has been a good wife to me. I admit to a certain curiosity about her father. Your reputation as a warrior and a conqueror are well-known, but she spoke so highly of you as a father, a man for whom family is important. I, too, wish to protect my family, what is left of it. She is my family, but so are you, honoured father-in-law." He bowed low. "I do not wish to war with family. If you allow us to reach the Winter Palace, we will set up court there, leaving these lands to you. The lands that remain to me will become a place of culture and learning, and no enemy to you. We will be allies, and I will instruct my sons in peace, not war."

"And what of your daughters?" the King demanded.

"Their mother will instruct them, for women are a great mystery to me. All I know is that it is a rare woman who thinks of war with anything but fear," Yun said.

"You have countrywomen who think differently. One who fancies herself a general," the King grumbled. "Cost me some of my best troops when victory seemed certain. There are witnesses who swear they saw her slay my son, their general."

"Da Ying? If you support me as emperor, I will make sure she retires from the army. I'll find her a good marriage where a husband and children will occupy her for the rest of her days. Consider it a favour to my father-in-law."

Ava's breath caught in her throat. The maids had told her stories about Da Ying, the general's daughter turned general. Though the stories Ava had heard included both a husband and child.

The King laughed. "So you wish to be emperor of half a kingdom with no army? You are a strange man, Prince Yun. I could kill you now where you stand, and take all your lands and people for myself. What is there to stop me?"

Ava couldn't muffle the squeak that came

out of her mouth at this. She felt both her husband and her father's eyes on her.

"Family," Yun said gravely. "Far easier to name your daughter Empress, with me as Emperor by her side, and you will always have allies at your back, leaving you free to conquer other lands wherever you choose."

"We have a bargain," the King announced. "As long as my daughter is Empress, and you do not raise an army against me, you may have the Emperor's throne and the lands that remain."

Ava breathed again. "Thank you, Father."

"My Empress prostrates herself to no one," Yun said, helping her to her feet. "Especially not when she carries the next emperor in her belly."

Ava blushed to hear Yun repeat her lie. Surely he didn't believe…

"Come, Princess. Your father is a busy man, and we have a long way to travel to reach the Winter Palace, with much work to do once we reach it." Yun tugged her arm, pulling her out of her father's tent.

He helped her mount her horse, before leaping onto his own. With his helmet on, he appeared every bit her bodyguard again. "Shall we go, Princess?" he asked.

Not trusting her voice, Ava nodded and nudged her horse into a walk.

Thirty-Three

After an hour's ride, they reached a stream, and Yun called a halt. He dismounted and filled their water skins. He passed Ava's up to her and she drank deeply, gratefully, before thanking him.

"So is there a baby?" Yun asked.

Ava reddened. "No. In the western kingdoms, they tell stories about a virgin who gave birth to a son, but I am not her. I…lied. I am sorry."

He swung back into his saddle. "I'm not.

Your lie won us an alliance."

Ava shook her head. "No, your charmed tongue pleased my father. The alliance is your doing, not mine. I merely bought you safe passage through the camp to my father's command tent."

"You bought me a kingdom that should never have been mine. Truly, you deserve to be its Empress." Yun brought his mount close beside hers and reached out to cup her cheek. "Empress Ava Asuka, the bird who flew from her father's court and will be the jewel of mine. The finest poets will proclaim your virtues, and every dancer in the kingdom will clamour to perform for you. I am honoured to call you my wife."

She raised her gaze to meet his dark eyes, and found she could not look away. "I'm not truly your wife yet," she whispered, before he cut her off with a kiss.

The moment stretched delightfully, until with considerable reluctance, he pulled away. "When we reach the Winter Palace, you will be, I promise."

A shiver of anticipation shook Ava from her head to her toes as she swallowed. "Thank you, my prince."

He laughed and spurred his horse forward. "We should hurry home."

What could she do but follow?

Thirty-Four

High in the mountains, huddled closely together to share the warmth of their tiny campfire, Yun waved at the city in the valley below. "The second largest city in my father's kingdom, crowned by the Winter Palace. This will be your home, my Empress."

Ava still wasn't used to the title. She doubted she ever would be. In her mind, the Empress was an incredibly courageous woman who had used her dying moments to save her son's life. And the traditional crowns of the

Emperor and Empress, which Yun had found in the saddle bags on the first night, were almost too heavy for her to lift, let alone wear.

"I am afraid," Ava admitted. "Afraid that I will never live up to the honour of the title that your mother held."

"You have nothing to be afraid of, my Empress. You are the fish who leaped to the top of the waterfall, and tomorrow, you will become the dragon herself." Yun held up her crown which featured a jewelled dragon and set it upon her head.

Ava removed the heavy gold crown and handed it back to him. "No one can fly with so much metal on their head. I would sink to the bottom of the river wearing such a thing."

Yun laughed softly as he returned the crown to its hiding place. "Tomorrow, you will sink into the Empress's silk bed, and as your Emperor, I will love you until your spirit takes flight once more."

He had said similar things every night, never pushing Ava about her promise to give him a son, and she had been grateful for it in the beginning. Now, she felt her courage build.

"I would like to be loved as a princess first," she said slowly. "Loved by a prince, just like in the stories my sister used to tell me in the women's palace when we were children. A prince who saves her, and loves her, and who will lead her to a life of happiness."

"Here? On the ground, without the silken sheets and soft mattress that a princess deserves?" Yun asked.

It was Ava's turn to laugh. They'd slept on the ground for every night of their journey, wrapped together in a rough blanket to share their warmth. She'd almost forgotten what it felt like to sleep in Yun's bed in the palace.

"Yes. Here, in my husband's arms, on our last night alone together before we become part of the world again. Tonight it will be just us – you and me. I am willing, Yun, more willing than I have ever been." Ava kissed him, untying the lacings at the front of her gown with the practiced skill of a woman who didn't need servants for such a thing any more. She shucked off her shift without a second thought, feeling only the joy of her husband's gaze on her as he devoured her body with his eyes alone before he moved in closer for another kiss. His hands on her bare skin felt heavenly. Ava tensed at the slight sting as he eased inside her, before her only sensation was pleasure. Pleasure at finally being one with her husband, and the spiralling desire he coaxed to greater and greater heights until she screamed for joy to the very stars above.

And when the first rays of dawn touched Ava's aching body, she vowed anew that the child they had created among the stars that night would live to see his parents live a long and happy life together. But first, she would wake Yun and enjoy his lovemaking for another hour before they headed down from the heights to take their places at the head of a new and peaceful kingdom.

About the Author

Demelza Carlton has always loved the ocean, but on her first snorkelling trip she found she was afraid of fish.

She has since swum with sea lions, sharks and sea cucumbers and stood on spray drenched cliffs over a seething sea as a seven-metre cyclonic swell surged in, shattering a shipwreck below.

Demelza now lives in Perth, Western Australia, the shark attack capital of the world.

The *Ocean's Gift* series was her first foray into fiction, followed by her suspense thriller *Nightmares* trilogy. She swears the *Mel Goes to Hell* series ambushed her on a crowded train and wouldn't leave her alone.

Want to know more? You can follow Demelza on Facebook, Twitter, YouTube or her website, Demelza Carlton's Place at:

www.demelzacarlton.com

More Books by Demelza Carlton

<u>**Colony: Aqua series**</u>

Halcyon (#1)

Poseidon (#2)

Apollo (#3)

<u>**Siren of Secrets series**</u>

Ocean's Secret (#1)

Ocean's Gift (#2)

Ocean's Infiltrator (#3)

<u>Siren of War series</u>

Ocean's Justice (#1)

Ocean's Widow (#2)

Ocean's Bride (#3)

Ocean's Rise (#4)

Ocean's War (#5)

How To Catch Crabs

<u>**Nightmares Trilogy**</u>

Nightmares of Caitlin Lockyer (#1)

Necessary Evil of Nathan Miller (#2)

Afterlife of Alana Miller (#3)

<u>**Mel Goes to Hell series**</u>

The Devil's Work (#1)

See You in Hell (#2)

Mel Goes to Hell (#3)

To Hell and Back (#4)

The Holiday From Hell (#5)

All Hell Breaks Loose (#6)

The Devil Goes to Heaven (#7)

<u>**Romance a Medieval Fairytale series**</u>

Enchant: Beauty and the Beast Retold

Dance: Cinderella Retold

Fly: Goose Girl Retold

Revel: Twelve Dancing Princesses
Retold

Silence: Little Mermaid Retold

Awaken: Sleeping Beauty Retold

Embellish: Brave Little Tailor Retold

Appease: Princess and the Pea Retold

Blow: Three Little Pigs Retold

Return: Hansel and Gretel Retold

Wish: Aladdin Retold

Melt: Snow Queen Retold

Spin: Rumpelstiltskin Retold

Kiss: Frog Prince Retold

Reflect: Snow White Retold

Roar: Goldilocks Retold

Cobble: Elves and the Shoemaker Retold

Float: Enchanted Horse Retold

Steal: Forty Thieves Retold

Call: Pied Piper Retold
Fall: Scheherazade Retold
Feather: Swan Maidens Retold
Cross: Billy Goats Gruff Retold
Weave: Rapunzel Retold
Claim: Puss in Boots Retold
Curse: Rose Red Retold